The Sleeping Phoenix: Part II
NAGODARA

A Transformational

Science-Fiction Fantasy

Epic Journey

ishKiia Paige

First paperback edition February 2022

Book design by ishKiia Paige
Illustrations by ishKiia Paige

ISBN 978-1-956297-05-8 (paperback)
ISBN 978-1-956297-06-5 (hardback - laminate)
ISBN 978-1-956297-07-2 (hardback - jacket)
ISBN 978-1-956297-08-9 (ebook)
ISBN 978-1-956297-09-6 (audiobook)

https://ishkiiastudios.com

Dedication

I dedicate this to my youngest son,

who transitioned from this life way too early.

The echoes of your song sing here in this series,

your message and purpose still live within me,

and you will never be forgotten.

Thank you for your gift.

Epigraph

The more you give the matched frequencies of
compassion, love, fortune, and joy into the quantum,
the more you will find the whole of all existence has
become more generous to you.

Their matching wave patterns will stream in from all
directions towards you. And your whole life structure
will go through a transformation.

There, also, the opposite is also true.
It is how the most heinous things in the multiverse
propagate and come to be.

~ishKiia

Letter from the Author

Dear readers,

Thank you for taking this ride with me. I keep saying that, but it is only because that is what I feel in my heart. Appreciation goes out to all of you with sincerity.

I would like to thank all those that were part of this book, including editors, beta readers, Patreon supporters, etc. It means the world to me that I am enjoying the ride with others, especially in a time when things seem rather dark in the Covid world right now.

I hope you enjoy the escape, have fun on an adventure, and learn a little something along the way too.

I hope you create an amazing day for yourself.

~ishKiia

TABLE OF CONTENTS

PROLOGUE

Aqum Interruption:
— Pausing time —
— Anxiously informing you with secrecy —
Revealing time period: Past
3 hours before the firehouse challenge on Earth
— Transmitting Event —

𒐫𒐫𒐫 *Rtu* 𒐫𒐫𒐫

Rtu looked at the screen and saw Rhom and Zreyas walking off the challenge node entity that Zreyas named Aqum. They walked out into the portal room, weirdly suspended in nothing. The no-walls room consisted of a floor, walkway, a single portal with space for two more, and a console.

Zreyas leaped over to the console, showing Rhom where it was, like a kid would show his father something he was excited about. Then he Q-leaped up on Rhom's shoulder, causing him to react with a jerk.

Rhom chuckled and shook his head. He said something to Zreyas with smiling eyes. Then they both looked down at the console.

"Seems our new little buddy is very useful. With the Dark One's challenge, he has been a powerful ally in landing that portal for us and that room that the Dark One won't be able to access. He has an expressed interest in making sure Ayya is safe because of his brother now merged into her gut, and he is fun to have around. What are we going to do with Rhom and Zreyas? Do you think they will win the challenge? I have to admit, I enjoy being

"

on their side more than helping the Dark One. I really hated working for him. It was all kinds of wrong."

"What's a war without turncoats, my dear son? I like this side better too, but we need to make the Dark One believe we are still on his side."

"Doesn't the Dark One know already if we are or not?"

Tulyata stopped her work on the scales, put her hands on her thighs, and looked at him. "I think there are higher powers involved here. Plus, it would devastate Rhom that we would side with the wretched creature no matter what the reason, just because of who he is and what he stands for. Anyway, the Dark One approached us when things were at zero percent success at helping Ayya. All the pieces of the game have changed since then, and I am glad we are back where we belong and of our own minds again. Zreyas does not know what he has done for us."

"I wouldn't want to be on the other side of his wrath, even if he isn't a visage." Rtu laughed and watched the two. "Besides, I like our little buddy. Can we keep him? *You* even like him." Rtu let out a mock gasp.

"Shut up, you," Tulyata said sourly as her beaded tassels from her head band whipped around as she turned her head toward him.

Then they both laughed as they watched Rhom and Zreyas.

Rtu sighed, relieved that there was no more demented connection to the Dark One. Feeling his power slowly heal and grow, he was glad to be free of that wretched entity.

"Who would have thought his pushing an aura of peace could break a bond of contract with the Dark One?" Tulyata said with wonder. "It still amazes me how we all just sat here and felt it all happen with him just sitting there on the couch. Who would have thought feeling at peace would be that powerful?"

x

Rtu propped his elbow on the arm of his chair, his conscience getting the better of him. "If they ever find out without us telling them first, it will cause damage without the ability to repair it—It will forever shatter their trust. I mean, I *am* his twin brother. You are his mother, and all three of us are close. Plus, it's not exactly a world where he has a lot of Viduri friends like he had in his incarnation anymore, so there are very few people and family he has in his inner circle. I mean, how would *you* feel if the only two family members, who happen to be your sons, would hold that kind of secret from you? That is betrayal through silence."

Rtu put his fist on his freckled cheek and sighed. "Do you think they will forgive us for showing the Dark One where Ayya is? Not that we had much choice at the time with zero percent chance of success. Even so, we *are* responsible for that."

"Let's not find out, because I don't know. Zreyas is not the type to forgive something like that, I don't think. He is likely to commit himself to revenge now, even *with* his improvement. He was, after all, a Janquar all his life and very conditioned to be so."

"He isn't Janquar anymore, Mother. He's morphed into something fascinating. What scares me is, I didn't foresee or create that variation of him."

"Let's just count ourselves lucky that Zreyas' powerful peace aura broke the connection and released us," said Tulyata, as she paused to work with her scales. He knew that look. She was checking out something she had just thought about. "We are no longer bound to him for sure. I just checked. The laws of balance say that since it was for balance, we made it. Someone else can break it for balance."

Tulyata rubbed her nose, slammed down her half-glasses, and continued. "That bastard Dark One is powerful! I'm terrified of that creature's potential to do things we never thought of. We lost a lot of power from that escapade. I can tell it in the checks and balances."

Rtu looked at his mother. "Don't worry about it. We are ourselves again, and it will all come back soon enough. I wonder though, can you check yourself with the challenge node again? I mean, you can get locked in maybe if you are under the max?"

"We can try. It is after the start of the challenge, though. So, if I grow in power later and go past the max, I just won't be able to go again. But it might come in handy until then."

She stood and moved into the challenge node entity and watched Aqum's purple mist rise. It flowed up the walls and into the ceiling. It finally stopped a few hands from the center.

"—Tulyata is an approved team member. Would you like to travel now? Yes or No."

"No, but is this configuration locked in for the duration of the challenge?"

"—One moment, please... We are replying with apologetic inflection—this team is not a permanently approved team."

"Reason: It was not locked in before the beginning of the challenge."

"Would you like to travel now? Yes or No."

"No, but remember me for future travel in case we are in a hurry, Aqum. Thank you." She grumbled as she walked to the desk. Just before sitting down, Aqum replied to her.

"—Replying with sarcastic gratitude to a grouchy Prime Visage—you are welcome... traitor."

Rtu bust out laughing hard as Tulyata spat expletives

that Rtu really couldn't hear over his laughing. "Oh, by the visages, I love you, Aqum!"

"—Aqum is saying with perceived aggravation—Shut your laughing yap, Rtukaiah."

Rtu blinked, but the traitor comment from Aqum stifled his laugh after he thought about it. He grew serious as his heart wanted to break about the silent betrayal. Most of the multiverse's largest betrayals he had ever seen with all the creations were silent ones in various forms. They did the most damage, yet almost never talked about.

Then he looked at his mother and thought about all her little secrets she was mounting up. This wasn't like her at all. There had to be a reason she was doing this. "You don't want them to know you lost power, do you?"

"No, because I don't want it to lead up to having to tell them what happened."

He tried to prompt some sense into her. "Wouldn't it be better to just tell them and let the news come from us?"

"I've looked at the checks and balances odds; it would not be good now."

"It's *never* going to be a good time. You are using your purpose of balance as an excuse again."

"The percentage chance we can awaken Ayya is much slimmer than if we don't tell them at this point in time."

"I'm not sure why you say they forced us into that decision to help when you made the choice to do it, Tulyata." Rtu sat strong, bountiful body straighter. "Just because you like balances, and living your life as a balance maker, doesn't mean that the odds can't change depending on someone's choice to grow or unexpected known circumstances that may or may not show up."

Growing more aggravated, he sat forward, propping his elbows on his exposed, dark knees. "Have you thought about factoring in your *own* growth? I think it is important that we honor the mistakes we made. Perhaps we can at least tell them we made one, but also say we can't tell them about it at this point in time to help with the balances."

Rtu leaned back hard. "At least we would have our honor on the table, even if we cloak it for a time, which you are so fond of doing to begin with. Are you sure you were released from that dark and cursed connection? This doesn't seem like you. You are normally fearless when it comes to facing—"

He looked at the expression on his mother's face as if she was hiding something of this nature. She hated dealing with her own heart. What had changed?

His face lit up with realization and took in a breath. "Wait... That's it! You are afraid!"

Rtu sat straighter in astonishment at his own realization. "Honestly, I'm scared shit-less, but you... You aren't used to experiencing fear because of the nature of what you do as a visage."

Tulyata froze and stared ahead, saying nothing.

He knew he had hit the mark with those words. Rtu thought she might be trying her best to decide if she would lash out in her bitterness or listen to what he had to say. But he decided to push because this was critical for her and everyone else around her.

"Remember what Rhom said about it being rare to see the problem, acknowledge it, and then put something into motion to work past it? Now might be a fantastic time to go by Zreyas' example. If Zreyas can do it at such high improbability, then why not visages?"

Tulyata stared at him, incredulous.

"You are so good at objectively putting things from everyone else on the table to guide us throughout life's choices. Now is a great time to apply that to yourself. I'm putting it out on the table for you, dear Mother. I'm calling you out and inviting you to step up. If you don't, I think your valuable contribution will deteriorate." Rtu paused to see what his mother was going to say, if anything.

Tulyata lowered her gaze.

Rtu knew his mother all too well. She was feeling the conflict and fully expected an explosion. But he had to try to push this. "Mother..."

He paused and took a deep breath, feeling the fear of his thoughts travel through his body with a death grip. "I'm afraid if you don't face this, you will begin festering and fall. The multiverse needs you right now more than ever. *I*... need you. But I think there is more at stake this time around. It's not because of the Dark One, not because of me or Rhom, but because you *like* Zreyas. That is in the realm of the heart, and that is an amazing miracle by itself with it coming from you. If you—"

"Stop! You are right, my dear. I'm not used to having issues because I'm cooped up at a desk with my mechanical-like design with only one friend—the scales. All I do is formulate strategies. I don't have to deal with real issues of living incarnate-like lives, in any capacity. I just don't know what to do. I feel... helpless."

A wave of shock ran through him, her saying those words. He just let her talk.

"There are some things about all the checks and balances I can't figure in, because it is all part of the quantum field. The factorable pieces from choices people make, no matter how hard I try to estimate, are almost never known until after the choices are made."

Hearing his mother's words made him realize he had no clue about what she was up against every day. He had his own problems in his role as a visage of earth and air in tandem with his brother creating universes, planets, stars, and the species in and on them. He didn't want the problems his brother had with his elements of fire, water, and aether, much less his mother's, being a Prime Visage of balance. Trying to balance things and still leave freedom with almost all of it not in her control because of others' choices seemed impossible.

Rtu felt compassion for her. "I do not understand what you are up against every day. I'm not sure I could take it. You do a phenomenal job, and much better than anyone could. You are the core of what makes up the balance of the quantum, yet you have no understanding of it much scientifically."

Rtu turned his body, leaning on the arm of the chair to make sure she knew he was sincere. "I know I seem like I take things too lightly and laugh too much, but I say to you with all my heart that you have balanced things I never thought could be balanced. It's just mind blowing. You care." He paused a moment for emphasis. "But you are not used to showing it because you are not a caregiver. There is a difference. It's a new adventure for you. I invite you to take it. Factor in what you can and live the rest."

Tulyata broke loose suddenly. "Enough of this talk! I'm your mother and superior!"

And there was the explosion he expected. Rtu held his hand up as if to signify peace. "You have your path... and I have mine."

— End of Aqum Interruption —

1 Inform

Rhom

Zreyas finished his list of questions as he paced on the back of the couch in Tulyata's dimension. He wasn't really asking the three visages as much as to sort things in his mind. Sometimes it just felt good to talk about things out loud to help work things out strategically.

Tulyata snapped and slammed a hand down on her desk. "You and your multiple questions!"

Zreyas whirled around to face Tulyata, narrowing his eyes. "Well, someone has to ask them! Besides, I'm just thinking out loud. I have a right to do that," he retorted defiantly. "Rhom says with my... design. I should inform people. Well, I'm informing you to set me down on a planet if you want me to shut up, because I am going to continue to think how I like to, and I'm not hurting anyone by doing it."

Rhom's eyebrow rose, and the room was dead quiet, his brother and mother frozen in surprise. Rhom couldn't help but grin, though admittedly, it shocked him, too. He couldn't remember a time when an incarnate stood up to a visage, much less so bold as an equal. He liked how Zreyas didn't cower just because of title and position. It was refreshing.

Zreyas pointed at Tulyata sharply, as if to punctuate his next sentence. "I'm *sick* of being treated like nothing much, even though I am nothing much in station compared to you. I might be a lowly incarnate, but I have every right to be respected as much as anyone else. I've done my part since that challenge node showed up, more than *any* of you!"

He paced as the anger simmered and warped around him, making Rhom almost chuckle. He had to cover his mouth, trying hard to suppress it because Zreyas showed no signs of stopping any time soon.

"I helped put Ayya and Aaru together and into her new body, I killed to protect Rhom even though I was still a mag-shit of a Janquar commander at the time, I've shrunk my ass to try and get away to help Ayya, I ran that ticking-challenge run to find the portal room and claim an extra node before anyone else did. I've been attacked by mag-shit-eating Dark One minions with thunder spears while helping to save Ayya... again, and... the worst one of all.... enduring *you* lately!"

When there was no response, he continued. "Well? Let me know now, because I got a lot of thinking to do. If you put me down on a planet, put me on the one you picked me up from because that is likely where another challenge node will be."

The room was silent, and Tulyata glared at him.

Zreyas stared back at her, unwavering.

The battle of wills in the room captivated Rhom. He knew Tulyata loved the boy, but he couldn't figure out why she had been so moody with him lately—more than usual, anyway. She wasn't a visage of the heart with a direct channel to voice it by design, but she loved deeply. As a result, Tulyata showed her affection with taunts. She had always called him names and asserted her dominance. But today... she had just been venomous towards him.

"You can call me all the names you want. I don't care!" Zreyas said with a flared war aura. "But I will not slink around here like a worm because *you* are ticking-moody as hell. In case you haven't noticed, I don't care about my life nearly as much as I do about Ayya and Aaru. Even though Aaru is... no longer with me. What he taught me is. So, visage-zap me all you want!"

Tulyata sat with a stunned expression, body rigid, and... silent.

Rtu widened his eyes with a respect that came through loud and clear in his expression.

Rhom couldn't ever remember a time that his mother was speechless, an anomaly itself. He grinned and sat back, crossed his arms, and looked at Tulyata.

After several long minutes, Tulyata broke the silence. Her whole body shook. Zreyas cocked his head and a look of concern filled his face, despite his anger.

With tremors in her voice, she said, "I have something to tell you... and I take no pleasure in this. It's why I have been moodier than the normal grumpy lately."

It was easy to tell Tulyata was under a lot of duress. She took in a shaky breath and seemed to choke each time she tried to speak. Rhom had never seen her like this before.

"I can't give you details on why this happened because of balances, and I'm already pushing the balance by telling you this. I'm putting my faith in all of you being better than me in the hopes it will not hurt our mission to save Ayya. But..." Tulyata swallowed and Rhom could tell she was clenching her fists and jaw, trying to control her emotions.

Rhom sat up, feeling a concern so deep that it almost made him feel a simmering panic. "I *knew* something had been bothering you. Take your time and tell us when you are ready. It is obviously something you care deeply about."

Tulyata took in another shaky deep breath and blew it out through her tight trembling lips. She looked down. He could tell she was trying to hide the tears falling. "When we picked you up, Rhom, we were basically..." She stopped and was visibly out of her element.

Rtu gently said, "I can tell them if you want me to."

Tulyata shook her head and took a deep breath. "Zreyas, you have no idea how you saved us all, and I want you to know I appreciate you. You will never hear this again from me, so enjoy it," she said as if she had acid in her mouth, yet it was sincere. She looked like she was going to explode from the words. "You are something... special. Anyway, when we picked you up, Rhom, we were under contract with the Dark One."

Zreyas froze sharply in mid-breath, then looked at Rhom.

Rhom didn't make a move and concentrated on Tulyata, hoping to show Zreyas it was a time to listen with the heart and not with the emotions. Sometimes it was difficult to teach by example because he had his own emotions pinging around inside himself, too. He really hoped when all this was over that he could take in Zreyas as an apprentice. He was rough, but he had what it took to replace him if something happened.

She continued, bringing Rhom's thoughts back into focus. "We were trying to figure out how to get out of this contract this whole time. But Zreyas broke it for us. That aura of peace was just too powerful to keep the link; and since the contract was under circumstances forced on us by keeping balance, the laws allowed the break of the contract to stand because it was broken naturally. But if we *hadn't* done it, there would have been *literally* zero chance of success in helping Ayya and Aaru." She took a deep breath and said with much speed, "I'm the reason the Dark One knows where Ayya is. There, I said it. I'm sorry."

Silence filled the room, and Tulyata sat back hard.

Rtu joined the confession. "I am not innocent either. I followed Tulyata's decision without question, and I think that was worse than choosing to do it myself. At least she had the balances in mind."

"It's probably why we didn't hear the voices when you were in that challenge run, though it is too late now to test it." Tulyata looked down at her lap, still visibly shaking.

"In her defense... though it was still her choice, when she found out there was a zero chance for us all to make it, she did what she felt was best. She tried to be a spy to help our cause. Tulyata did it in the hope of having enough will to work against the Dark One's enthrallment. But it was also how they found out where Ayya was so fast, through her inside connection. I apologize as well, though it doesn't help. I just ask for your forgiveness."

Zreyas stood there with wide eyes, then his expression morphed into a hot fury. He visibly forced himself to breathe.

Rhom admired the composure, since he knew it was incredibly difficult for a Janquar to hold their temper when even slightly agitated.

After a few moments, he turned to Rhom. "That tryst

you gave me to find Ayya... Can I have it again?"

"You already have it, remember?" Rhom knew what he was going to do, and he felt an immense heavy sadness fill him. It was like watching the son he never had, leave to go into the jaws of death, and wanted so badly to plead that he stay.

Instead, he looked over his shoulder to Zreyas, feeling the waters within him churning like angry rivers of panic. He nodded. "We have upgraded yours through a crystal Rtu made." Rhom swallowed. "I was coming to find you to upgrade it when you ran into my foot. The new one will also signal me, and only me," he added, "to know where you are, and a few other things to make it more helpful for you."

"As long as it lets me know where Ayya is, that is all I care about. I will find a way to protect her. Put me down on that planet. I've had about as much visage-ness and hypocrisy as I can stomach right now."

Tulyata silently started messing with her scales.

Zreyas leaped down from the back of the couch he and Rhom were sitting on.

Rhom reached into his leather pouch and pulled out the innate crystal that Rtu made to upgrade Zreyas' tryst. The one he had was lifeless and useless, but he wanted to keep it, anyway. He remembered the wonder he felt when Rtu had given it to him as a Viduri incarnate. It was also why he was able to find Zreyas again. Both of them, the discovery, wonder, and fascination of those times, were something he didn't want to forget. Those things could only be experienced as an incarnate, and he didn't want those body and mind memories to fade.

His heart felt like it was breaking inside. He could barely contain his tears trying to push out in a torrent. "Be safe, my boy. I will miss having you around. I'm still going to keep my promise to you. You are not alone, and I will be there for you. I've never betrayed you and don't plan to, and I'm sorry you had to see the dark side of being a visage... We are no different from incarnates, really. I was also serious about apprenticing you in the future, if that is something you ever want to do."

Suddenly a door opened in the room's side, opposite the node, revealing the surface of Tarq. Zreyas was familiar with this section of the planet, at least in part. Though he had no idea he had shrunk himself at the time going through that fracture, he managed to fight giant hostile animals, survive, and make his way to him. Zreyas was a natural at survival in nature.

But Rhom knew the dangers on that planet that Zreyas didn't, but he had to stay quiet for the balances that needed to be kept, else he would doom them all by tipping them giving a recoil of exponential advantage for the Dark One that had escaped his dimensional prison. His soul wanted to cry out to warn him, but he couldn't. He understood why Tulyata had to do what she did.

Tulyata looked at Zreyas with open sincerity for the first time. "For whatever it is worth, thank you for all you have done."

Rhom looked over at Rtu, who was trying his best to open his mouth to say something, but tears flooded out instead.

Zreyas turned and stormed out of the dimension, down the ramp she had provided, and onto the planet, never looking back.

Grief and loss ripped through Rhom as he looked at him walk away onto that beautiful, lush planet. He felt the tendrils of the Dark One's energy and it made him shutter. As the door shut behind him and all went silent, he figured the next thing that would happen was that Tulyata would change her dimension pocket so she could hide where they were.

Then Rtu distracted him with a cracked voice. "I'm surprised he didn't tear us apart."

Though clearly upset, Rhom could tell he tried to keep things light, but he had no patience right now with making things flippant.

"I'm not," he said sourly. "He is a *master* at using his anger. And he has learned enough from his brother and me to channel it. You two are so busy being so flaming pompous that you have lost all compassion!"

Rhom sliced his hand in the air, palm down from one side to the other, leaning his head forward. "*Never* tear him down again with me around, or we will have a serious problem, and I won't bother to contain my anger! He is better than any of us at this point. At least he has integrity with no big secrets."

Tulyata looked up to the closed door, then watched Zreyas on her screen, clearly upset about losing Zreyas as well.

"Noted," she said blankly.

Rhom felt Tulyata's crushed spirit, but he was still so angry he could barely contain himself. "At least your little secret is out, and maybe one day he will forgive us." Rhom sighed. "Thank you for at least letting us know, rather than us finding out some other way. You would have been dealing with a raging son, and it wouldn't have been pretty. We have done him so wrong on many levels."

"Us? You did nothing wrong," Rtu said.

"I'm associated with you, and he knows I cannot leave with him because of who I am. He was angry at me because I'm one of those visages that deceive in his eyes. I know he loves me, and that somehow makes it worse."

"I'm sorry, son," Tulyata said, looking up to face him,

her face tear-stained and still crying silently. "I didn't mean for all this to happen like it did."

"I know. We just need to stop and remember, no matter what we are, no matter what our gifts are, just because we are in a higher station or different species, it doesn't mean we are the better being, the better opinion, or the only right way!"

The more he talked, the angrier Rhom became, despite Tulyata transitioning into a full cry. "You two have cost me my friend because you didn't factor in your own processes, choices, and growth in the balance. You were too busy being... *entertained!*"

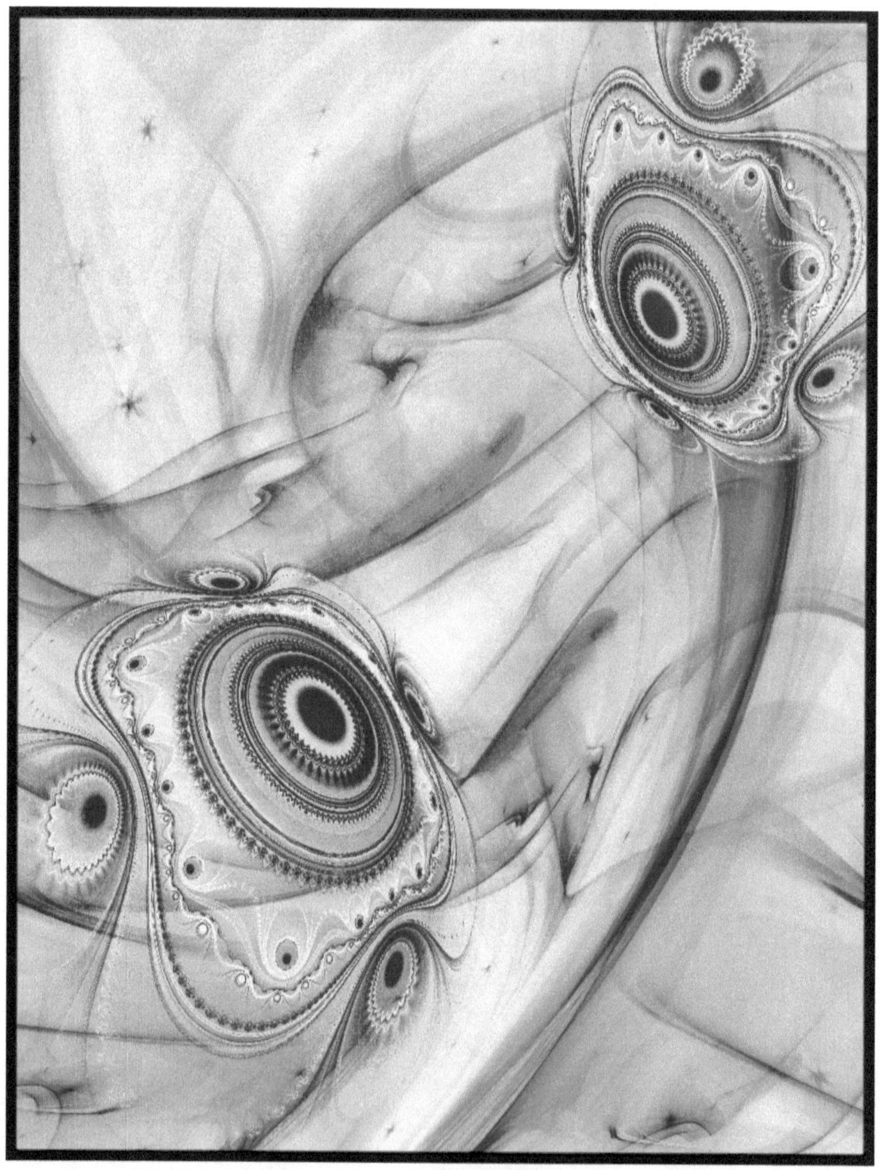

2 You Can t Use Me

Rhom

Rtu's radiant dark-skinned face turned sullen and his large dark freckles seemed to melt down his face as his features drooped. He looked at Tulyata, crying as his own eyes filled. He pulled a handkerchief out of thin air, and reached over to hand it to her, then did the same for himself.

Rhom didn't hold back, though. The more he thought about the damage they had done, the more the anger filled him. "It also cost Zreyas three friends, his brother, and his only chosen family... us!"

The grief just about overwhelmed Rhom and his heart was painfully ripping apart. He realized Zreyas' description in the dying dimension of his chest cracking almost made him chuckle because of its accuracy. He felt his eyes fill, and the torrent of his water element was about to break open.

Rhom took a breath to calm himself, trying to focus on the grief and anger. "He and I talked about what chosen family was—he told me when we were at the console that he wanted to believe that you two were part of our family too. Then you cost him something even more precious. You cultivated the circumstances and environment for him to choose to lose faith in good people, visage or not! And that is just the beginning of the list!" Rhom stood and paced.

Tulyata's eyes filled all over again and ran down her face. He had never seen his mother like that before, but it was about damn time she and his brother rekindle themselves a little. She looked down and wiped her face with a handkerchief Rtu had given her.

Rtu looked shocked and had tears dripping onto his firm belly.

Rhom checked his emotions before he did any unrepairable damage. He took a deep breath and let it out slowly, remembering his love for them. He needed to talk in the realms they were more used to. They weren't visages of aether. They experienced them, but he had to remember that was not their realm.

"All that said, I know that despite our mistakes, he's going to change the game, and he doesn't even realize it. And it would have happened whether you sided with the Dark One or not."

Rhom scratched his head over the top of his right ear, then looked at his mother and sighed. "Thank you, Tulyata, for having that courage to tell us that horrible news. I know it must have been extremely hard for you. It would have been for me as well." He turned and looked at his brother. "Thank you, Rtu, for telling us your part as well."

"You are both hurting. Rest a bit. I invite you to recharge and take some time alone. Zreyas will not abandon his promise. He is still in the game with us. To his credit, I could tell he didn't want to blow up, and the best thing he felt like he could do was focus on his task and strategy rather than show his hurt. That trial he went through and his successful find of that portal room for our challenge was an epic effort of will, steadfastness, and heart. If anything, we should be following him and his determination. He has shown more respect, strength, commitment, and heart than any of us."

"It's good to know that not all is lost," said Tulyata quietly. "I don't have to check balances to see that from what you said. I have faith that you know the boy enough to say what you did." Tulyata stood, waved a hand, and opened the door to her chamber room in the back of the room and walked in. The door shut behind her, leaving Rhom feeling a loss approaching that he couldn't put his finger on.

"That... was intense," Rtu said, looking down at his feet.

"I liked you better when you were laughing and honor-bound. You got lazy in your visage-hood, dear brother. What happened?"

"Though it isn't an excuse, I missed you. We were a team, and suddenly we split for the cursed balances and I was alone. I guess I used Mother as my companion, and it was just easier to go with the flow. I'm not proud of it, and I won't make excuses. But I know I won't ever do it again. Besides, you are back."

"Rtu, you can't use me either. We are separate visages now—different individuals from the same source, just like all the Janquar, Humans, Viduri, and so on. It is no different with us. In a way, we are incarnated with a different role and set of rules. Truth be told, I'm quite lost myself, but we must find our own way and live according to our own design."

Rhom scratched his head just above his right ear, then rubbed his face for a moment. "When we don't live our design, disaster will always be on the way. Believe it or not, Ayya and Aaru taught me that, and then the incarnated Rhom put the ultimate lesson in for me. I understand the power of incarnating now. Living that incarnation taught me so much. Now I need to integrate it better in my current form. I won't lecture anymore about this—you know this already."

Rtu was silent and rubbed his dark freckled face, adorned with sadness, then nodded. "You are right, brother. And I have missed you terribly. I checked in on you every day. And you were superb in what you did! I was always in awe at how you handled things, even though you were suddenly this huge spirit of a visage stuffed into a cramped body." Rtu chuckled sadly, "I always secretly hoped you would explode or something so you would come back, but I couldn't help but admire and watch you. You made an outstanding teacher and father. Ayya didn't have a father, but you were just like one in her life. She adored you, even though she was definitely a rebellious freethinker."

"As she should be. She is to bring in the new age, not just save the Viduri race. Though we all have a part in doing that, there are certain ones that will bear a lot of the weight. She and Zreyas are two of them. Change *has* to happen... and unfortunately, she ran out of time to get those changes in place yet, so now everything has to be done the hard way. I keep going over in my mind, wondering how I could have done things differently and assessing mistakes I made in the past as an incarnate."

"Mother checked. If you had sped up her ceremony earlier, the acceleration would have met the pace. If you had put it off, then it would have come at the same time. It was alarming to her. That is why she did what she did, although it wasn't the best solution, maybe. It provided us with a powerful lesson in responsibility and not taking visage-hood for granted, though."

"All forgiven by me. But let's talk about this a little because you have been so distracted by living someone else's decisions, you haven't really looked at the whole picture, and it would do me good to look at the whole overall picture again myself."

Rhom sat down at the edge of a chair and leaned toward his brother, resting his elbows on his knees. "A few hours ago, I dispatched the light warriors back to Vela to inform the Viduri they needed to evacuate to the stronghold on their backup planet in their system. It's not an ideal environment, but at least the stronghold city was built long ago for such situations as we are having now. They can live and thrive while they do their best to survive and keep light and higher frequencies alive. Let's hope that they can also rebuild. Without them, neutrinos would—"

"Let's not think about that. I get the picture of cascading doom, dear brother. And you are right, I have lost all perspective on the whole picture, getting wrapped up in a smaller, up-close situation."

Rhom scratched above his right ear. "Let's look at this now with fresh eyes. As much as I love Ayya, she is not the most critical player anymore. Through our actions, we have put that burden on Zreyas inadvertently. But I think these elusive powers that are behind all this knew it would happen. Zreyas has taught me many things, one being a little strategic thinking."

"If those so-called higher powers behind all these events let this go bad to the point of non-existence, then they wouldn't exist either, or at least have a reason to. We are all connected in this chain of existence. I think they adjusted for this. I know I might be hopeful, but we know from the work we do. There are almost always alternatives we can see, even if we don't like all of them; which means there are more we can't see, so living with hope is just going to put good energy out there into the quantum for us to come back to us, and that makes life more enjoyable and fortunate, even as visages."

Rhom stood. "I have made my mistakes and I'm sure I will make more. Those Janquar will not take their time. I'm going to go back to the portal room and check the time slots of when would be the best time to give Ayya her second sign to awaken. Though not as critical as Zreyas right now, she still is very critical. I miss the little phoenix." Rhom put a loving, hard-handed pat on his brother's shoulder before turning and heading to the challenge node.

Then he heard Rtu's voice say with deep sincerity, "I'm sorry you lost Zreyas. I know he is like a son to you."

Rhom stopped for a moment, feeling the ball and chain of anguish sink down on his chest, but he never turned around. He walked into the challenge node, and it wasn't long before he disappeared.

Rhom landed in the exit node and noticed he could hear his brother through the aether crying softly. They still had a connection, so it didn't surprise him. He turned to look up toward where he was, though he didn't physically see him. Over time, his brother's soft cry morphed into a full, sobbing cry.

"I'm sure many places in the multiverse will have heavy rains today, dear brother."

3 Death Crawls

Zreyas

Zreyas stomped off the ramp of Tulyata's dimension, wanting to hit something, but he knew he needed to calm down. If he didn't, the Janquar would find him faster than he was ready for because his war aura signature would flare in their communication network and give them a location of where he was. It was just a matter of time till they did, anyway, so there was no need for him to speed up the problem.

He scanned his surroundings to determine where he was and recognized a familiar landmark—the small pond where he washed his armor off the last time he was on Tarq.

Zreyas could see better this time, because he was twice as tall. He couldn't believe how much difference an extra fifteen centimeters made. A small portion of the plains' foliage was shorter than him now. In his mind, it was perfect and more manageable.

The plan, for now, was to get back to the coast where they wouldn't think to look for him so quickly, taking advantage of the fact that all Janquar hated water because their eyes were so vulnerable to it. He would set up a base of operations for himself there.

First, he would fill his water-skin and drink his fill as well. *I guess I should have asked for some supplies first before leaving.* He walked over to the pond. The water was crystal clear today; it made him smile.

He sure wished he had his bow with him. He missed that weapon but he didn't have time, nor the proficiency, to make a new one. The artisans always did it for him. He missed having someone do things like that so he could concentrate on what he needed to do, and it made him have a softer spot in his heart for the artisans. Only now did he realize how important they were to him and how well they treated him. That was probably the only thing he missed at all about the Janquar Nation other than his brother.

Zreyas started laughing when he thought about how small he was and how the bow for someone his size would affect something he shot. His arrows would be like a little splinter to most, if it penetrated at all. There was no way a bow for his size would penetrate a Janquar as hard as their skins were.

Zreyas realized how much he missed Rhom already. He even missed Rtu and Tulyata. He was glad he said nothing he regretted to them before he left. Zreyas filled up his skin again.

He reached into his pocket and pulled out the modified tryst Rhom had given him. He held it in his palm after looking around to make sure nothing was approaching. It looked far more vibrant than it had before. It must be the enhancement that Rhom told him about. But he still didn't have a clue about how it worked. The living rhomboid-shaped neutrinic-gleam pendant with an inset triangle swirled within itself like normal. Three points in the inset triangle had channels between them, making the outline of the geometric shape. The points and channels were blank except for the one dot representing him in the bottom left corner. The glowing cyan dot bled into the two channels slightly that went out to meet the other two points.

Feeling ridiculous, he spoke into it. "Rhom, I'm not sure if you can hear me, but giving the thankings to you for everything. I shouldn't have stomped out of there so fast, but it was better than saying or doing something I would regret. I'm going to find out what I can about their node and see if I can sabotage them a little while I'm at it. It might be crazy, but it's the only plan I have right now."

Sitting back on the grass, he looked around him. It was mid-morning, and the breeze blew gently. His chest filled to cracking as he thought about how hard it must have been to talk about what they had done. He wanted no more regrets in his life. He had never had them until several days ago, and they were debilitating.

Speaking into the tryst again, he said, "Tell Tulyata and Rtu I'm not angry at them because I know they meant well and did it for balance—but I *am* angry at the results. I understand they were facing extreme circumstances, but they still made choices that ultimately killed my brother and jeopardized Ayya, too. But, I know I will make mistakes too. I just hope I'm forgiven when I do. Ticking-hell, sometimes life seems too hard to make any sane decision."

Zreyas rocked back-and-forth, feeling awkward. He was new at this heart talk. "In case I get myself killed, I want you to know, Rhom, I'm always there for you too. You are not alone, and I... I am giving the lovings and missings to you."

Putting his tryst back into his pocket quickly, he shook his head. "Ticking-hell, that's enough of that. It was worth it, though. I got no regrets now."

He stood up and faced the direction where the fires of the Janquar would be. He stared blankly for several minutes. Zreyas took deep breaths to ready his mind for what he was about to do. Then, he grinned the best grin he had ever done in his life. "I got a pile of mag-shit to stir up by stealing their most valuable resource."

Zreyas packed up his things, drank more water, and made sure his water-skin was full. Then he tuned in with his instincts. He brought his war aura up, gently pushing it out to feel the surrounding environment. Turning as he looked, he took in the flat grassland toward the ocean first. He listened for the ocean life and heard the wind, distant waves, no life. Then gradually turning around to face inland, the forest blocked any long-range view. He heard and felt a breeze and rustling leaves. There were no signs of approaching dangers and no life approaching.

As he made sure he left nothing behind, an odd energy surrounded him that made his skin feel mucky, and it took him by surprise. He wanted to wipe it off, and tried, but there was nothing there. *That s odd, I ve never done that before. Ticking-hell, I ve never felt anything like that either,* he thought. He shrugged and told himself it wasn't a bad thing.

As he jogged toward the familiar coast, his curiosity grew at how everything here seemed different this time. It hadn't been that long since he was here. Even with his time in Tulyata's timeless dimension, only a few days up to a week had passed. He reasoned it felt longer was because his body was changing inside and out, as well as his mind. Everything around him seemed to have a—. *Ticking hell, I don t know what to call it, but Rhom probably does.*

It felt good to jog again. Zreyas was used to being

active, and his body needed the release of the stress of his upside-down life. His body needed it, especially his eyes. He found he could think and see better from the activity, too.

Zreyas looked toward the water. He smiled at how much it had become his friend when he was here before. He thought about how weird the Janquar eyes were—not able to tolerate exposure to water and another vulnerability he had not thought about in varSas. Lack of physical activity would make them swell. Zreyas transitioned his jog into a run as the fear of that happening to him wafted up through his body.

A Janquar warrior from his homeland came to mind that had a horn array that had been immense—an indicator that his war prowess was extremely strong.

One day, he had come back from a war with his legs cut off, but survived. The warrior had been so strong a fighter that when other warriors had tried to kill him; they had been the ones killed.

The healers had been afraid of him, so they had healed him, going against Janquar protocol. Most warriors would have just killed themselves if they couldn't fight anymore, but he hadn't.

He had been a trainer, so he took up that role full time. He had stayed active, but not as much as he needed to be. Every Janquar's horn array needed support just as much as their bodies did. But, because of the inactivity to support his body and horn array, his eyes had swollen, until one day they had burst. Then he had killed himself.

What is it about our eyes? Are there more weaknesses I don t know about?

Zreyas spotted the sleeping rock formation that he had ended up on after his battle with the aramzu that had tried to eat his armor while swimming to shore. The water had sealed his eyes shut as a defense.

He couldn't seem to get his mind off the eye issue. Obsessed with it, he analyzed the frailty while he slowed to a jog. He realized it didn't happen to the artisans, workers, and cooks with blue skin. And most of them had no horns. If they did, they weren't big. He wondered if it had something to do with their yan.

Zreyas had recently explained what yan was to Rhom while they were in the dying dimension. It had been the first time he had explained it to anyone in a long time. Rhom had said it translated to him as 'the intention of the soul' of a person.

Now his body was light blue, rather than a navy-black, and operating at a higher frequency. His intentions were totally different now. That would mean his yan had changed. He used to kill for the thrill and because he was told that everyone but the Janquar was a threat. But now, he didn't want to kill anymore unless it was for a good reason. *Even I can see my yan is different from what it was several days ago.* Had it really only been that long?

He remembered he had been glad he had talked to Rhom about yan in the dying dimension because it gave him more understanding of his own species and why the Janquar were different from others that he hadn't fully understood before. He had only associated it with the color and texture of the horns and skin. Rhom had said yan had a frequency. He didn't understand soul much, but he understood how much different he was now versus back then.

Zreyas stopped jogging as he neared the shore at the edge of the grass where the sea oats grew. He noted that there was no one east or west down the beach. It seemed a little eerie, everything seemed way too... quiet.

Maybe it felt that way because he was so used to being

around crowds of people, he reasoned. He felt the surrounding air again, feeling compulsive about it, war instincts kicking in. *Something is going on, or something is nearby. And whatever it is... it s not good.*

Zreyas took his time walking the rest of the way to the rock formation that had a small cavern in it. It wasn't big, but it would be enough shelter, and it would protect him more than being out in the open. He had never really looked at it close the last time he was here because he had been trying to get off the beach and away from the Janquar without being seen.

All ticking hell would break loose soon enough, so he figured he would just enjoy the peace for now. The weather was beautiful. He couldn't help but wonder how often it rained here. The Janquar hated rain. They couldn't do much in it because of their eyes sealing shut at the most inopportune times.

Their home planet was sterile, and it had no weather other than hot and sunny. So, they had never worried about their eyes sealing there. They carried water protection for the eyes when they had left the planet. It would be the perfect time for him to really do some harm to the Janquar during the rain—if he could keep the water away from his own eyes.

"So, this is Tarq," Zreyas said, remembering the information on this planet that he had seen on the charts back in Tulyata's dimension. "You are a beautiful planet, and I am giving the lovings to it here."

As Zreyas entered the cave, he continued to talk with the planet, glad no one was around to judge him crazy. "I don't know what is going on here, but I hope the Janquar don't mess you up. They tend to destroy everything they touch. If they do, I say to you now what Rhom calls a 'pology' and say to you the sorry. I *think* that is how he had said it. If it is wrong, I make a... plop-o-logize and say the sorry for that, too. My people weren't very nice, so this is all new to me."

Zreyas estimated maybe three large Janquar warriors could fit in the cave standing up, but cramped. It had many natural shelves in the walls and had two openings in the top. Though rain would come through, it still made the cave open, aerated, and easy to see details. He found he liked well-lit places, rather than dark.

There was a ledge up high. It was big enough he could sleep on that wasn't under an opening. It felt cozy, and it was perfect for him.

He exited the cave and climbed out over the rocks around the bottom of the tall formation, making sure he stayed hidden as much as possible so the kuravy birds wouldn't eat him as a snack. He didn't hear any of them above him and didn't see any on the formation across the water, either. That was just eerie. Just days ago, they had been on every formation around, especially since they had laid eggs. Where had they gone?

He reached the place where he had crawled out of the water. There were a few crabs on the rocks eating what was left of the aramzu he had killed last time he was here. "Enjoy your meal. I made it myself. Ha!"

The crabs scuttled off the formation and plopped into the water below.

Zreyas noticed it was low tide. "Okay, I can take a hint... my laugh is a little scary." He looked around for the petrified wood spear he had left. His hopes started waning when he couldn't find it. He thought about it as he scanned the area. It would be smaller for him now that he had grown a little, but it would still be handy.

Zreyas resigned to the fact that his petrified spear was a loss, but he would make do. He climbed back over the rocks, making his way to the cave again. He decided he would rest for the last part of the day so he could do some scouting around that night.

Something about this place feels weird now, like it s growing sterile, slowly. Zreyas climbed and Q-leaped up to his new sleeping place. It was plenty big for him. It was a nice, breezy, and a cool place to be. He looked at the cave ceiling, watching the rays of light coming through the holes, and thought about how it was too quiet. The surf and breeze were the only things that made it feel okay.

He had one more thought before he fell asleep. *No—it s worse than sterile. It feels like death is crawling on this beautiful place. And everything in nature is hiding from it. Yes, that is what it feels like. Tarq, I m saying the sorry to you that this... death came to you like this. It seems we have all been caught up in something big and evil.*

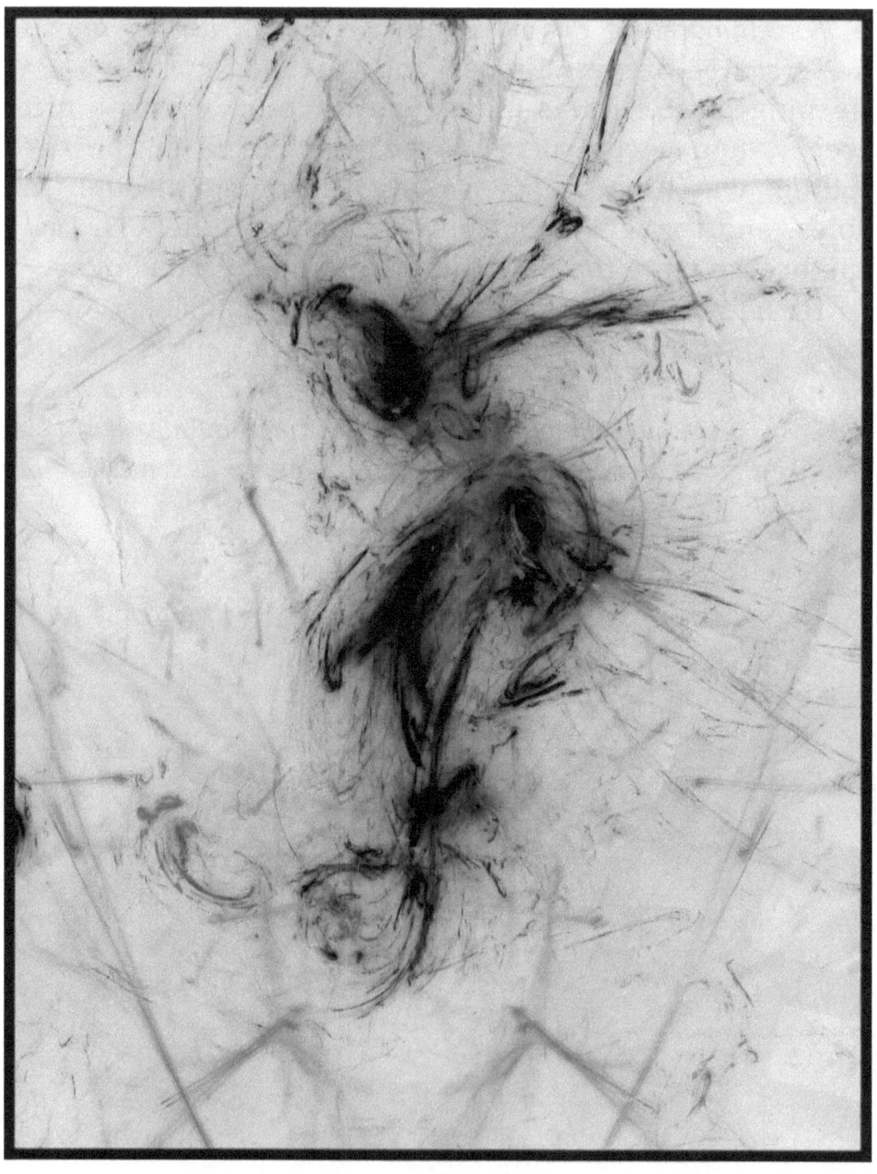

4 Dark Quantum

It had taken Zreyas several hours to find the Janquar Nation again. It surprised him the Janquar moved so far inland. There had to be a reason they went past a large wood source and never touched it. This would be the second move in just a few days. His educated guess was that there was a challenge node they found here. Emperor Rok Phaar would be nearby, too.

Zreyas was glad he started hiking inland before dusk because he still had quite a distance to cover. He took the opportunity to practice his Q-leaps. While he did so to save time, he thought about the first time he had done one in the dying dimension trying to escape by running toward a fracture that was closing fast. He remembered thinking he needed to be ahead while he thought about the lesson Rhom had taught him. It was about how the mind and brain sent out impulse signals into the quantum, and how his heart drew in the new reality that the mind and brain prompted to create while his war aura was going. At first, he ran faster. When he realized it worked, he focused on the fracture, thinking he needed to be small so he could fit through. That is when he Q-leaped for the first time... and apparently shrunk himself too.

Arriving at the outskirts of the Janquar Nation camps now, he realized if it wasn't for Q-leaps, it would have taken him an entire night to find them, if not longer. Zreyas made his way as close as possible without being seen or sensed. His size was proving to make things like that much easier when it came to sneaking around. He wanted to get a picture in his mind of what their situation was like, and hopefully, find what they might struggle with.

He climbed a large tree, using the rough bark as hand holds. He didn't want to use his Q-leap and take the chance of missing a branch right now so close. Zreyas was at the top before he knew it. Then he thought about the *silent* Q-leap and that there was no better time to hone his skills when under the pressure of not being caught. His mind was sharp now. *It feels so good to climb again;* he thought. He reached the top-most branch and moved as far to the end as possible. Zreyas sat cross-legged, using the forks in the branch as a seat.

His first task was to find out where the emperor might be. Security would be higher there. *It shouldn't be hard to find the pompous bandhula. He always elevates himself in any way possible.* Commanding intimidation was a skill the Emperor was very good at. He would take the emperor over the Dark One, though. *I wonder how much of the real emperor remains now that he has the Dark One using his body, too.* He started scanning the massive sprawl of clustered sections of the vast camp from right to left. There was so much to see, and his sitting spot was perfect.

Zreyas noticed several fights, customary for the Janquar's culture for dominance. It surprised him they had the mass numbers their species did. Most of their deaths came from their own people, and he was glad he was no longer part of that culture.

He might not know what species he was now with all his body changes, but it was better than that life. He instinctively knew that he was different even than the blue Janquar. Looking at himself, listing the changes in his mind as he scanned the camp. Besides now being light blue, thinner, and pliable, his golden horns used to be nicely sculpted and harder than stone. They had been a great protection for his head. Now they were no longer sculpted and just limp horns that were more like several fat pieces of hair that fell on each side of his head. At least they were still gold, he told himself.

But he had one thing he never thought he would experience—the freedom to think on his own. He had learned about the quantum from Rhom, how to laugh from Rtu, and that he didn't mind being called a ferret by Tulyata because it was her way to show that she had liked him.

Zreyas found his first focus as he scanned a supply cart in an area being turned into a permanent hub for artisans and cooks. He continued to scan to see how many supply carts or wagons he could find. The best way to find them was the color of the Janquar near them. The blue camps, at least, that is what he called them. They were always around supplies and food because they were the cooks, workers, and artisans.

The Janquar hadn't had to pack the carts and wagons for travel because the Janquar always kept at least one cart per supply type packed, per camp region, and ready for war. He had never packed them before except a couple of times when he was only a few varSas old.

If he could mess up their supplies, it would hurt them.

If he could kill the blue camp members, it would cripple them and many would die. They would fight for dominance over who would lower their rank to do blue camp members' jobs or to eat other Janquar for food. He had seen it happen before.

Zreyas felt conflicted. Part of him said yes to hurting his old nation, and part of him screamed no. He smacked himself in the face hard, then had a furious chat with himself. *They have done nothing but hurt anything and everyone around them just for the sake of their dominance, hate, anger, and jealousy,* he thought. He felt himself transform the conflict within himself into a pure and focused determination. *That mag-shit needs to be cut back!*

His mind started calculating strategically. It occurred to Zreyas that he needed to either kill them or change them... either way, the problem was solved. He was no visage and there was no way that they would change. *So it looks like I have no other option. Unless—*

With a renewed focus, Zreyas started scanning again, not on the supply hubs, but on the blue skins, small horns, or no horns—indicators of supplies, cooks, workers, and artisans. *Maybe, just maybe, I can help some of them save themselves. I m not Rhom, but if he can help me change, why not help who I can before it s too late? Besides, I can t do this alone. I m good, but I m not that good.*

He deflated a little when he didn't find any of the blue. Zreyas checked the one spot he saw the first wagons and carts, but there was no blue there either. In fact, he noticed warriors camping at the supply hubs being made.

Stunned and curious, Zreyas whispered, "What the ticking-hell is going on? They never camp like that. Where are the blue?"

Then he found the Emperor's camp. They had already constructed it in a permanent nature, and they were still working on it. They made it of logs and stone with absolutely no style. But, again, no blue artisans.

The artisans must be somewhere, or they wouldn't have gotten that far. There was no way the warriors worked that fast. He mentally made a note of where everything was that he had spotted. Zreyas was about to climb down to look in another place when he saw a satellite camp off in the distance. Though he couldn't see any detail, he saw the light of the fires.

Zreyas tapped the trees as far as he could to get closer. He used his newly acquired skill of Q-leaping silently that he'd grown to love. He loved the fun challenge, and he wanted to do it without thinking by default. *Sometime, I will have to try it with as much sound as possible. That might come in handy strategically, too.*

He reached the end of the tree line and he understood now why he could see that distant camp. Everywhere he looked, there was devastation—of the trees and of the life they provided for so many creatures. Zreyas only saw marred ground and stumps. Off in the distance, they had laid the foundations for a tower further inland.

"Ticking hell. Look what they have done to this place," Zreyas said softly, feeling sick to his stomach. He had grown up and lived in a desolate, sterile place, so he wasn't sure why this bothered him so much, but it bothered him a *lot* now. Maybe because he got to experience what it felt like to live in a place that had a lot of life—but right now, he felt the devastation to his core, and it made his chest feel like it was cracking inside. Then he felt anger build, and it made him more determined to do something, though he didn't know what.

"That's where their challenge node is, I bet," he said under his breath. "I think the other place was temporary. What do you think, Aaru?"

Zreyas caught himself. He needed his sanity and the determination to let Aaru go. Aaru wasn't with him... Rhom wasn't with him... No one was with him, and he needed to face that. He might not always be alone, but no one was with him now.

He let out a low, long, and menacing growl from the anger that filled him about what the Janquar were doing. He did his best to release the pressure of his war aura slowly, so they couldn't sense it.

This new way of thinking was confusing to him. Right now, he was angry at the Janquari destruction. Balances, Aaru, Ayya, Rhom, and Rtu be damned. Right now, at this moment, he was going to fight for Tarq. Zreyas would do what he could to help those that wanted help, but his priority right now was to help Tarq and destroy the Janquar.

— Be careful of the waves. I am with you.

Zreyas whipped his head around to find the scratchy static voice, then realized it had been the same voice he heard when he was in the challenge dimension, trying to find his way to a room that had a portal to Earth to help Ayya. He remembered the hall that had blasted energy waves every few minutes that made him feel different emotions. It had taught him it was strategic to have patience and wait for the waves of emotion to flatten and smooth out for the right time to decide or act. *I remember now about waiting for the silence. Who are you?*

No response.

He calmed himself and let out a breath.

Once his emotions evened, he refocused on the camp in the middle of the wasteland. Once he got close enough to see, they looked like demoted warriors. The closer he looked, the more he recognized who they were.

They were part of his own Rittak line. They had been

at the top of the line in the Janquar Nation. Zreyas wondered what terrible thing had happened that was so bad that they had gotten demoted. The more he thought about it, he was likely the culprit when he attacked his father for attacking Aaru.

One thing was certain, those men were why they flatted the massive forest so quick. They had probably used their anger and war auras to chop those trees down because they had plenty to be angry about. There were piles of sorted logs, kindling, and branches. But those were not the true artisans. They were only there because they had no choice. It wouldn't be hard to turn them, but they would not be loyal or care about the cause. They would only be loyal enough to gain opportunity. Maybe in time they would soften some.

"That can't be all of them," he said under his breath. Zreyas used his eyes like a dragnet, looking for blue camps. At the edge of the cleared land, just inside the forest line several meters back to the south, he saw firelight.

He wasted no time tapping the trees around the edge of the clearing. It was longer than cutting across, but it was safer. He wasn't about to take anything for granted, being so close to his old angry line that was so attuned to him. If he was the reason the Emperor demoted them, they would rip him apart if they found him.

Once he arrived, he stood high above them, close enough to see detail, but high enough they would never notice him, even if they looked up. He stood there, stunned at how many there were. He recognized some of them, though he had never spoken to them enough to know their names. Zreyas sighed at how he used to live and treat others. He knew he was still rough, but he vowed to make extra effort to always ask someone their name from that moment on.

Zreyas decided the best thing he could do was take his time and watch, just like he did in the challenge at the hall of waves. He was in no hurry right now. Information was the most valuable asset he could get. He was only one person. He had to do things strategic and smart. The biggest thing he could do now with the situation he was in was to sabotage the Janquar to decrease their numbers.

There were no birth tunnels here, so they couldn't replenish numbers. His plan was to kill them off slowly. It would slow their progress to hurt Ayya or get Aaru within her to fulfill his commitment to his mission. It was ticking dirty that the Dark One tricked him into making that pledge.

He watched for hours, noticing the dynamics. It surprised him how different their culture was from the way things worked when he was part of the Janquar. The warriors were all about domination and killing your way up the command line. The blue camp was different. They were like a cooperating community. They helped each other. The members didn't fight the same way. All their skin was medium blue to light blue with small to no horns. There were hundreds of them in this one camp.

He watched their tendencies and behaviors. *There is hope, Zrey. I will keep and hold that hope for them in the quantum, just like how I Q-leap. When they are willing, it will be there for them. Rhom and Aaru did for me. I can do it for them.* He got a section count of the heads in that camp and then did some multiplication to get a general head count. Some looked like they were getting ready to move camps, some did not. *Hmm, but what if... what if they joined us?*

As he thought about that concept. It was a much better situation, rather than killing them, in his mind. Then he started going over what he knew about the artisans and workers. They weren't trained for instincts, for one. In addition, when they slept, they slept hard after long days. They always had protection, almost as much as royalty because of their value to the Nation even though they didn't treat them like it. The only thing they were attuned to was instincts about something that wanted to cause harm. Well, he didn't want to do that if possible.

Zreyas spotted a tree-climber scurrying near him. He pulled his knife out and Q-leaped across to the next tree over and ran it through its temple. Its bushy tail twitched a few times as he held the scruff of the neck, then it went limp. *I need to eat, I'm saying to you the sorries, but also the thankings to you.*

He put the knife back into his belt, used the tail to secure the dead climber to his belt, and decided it was time to leave. Zreyas put a fist on his chest and faced the blue camp. *I'll be back. I want to make sure you have every chance to have something better, just like I did.*

Zreyas Q-leaped to tap a tree nearby. He made an abrupt stop. Something felt different about that Q-leap. It felt... wrong. Zreyas Q-leaped again with more attention, but that was a mistake.

As he moved through quantum space, he felt like he was being dragged back. It was as if he was stuck within the leap itself... suspended. The black space of the quantum now contained an inky mist—tendrils of it were everywhere, like a web. Then he noticed one was attached to him.

His eyes followed the tendril and realized it wasn't him it was attached to. It was the tree-climber. It hadn't quite left the dead body yet. He replayed the memory of when he had first seen the tree-climber. It hadn't seen him yet before he had killed it. Relief washed over him and comforted his mind when he realized the implications if it had.

He tried to exit the quantum by imagining that he was already out, but it wasn't working. All this confused him and he didn't know how he would get out. *Think, Zrey. Think.*

Zreyas paid attention to his surroundings. There was the web of tendrils, but he saw nothing else anywhere. He knew he needed more education from Rhom on the Quantum. He had seen nothing like this before in his Q-leaps.

A wave of horror ripped through his body. *The Dark One is using the Quantum! Is he doing something to it?*

Then he remembered what Rhom had told him when he was going to conceal them in the Quantum. He had been very adamant when he had said everyone needed to be willing. He looked down. And though the tree-climber was dead, the Dark One attachment to it was not. Zreyas doubted it was willing.

The area immediately around him had no web of tendrils in it other than the one attached to the tree-climber. *What is this? The Dark One didn't have tendrils like this.* His were black and opaque—these were a dark, sick, muddy-green-purple, and misty.

Zreyas felt himself waning and slowly watching particles of himself dissipate. He instinctively knew the frequency and space of the quantum was not a place for a dense body to stay long periods at his frequency. He watched the situation longer and thought about how Tulyata and Rtu had been bound in contract with the Dark One. As he followed the tendril to the tree-climber that was dissipating as well, he wondered if Tulyata and Rtu had one of these tendrils attached to—

Then he realized what he was seeing. He was witnessing the web of enthrallment the Dark One had on everything on that planet, including the living parts of nature like the tree-climber, trees, and even the grass. The grass had a vague mist laying on it. Though he couldn't see the actual grass, he could make out the scenery just by looking at the web and a general level. The Dark One had enthralled everything in this area. He turned toward the general direction of the blue camp. There was an enormous gap where they had been.

Zreyas turned to face the representation of the tree-climber and sent the mental signal out to let it go. In his heart, he knew he had already let go to draw in the reality so he could be released from the Quantum.

Zreyas felt the sensation of falling. He watched branches whizzing past his face. His hip grazed a branch, throwing him into a spin. Trying to orient himself from exiting the Quantum, he didn't think fast enough, and his chest hit another branch, knocking the wind out of him. His body bounced off the branch before he could grab it. The tree-climber's body smacked into his shoulder just before he landed on another branch. And ticking hell, he landed in a straddled position. Thankfully, it was large for him, so his legs took more of the brunt of the hit. He immediately broke into a sweat. He closed his legs and arms around the branch as soon as he could, trying his best not to make a sound.

Zreyas watched the tree-climber hit the ground below, causing the blue camp members to look toward the noise. He carefully unwrapped himself and laid on top of the branch to be as hidden as possible. Two Janquar walked right under him, almost touching the branch. He didn't let himself even breathe and stretched his body along the branch as thin as he could.

"What is it?" asked one of the Janquar in the camp.

His axe fell forward in its sheath, almost hitting the head of the Janquar closest to him. Zreyas reached down and slowly pivoted it back up and secured the axe between his body and the branch, making his hip cock oddly.

One of the two Janquar that came to investigate answered, "It's just a tree-climber that has gone and killed himself with a fall."

The second investigator looked up the tree toward Zreyas, "It is unusual that a tree-climber would lose their footing."

"There is a load of mag-shit happening in this place since the Emperor joined us here. Just add it to the list. Come on, we got work to do before we can sleep," waving the two back to the camp.

One of the Janquar kicked the tree-climber away, and they both walked back to the camp. Zreyas breathed a sigh of relief, grabbing the branch to sit up. He sat there for a few minutes while he let all that happened sink in.

Now he understood why it felt like death was crawling all over the planet. He was feeling those tendrils of enthrallment. That enthralled tree-climber could have been a scout looking for him.

He watched the camp members, and it was the area where there had been no web of tendrils. *They are not under his influence!* Hope filled Zreyas' heart. He Q-leaped out where the tree-climber was and looked at it. He no longer felt the energy of the Dark One on it. Zreyas picked it up and raced toward his camp. He had to think and plan carefully with all this new information. The last thing he wanted was to be seen by something that the Dark One was using as its eyes. Nothing was safe anymore.

As he gathered sticks and kindling for a fire on his way back, he couldn't help but wonder how he could now feel those tendrils. He needed to talk to Rhom.

When Zreyas arrived at the cave, he looked it over. He wanted to make a small fire to cook his meal. The tide was coming in and almost covering the cave floor, but it wouldn't fill the cave much. He made a fire on one ledge inside close to one of the openings facing the ocean. He kept the fire small and humble, but hot enough to cook meat.

He skinned the climber and prepared the hide to be dried while the fire got hot. It would need salt, though. Fortunately, there was plenty of that in the water.

Zreyas didn't know how long he could be here or what the seasons were. He would not waste something that might keep him alive in the winter. As he tended the fire and cooked his meal, he used the time to think.

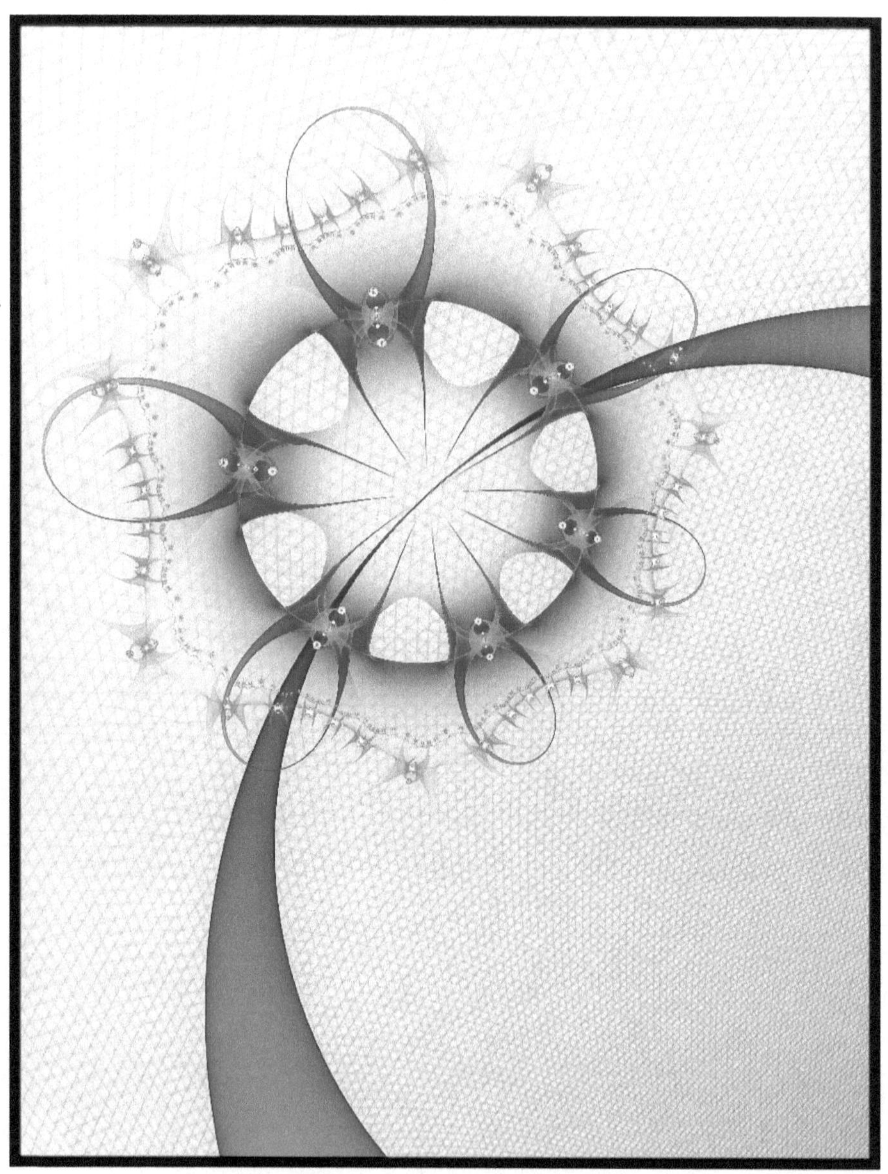

5 Blue Dreams

As Zreyas jogged back toward the blue camp, he tried to think of a meeting place that he could use if the crazy plan pinging around in his mind worked. He was counting on a lot of factors he knew nothing about. All he had were bits and pieces of Rhom's science talks and pure gut instinct. There was so much he didn't know and wanted to learn. He told himself he needed to be patient and think this through, because this kind of plan was different. This plan didn't include threats or killing—something he wasn't accustomed to. It was the most peaceful and crazy war plan he had ever come up with.

A creature with oddly shaped horns neared him as it grazed, walking on a well-worn animal trail. It was likely on its way to water. Zreyas felt the tendrils of enthrallment on it and quickly hopped into some brush to hide. It might be enthralled, but it was a creature with normal senses for its kind.

As he waited for it to move along enough that he could sneak past, he couldn't help but think about Rhom and the time he had spent with him in that dying dimension. They had fallen from the sky and lived, thanks to Rhom.

But he had wanted to rip Rhom apart and only went along with him, because he had hoped he would find Aaru. Rhom had respected him as he was, though, and that grabbed his attention. Zreyas was awestruck at how he saw him as a friend right from the beginning and realized he had been afraid of Rhom.

As he watched the animal walk past him, he wondered if it was afraid. It had to know instinctively something wasn't right. Animals were much smarter that way. *Maybe Rhom was afraid of me too, but his concern was for Ayya, just like I was concerned for Aaru. That kept us working together. Fear of what we don t know is real. It rules the Janquar Nation, and it ruled me all my life—and still does, if I m honest with myself.* He knew he left Tulyata, Rtu, and Rhom, more from fear than anger.

Rhom had told him that his war aura and anger were intimidating and harmful after he had bombarded him and his light warriors with it. If he was afraid, it was more like a healthy apprehensive respect than pure fear. *One day, I would like to meet the Viduri people. I wonder if they are all like Rhom and the light warriors.*

Well, Rhom wasn't Viduri anymore. He and his brother split into two visages and incarnated for balance. He doubted he had been a typical Viduri. In fact, he couldn't imagine him being typical of anything.

When the creature was far enough away, Zreyas slipped out of the brush and continued his jog once it was far enough away. He realized then that the safest place they could meet was at his cave. It was at the water and secluded from the Janquar. Also, there didn't seem to be enthrallment going on that far away. He knew this time of night the blue camp might still be up, but he would wait it out. As he reached the vicinity of the camp, he saw they were bedding down for the night, earlier than the warriors ever did. They had to be up early to fix meals and prepare whatever it was they needed done for the warriors.

Zreyas stalked close to the camp behind a tree and waited for them to sleep. They all looked dead tired. It wasn't long, and they were all snoring in staggered unison. He waited while he decided what he was going to do exactly. He had the plan to meet, and he knew they weren't enthralled, but he didn't know the details of what he would do to get this message to them. His first idea was to write something on the ground, but all of them were illiterate. *Ticking hell, I m not even literate. What was I thinking? Okay, Zrey, that plan is mag-shit.*

Zreyas watched them sleep while he thought. One turned over and mumbled something in his sleep and the one next to him responded with a mumble, almost as if he was resp—

That s it! I ll talk to them in their sleep! He just needed words that would stick in their head.

He thought about this plan. Thankfully, the Janquar have a habit of sleeping in circles with their heads being toward the center of the circle. They call it the stars of sleep and everyone did it when they were away from home. It was for being quiet on a hunt and still being able to plan or warn each other. They would lie on their stomachs with the circle of ground between them. When they planned, they drew basic pictures and directions on the dirt between their heads and whispered. It was just part of the Janquar habits. They geared everything they did toward war and hunts. This habit would work to everyone's advantage this time.

Zreyas padded up to the first star of nine, knowing he could never get away with this if these were trained warriors. He carefully passing the bodies to reach the middle of the star. He stood in the center and drew a simple image of the cave with his foot. The words he wanted to say still didn't come, so he thought for a moment. *Ticking-hell, I ll just make it up as I go along.* He took a deep breath, and a thought occurred to him about his pushing aura. Rhom said it pushed out. *Let s see if it helps with the communication.* So, he concentrated on using his aura along with his low voice to send the message.

> "If you know things aren't right,
> Heed the call tomorrow's night.
> Due south is kuravy's landing,
> Where the tide's crash is ever branding.
> There, you will find a better offer,
> Far better than your current coffer."

Zreyas palmed his forehead at how terrible his rhyme was, but recited it again, intending to reach their minds. *At least it is somewhat catchy... maybe?* As he recited the next-to-the-last line, one of the Janquar in the sleep star woke up, blurry eyed. The Janquar looked straight at him as he said the last line. Zreyas kept his cool, and after a pause, he did a Q-leap out to the nearby tree and hid.

The Janquar rubbed his eyes, looked around, saw the image in the sand, then waved a hand dismissively. It wasn't long, and he was asleep again. There were many sleeping stars, and he knew he needed to work fast to do as many as he could before they woke for the day.

To save time, he decided he would Q-leap to the center of the next star instead of hiding, making sure he Q-leaped as quiet as he could.

More practice.

He repeated the process of the rhyme. The second time

through, to his surprise, one of the Janquar woke again, just like the first one. He finished the rhyme and again, Q-leaped to the next star, out of blurry-eyed Janquar's view. *What the ticking hell? Twice in the same place?*

Now curious, he repeated the rhyme again with the third star; and yet again, one of the Janquar woke, dismissed it, and went back to sleep. Zreyas just shrugged his shoulders and continued the process for all the sleeping stars. With every one, but two, someone woke up.

He reached the last star, and it only had three in it. During the second time through, *all three* woke up blurry-eyed. When Zreyas finished the rhyme, he Q-leaped away to the outskirts of camp. He watched them go back to sleep. It stumped him, but assumed it was because of his size that didn't make them wake up, fully aware. He felt grateful it all got done without a problem. They were still Janquar, but he didn't want to hurt them if he didn't have to. He just wanted to give them a chance.

If it didn't work, he would have no problem slitting each of their throats. It was all he could do not to do it now, but it just didn't mix well with his guts. He was walking in a world he never knew existed with the blue camp members. It fascinated him.

Zreyas started the jog back to the cave. *Time for me to get some sleep now.* Rhom would be proud—he was doing science experiments. Tomorrow night, he would see the test results.

The blue camp members were still Janquar and could be nasty in a fight. He knew he best make sure not to take them for granted. They wouldn't roll over for anyone that spouted out an aura. The Dark One hadn't enthralled them for a reason, and it wasn't because he didn't try. In his mind, there was strength in them, but of another kind. *Hmm, if they join me, what are we going to do? I need to think about that one. I have no ship, no way to get off Tarq, no authority anymore, no nothing to offer.*

Zreyas reached his cave, slightly dejected at *that* thought. But... he also had hope. He stoked the coals of his fire that were drying the meat he had harvested the night before and sat, staring into the embers. He was pleased he had no incidences with enthralled creatures, at least that he knew of. After a short time, he covered the coals and leaped up to his sleeping spot, drank some water, and ate some of the meat.

Zreyas laid down, tired. Then he thought about the tryst. "Well, if worse comes to worse, I could always call Rhom... I think." He sighed and closed his eyes. "Good night, little brother. You might be gone forever, but I will still miss you forever."

Zreyas woke, having slept like a deadwood log. He listened to the haunting sounds in the cave with the wind and water coming in and out of it. It was comforting, fascinatingly new, and strange to him. The sounds vibrated his innards. Zreyas thought about how nice it was to sleep as well as he did last night. He wasn't sure if he ever slept that well. He sat up and picked up the last of his food and water-skin.

He looked down and noticed the tide was going out because the floor of the cave had no water in it now. He hopped down, made his way to the mouth of the cave and looked around leisurely, holding his breakfast. *It was all so deceptively peaceful. No one would ever know almost everything here had been enthralled by the Dark One.*

Zreyas walked over to the rocks in the sun, sat down, and ate. The formations across the water from him, where he had landed on the planet the first time, still had no kuravy flying around or roosting. This disturbed him. They were higher on the food chain and in elevation. Even if the Dark One enthralled them, they would still be around.

Zreyas reminded himself that he was on a strange planet and there may be something else higher in the hierarchy than them. But he knew the Janquar wouldn't have killed them to eat. They didn't bother with a bird for food, and they would be too difficult to kill for the feathers. He shrugged and put the nagging feeling aside that something was more wrong than he could see—at least until he could do something about it.

He couldn't help but consider why the Dark One would do what he was doing, why the Emperor would allow that thing to rule him, and why the warriors would follow such a thing. It all seemed to come back to one thing. He had lived too long in fear and there was an entire nation over there built around it. Fear... word had more significance than he ever believed it could have. *I m no different, really. I m just choosing to break the cycle. With any luck, some of the blue will join me in that.*

Zreyas finished eating. He reached down and got a small hand-full of ocean water and put it into his water-skin to mix with the rest of the fresh water he was about to get for nutrients.

He walked back into the cave and picked up a stone he found half-exposed in the sand just outside. When he entered, he paused. He realized he really liked this place. It was only a cave, but he found peace in it, and the light shining through the top in places made it seem magical.

Zreyas leaped up to the ledge that had the hide on it

and used the rock to unroll the rest of it that wasn't already pinned down. Cross with himself for not taking care of this hide better, it surprised him it was doing as well as it was with no salt on it. Then he remembered the sea air was full of salt. Though not enough, it bought him time. But he needed to soak it, then scrape it, and soon.

There was no real time for it now, though. At least the hide would be good enough to lie on, even if it wasn't good for anything else, when he was done with it. He figured he would worry about it after tonight if the blue members didn't somehow kill him—after all; he had invited them to his new home and hiding spot.

Zreyas picked up his water-skin and made sure he had everything armed and ready. As he walked toward the freshwater pond to the northwest, he realized he had never taken his weapons off last night. No wonder his back was a little sore. Sleeping on his crossed swords wasn't exactly amazing bedding. *I must have been tired last night.*

He decided to start a new ritual today as he thought about the habit of doing the Janquar morning rituals. Instead of rituals that were all about crushing every species that came within reach to supposedly preserve their Nation, he would talk to his friends and honor Aaru's sacrifice.

Zreyas took a deep breath and let it out just before he started jogging leisurely and thought about how lucky he was to have met Rhom, Rtu, and Tulyata—even though he was alone now. Each visage had their personalities, strengths, and weaknesses. It was refreshing to Zreyas to just allow them to be them and not make them live by Janquar rules, or kill them because they were not. He wished he had done that better with Aaru.

"Aaru, I don't know what you had in mind when you

wanted to help Ayya, but I respect it. Thank you Ayya for what you will do for us in the future—whatever it is you need to do for the multiverse. I can't even begin to understand all this. It doesn't make sense to me right now."

Zreyas looked around to check for problems, but there weren't any, and he felt no enthralled entities anywhere nearby. He wasn't willing to take that for granted, though.

"I don't know why I'm in this kind of mood, but sending you the thankings Rhom for all you have shown me. You saved me just by being you. I understand now what you meant when you had said Ayya never let you down just because she was being who she was."

He saw the pond ahead and stopped to make sure no wild animals were there that were enthralled. He did a small Q-leap, intending to pause in the quantum space like he had been forced to do two nights ago by the enthralled tree-climber.

Zreyas didn't do it successfully, but he saw enough to know there were no enthralled creatures nearby. He wondered if he was visible when he paused in the quantum. Without someone here to tell him, there was no way of knowing. He practiced trying to pause a few times as he continued his walk. He had success once, that lasted what he estimated as may be a second.

"Just in case you can hear me. I'm giving you the thankings, Tulyata, for your confession. The courage it took to do something like that was... big. I'm not sure I would have done the same—I hope I never know. Thank you Rtu for teaching me the ways of joy and laughter, even if you laugh too much for my liking. It felt strange at first, but now it feels stranger without it. I haven't laughed since I left the three of you."

6 Nagodara

"What is he doing? Has he gone mad?" Tulyata remarked, fascinated, as they watched the large screen that wrapped around three walls in her dimension at one end.

Rhom scratched his head just over his right ear, gawking while he watched him say his rhymes, Q-leaping all over the place without hesitation. He leaned forward with a huge grin, exhilarated by Zreyas' genius. "He's not mad. He's giving those guys a way out! If they take the bait, that will cripple the Janquar for a time and he just might gain allies." Rhom clapped his hands together in celebration. "Woo!" and leaned back hard in his seat, letting his arms flop down beside his legs.

"If he is successful, with even *one* of them, he will be my teacher and pseudo-visage of awesomeness," said Rtu. Then he laughed with an expression of wide-eyed wonder.

Tulyata rolled her eyes and flopped one hand over

in the air casually toward Rtu. "What if the little ferret does? How is he going to do anything with them? That big-ass group of Janquar are bound to know something is up if they are all missing their meals and no one is around to fix their armor, sharpen their weapons, feed them, build their buildings, and wipe their asses."

"I might be a little over-confident in his abilities, but knowing Zreyas, I have a sneaking suspicion that he is counting on that. He might not be all-seeing, but he was born into tactics and planning—and apparently excelled in it. There was a reason he was second in line for Emperor as small as he was, compared to the others. Also, part of his talents comes from many years of the necessity of trying to protect Aaru amongst everything else he juggled. He led tens of thousands of men, if not more. It definitely didn't hurt him to learn *those* skills. Zreyas didn't realize he trained in subterfuge, I bet."

Rtu pinched his dark freckled cheek idly, "Don't you have a ship, Rhom? Didn't you build one using element eighty-seven as fuel in one of your cockamamie experiments a while back?"

"Oh, yes, I do! I just got done testing it when I had to incarnate for the balances. There is only one problem with that, though, a big one." Rhom went silent to contemplate how to fix the problem automatically. *Maybe if I built a—*

"What big problem?!" Tulyata impatiently blurted.

Rhom looked at Tulyata. "As you know, he is not a visage. Element eighty-seven has to be handled quickly and carefully. In physical science, it only has the half-life of about twenty-two minutes in raw form, not to mention the extreme explosive aspect at the *end* of that time. He won't be able to transfer it in the special containment fuel pod that puts—"

"Yeah, yeah, okay," Rtu interrupted. "We don't need to hear your entire thinking process. Did you build a refueling station for it? And how long can it run if the ship is full of this E-87? Also, if the station is full, how long would that last?"

"I started a station, but I never completed it. Also, I wasn't exactly sure where to put it without others finding out about it. It's not that I can't *create* a place, it's just that I hadn't gotten that far to figure it all out when I had to leave."

"Well..." Tulyata started frantic balancing, the scales tipping from one side to the other so fast they blurred. Rhom thought her scales might smoke any time now.

Rtu looked at Rhom to get his attention, then darted his eyes toward Tulyata as he leaned sideways in his chair, propping his cheek up on his fist. "I think she likes him a little—enough that she has something up her sleeve."

A 3-D holographic set of blueprints appeared in front of Rhom as he made a casual hand gesture as the brothers chuckled. Rhom rotated the blueprints as he contemplated how he could create a fueling system where no incarnate had to expose the fuel or the containment system during the re-fueling process. Incarnates had a way of building things with weaknesses that malfunctioned too often.

The more he calculated, the more his chuckles died off. He felt his excitement grow as he focused. This was what he loved to do. "Give me a bit of time. I will come up with a few solutions and then we can check balances. Even if this ship doesn't work out, I have many ships... But, this one is... special, and not just because of the fuel." *I wonder... is Zreyas the one destined to have her? I should ask her.*

Rtu nodded, then asked him, "Not to change the subject, but I'm going to change the subject." He laughed, then continued. "So, do you think you got Ayya to wake up a little when we saw her at the fire station the last time? I'm glad for that short time I didn't have all my power back from that horrible bond mother and I had with the Dark One. It gave me a chance to work with you, bro. I liked the cookie baking part! And she was so cute. I've never gotten to mingle with the incarnates directly before as a pseudo-incarnate. It was fun!"

"Yes, I think so! As they were leaving, I called her little phoenix. She paused her walk. The timing was too exact to be a coincidence, and I felt her shift inside. Because I was there as Paul, it was difficult to tell without my normal skills. She had to be prompted by her mother to wake up from the daze. I really like Lanna, but she is in for a bumpy ride with that husband of hers, I think. And that means Ayya will, too."

Tulyata said with a distracted voice, "A small, yet massive, step. I checked the balances when you got back. It was a huge win. Nice work, boys!"

"We will take what wins we can get!" Rhom shifted the conversation back to the current situation. "Zreyas has definite leadership qualities. I recognized them when we were in that dying dimension."

With obvious glee in his voice, Rtu said proudly, "Look at what he has been doing on that planet, too. My little buddy is rather talented and creative! I know he has never had to do most of that before, but he just seems to know how to do it. Amazing!"

"Honestly, he trained for survival, but even some things he is doing are all instinct at this point. I know I had to do the same thing when all that mess started in the dying dimension. I didn't know what I would do next half the time. Sometimes you just have to do something that makes no sense, just because it feels right."

Rtu leaned forward. "Zreyas wants to give those blue Janquar a chance and I feel like we need to do all we can to help him. He's going way above what he needs to do. He is respecting nature, and even his enemies."

"It *should* be rewarded. That is love at its highest level, though don't tell him that. That had to be scary, and it took guts. He might get allies from it, but it wasn't the first thing on his mind—their wellbeing was. It would have been much easier to kill them to hurt the Janquar. It takes something beyond descriptive words to do what he did."

Rtu shook his head with an enamored expression. "Though I got a sample view being incarnated on earth with you for the challenge, I still had my mind and awareness. I'll have to take your word on what you say, bro. Having never incarnated, I really don't know what it is like to be up against something like that. I'm a visage of simple elements, not the visage of souls and aether."

"Don't sell yourself, short Rtu. But incarnating *has* given me a multi-dimensional view on things. The more perspectives you have, incarnated or not, the more opportunities, insight, and wisdom it gives. It's made me a better student of the Universe."

"That is an interesting way to put it," said Tulyata. "I never really thought about it like that." Tulyata gawked at her desk screen and remarked with panic in her voice, "Oh, no!"

Rhom jerked his head toward Tulyata with silent suspense while his brother said, "What's wrong?"

"Look at this..." Tulyata pointed at the screens in the room and put the scene up she was looking at so they could see it play out.

⊡⊡⊡⊡⊡ ⊡⊡⊡⊡⊡

Emperor Rok Phaar called for one of his commanders waiting outside the room. The black inky mist of the Dark One, sliding in and out of his eyes, gave Rhom chills.

A commander entered and put his fist to his chest with head high. "Wartok!"

"Activate the dark portal and release a small group of the nagodara. It seems we have two unwelcome guests on our planet. They are a threat... eliminate them, Zreyas is top priority!"

The Commander, visibly shaken with apprehension written all over his face, replied. "Yes, Emperor. But how do we keep them from—"

"*Now*, Commander!" the emperor barked.

"Right away, Emperor!" The Commander put his fist to his chest. "Wartok!" Then he turned on his heels and left immediately.

The Emperor turned and made his way down the hall and entered his private chambers, still roughly framed in and covered from early construction. He paused a few seconds, then walked toward a mirror. Rhom noticed it was strange and not of Janquar's origin. The reflection did not bear his own, but the image of the Dark One, eyes bright red and body more spread out and misty than the last time he saw the Dark One.

The Emperor bowed. "I have done as you have commanded, my King."

"Good, I want them dead before they discover each other."

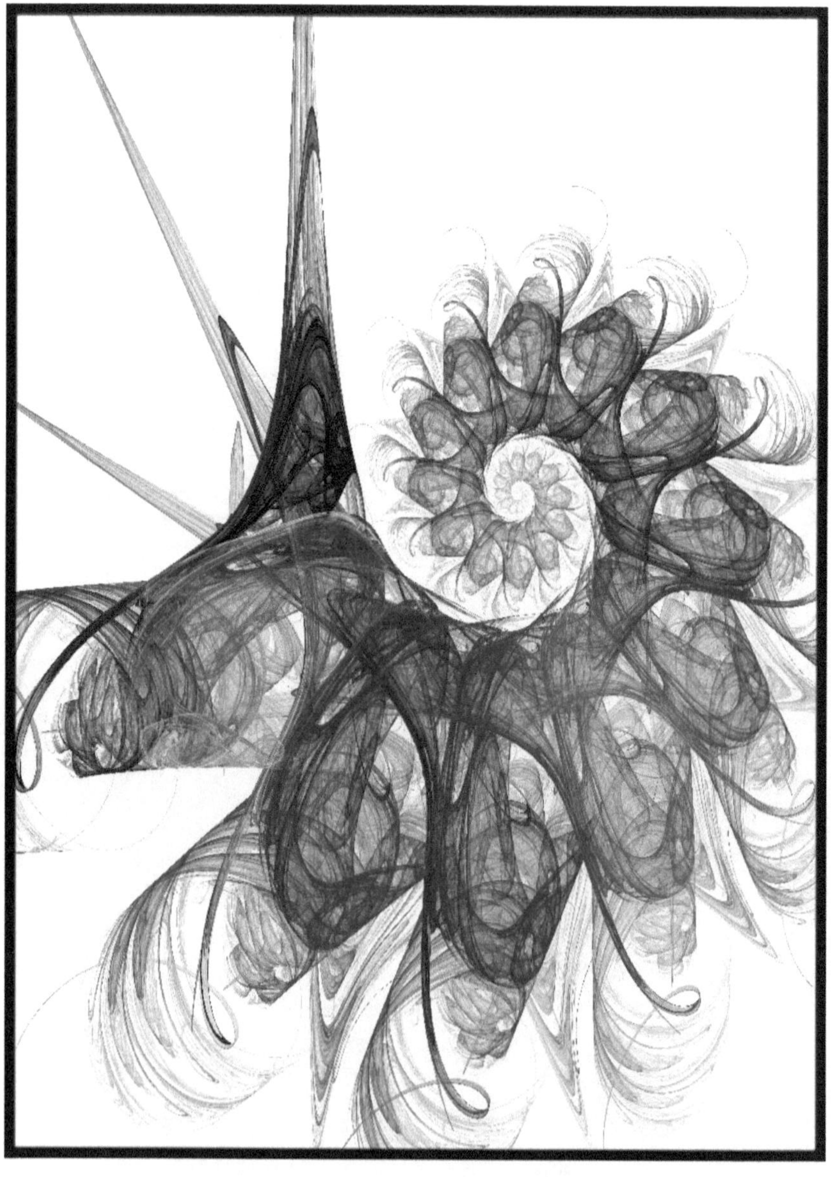

7 Quicker and Cleaner

Zreyas

Zreyas arrived back at his new home an hour before dusk. He made a fire on the rock formation outside. High tide would wash the rocks, eventually cleaning up the meat scent, but for now, the tide was going out and there would be plenty of time to let his meat dry by both the heat of the fire and the sun. While the fire burned hot, he cut the meat into strips for drying. He found also several shells. He thought about how large they were to him, and couldn't help but feel humor. "Ha!"

He used the shells as pans and cooked his meal, letting the grease pool inside with the meat. With the other meat, he soaked it in the sea water a short bit for taste and salt and lay each one on the shells with the bowed side up. That would allow the grease and moisture to drip away onto the rocks. He didn't have a rack made yet, so he would turn them every few hours.

Zreyas ate his cooked meat with berries while he dried the rest. After he was full, he maintained the fire and let the meat dry out. He didn't have to worry about animals trying to get at it because there weren't any around. It was convenient but disturbing. He left periodically to get more wood and shells as he needed them.

When darkness fell and the tide came in, he pushed the fire out into the water and packed everything in his pouch. He knew the blue camp wouldn't be here this early. They were in the thick of their duties at this hour. Zreyas decided to fill his water-skin up again and have a good shit before things got crazy. There was nothing worse than being in the middle of a fight or something important and having to take a shit.

When he got back, he sat down and dozed off while he could. After he woke, he stood at the cave mouth, hoping someone would come from the blue camp.

Suddenly, he felt very alone, but wasn't lonely. This puzzled Zreyas. Normally, he felt great alone. However, he seemed... lonely. *I guess it is because I m waiting for them to show up and because this whole new life is... too new. If they don t show, I ll kill them and find their challenge node.* Zreyas strategized he would destroy it or exploit it. He wasn't sure if he could do it, but he had to hinder their progress. Either way, he knew one thing: he would mess with their supply line first so things *would* get crazy.

Zreyas heard rustling and scratching nearby. He ducked into the cave and Q-leaped out of one of the ceiling holes to stand on the top of it. He couldn't see it yet, but he felt the enthrallment of it. Zreyas crouched and finally found the source of the noise. It was an odd animal that he had never seen before. It was furry and plump, with a ringed, fluffy tail. His face looked like it had a mask on, like the shinits. But it looked nothing like a shinit.

The little fat animal waddled up to a clam sticking out of the sand and used its hands to pick it up and crack it against the rocks nearby. After he ate the meat out of it, he continued along the beach, headed west. *Handy, that one.*

Normally that would have been a small animal to Zreyas. He considered this. With his size now, it was bigger and weighed much more than him. It would be a perfect fur for two things... winter and disguise. He had to survive, and he had to find some way to exploit or destroy their node.

Zreyas looked around to make sure no one was coming yet as he pulled one sword from his back. He let a subtle aura of war surface. *Sending the a-plop-ogies, you are enthralled, and I need to survive. I'm giving you the thankings for your gift.* He aimed his Q-leap just to the side of his head so it couldn't see him, but facing the animal. He imagined his position, and that he was already there and done what he needed to do, then Q-leaped ahead.

He landed precisely on point, just out of eyesight, grabbed its nose and drove the sword upward from the underside of its jaw into the brain. *Now you can fly, you are no longer imprisoned.* In his other life, he wouldn't have thought a thing about killing something. He would not have regarded its life at all. Zreyas whispered to it. "I just want you to know that you will help provide food, but most importantly, a disguise that might help save others from the Dark One. I honor your gift of help this day."

As it twitched one last time, he felt the thrall struggle to reach out, then he felt it leave. He pulled the sword from it and looked it over. He felt solemn, but he also felt peace.

Zreyas picked its head up by the jaws and struggled to drag the carcass into the tall grass nearby. It was ticking bulky and awkward with the size compared to him and gave him quite the challenge. Zreyas drug it past the dunes, where he was more hidden. He set it down and ran back to soften the sand marks. He could still see his cave, so, if the blue camp members showed up, he would know.

He worked quickly with precision, but also carefully. Zreyas took extra time to preserve the integrity of the hide, including the legs, head, and paws. He took extra care to pull the bones out of the limbs without cutting the hide too much, leaving loops of hide intact so he could put his arms and legs through them later, since he didn't have the tools to do proper garmenting. It would be tricky to tan and cure, but it was doable. It took a while to clean out the head with his hands and dagger, but it would be worth it. He didn't have the right tools for this kind of work, but he would make do. Zreyas definitely needed salt to prepare and preserve it properly, but he would wrap up the brains carefully so he could soft tan it. He needed to keep it pliable and soft so it wouldn't crinkle when he moved in it.

If it all worked out, he could slip his arms and legs through and wear it. If it didn't tan well or something went wrong, he could always make thin rope ties. But that would make it more conspicuous because it would pucker in places whether he stood or moved. He would be exposed on his underside and in the neck area, but for the most part, if he could get his movement down, he could fool someone that spotted him. If they were too close, they would know it was a disguise, but he didn't plan on being that close.

By the time Zreyas got the carcass separated and

cleaned, it was well into night time. He picked up the entrails and threw them into the water for the crabs. He needed to dissipate the scent as quickly as possible because he didn't want wild, enthralled animals near his home.

He moved the hide and carcass in manageable parts to the tall grass closest to his cave and scraped the hide down thoroughly, using his dagger.

Since there were no visitors yet, Zreyas figured they weren't coming. Sadly, he would have to kill them. *Well, it was worth a try. Sorry, blue, it s nothing personal, but you are supporting something... ticking evil.* Zreyas scooped up the remnants he scraped off and threw them out into the water. He moved the segments of the carcass and the hide into his cave.

Zreyas set both on the ledges at the top area of his cave temporarily. He didn't have a proper container to boil water, but he had nature. A walk down the beach would solve his problem. There were always shells.

After a few trips, he had a pile of very nice ones, some deeper than others. He set out to fill each one up with sea water and sat them carefully on the ledges of the rock formation, making sure it would withstand the breezes. The water would evaporate, leaving a film of salt. It would be tedious to refill them and scrape out the salt, but it would work. He had no pots to do it with and he had seen no clay areas yet on the land. It would go faster in the daytime with the sun. He would have to be diligent in scraping the film off and refilling the shells every few hours.

The deeper ones he used for the water, the shallow ones he would use for drying his meat along with the bones. He ended up with thirty shells placed for evaporation. It was a good start. As he found more shells, he would add to the spectacle on the rock formation. If he was to stay here for any length of time at all, he would need to make a water distiller and filter the salt out, and do it right.

As he started a fire at the usual spot, he kept his mind busy while he dug a hole in the sand. The surf barely touched it so it would fill but not get washed flat again. He tried to think if he had seen any high clay content soil anywhere while he retrieved the hide back and set it in the hole and let the hide soak in the salt water. Then he shoved sticks in deep all around the hole, forming a cage of sorts, just in case a wave came in and washed it away. He needed that hide.

He ran and got more wood and found a reed that would be handy for many things. He cut it off as long as he could, digging down into the sand at the roots.

He couldn't help but look toward the blue camp in the hopes they would show up as he did his work. Though that was disappointing, he found he was enjoying this peaceful work and wondered if the blue camp artisans, cooks, and workers felt the same way when they did their work. Their reasons might be different, but he hoped they enjoyed it as much as he did. He loved survival crafting in nature. He just wished he had been strong enough to admit it while he was with the Janquar. It might have led to appreciable change. Remembering, he painfully sighed because he had even mocked them.

Zreyas realized unless he got himself set up properly, he would never be able to do what he needed to do in order to survive. He was going to have to take a little extra time to make sure he got all the necessary tools. If this place had a winter or a scarce season, he would be in trouble. There was one way he knew of to find out if there were winters and he would check for it after he finished a few other tasks. There were probably more ways, but his knowledge was limited. It was almost dawn, and he had a lot of work to do.

Over the course of the morning, he scraped the membrane off the hide, and repeated the process of soaking, stretching manually, and scraping. He also cut the meat up and saved the bones, stacking them higher than the waterline on the huge rock formation to dry. Then he started drying the meat using a frame he built to hang the meat near the fire. Though the shell method worked okay, it was less susceptible to crabs, quicker and cleaner.

Zreyas went back and cleaned all the bones so there would be no insects. At his size, a lot of insects would be a life-threatening problem. He used one of the smaller bones to grind against a smooth rock to expose the marrow, dug it out and ground it down more to make more of a slightly rounded spike. He wished he had pots to boil the bones, but that was another thing on his list.

He ground the end of the bone to make a point to shape a needle. Then he snapped the length of the bone down to one third the length so he could make the eye, then carefully used his dagger to turn it to create an eye. Then he made two more, just in case one broke.

Zreyas decided to sleep before he made his next trek out to get material for rope, and to find out if the land had a winter. He had no way of knowing how fast the planet rotated its seasons, so he felt he had to concentrate on making sure he would survive so he could live, sabotage the Janquar, and find Ayya.

Sleeping in the afternoon would be nice in the cool cave. After he put everything away inside the cave temporarily, he hopped up on his sleeping ledge. Zreyas ate and drank while he relaxed a few moments, feeling good about what he got accomplished. He leaned against the wall, watching the surf through one of the holes on the other side of the cave.

Zreyas was tired, but it was a good kind of tired. He didn't intend to, but he fell asleep while sitting up, food and water in hand.

Several hours later, he woke with a stiff neck. All his water had spilled out of the water-skin. "Ticking hell," he mumbled in frustration at himself. "Ah well, I know where I can get water."

He was getting a bit rank with all the work. He washed his vest and under-clothes and wrung them out. Zreyas hung them inside his cave, half out of the holes at the top. It wouldn't be long and they would be dry with the breeze and sun. He got his pouch cleaned out and repacked while he waited.

Zreyas rolled the larger hide he wanted to use for both winter and disguise up damp so it wouldn't dry before he had the chance to properly stretch and dry it. He cursed he didn't have what he needed to do it now, but he would by the time he got back. He would roll it out and hang it inside the cave for now to keep it from molding. It was dusk now and it wouldn't dry fast without the heat of the day as thick as that fur was, anyway.

He put his clothes on, still a little damp, and left his armor. His weapons were going with him, though. He was just going to get water and come back before his two-purpose trip.

Zreyas headed out to get water. He felt good, though it felt odd to be free of his armor, and he Q-leaped silently here and there for practice. Just as he approached the larger of the two ponds, he watched a group of Janquar walking away northward, just before disappearing into the night past his night vision range. *I guess they need water too.* Once they left, he approached the pond.

He stood there, stunned.

The entire pond had been drained. Fish were dead at the bottom, and a few still flopped and twitched in their last gasps.

Zreyas couldn't believe what he was seeing. That pond wouldn't be a drop I in the bucket of what that Janquar nation needed to water them. They had to be using another water source. He couldn't understand why they drained the pond.

He walked to the smaller one ten minutes from there to see if they left that one alone. He arrived to see the same thing. They had drained it, too. Well, his trip the next day would have more objectives now. He had to make his drinking water unless he could find a fresh running water source.

He checked while he was there to see if there was any clay content soil around the ex-pond. He saw none.

Zreyas used his hand to make a trench for the wet mud to drain water into it. After it pooled up inside the trench, he fed it into his water-skin. He might be desperate before he got more drinking water, and it would be better than nothing.

As he walked back to his cave to conserve energy, he stopped again at the larger ex-pond to check that soil for clay content. He bent down, grabbed some soil, and gripped hard. When he opened his hand, it crumbled loosely. He shook his head. Though he expected it, he sighed—no clay. He stood and made his way back, planning as he went.

Though that was his first home here, he would pack everything up and take it with him at dawn. If the blue camp came to visit after that, he would just have to miss them. Someone knew he was there. He wondered if the blue camp reported his strange visit. Zreyas shook his head. "They are in as much trouble as I am," he said out loud.

He reminded himself that he had to stop thinking about *them*. Right now, his focus *had* to be survival for himself. The rest would come later.

8 First Encounter

Now armored and ready to go, Zreyas looked around for his rope, then remembered where it was. "Ticking hell, I left the rope I made in Tulyata's dimension." As he started his walk east, he continued to talk things through with himself, making hand gestures.

Zreyas had known he would need rope, and he wasn't sure yet if the planet had the plant die-off from seasons yet to make it. It was a durable rope with a lot of tensile strength. He wasn't sure they had the same ones here. *I better go with what I know—I m in a race for survival, and that shinit fur worked well. I hope they remember me. They helped me once. Let s hope they still want to again. I really don t want to kill them.*

Zreyas arrived at the shinit cave formation focused. Somehow, coming back here made him feel like he was coming home. It gave him a small measure of comfort in this chaotic race to survive in unfamiliar territory.

Zreyas smiled—he didn't have to take his armor off and swim this time. It took three Q-leap hops from rock to rock and he was back at the exit that he took in the rock formation. He climbed back up past where he had slept his first night and arrived where the shinits had tried to feed him.

Something wasn't right.

He didn't feel them, and the smell here wasn't the same. It smelled of death. Then again, everything smelled and felt like death crawling over everything here now, thanks to the enthrallment of the Dark One.

Zreyas crouched and pulled his two swords off his back. *Ticking hell, this is eerie; something has gone terribly wrong here.* He stalked quietly into the area that he pulled so much fur from. There was no life. He checked all the pockets that they previously used for bedding and where they eliminated. Nothing living. *This is not good. This is a bad omen.* Zreyas noticed his body sweating and palms getting slippery. *I am more than nervous. Something is near, but I can t see it.*

He sheathed his weapons long enough to climb with quiet care to check outside from the top of the rock formation where he had seen the kuravy nesting before. But that hole was so high for him to be quiet. He decided to Q-leap to the top hand hold and grab onto the ledge.

Thankfully, he got lucky and did it perfectly. He peered out of the hole first, then lifted his body up. His breath caught as he stared, trying to grasp it in his mind.

A single head of one of the beautiful kuravy was laying there on the rock. All the eggs had been broken and emptied. Something had torn apart the nest. He let out a whispered under his breath, "What the ticking hell did this?" That was when he spied something truly odd. There was a glowing dark-purple and green-marbled, thick slime of some sort. He picked up a stick and touched it. The stick smoked and sizzled. It ate away at the wood but didn't eat at the stone beneath it. He laid the stick down carefully so that it wouldn't splatter.

Zreyas turned slowly to look back over the hole he came out to see on the other side. His jaw hung slightly, and panic filled him. VarSas of training were the only thing that kept him focused; he immediately felt and heard the pulses of his circulation in his ears and was acutely aware of the alarm running through every muscle. That triggered the filling up of his war aura compartment. His fists clenched firmly, and he felt the sweat bead on his forehead. He was in war mode now, but out of pure fear. He wanted to run for the first time in his life.

In front of him stood a creature with most of its body covered in fur. Its body structure was like a rodent. The hind claws were long, black, and the knuckles seemed almost mechanical, but still fleshy. The clawed feet were built for torque, and they were needle sharp, designed to rip flesh up. *Ticking-hell, what is this thing?* As intimidating as its claws were, that wasn't what was causing the fear. What it was doing was what had him in war mode.

It still had not noticed Zreyas—he hid behind a rock near the hole and slowly lifted his axe and dagger out of their sheaths. He was afraid to pull his swords because of the chance of noise. The front legs of the creature weren't really legs at all, they just hung there. They seemed too tiny and useless for the rest of its body. As odd as what he saw was, seeing the rest of the creature gave Zreyas chills.

Webbed fish-like fins stretched out like wings on both sides of what its neck would be if it had one. Its eyes and slitted nose seemed to sit just above its mouth. The fins would fan periodically, pushing air forward and down like wings. The bones that supported the webbing of the fins ended in sharp talons. At the base of the fin against its head on both sides, there was a fleshy valve that opened periodically, emitting a fine purplish-green and black puff of mist barely perceptible.

Zreyas shifted in his position carefully. It had raised eyes like a crab, but with vertical slits. The seeing holes got wider from time to time, emitting the same mist. As the creature turned slightly toward him, terror rose inside him as he got a good look at the face and mouth.

He instinctively created a war aura, pushing out a warning before he could stop himself.

The creature turned to face Zreyas, now aware someone was there. It wasn't intimidated at all from his aura. Its mouth was round, made up of six circular rows of sharp serrated teeth. It looked like a circular grinder that you would feed something into.

Each row of teeth moved independently from the row next to it in opposite directions and started oscillating back and forth. They were designed to rip and mulch, and they were covered in blood.

Zreyas gripped his weapons firmly, readying himself for a fight. As he peripherally looked at his surroundings. With fur, tails, feathers, talons, and beaks scattered everywhere, he realized why there was no life in the cave. *This piece of mag-shit creature is not natural.*

Then Zreyas watched the oddest thing he had ever seen. He didn't know the word for it. The creature's eyes opened in the black middle where its eyesight should have been used. Then it started emitting a dark black mist. It made his skin crawl, being so empathetic to eye problems of the Janquar.

Zreyas stumbled back and almost fell on his ass when the wings and eyes slid backward over its body, turning itself inside-out, revealing more rows of teeth in its round mouth.

It continued, revealing more teeth. Now he understood why its front legs were tiny—the mouth covered the ticking things up, sliding back around its body. He realized the entire insides of this creature were rows of teeth that were now becoming a defensive armor, as well as what he thought might be some sort of way to engulf its prey. As it turned inside out, mucus remnants of meat and blood oozed out and fell on the stone. The creature stopped turning inside out when it reached its hind legs. The smell almost made Zreyas lose his stomach's contents.

"Ticking hell! What are you?" Zreyas felt the anger surge from a pure fear that he felt for the first time in his life. He had always been angry inside all his life about most things. But this... it was clear, unadulterated, and raw fear that ripped up through him, creating the anger surge. It took his breath and disoriented him a few moments.

Just as Zreyas thought he had seen all the creature's features, another one revealed itself. The middle spikes in the wings started extending five long spindly knuckled claws almost as long as the creature that seemed almost mechanical. Zreyas pulled his head back, appalled.

More mucus emerged between the teeth, dropping to the stone under it. Some of it dropped on part of a carcass that it had been working on when Zreyas had gotten there. The carcass boiled and sizzled from the contact and he felt extreme heat from it. Zreyas' eyes widened and another wave of terror ripped through him.

The creature's spindly claws retracted back into the wings slightly as it sat back on its back legs. The wings turned toward Zreyas like it was honing in on him as more mist started wafting out of its eyes. He realized what it was going to do just as it started beating the finned wings furiously.

Zreyas Q-leaped out of the way to avoid the spray just in time. And anger surged violently as he thought about what this... abomination had done to all these beautiful creatures here on Tarq. He knew he had to kill it, and quick.

The creature hissed out syllables he didn't understand, spitting mucus in the process. This thing had a feeling about it that wasn't natural, made of pure evil, and it made his skin crawl.

"Who sent you? You are one ticking-evil piece of mag-shit!"

Zreyas stepped back, staying crouched, almost falling back as his heel hit a loose rock, but he regained his footing. *Think, Zrey. Think.*

He wanted to see how good its reflexes were before he did anything drastic just to get himself killed. He needed to understand this foe, because if this one was here, there would likely be more.

Zreyas reached down and picked up the rock at his foot. Immediately, the mucus flowed and the wings beat. He Q-leaped out of the way, again. It immediately turned. There was no acceleration time, no deceleration either. It was on or off as if it used the quantum, but it wasn't quite the same.

He Q-leaped again forty-five degrees over, let his anger flare just as he landed and threw the rock hard straight toward it.

The creature's wings beat, teeth rotating, and the spindly claw extended at lightning speed, grabbing the rock. As it pulled the rock into its stomach, the animal reversed its inverted state, engulfing the rock.

As Zreyas Q-leaped again to its side as far as he could away from it, he could hear the scratching of its teeth grinding the rock in its belly. *This creature is not of any universe—it s from ticking-hell. Surely Rtu didn t make this.* Zreyas narrowed his eyes in resolve. "There is no way I am letting you get away alive, you sick ticking bandhula—let's play."

Noting his surroundings at an acute level, his eyes looked straight at the eyes of the creature with razor sharp focus and let his war aura push out without reservation. Feeling the bounce-back of his aura gave him more detail, instinctively of what was around him.

It was odd, though. He noticed he felt it more acutely this time than he ever had. He would not complain, he had a kill to execute, and he wasn't messing around.

The vertical slits in that thing's eyes opened, and black mist released again. Zreyas knew what came next. If nothing else, the creature was predictable. He understood there would be dire consequences if he was in the way of that blast that it was getting ready to push out. *This has to be some minion of the Dark One.*

Zreyas' anger compartment filled and rose so fast and full that he felt like he would burst.

"You may be confident in what you are and what you do, but you have one tremendous disadvantage, you ticking piece of mag-shit. I'm not confident. I'm just learning about myself."

As Zreyas attempted his distraction of talk, he started using his newfound skill of frequency conversion, like he had done for Rhom in the dying dimension. It made his war aura exponentially more powerful and a much higher frequency. That rot-snot creature was definitely not high frequency, and he was going to use that against it.

The creature paused and made a questioning hissing sound.

That confirmed it for Zreyas. That thing knew what he was saying, and he planned to use that to his advantage. He thought about that doorway exit of his compartment and focused on it to do the conversion. Zreyas thought about Ayya, Aaru, and Rhom and the love he felt for them. As he let the anger go through the conversion doorway that he had set up to convert the frequency, he said, "Oh, interested now? Well, let me tell you all abouuu—"

Zreyas let the aura go with his word and blasted the high frequency aura forward to hit the nasty creature. He let it out as hard, focused, and fast as he could.

The thing's eyes splattered with such force that the remnants only barely hit the rock behind him before flying off the edge of the rock formation.

The creature let out an other-worldly screech that might have incapacitated him had it not been for his aura pushing out with the force it was.

Zreyas Q-leaped behind a rock that was behind the creature, letting only his head show and said, "You ticking killed my animal friends, and you got no idea what I can do, you ticking-bandhula."

The creature used the quantum to turn around to face him. The spindly claws ejected with lightning speed and grabbed Zreyas' head, mucus splattering on his armor. He smelled the sickening burn of his armor as it started slowly melting.

Zreyas wondered if he had come all this way, just to die in the mouth of this... *thing*.

9 No Bleeding

Zreyas

Zreyas' head jerked forward, body following violently with it. He found himself dangling by his head. His eyes widened when all he could see were rows of teeth, as he felt the single claws of each finger puncturing his head for a grip.

He let out a war aura and quickly slashed both weapons inward to cut the ticking-spindly arms that had a hold of him. The axe cut one, but the dagger wasn't quite the right tool. But it was enough to free the one side. As he fell away from the once-piercing death grip, the other claw gouged the skin on his face on the way down.

Zreyas Q-leaped to the other side of the formation behind a rock as the creature screeched, emitting a loud piercing sound that almost made him lose consciousness. He scrambled to get his armor off as fast as he could, careful not to let it touch his face or neck. The chest piece was first. As soon as he got it off, he threw it with all his might at the creature. As luck would have it, he hit it, knocking it off the edge of the rock formation.

He continued to take off his armor as quickly as he could. The burning smell seemed to have an effect on him.

His suspicions were confirmed when his sight blurred slightly and he felt woozy. He needed to get away from it, so he staggered away from the armor he had dropped while he took the rest of his armor off, just in case, as he went.

Zreyas shook his head to try and get his wits back as he walked toward where the... thing fell off the ledge.

He realized the true power of the mucus now. It wasn't necessarily the acid, though that was definitely powerful. It was the smell of it actively eating away at something that was the dangerous part. If he had not Q-leaped away and immediately taken the chest piece off, he would have been dead—either by whatever caused the smell, or the creature itself taking over where the smell left off. He wondered if eating away at different materials made a difference in the smell.

Putting his hands on his knees, bending down to rest and calm himself down for a few seconds, he checked to see if he saw or smelled any more of himself that was being eaten away.

After a few seconds of assessment, he decided he must be okay. He didn't feel anything burning on himself. He had gotten lucky... again. "Ticking-hell, what was that thing?"

Thinking back over the fight was something he always did for learning strategy. It's one of the things that made him get so proficient at tactics and fighting as he did. Without that extra work in his mind, he would have just been another Janquar warrior in the middle of the line.

There was one thing that came to him as he looked over all the pieces and parts littered on the top of the formation. That creature didn't bleed when he cut its spindly arm off, which was odd. He examined and sheathed his weapons. As he did that, something came to him. He had killed many things in his life and never once did he see a body not bleed or seep fluids when it was opened or killed.

He froze in realization. "That thing isn't alive—at least not in the sense that I know."

Zreyas whirled around to look over the edge of the formation.

Rows of teeth were suddenly a quarter of a meter away as if it Q-leaped there. Rows of teeth slid back over its body as a loud screech invaded his body so loud it made the teeth and his own body vibrate and shudder. Something about this screech seemed familiar, but he couldn't think.

He felt blood trickle down his lip from his nose. Out of pure reaction and body memory from what he remembered now in the hall of statues, he let his war aura go but concentrated on converting it immediately. Though still new to him, he figured his body already remembered what he did to counter it.

But he didn't want to just counter it... he wanted to kill this ticking-piece of evil mag-shit. His anger grew, and the conversion started its eruption. He let it go.

Then a spindly claw slammed into his body and face so hard it threw him over the edge of the formation. As he fell, his mind put together that the thing could fly. The rocks came fast as he watched the water. He noticed the thing coming behind him because of its shadow, still screeching.

Zreyas had an idea, and he went ahead and acted on it. It could fly, but could it swim? He aimed his next leap, a destination, a meter or so deep, near the rock that he had clung to when he first came to Tarq trying to get away from the Janquar.

He Q-leaped. Landing in the water as intended, the

inevitable thing happened. His eyes sealed. He was grateful the creature's screeches garbled. He could think straighter. But he could tell it was hovering above him. It was waiting for him, and he knew it was a matter of time till he would have to come up for air.

This... *thing* had intelligence. He wondered if it could see him, but at least he knew it didn't want to swim, or couldn't.

Swimming deeper, he listened. The screech faded slowly. He had about half his time left when he stopped and waited, trying to keep himself from floating upward. He could still hear the screeches, but they were now coming in sessions that were divided by silence.

At one-quarter air left, he knew he would have to use his converted aura to speed up to get out of the water in time. Since he couldn't see, he didn't want to risk Q-leaping and take a chance on ending up in the middle of the rock somewhere, or too high, and killing himself.

It was time.

Zreyas started letting his war aura go with the anger of what that nasty thing was doing, converting it like he did for Rhom in the dying dimension. He aimed for where he heard the screeching come from in the hopes that when he got to the surface, he would hurt it at least.

To his surprise, he felt the water around him start to flow strongly. It flowed upward, making his swim seem effortless. Before he knew it, he was flying out of the water. Flying through the air, arms and legs flailing, he felt his ascent crest, then start his descent.

"Oohhh, Sh ii-ii-iit!"

As he descended, he wiped his eyes frantically, trying to get the water off them. When they opened, he was just a second away from smashing into the bottom section of the formation. He immediately Q-leaped into the space just over the water in the tunnel he came out of on his first Tarq landing.

After coming out of the leap, he fell into the shallows and scrambled up into the formation as fast as he could and looked out of one of the open holes to see the creature flying awkwardly away inland, then it fell to the sand, struggling to walk, but still heading inland.

Zreyas started to pull his weapons and go after it to make sure it was killed, but a small opening in the air opened, and it had a dark blackish-red environment on the other side. Then it disappeared.

"Ticking-hell, what are we dealing with here? This is beyond natural life." He felt so dazed he realized he might have some serious post-battle shock going on. he realized he was afraid of that thing, and he hoped he would never see another one of those monsters again, because he might literally lose his shit over it.

The first thing he wanted to do was check to see if there were any shinit survivors and help them if they needed it. Throwing caution to the wind, he raced his way up through the cave system, past the alcove he slept in once and where their dens were, and into the den to the right.

Nothing, no life. Fur was laying in many places, including the walls, but no one was there.

He turned to go back to the other den he wasn't as familiar with. It was much larger than the first. With sadness, he realized there would be plenty of fur for rope here, but the supply would be limited now because there were no more shinits.

Anger rose and tears of fury filled his eyes a little as he ran into the area where he had made his rope the first time under the opening of the top of the rock formation. He felt himself shake at the thought of going up there, and that made him even angrier. He thought back to all the Janquar that had gotten battle-shock and what happened to them.

"No ticking-way! I will not let that happen to you, Zrey!" he shouted to himself. "Face this!"

Zreyas paced around the room until he finally moved to the corner where he made his first shinit rope and faced the corner. He stood there breathing hard and fast, sweating. He felt like he would pass out at any moment.

All the times he judged other warriors for battle-shock came crashing back into his mind. He remembered one warrior that couldn't even go to war because he was so afraid. He had put that warrior to death with his own hands. On top of his fear the guilt flooded in.

He started growling in the pain of his cracking chest. As he pushed his forehead against the rock, the longer he growled, the more it turned into a roar. The anger at himself for the things he had done, coupled with the experience he had just had, felt like it would rip his body apart and shatter his mind.

No matter how hard he tried, he couldn't see how to get through this. Every time he closed his eyes, he would see those rows of teeth or putting that warrior to death. Zreyas opened his eyes to stare at the rock wall, but it made no difference. All the images of fights throughout his life came along with it. He watched everyone he had put to death—kills he had long forgotten about. He tried moving his eyes around and blinking hard, but he couldn't get away from the images.

It felt demented in his way of thinking that he didn't want to turn away from them. In a way, he felt like it was comfortable. This new life was uncomfortable. Maybe that is why he got to be such a hardened warrior. He had just been pocketing every memory, fight, kill, and trauma. He felt like he might deserve all this, so it would be justice.

Zreyas moved his hands to press against the wall and lean on it. There was no way he could help anyone because there was no trusting him now. He didn't even trust himself anymore. Fear had gripped him in ways he never thought it could. Maybe he would just stay here in memory of the shinits. He liked this place anyway. And when the Janquar caught up with him, he would be okay with that.

As he watched all the scenes play in his vision, he thought about the warrior that had his legs cut off and still went on to train other warriors till his eyes failed. He wondered if the warrior stood in front of a wall and panicked behind walls out of fear, like he was doing. His wall kept showing the round rows of teeth, making him flinch and jerk.

Zreyas wished with all he had that he could talk to that warrior right now. He tried to put himself in his place. He should have been put to death. Most Janquar would want it, but he didn't. A memory came back to him in between the flashes of kills and rows of teeth.

He had come to check on Aaru, who had gone to learn a few techniques from the warrior trainer by his command. They were having a conversation. Aaru, being who he was, had asked him why he didn't want to die. The warrior grunted and simply said, 'Because I have figured out what I wanted to do more than smash my face up against a wall and give up.'

Zreyas' breath caught. Was that what he was doing right now? Was he throwing his face up against this wall to die? For the first time since he had been in the room, he looked at his hands, still up against the wall.

Between his thumb and index finger, his skin had darkened. There was his answer. The warrior's response to Aaru, and the dark skin signs, was saying he was dying inside already, little by little. The flashes and visions didn't stop, but he noticed his breathing had slowed. He wasn't sure how he would get out of this. He knew he didn't want to throw his face up against this wall and die. At least he knew that.

But it wasn't enough to know what he *didn't* want because he would keep thinking about it. *That* would go into the quantum... not what he wanted. He would get what he didn't want stronger, everywhere he turned. Rhom had said it was science, not magic.

"The dark side of the quantum, Zrey... what I put into it." He just wasn't sure how to stop. He didn't want to look at the wall anymore, but he wanted to see the sky more, and there was the starting key.

Zreyas turned and leaned against the wall, putting it behind him, and looked up through the hole to the sky. He still imagined that creature looking in on him with all those rows of teeth and the spears of its claws pushing into his head, but at least he was seeing the sky.

He sat down hard, propping his forearms on his raised knees. At least he turned to something he wanted more than the wall. It was a start. "I have people that have the likings for me and I got a lot to do to save Ayya and Aaru!" he tried to tell himself. But he was so tired and didn't want to fight it anymore.

Zreyas pulled his knees up to his face and his chest cracked up into his throat, and he let the tears come as he shook uncontrollably.

10 Weet! and Water

ꙮꙮꙮ *Zreyas* ꙮꙮꙮ

He examined the splattered mess all around the top of the rock formation and grieved at the loss of life, and for the future—life that would never breathe air. He had no idea how to clean this acidic mess up.

Zreyas took out the tryst in his vest pocket as he sat against the rock that hid his melted armor, not sure if what he was about to do would get through. He held it in his hand and spoke into it as he sat down, facing away from the mess to look out over the sea. "If it is within the balances, Rhom. Can you see if Rtu would find it in his heart to clean this mess up so no unfortunate living being would die from this... whatever this mag-shit is? I'm not asking for myself."

Zreyas really didn't expect a response, but he sat back and calmed his breathing down. He didn't want to touch that mess, but also wanted to clean it up somehow. But he needed to recover a little.

He stood after a few minutes and turned, laying his eyes on the devastation. Then, right before his eyes, the mucus gradually disappeared. The dead victim parts stayed and were dried like they had been burned or dried in the sun.

Zreyas sat down on the rock again and breathed a sigh of relief. He put a fist to his chest and looked up. "Sending the thankings to you. I'm not sure if it was you that did that or if it was by its design. But, I don't think that thing was natural, and there is no way I can believe that Rtu made that."

Zreyas looked closer at the parts of the bodies left behind, staring at the crinkled burned skins, at least the parts of the skins that were left. Then he remembered the heat he felt when the flesh burned from the acidic mucus. It resembled a bunched-up pile of skin. He used his dagger to move it, and he felt something small inside, like it had shrunk from—

Horror ran through Zreyas, and he took in a sharp breath. He removed the skin; it looked like a tiny burned and dehydrated version of the body parts of the creature's victims that were left.

Zreyas sat down hard, stunned. He started talking to himself. "Ticking-hell... Rhom, Tulyata, and Rtu need to know about this."

Something must have made these creature things. Aaru had said something attacked them. Though they didn't look exactly like this, it was too similar to ignore. If something attacked Ayya, and Aaru gave his essence to keep her alive, then he might have prevented her from being killed from those things, or becoming one?

"Okay, my imagination is working too hard again."

Determination filled Zreyas as he took his water-skin out to get a drink. That was when he remembered his dire circumstance of not having water. One of the artisan grandmasters that taught him survival skills had once said, 'Survival is busy work... always busy, and always a taskmaster.'

Zreyas thought a moment while he filtered the water with his lips and drank. Then he capped his skin again, rolling it up. "It seems there might be more than one kind of survival, and water and food seem to be the easier of them."

He couldn't help but chuckle, thankful he was alive to live the simple work. He would focus on that and why he wanted to not pound his face into a wall and die.

As he stood again and put up his water-skin, Zreyas realized he had gotten lucky several times today... very fortunate. He doubted he would be that lucky again if he ran up on another one. It was too intelligent, and he was too afraid of them. They would take advantage of that.

Zreyas went back into the cave to get back to his mission, to find as much fur as he could for rope. When he dropped, he looked around, feeling sad. "I'm sending you the... aplop-og-ees shinit family that I couldn't protect you and also giving you the thankings for your strong and pliable fur."

They must have shed constantly, and rubbed up against the walls to get rid of the extra fur with the weather as warm as it was. Maybe they didn't have the shedding mechanism most hairy creatures had.

He pulled out his pouch and began the peaceful work of stuffing it in neatly, packing in as much as he could. He had more things to put in there if all went well. After picking up all the fur he could find in that room, he moved into the two dens the shinits used for bedding at the left and right sides of the tri-fork.

He squatted down to grab the last tuft of fur he saw and realized his pouch was over-full. When he had been here before, he had just made the rope as he picked it up.

He didn't think this rope would be as long, but it would be better than nothing. It was always a handy tool, no matter how long it was.

A high-pitched call sounded and echoed through the cave and Zreyas jerked his head toward where it came from, immediately trembling. He closed his eyes and talked himself down and remembered why he wanted to live and made the effort to focus on his curiosity that fed his adventurous nature.

He stayed in his squatted position, reaching for his weapons. The creature he had just had a run-in with was too fresh in his mind and body, so he felt the electric surge of a startle inside.

Zreyas stood as he scanned the cave. Then he heard another one and followed the sound, relaxing more because it was definitely not the acid-toothed creature. He arrived at the back wall of the den and saw nothing. The 'weet' sounded again. It came from below him.

"I'm trying to find you, little one. Keep calling."

Zreyas squatted and wiped debris on the floor away from the area. He saw a small crack he could get a hand through. There was a small area through the crack he could see through. Zreyas adjusted his vision to see in the dark, but he still couldn't see anything in there.

He knew what he was about to do was unwise, but his instinct told him differently. He felt pulled to do it. Zreyas reached into the hole, more than a little leery after what had just happened. *Who knows what is down there?*

Feeling around in the little compartment of the cave, he no longer heard the 'weet' call. Zreyas pulled out his hand, sat on his heels and listened.

"Weet!"

Zreyas looked down through the crack in front of him, again. A large furry paw with unusually large taloned claws popped out playfully.

He grunted at the creature. "So you want to play, do you? I'm new to this playing thing." He placed his hand back down at the edge of the crack, and the paw popped out again and gripped Zreyas' hand, covering it up. Though still playful, the razor-sharp talons pierced through his skin. He had forgotten he no longer had armor, but at least his skin was still thick.

Zreyas resisted the urge to jerk back. "Ow, those claws are ticking sharp. How long have you been down there? Come on out. I will help you."

He put his hand back down, relying on the creature to grab him again. "Grab my hand and hang on." The pure white paw with sparse flecks of iridescent silver popped out and grabbed his hand.

"You are good looking! Let's see the rest of you."

He felt it pull against his hand, trying to pull itself up, so he slid his hand back slowly to help it along. "You need to do it to get stronger. Pull yourself up, young one."

It wasn't long before he saw an elbow and shoulder. Though young, the muscle structure was strong already. Then the eyes peered through. It stunned Zreyas momentarily. They were round, large, and ice-white around the seeing-circle. He knew there was a proper term for that, but he didn't know what it was. The eye color constantly swirled around as if it was a universe itself. Its brow was predatory and intimidating, even as young as it was.

Zreyas sweated at the effort of helping it out. It was a good thing he came along because if it grew anymore while in there, there would be no way to get it out, aside from ripping the rock apart.

He put his foot up against the wall for leverage. "You are heavier than you look! Then again, you are probably bigger than I am, judging from those paws of yours."

It called out, "Weet!" as it struggled up, revealing its sharp hooked beak, designed to rip and shred.

Zreyas almost let go seeing it, but helped it until it let go—he felt no threat. By the time he got the thing out of that crack, his whole body was shaking from the strain. He sat down, breathing hard.

Then Zreyas gawked.

As it shook out its muscled feline body clumsily, it almost fell over. It shocked him it didn't have a feathered body and assumed it must have just been born recently.

It had silky-furred pointed ears that were sideways rather than straight up. They seemed to make room for that wild tuft of hair at the top of its head.

"Well, you are not like the other birds that were here earlier—in fact, you aren't a bird at all. Where did you come from?" Not really expecting an answer, Zreyas grinned at the tuft of pure white long hair on top of its head, sticking straight out in all directions except forward. Watching it just made him feel joy and wanted to laugh in the middle of the chaos. *This little thing is another reason to want to move forward, Zrey*, he thought to himself.

As it turned, it seemed like it was showing off. It paced around the cave room. It was majestic, and Zreyas started seeing gold flecks mixed in with the silver. On its shoulders, he could see a patch of scaly skin and feathery down sticking out of it.

"That skin on your shoulders looks like mine did before my horns came out. Are you going to have wings? You are ticking-impressive!"

It looked at Zreyas and stalked slowly up to him like a predator focusing on prey, but Zreyas felt no threat. It sniffed him. His fur shimmered a moment, then he sat down, staring eye to eye with him.

It cocked its head. "Weet!"

Zreyas realized what it was prowling toward. "Are you hungry?"

"Weet!"

Zreyas reached into his pouch and pulled out the meat he had with him. He opened it carefully, put a piece in his own mouth.

The creature growled.

"Ha! I was messing with you. Here you go." Zreyas put half of the meat he had down to share and slid it slightly toward his new friend.

The creature reacted defensively. All the hair on its face stuck out, and he screeched a warning hiss with vibrations and 'weet' sounds mingled in.

"That was an unusual warning growl. It's okay, I'm not trying to hurt you. Don't feel bad, I'm scared around here too. Did that evil creature or slither scare you?" He stepped back and ate his own meat to give it space while it watched Zreyas eat.

Eyeing him, the creature lowered its head down and sniffed. A second later, it was using its claws to hold the meat in place while the creature ripped it apart with its beak and then gulping it down.

"I'm not sure how to get you out of here. You are just as big as I am. It's not like I can carry you. I hope you can swim. It would be nice if you could Q-leap like I can."

Zreyas waited for the creature to finish eating so he wouldn't startle it. When he finished, Zreyas put his meat away and stood slowly.

"I have to go. If I don't get some suitable water made soon, I will die. I have a lot to do. Good luck. I hope you make it." He stood and walked to the drop-off and looked back. The creature's icy-white eyes were staring straight at him. There was something about that creature that made him pause. After a few seconds, it cocked his head, making the tuft of hair on its head very active.

The tuft seemed silky and soft, but it was stiff enough that only the top two-thirds of it swayed with its motion. That, combined with his wide and round eyes, almost made him laugh, despite the intimidating, predatory face.

Zreyas grinned and climbed down the drop-off, past the shinit den alcoves. "This is a good place to sleep if you ever need it. I slept here once and the creature that lived in it is now dead." On the way down, Zreyas could hear the creature's claws on the stone, trying to climb down. He knew he had to let it be independent, or it would die. Its chances were slim anyway, but impossible if he did too much for it. He wasn't a master of animals, but he had a lifetime of training Janquar.

He approached the mouth of the rock formation, then turned slightly. "Good bye, my new friend. I hope you live to show this world how impressive you are." Zreyas turned and Q-leaped away stealthily onto a nearby rock on the way to shore. He wanted to be quiet so he wouldn't startle it.

Zreyas turned and yelled back to it. "Just in case you understand me, you have made my day in the good range of frequency by meeting you." Then he Q-leaped to the shore and began walking down the beach.

This time, he wasn't going back to his home cave. Zreyas was making his way west... well, further west than he had been before, in the hopes he could find the materials he needed for making fresh water and find out if there were winters here. He smiled and thought about how he would get a fresh water solution on his trip, though he wasn't sure why.

As Zreyas walked past his cave, he paused long enough to make sure he had everything he needed. As he made his way west, he made a rope. It wasn't long, and he felt a dull headache that grew with intensity due to lack of water.

Zreyas knew where the Janquar Nation's new permanent location was. There had to be fresh water somewhere near that new one—and a challenge node. If he was going to die of thirst, he might as well go out, hindering their effort. He was fed-up with all the damage they were causing, especially that... *thing* he had just fought with today.

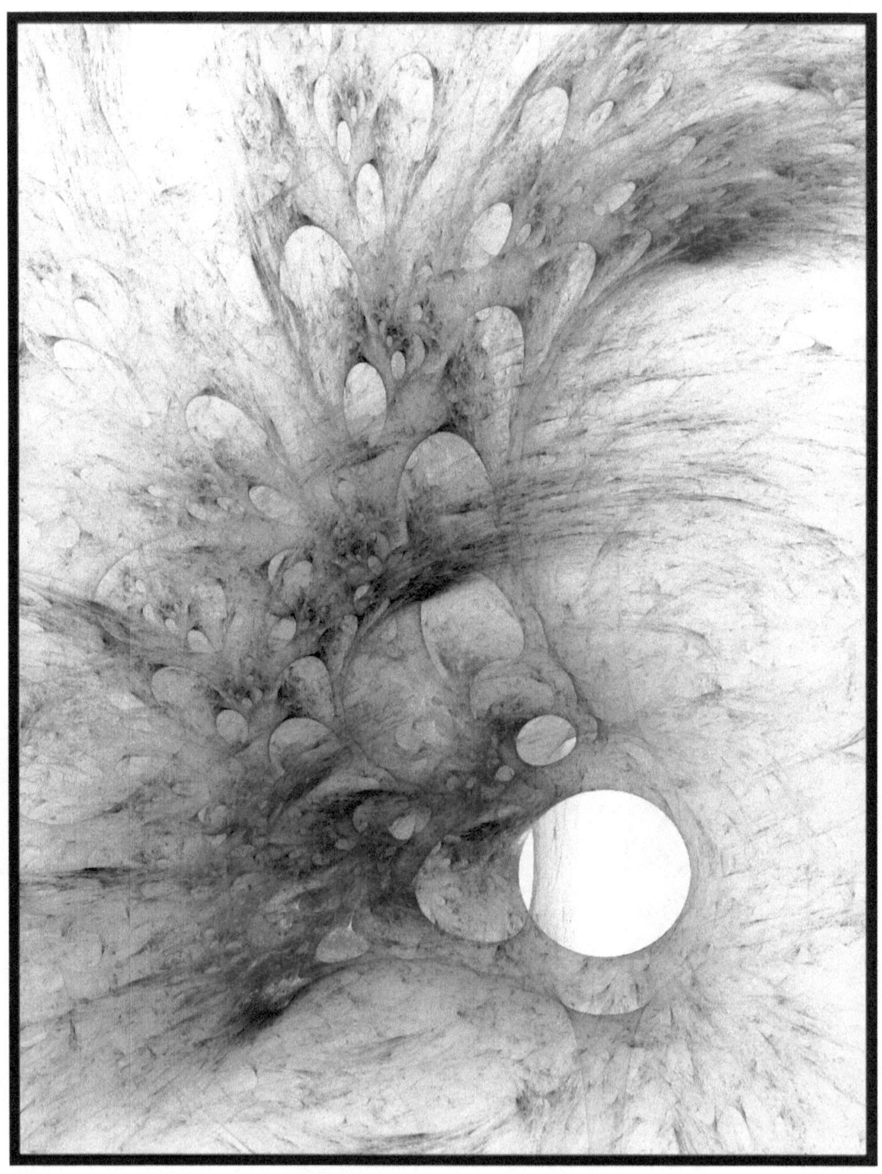

11 Finally!

Zreyas

After several hours of hiking, no water, and no sign of the Nation, he decided it might be wise to find a tree in the forest he was hiking through now. He needed sleep. His body was depleted, and he needed to be careful. He quit trying to Q-leap because he was too depleted and tired to even get angry or upset about something to fill his chamber. No water for this long was really tearing it down. All the extensive walking wasn't helping.

He looked around for a good strategic tree to sleep in. Just as he was about to climb it, he heard rustling behind him. Zreyas Q-leaped up into the tree and walked out on a branch. He pulled his two swords off his back quietly and waited.

He listened for several minutes, but the rustling had stopped. Out of the corner of his eye, he noticed the branch next to him bend slowly as if it had something heavy on it, but saw nothing. He felt no threat, but seemed odd.

He needed sleep, and it was as good a time as any to get some. He would rather lay down and sleep than stay defensive all night. If he died, he died. He was too exhausted and lethargic to care.

Zreyas made his way back to the center of the tree, where a large branch attached to the trunk grew. It had a nice curved dent at the joint, and he laid himself down in it and used his rope to secure himself, just in case he rolled off in his sleep. He looped the other end on a branch stump that must have gotten broken off in a storm. As soon as he laid down on his stomach, arms and legs dangling, he was asleep.

Half way through the night he heard footsteps. He woke, lifted the loop of rope from the branch, and looped it over his shoulder quickly. Watching closely, he slowly edged himself out further on the branch, drawing his dagger and axe. As he did so, the branch next to him slowly bent. *What the ticking hell!?*

It wasn't long, and he saw a small group of blue camp members tracking something and headed his way. They eventually made their way right up to the tree he was standing in. No one said a word, and one of the Janquar walked around the tree and started looking up.

Zreyas' adrenaline rushed through his body, revitalizing him a little. He hopped down from the tree right in front of him, startling the Janquar, unafraid of the blue by habit. After he landed, he realized they could just stomp him out pretty easily in his state. His best strategy now would be to act like he was still unafraid. "Is it me you were looking for?"

They all looked shocked. Zreyas imagined it was because of both his size and voice change. One of the blue walked forward a few steps to look closer. "Are you *Zreyas*?" His face had incredulity all over it.

"I am, but no longer the same Zreyas you might have heard about." He fell right into his old role just being around his people again, despite the size difference. He stood with a commanding air about him. "What made you track me down?"

The Janquar that had stepped forward and said, "We went to the cave like the picture in the sand, but no one was there. But I could tell something had been. Then our tracker picked up your trail, and we followed."

"Ticking hell, you finally came." Zreyas sheathed his weapons as the blue camp members looked at each other. "I have asked you here because I want to see if you are as different from the others as I think you are. *Why* have you come? Sit... if you want. Is this the entire body of the blue camp? There *were* more of you last I saw." Zreyas sat, wanting to show them he was not the same Janquar he used to be.

"Blue camp?" one of the Janquar asked.

He pointed to his own skin on his face. "Look at your skin. You can't tell me you haven't noticed that your skin is blue compared to the rest of the Nation. There is a reason."

"Yeah, we know. We are weak," the spokesman said with exasperation. Then he sat awkwardly in front of Zreyas, clearly uncomfortable by the way he shifted his body and looked around. The others followed his lead.

"No, that is incorrect." Zreyas let that sink in. "They can get more out of you if you don't know the real reason. Plus, they are afraid of anything that is different, hence why they kill everything in sight. They want you useful to them, not independent and confident. They want you to clean their ships, weapons, cook their meals, and clean up their shit."

Zreyas paused a few moments as he rested his elbows on his bent knees. "They thought my little brother to be weak, too. In fact, they were going to send him off on a mission to kill him in an ambush to save face for the Rittak line. Though he was a prodigy fighter, he thought differently, so they didn't want him to *threaten* what the leaders had established and give up power over you."

"Your brother was Aaru?" another of the group asked.

Zreyas painfully looked at him and nodded. "Yes, yes, he was. Did you know him?"

They all looked at each other as if they were not sure if they wanted to confide in him.

"In case you haven't noticed, I'm not exactly the size I used to be and my skin is also blue, though it didn't use to be. In fact, I was in line to be my commander's successor until I tried to kill him to protect Aaru. He slid through a portal before I had the chance to kill him. My other brother, Nat, tried to kill Aaru. When I defended him, my father tried to finish the job—I didn't let him."

They started whispering with each other, then one spoke up. "So you really are the one they call Zreyas that has caused so much uproar."

"I guess so. But I would do it all again if I had to."

"We liked Aaru. He is not with you, so does that mean he is... dead?" asked the same one that seemed to keep speaking for the group.

Zreyas crossed his legs tighter and let out a sigh. "Yes." He paused a moment while they gasped and started whispering to each other.

"And no." He rubbed his temples and let his hand drop. "I'm not sure how to explain this other than just come out and say it. But first, I need to ask, is the main camp going to miss you all? If so, we need to pick more of a hidden place to talk."

"No, I don't think so. They released some nasty rodent monsters called nagodara to find you and another. But they turned on us and killed a lot of us. The warriors killed four, but one escaped. They didn't bother telling us to move."

"So that is what they are called."

"You saw it and are still alive?" the lead spokesman said.

The members looked around at each other, amazed.

"I got a little lucky, but as you can see—" turning the gouged side of his face toward them, "I didn't fare that well. If I hadn't used a new skill I discovered in a dying dimension, it would have killed me." After they prompted him, Zreyas spent a few minutes telling them about the fight.

"Wow! If you knew how many of our people they killed before they got them killed, you would be amazed."

"After seeing what it did to the creatures around there, and what it was about to do to me, it wouldn't surprise me."

The leader of the group cleared his throat, still showing signs of being uncomfortable. "While we were cleaning up, we started talking about all the weird stuff going on, and one of us mentioned having a strange dream they had about a poem, directions, and a little Janquar that disappeared like a firelight fly. Then others started talking about how they had the same dream. When we went to the place you talked about, our tracker found activity and your foot prints... and we decided it had to be important. Is it?"

"And I thought it wouldn't work, but figured it was worth a shot." Zreyas let out a single, "Ha," almost resembling a chuckle. "And yes, I think it is important because you won't live long if you stick around here."

"That took balls and steel guts to take that kind of risk as small as you are. We could have roasted you for a snack."

"No ticking-shit! I kept wondering what the ticking

hell I was doing." Zreyas laughed hard this time. "Ha... ha... ha!"

The others just stared at him like he had gone mad.

Zreyas looked at them, unaffected by their shock. He shrugged. "A new thing I just learned about; you should try it. It's called laughing. It will make you feel weird at first because you are not used to it, but it's freeing... ah, never-mind, you wouldn't understand... yet."

He stood for emphasis and motioned for them to stay where they were, "So, you are a group of blue skinned Janquar that think they are weak because that is what you were told, but I want you to know you are the strongest of them all."

"Maybe, if we knew what you were talking about. But we don't care about you. We want to tell you about Aaru. That is who we care about. It is our tribute to his death. You are the only one that would listen to it."

"Fair enough, but I don't have patience with talk like that. I don't care if you don't like me or don't care about me, but I deserve respect. I'm not lesser than you because I'm small. Just like you are not less than the others because you are blue."

Zreyas whirled around toward the one that had said he didn't care and glared. "You forget, you ungrateful bandhula. I cared enough to attempt to help you, at high risk to myself, rather than slit your throats to hinder the progress of the Dark One and the Janquar."

He walked right up in front of the Janquar, just in front of his crossed legs. Then, for shocking emphasis, he Q-leaped one inch from his face and said, "You—" He immediately Q-leaped back in front of his legs again as the group gasped.

"—can at least ticking give me a little mutual respect, or I can kill your asses and put you out of your misery before you fall to the Dark One." Zreyas sat down and waited, staring into the now silent Janquar's eyes. "Either way, I will honor my brother by listening to you. It is rare someone talked anything but mag-shit about him."

The blue camp members looked at each other.

Their leader swallowed, then spoke. "Aaru always came to visit us. He would sneak in during his free time and see how we were doing. He would even help us out of predicaments were facing."

Another member chimed in and added, "Aaru always seemed to show up at the right time. So, we gave him food or mounted up favors and boons he never collected on."

The leader spoke with that typical Janquar edge. "We owe him many times over. Tell us what happened to him."

Zreyas spent the next several hours telling them the story of what had happened to Aaru since the fractures. He told them about the two galaxies that had split in this universe and how this planet was in one of those new ones called Proioxis and that the name of this planet was Tarq.

After they told him they wanted more information, he gave them the details of the Emperor's challenge that included the entire multiverse and deities. Zreyas told them about what Rhom said about how he thought Zreyas may have been Viduri long ago. "That means you likely were, too." Then he told them how he watched Rhom transition back from an incarnate of a Viduri High Seer to a visage and that he had incarnated for the balances of the multiverse. He knew it sounded so crazy, but he would not hold back.

He let them absorb some of it, then Zreyas also explained why their skin was blue and that it was a gift, not a curse. Then he gave them the short version of what he had learned about frequency.

Zreyas didn't say a word when several of the Janquar

grunted or balked at anything he said. He knew it was a lot to take in. It sure had been for him. Then he finished the explanation by telling them about how the Emperor was now possessed by the Dark One and the signs. "I know it is a lot to take in, but we are in deep ticking mag-shit right now in the multiverse. I don't know a lot about technology, but I have gathered enough to know that we are very behind the rest of the multiverse and that they were a primitive species."

The dawn started breaking and Zreyas got up. "Think about it a while. I need to find water or make drinkable water. You all drained my only water source, and I haven't had fresh water for almost two days now."

The leader piped up and said, "I believe you."

Zreyas started to turn around when he heard the leader speak up again.

"Aaru talked about you all the time. He described you and put you up on a throne. He said you would help us if we just asked, just like you did him. And honestly, no one can make that pile of mag-shit up. And it all makes sense. I've seen that black inky mist in the Emperor's eyes and it started showing in other warriors. I believe you."

The others murmured their agreement.

Another asked, "I ask you to show us this disappearing leap again you talked about learning. Then the converting one. I'm curious."

Zreyas lowered his head, thinking about the deception of the Janquar and how they had all lived in it for so many varSas. "Hold your hands out in front of you, palms up."

He did so.

In a matter of a second, his inner chamber was full of rage. With tears in his eyes from the love he had for his brother and how he affected so many, he opened the anger and converted it to all the love he was feeling for an explosive power. He sent the signal out with his mind and his heart pulled in the wave pattern of the place and state he wanted to be in.

With a soft crack, he was immediately there in front of the leader, standing on his palms. He looked into his eyes with care and honesty... open for all of them to share. His aura pushed it all out to them and they seemed stunned at what they felt, judging from the wide eyes, gasps, and frozen nature of their bodies.

Zreyas bowed slightly and Q-leaped back to where he stood before. He wasn't sure the Janquar would appreciate someone being so close to them.

After a few minutes of gathering themselves, the leader said, "We didn't drain the lakes to hurt you. We drained them because we didn't want that water to be corrupted like the Emperor did with the water to the north. We didn't want to drink it. What do you want from us?"

Zreyas looked at him. "I don't want anything from you, only to give you the chance to understand the truth so you could make your own decisions about your own lives. I didn't want to hurt you either, because my plan is to do as much to hinder their progress in the challenge as possible and find that node and obstruct it—or destroy it somehow."

He scratched his head and dropped his hand down to slap his leg. "How? I don't know. So there you have it, all the truth and why I came to you. It just felt wrong to lump you all in with the rest of them when you are more than you ever thought possible. You care, so there is hope."

The leader grunted, as did the others, nodding.

"All I know is, if I don't at least try to help, we are all doomed no matter where we run to. Good day, my new friends. I need to find clay, since there is obviously no clean water around. You know how to track me if you decide to join me."

"There is clay northwest from here. Will you come back to your camp?"

"Yes, when I get what I need and make what I need to get fresh water from the sea. But if you are limited in water, you probably better look for clay too."

The leader nodded, got up in silence. The others followed his lead and got up as well. "We don't know what to do about water, either."

Zreyas turned northwest and started walking. "Then you better send someone with me to help because I am too small to make shit for you."

"Hey, I will go, and I have some water here," said one member of the group.

"I'm giving a real thanking to you," and held up his water-skin for him to fill.

They seemed puzzled at his response, but he pulled out his own water-skin and the Janquar filled it for him from his own waterskin. He motioned to one other, and that one nodded in consent to come as well. "Drink, and I fill again."

Zreyas nodded, drank as much water as he dared to drink at once before he got to the point he would throw it back up. Then they filled it back up for him.

Two Janquar walked up to him and stood waiting. They looked down, and he said, "We go with you." He thumbed back to the leader. "He will go back and tell the others where we are and what we are doing."

Zreyas nodded and started walking with the two large Janquar behind him heading northwest.

12 The Humming

"Ayya, you have *got* to stop that humming. You can't hum all the time," her mother pleaded with her.

"Why not, Momma? It feels good and makes the happy come," Ayya returned in dismay.

"There is a time and place for everything. School is where you are going, and they won't like it if you hum. It will distract the others from their learning. You got away with it in kindergarten, but first grade is much different."

"Hmm, why does it have to be so different? Can I stay home with you, Momma?"

"No, Ayya, you can't stay home with me, because it's important that you get a serious education."

"Nuh uh, I don't want serious and important if I can't hum," she retorted.

Her mother grabbed her arm and turned her to face her toward her, looking like she did when she took off her clothes when she was outside. "During class is not a time to hum. If you get in trouble at school for humming, you will get in trouble here when you get home, too."

It surprised Ayya at her mother's mood. She raised her shoulder to ease the slight pain of the grip. It jolted her insides, almost like something was inside her that wanted to come out. It was unusual that her mother reacted like that, and it confused her.

She looked at Ayya with firm eyes. "If you get into trouble for humming at the wrong time, I will make you stop humming here, too. You *must* learn to live in *this* world being considerate of others, not just in your own world."

On the verge of tears, she stood on her tiptoes to ease the grip a little. "Okay, Momma." Ayya's heart ached as she looked into her mother's eyes, but wasn't sure why. Something was wrong.

The bus drove up to the bus stop, and her mother hugged her. Ayya saw tears in her mother's eyes when she said, "I love you."

"I love you too, Momma. I will miss you." She hugged her mother's neck tightly once more. Her mother peeled her away from her.

"Now go have fun, big girl." Her mother smiled and patted her butt once.

Ayya turned and climbed up the stairs of the bus, pulling on the rails to help her up. The steps were huge for her, but she would be six in a few weeks and she would grow on her birthday. She was sure of it.

Rhom

Watching the scene unfold in Tulyata's dimension, Rhom shook his head with a sigh. "She's so little. Her humming was... *extensive* when she was a Viduri. I understand how maddening it can be at times. I know there is nothing I can do, but I wish Tulyata was here to run some checks and balances."

"Times are different, culture is different with each place," said Rtu. "Even for *that* culture on Earth, she lives in an ultra-conservative area of the globe during that time period. Kids were birthed to work the fields on the poor side, and for the medium to higher classes, they were to be looked at, not heard. She also lives in an area of the globe where humans of different color skins are only beginning to integrate for the first time in schools."

Rhom leaned forward over his lab desk to watch her as he listened to Rtu.

"She also lives in a very conservative religious belt on the continent she is on. In addition, there is a war going on! She isn't growing up in the best of times, especially since she will never fit in. It's my hope it will strengthen her though—if it doesn't kill her."

"I forget you are more adept at certain parts of creation than I am, Rtu. This entire culture, segregation, integration, etc., I just don't get why people treat people differently just because of the color of a skin, if they have horns or not, or more legs and arms than someone else. I just don't think about it. I mean, look at us. We used to be the same visage but when we separated, we ended up with different color skins."

"Yeah, you noticed too?" Rtu laughed.

Rhom chuckled. "Look at the Janquar. They hate everyone that isn't dark skinned."

Rtu spoke with compassion, yet a tone of fairness and balance. "And on earth, they have prejudices of skin color from all sides. It isn't just one skin color that prejudice against the other. Though they don't admit it, the prejudice is equally bad from all sides, no matter where it happens. Because of conditioning, humans have this tendency to want to judge themselves better out of insecurity or some other conditioned reasoning. It's not just skin color, it's everything from gender, money, or which side of a sporting event they cheer for."

"I just don't understand it." admitted Rhom. "Then again, I'm a flawed visage."

Rtu chuckled wryly. "But anyway, I'm not worried about Ayya's mother treating her badly for humming; I'm concerned about her father, and what he is doing to Lanna."

"She is the only thing keeping Ayya safe now, and a little piece of Lanna dies every day. She keeps Ayya dampened so she will not get out of hand, and she keeps her husband dampened from doing the same thing. One day, his mental abuse might break Lanna and Ayya both. And by the way, she has another child on the way."

Rhom extended himself to Lanna's husband to see the situation clearer, then asked Rtu, "He hates Ayya unconsciously because of who he used to be, but it is slowly surfacing. His design has a defined ego with a direct connection to speech. He has to pretend to be certain about things. Normally, this wouldn't be an issue, but that commander in him is not a normal incarnation. The poor soul's incarnation body was stolen from him and now the commander is operating in another's design."

"Yes, the commander's incarnation design was a very ego based manifestor design. Ayya's father has a body that has a generator design. Those auras are complete opposites, so their auras are constantly fighting each other. He unconsciously knows who she is and what she is... also what she is not. Her successes and confidence makes him feel outdone and gives him the illusion that she threatens him. As long as her mother and siblings don't touch that same nerve, he will not mistreat them, though not necessarily love them. Besides all that, it also upsets him she is not a boy and he will do many things to show that."

"Yes..." Rhom said, considering the situation and investigating them further. "Yes, I see what you are saying."

As Rhom looked at their designs, thinking he was missing something important. "Look here, brother," pointing toward them, "it is also interesting to note that Ayya's Vidurian Tantra design was a-sexual and an all-encompassing generator type that is not duplicated anywhere else in the multiverse, meaning all centers were authoritative and generative. When the fractures happened, two of the centers slash galaxies split."

Rtu scooted up in his chair, leaning forward. "I think I see where you are going with this. Go on, I'm interested because we didn't make the Viduri and come up with designs originally. We just picked up where whoever-it-was left off when the need arose. Also, I think that fracture event was right about the time on Earth when human centers evolved too, around... 1781."

Rhom nodded, glad for the information. "That is good to know. You just saved me some research. Now for Aaru's design. He was truly male in both gender and sexuality preference. His design is manifestor, as you know, and design was of the ego but channeled through and centered in love, direction, and identity. His downfall was not knowing when enough was enough and holding on to what wasn't good for him, so he put up with this situation for far too long. When he met Ayya in her ceremony, however, he shifted and made his decision, and his stubbornness in his identity and purpose shifted.

When I put them together, her body gender should have been male. She will have a hard time identifying her sexuality. Also, when I had to flip Aaru's design polarity to make it work with Ayya, it created a design of a manifesting generative type. Thankfully, her new design now matches the body she is in closely, thanks to Aaru showing me how—through Aaru's example of how he kept her alive. At least her conflict isn't as extreme as her father's. I'm surprised he hasn't imploded with the aura conflict."

"It goes to show you, dear brother, how resilient the human form is. It will conform and adapt to anything, even if it is bad for the body if it is repeated enough."

ꡖꡖꡖ *Ayya* ꡖꡖꡖ

Ayya arrived at school and would soon be ushered into her first-grade homeroom class. She was excited and full of cheer at the new adventure. Following instructions, she got in a line to walk into her new classroom.

The teacher introduced herself. "Children, I'm Mrs. Haskel. Get in line starting," she pointed, "here in front of me as I call your name."

She looked like a grandma to Ayya, not a teacher like she had in kindergarten. She was small-framed, wiry, thin, and seemed nice enough. Ayya cocked her head, waiting for her to smile while she called names out. It never happened.

When Ayya's name was called, she moved as she had been told to the last position in line. Then Mrs. Haskel told them to follow her and to stay in the line.

Once in the classroom, the teacher told them they had thirty-seven in their homeroom class. Then the teacher started giving seat assignments.

Finally, Ayya got hers right in the middle of the room—row three, five desks back. Ayya skipped down the row and met her newly worn wooden desk. She looked at the old desk and spoke to it softly. "I like you Mr. Tree. I know you are listening even though you are not there. I promise I will take good care of you."

She put her lunch pail under her seat and caught herself humming. She immediately stopped, looked around, then sat down, relieved the teacher didn't catch her. *No humming, no humming.*

Ayya tried just humming in her mind, but that didn't work because she heard herself humming again and wasn't sure when she started doing it. *No humming, no humming!* She felt herself tighten and go stiff; so much so, she had to pee. She got up and ran to her teacher, still busy with other students.

"I have to pee, Mrs. Haskel. Can I go, please? Where can I pee?" Ayya couldn't help but wiggle, body going stiffer, trying to hold it in.

Mrs. Haskel took her by the arm, and that is when the teacher showed that she wasn't very happy with her. "It is rude to interrupt, girl. If you do it again, you will get a paddle." The teacher walked her aggressively toward the door.

"Yes, ma'am," Ayya said, as she felt a little pee leak. *No, no, no, please hold it.*

The teacher pushed her across the hall to another door and then pushed her inside. Ayya did not know what to do. She had never been in a bathroom like this. There were many sinks and doors.

"Where do—"

"In there!" the teacher spat as she pushed one door open with a slam, making Ayya jump.

Ayya lost control of herself, still holding it as much as she could. Now afraid of the teacher, she pulled her skirt up and sat down and peed right through her underwear.

She cried silently. Well, as quiet as she could.

The teacher started yelling at her, then she turned and slammed the door shut.

Ayya cried as she finished peeing, feeling her underwear totally soaked. Someone else opened the door as she held her legs apart and flushed the toilet. She walked out of the stall door, still crying.

Another teacher she didn't know was waiting patiently with a bright smile. She was a heavy-set and dark-skinned lady with kind eyes. What caught her attention was her large black freckles on her cheeks.

"I'm sorry, I didn't mean to," Ayya said, shaking all over, feeling her wet underwear draining down her leg.

"Oh, sweetie, it's okay. It happens sometimes! Let me help you."

Ayya looked up at the plump lady, feeling the tears drying on her cheeks, "Yes, ma'am. Thank you, ma'am."

The teacher helped Ayya wash out her panties and wash after she instructed her to take them off. "We have to make sure you are nice and pretty for your first day at school. It's time to have a good time, don't you think?"

Ayya nodded with a sniff.

"We are starting new again right now. How does that sound?"

Ayya nodded again, feeling excitement, smiling through the remnants of the tears in her eyes.

"What just happened is no longer here anymore, okay? And right now we are just having a chat."

Ayya smiled brightly. "Yes, ma'am. Thank you, ma'am."

The kind teacher reached into her pocket and pulled out a rock with a smiley face on it. "Here, I have something for you." It was smooth and small. She gestured for Ayya to take it.

Ayya was unsure and looked up at the lady's smiling freckled face. She reached out and opened her hand, and she set it on Ayya's palm. The hand painted rock felt good to hold. It felt like it filled her heart, and Ayya forgot about what happened. Happiness came back again.

"It'll be with you all day, okay? You can pull it out of your pocket any time you need help and it will make you feel better, at least a little," encouraged the nice lady.

Ayya smiled gratefully and wrapped her hand around the rock. It fit in her palm perfectly. "Thank you, ma'am. Can I keep it till tomorrow?"

"You can keep it *forever*," said the smiling woman.

"Thank you, ma'am, and I like your happy freckles."

The lady laughed. "You are very welcome, Ayya, and thank you! I like them too."

Ayya held the rock with a cherished grip. It was almost as good as the camel saddle cap at home she liked to hold— nothing could ever be as good as that. Then she looked up at the smiling lady and said, "I love you, ma'am."

"I love you too, little one. Don't forget, no matter what, that someone loves you."

"Yes, ma'am. Thank you, ma'am."

"Time to get to your class and start learning all kinds of fun things. And Ayya..."

"Yes, ma'am?"

"Sometimes, some people are not happy inside and they just don't know what to do. It's sort of like how you peed when you got scared and didn't know what to do. Grownups can be like that, too. They just might show it in other ways, like getting angry. Sometimes they yell or do other things that don't seem right. Just remember you love them, or like them. It will be easier."

"Like Mrs. Haskel or Daddy?"

The lady radiated a smile. "You are wise for your age.

Did you know that?"

"No, ma'am, I didn't." She opened her hand to look at her new rock and noticed it had freckles on it. Ayya smiled and thought a second, then said, "I like your smile. It matches the one on my gift. Thank you."

"My pleasure. Are you stalling?"

"Oh, yes, ma'am!"

The lady laughed and opened the door. "Let's have fun today."

They walked out of the bathroom and back into her classroom. Ayya turned around to wave bye, but there was no one there. Ayya put the rock in her pocket and immediately took her seat for her first day at school.

Her teacher gave them work to copy A, B, and C from the board onto their paper. She found she enjoyed drawing the letter pictures.

Ayya's body jolted when she heard the teacher scream, "Ayya! Stop humming!"

"Yes, ma'am, I'm sorry. I do it without thinking."

No humming, no humming. Ayya pulled her little rock out and smiled at it, held it to her chest in her gripped fist, then put it back into her pocket.

She drew out the letter B and smiled, proud of herself. Ayya started on drawing the letter C. She formed it halfway down when her ribs suddenly felt like they just cracked apart, pencil flying out of her hand.

It took a few jolts of being shaken before Ayya realized the teacher had her arm up in the air, body off the ground, shaking her violently.

The lady walked with her like that all the way down the hall, screaming at her. "You will never amount to anything good acting like that! You have interrupted my class for the last time!"

Ayya felt her body crunch as her ribs and back pulled

apart with every shake. Her shoulder felt like it was going to rip loose any time. She couldn't understand why she was in trouble. She couldn't think. All she could do was feel the panic and cry silently.

The teacher dropped Ayya hard into a wooden seat in the principal's office. "This girl refuses to stop humming!"

Oh, so that s what I did.

The principal was scary to Ayya, even scarier than Mrs. Haskel. He talked to her with a pleasant voice, but there was something about him that seemed scary... and familiar.

Ayya felt a jolting inside her several times again, like something was trying to get out.

The man smiled, but it was different from other people's smiles. It seemed slimy and icky, and she could have sworn the man had black mist around his eyes. Ayya rubbed her eyes and looked again.

The man picked up the receiver off the phone. "It's too bad that you won't get to hum at home either, you naughty little—"

The principal never finished his sentence and grinned. Mist started sliding in and out of his eyes, "Darling."

Shivers rippled up her arms and legs as he called her mother.

Momma must have talked with him ahead of time about my humming.

After reporting what Ayya had done, he slammed the receiver down hard and looked at her. "Next time, you will get the paddle," he said, as he pulled out a wooden piece of wood with many holes throughout it that had a handle.

Ayya did not know why the wood had holes in it, or its significance, but she knew it wasn't good. She swallowed, needing to pee again. "Yes, sir," Ayya croaked.

The principal rubbed the paddle affectionately like it

was a pet rabbit. "Go back to your class," he commanded.

"Yes, sir." Ayya stood and walked stiffly just outside the doorway. Her body hurt. She looked both ways, trying to get her bearings. She reached into her pocket and gripped her rock. All she wanted to do was to get out of that room, but she was not sure which way to go. She looked back into the office and he pointed in the direction to her right.

She wasted no time and left, though she had a hard time walking and breathing. Her panic wouldn't leave. Her armpit and ribs were on fire and her shoulder hurt so much she could barely move her arm. She walked into the door of the classroom with her head hung low, looking at the floor, and made her way to her seat.

Ayya wanted badly to take out the little rock, but she was afraid the teacher would see it and take it away from her. So, she just *thought* about holding the rock and remembered the smile of the lady that gave it to her.

෩෩෩ Rtu ෩෩෩

With tears running down his cheeks, Rtu said as he waved a hand to stop the vision he shared with his twin brother, "We will stop this here. I don't want to watch the rest, nor do we need to. I will say, though, she never hums again that I can foresee, unless prompted, with the present balances and current awareness. That teacher and principal broke part of her that day. She will have problems because she has cut off access to the sacral part of her."

Rhom's face showed the fury he felt from his brother. By his knitted brow, he could tell Rhom could barely keep it contained.

Rhom finally said, "She drove me crazy with the humming because she did it just to avoid listening sometimes, but it was never something that was annoying to me in general."

He understood Rhom's anger. "It's not fair, I know. The more I think about it, the more infuriated I get, too. She didn't realize she was humming. What is wrong with being unconsciously happy?"

Rtu found the more he talked, the angrier he got, seeing the implications of the system Ayya was living in. "Why are they sent to a place like that to learn to draw letters without learning to teach themselves happiness too? Teaching too much about letters and numbers, without teaching them to be a naturally whole person, just homogenizes them, making them all carbon copies of mindless unhappy people!"

"*Now* who's getting upset!" Rhom chuckled, with fury still coming through his voice. "It's like how Zreyas grew up too. Every day, for many varSas, they trained to fight so much that they turned into mindless armies. It's the same thing. It happens almost in every society, no matter the species. Organizations, governments, and churches don't want them if they can't manipulate them because they are strong in who they are naturally. I'm getting too out of hand on this perspective, though; there are good things about schools, governments, and churches, too, but they aren't adjusting to the current times and awareness."

"You are right, brother. And I'm feeling your overprotective nature over her. I understand now, at least a little. I felt it with my little buddy, Zreyas." Rtu grinned as he sat back and propped his head on his fist. "Funny thing, that teacher that gave her the rock. There is no teacher there like her. I think she might be the best teacher in history, though!" Rtu smiled broadly.

Rhom laughed and shook his head. "That was a well-spent challenge-portal run. I'm glad you did that. You did a great job with her, too. You would make a fantastic father and I'm grateful you were there."

Rtu chuckled. "Hey, hey, what can I say? As Zreyas says, 'it's what I do!' Maybe Ayya will see her again next varSa as a proper teacher. She will need a lot of support."

"Why am I not surprised? Thank you for watching over her. I've already picked my own next run there. Can I have one of your smiley rocks?"

"I will laugh in honor of my little buddy." Rtu paused, cleared his throat, then let out a single, "Ha!"

"You really do miss that boy!"

They both laughed.

As Rtu's laughter died, he felt that sick nagging heaviness again that he had been feeling ever since Zreyas left. He knew he wasn't under contract with the Dark One anymore, but it sure felt the same. Rtu wasn't sure he should say anything and decided he didn't feel like going back to help Ayya until he felt better. He wasn't used to feeling bad.

Suddenly, they heard Tulyata's voice. "Before you tell me I should rest, look at this event. Ayya is in trouble again. That commander is emerging, but so is Aaru. You boys have work to do."

13 Team of Choice

"So, what do you two specialize in?" Zreyas asked out of curiosity as they hiked.

There was a long silence, so Zreyas just said, "Well, if you will not talk, walk ahead as fast as you can. We don't have that much time. My gut is telling me something is wrong, but I just don't know what it is yet. We need fresh water soon. If you don't want to choose to work as a team, fine, but this would go a lot better and quicker if we did."

The two Janquar quickened their pace and Zreyas Q-leaped to keep up with no problem. He had never done an endurance run with the Q-leaps, so he thought it should prove interesting.

"I'm an artisan, and I don't specialize in anything. But I do know clay. That's why I said I would come, but I don't know what needs to be made to make the fresh water."

"It's okay. I can show you if you like, though you would probably execute it better than I would. I have the knowledge. But I have not yet had the time working with clay to become accomplished at it like I have fighting."

The artisan grunted and nodded. "Yeah, I would like to learn to make water. I like this teamwork by choice."

Zreyas watched the Janquar look over to the silent one. The artisan raised his head up in silent pride, then looked ahead.

After an hour of hiking, the silent Janquar pointed. "We are almost there."

"Good." Zreyas thought a moment, then asked the artisan, "Is the clay hardened and packed, crumbly, or soft?"

"We broke up quite a bit of it because we had planned to use it, so it's like gravel or larger chunks."

"Then we will need to do our work nearby. Can the Nation see a fire from there?"

"There is a cliff that goes higher than the rest of the plateau that could hide us from that side."

"Good! This will be fun!"

The two Janquar looked at each other with confused faces.

Zreyas felt for them in their confusion. He knew why. As thirsty and headache ridden as he was, it was great to be back with his people again in a unique setting. He knew they thought he had lost his mind, but he didn't care. Zreyas took his water-skin out and drank some water. He wanted to so badly to gulp it all down, but he resisted.

The others did the same.

Zreyas put his water-skin away and looked at them. Both were already watching him. "For the first time, I'm with my Janquar people working together by choice. I'm having fun and enjoying my life with you."

The two Janquar looked at him like he had grown two heads.

He shrugged. "I have learned something valuable—Anyone that has good intentions and cares about others, they are my people. It doesn't matter the color of the skin, species, or what their profession is. I wasted most of my life living in fear of one thing or another, or fighting to kill what I knew nothing about because I was told to."

Zreyas stopped in his tracks. "Hey…"

The Janquar stopped walking and cocked their heads slightly.

He looked up at their confused faces. "I'm giving you the thankings for everything you did for me, directly and indirectly," he said with sincerity. "I didn't see you, but I always had what I needed. I just want you to know that I… am giving the appreciate now."

Their faces went past confused and hit the level of perplexed shock, wide eyes and sliding their heads back on their shoulders. He knew no one in their life had ever thanked them or appreciated what they did, except Aaru.

"There it is!" Zreyas Q-leaped ahead, pointing at the broken-up clay, leaving the shocked Janquar behind.

When Zreyas arrived at the area, he immediately found a flat rock nearby. He picked up another rock with a flat side in his hand and grabbed a chunk of high-content clay dirt. He laid it down on the flat rock and started crushing the chunk of clay into powder.

After a few minutes, two enormous sets of Janquar feet stopped right in front of him with a 'thunk.' It vibrated the ground all around him. Then a huge chunk of clay landed right in front of him, startling him.

The artisan let out a single "Ha!"

Zreyas looked up with a grin, hearing the attempt to laugh.

"You will take forever, move."

Zreyas laughed, "Ha… ha," then Q-leaped to the top of the artisan's shoulder, startling him. "Ha! You just laughed."

"Well, it was a ridiculous sight, you trying to make powder for a Janquar project. It's like a tiny drop of mag-shit attempting to make a tower."

Then he heard a deep rumbling and dry, "Ha! I laugh

too," from the quiet one. "You just tell what we need to do with your big-little voice."

"Okay. First, we need a large pot. The lid for it needs to fit well without gaps and needs to have a hole middle way up with a casing that is big enough for a reed to fit through horizontally."

The artisan grunted and nodded. "Easy enough, go on."

"Then we need another pot exactly the same, but it doesn't have to be as big if you don't want... unless you want to store more water. The first one is for the sea water, the second one is for the purified water."

The artisan nodded with lit up understanding in his eyes. "Choice of teamwork. Once we crush, I make pots for Janquar. You make pots for your size in case we are not around anymore. You teach us how to make water, I teach you how to make pot better."

"I will help him crush," said the quieter one. "You find some kindling you can carry to start a fire. I find big wood."

The artisan looked at his comrade and nodded. "Yes, good teamwork by choice."

Zreyas nodded with a grin. "Sounds like a good plan."

He scanned the area for dry grass and small twigs that were like fire logs for him. Zreyas stacked them up near the cliff that matched the description they gave earlier for hiding the fire. He rubbed his head, feeling light-headed from the lack of water in the heat and exertion. After a couple hours of work, he drank some water in his pouch conservatively.

He walked over to the ledge of the cliff for the first time and saw an entire massive lake. *What the ticking hell, there is water there!* That is when he noticed the black mist hovering over the water. He guessed the drop was seventy to eighty meters and when he looked down; it caused him to take a step back instinctively.

"Long drop," a voice said that was *not* one of the two Janquar with him.

Zreyas whipped his head around to see who it was, but there was no one around. The two Janquar were crushing an enormous pile of clay silently. He walked over and asked if they said something to him. But they just shook their heads.

The artisan looked up and stood. "This is for making water? And you are sure it will work?"

"Yes, and I'm positive it will work. *If* the lids fit well, it will be more effective. The more they seal, the better it will work. We just need the reeds to fit well. If they don't, we can seal them with mud around the seams."

Their faces looked impressed. Then they looked at each other, then back at him.

"Then I take the risk." The artisan squatted at the powdered clay, made a bowl in it with the back of his hand, and drizzled his only drinking water in and mixed it carefully a little at a time.

Zreyas knew he was trying to make sure he did not waste the water.

His chest cracked a little that he would risk himself for his people. He opened his little water-skin, took a drink, then poured his water in with it. It would show them he was willing to take the risk too, and that he was confident. They spent all their lives being made to do something and take risks like animals, and he wanted to show them he was different.

"Before you put more in, how far is the sea from here?"

The smaller, quieter one of the two with smooth blue skin and no horns spoke up first. "Not far."

"We can use sea water to mix the clay if we need more. I wish I had known. We could have just gone to get it rather than use drinking water."

The artisan nodded. "Yeah, but then we would have used the water anyway to replenish ourselves for the walk. Not far to him is half day's walk one way."

"Oh, okay." It made sense to Zreyas and was surprised he didn't think about it.

Once the artisan used up his water, he handed the skin to his comrade. And then the silent one gave the artisan his water-skin.

Zreyas followed their lead on learning how to work with clay better while he made his own set, and Zreyas gave them instruction on the features needed in the pots. Over the course of the rest of the day, they made the pots they needed to distill the sea water into the fresh water and salt they all would need.

They set them in the sun to dry enough slowly so they could fire them later. The artisan would water them down periodically so they wouldn't dry too fast and crack. At one point, one of the large lids cracked and the artisan just filled it patiently.

While the pots dried between tending, they all got a fire pit ready together. It was well dark then, with only moonlight illuminating the area.

Zreyas was grateful for the cool air.

"We will have to wait till morning to fire them." The artisan sat up against the cliff face that was protecting the fire and closed his eyes.

The quiet Janquar did the same right next to the other one. Then he said tentatively, "I'm a worker, the lowest of the low." Before Zreyas could say anything, he continued. "But Aaru taught me tracking to help elevate me in my group. He said you taught him." He paused. Then he awkwardly said his next words, "I give the... ap—appreciate to you that you taught Aaru."

Zreyas nodded and smiled.

The two Janquar then leaned on each other, touched heads for sleeping stability, resembling the star sleeping pattern, and fell asleep almost immediately.

Zreyas' chest cracked and eyes filled, causing them to seal. *I didn t know that I indirectly helped anyone during that piece of mag-shit kind of life I had with the Janquar—except for Aaru. I guess we never know just how much we do for others, bad or good, and I was lucky enough... again, to find out.*

Those two were much larger than he was when he was of his normal size. Zreyas had been small for a Janquar, but that didn't hurt his fighting skills. He had just adapted to it and fought differently. He wasn't sure why, but he didn't miss being that big. And when he thought about it, he never really did deep down. It just seemed like an unfamiliar experience. Then again, at first, he didn't know he was tiny, so he had already made the adjustments by the time he found out.

Zreyas quietly Q-leaped right on the touching shoulders of the two Janquar. He looked up at the two snoring heads leaning on each other above him, cheeks vibrating over him as they snored. He wasn't much for noise while he slept; but this time, he didn't think he would mind. Zreyas laid down and fell asleep with a smile on his face.

14

Eyes Don t Have It

The two Janquar apparently woke at the same time and sat up straight, dumping Zreyas between them, hitting the ground hard. His instincts kicked in and Zreyas popped to his feet, drew his weapons, and threw out a war aura.

His two new friends pushed their backs against the rock wall behind them, holding their hands up.

"We didn't know you were there. Don't kill us," pleaded the artisan. "We always wake up at the same time in our sleeping star."

Zreyas realized what happened, sheathed his weapons, and wiped his eyes. "It's okay. I just don't normally wake up by getting dumped to the ground. I just didn't know what happened and trust me, I don't want to kill you for something like that."

"Anyone else would have," said the tracker.

Zreyas looked up at the tracker, "Well, I'm not everyone else... anymore." He smiled. "It was an accident. They happen."

The two exchanged glances, then back to him.

Holding his hands up, stretching and bending his body

back and forth, Zreyas asked, "So, let's fire the pots and get back, what do you say?"

The artisan looked shocked and said, "You are asking *us*?"

"I'm not your commander. You haven't signed up under my leadership. This is a team of choice. I'm asking you if that is what you want to do as a team."

Both nodded, paused, and looked at each other. They both grunted in unison as if they were mirror images.

They stood and started checking on the pots for cracks and structural integrity. The artisan tested them several ways. Then he nodded and placed them at the heart of where the fire would be. They all worked together to build a fire around the pots with care.

The artisan stopped and asked, "Are you sure you weren't an artisan? You sure know what you are doing."

Zreyas looked at him, "No, but I loved survival, so I learned everything I could from the grandfather artisans, so I could teach the others under me."

"You took the time to learn a low-life's tasks?"

"They aren't low-life! They are important!" Zreyas Q-leaped on top of the artisan's head, knocked on it constantly while he said, "Hello! Wake up! You are not a low-life! You are important! What you do supports life itself! Without you, none of us would be here now!" Then he stopped knocking on his head.

The other Janquar couldn't help himself and he blurted out as he pointed at the artisan, "Ha!... Ha!"

Zreyas didn't want to leave him out either, giving them an equal message. He Q-leaped to the tracker's head and knocked on it with his fist, "And you, no matter what job you have, it's important. A position of profession doesn't make you less or more than another person!"

The artisan then started his awkward laugh, pointing

at the tracker, "Ha! Now I know why you 'Ha'-ed at me."

The one Zreyas was standing on bent over slightly, and Zreyas Q-leaped off his head to the ground. He scratched his head, watching them with a grin. "Well, as long as you get the message somehow... you are as thick headed as I was about similar things."

After a short time of watching them punch each other with a lot of grunts, he said, "Okay, okay, I am going to start this fire. But you two got to put the large logs on. I can't do that part."

It took till late afternoon for the pots to fire and cool. They wiped them off the best they could. Much to their surprise, none of them cracked on the first attempt.

Zreyas felt proud. He could tell the other two were proud of their work by the way they held their expressions and body, not to mention their satisfied grunts and nods.

He grinned and said, "This is a good omen. Let's pack them up carefully and get back to the coast. We can walk back along the shoreline to keep from being seen so easily. There won't be as many enthralled creatures and no Janquar nearby."

The Tracker paused. "How do you know they will not see us on the shore?"

Zreyas paused a few moments, considering if he should divulge his simple strategy. He took a couple seconds to work it out in his mind, and he decided to tell them. "I'm going to give you the trust I think you deserve. It's about my survival while everyone is still highly attuned to me from being their commander for so many years. You know as well as I do that, I'm easy to track because of the internal war communication imprint, even though they locked me out of it."

They nodded their agreement without their typical glance between them. *You would think they were split into two bodies, like Rhom and Rtu, the way they interact. They seem like they share the same mind or something.*

Zreyas nodded back to them. "How many Janquar do you know that want to look or go to a large body of salt water?"

The tracker and artisan exchanged glances, then back to Zreyas. Both shook their heads.

"Exactly! How do you think I have been able to avoid and slip past the Janquar on the beach when you were all there?" He didn't wait for an answer. "And guess what? I landed on this planet just meters away from you. But I stayed in the water."

The tracker grunted. "So that's how you stayed hidden from us all this time."

Zreyas nodded. "And I learned quite a bit having to swim in water."

They gasped with wide eyes.

"It's not so bad when you learn to work *with* our eye problem, not against it. It's sort of like clay. We gave that clay the right environment and approach to work with it to make what we needed, yes?"

That seemed to ring a note for them. They perked up, and both nodded and gave a grunt of understanding.

Zreyas began to see the differences in their grunts and what they meant in their blue culture. It was interesting to see how they communicated since he met them at the tree just two days ago.

They must have had to do a lot in silence. No, that wasn't right, he realized. It was a way to communicate that was part of their culture he had never had the privilege to see before. They didn't *have* to use words. The strategy in that was immense in Zreyas' mind. It kept them open to receive sensory input.

He enjoyed being silent. Zreyas remembered how he

used to communicate with Aaru without words. He could still stay aware and keep his senses sharp. As he considered it, Zreyas chatted with the two Janquar as he thought this out. He realized that as he spoke, he couldn't listen with all senses very well, much less pay attention to his environment with them. For him, it was like putting a pause on the instincts. *Interesting. It could be strategic, too.*

After they packed everything carefully, each Janquar had one large pot each, and he had his two pots.

The artisan looked at Zreyas doubtfully. "How will you carry your two pots?"

"I made rope! Watch." Zreyas tied both pots carefully on each end of the rope, wound it around the pots to keep them from hitting something directly and draped it over his shoulders, a pot dangling from each shoulder.

Both grunted and started walking. It was awkward to keep up with the two Janquar, though, with both pots, trying to keep them from hitting each other... or him too hard. He knew he was slowing them down, but he didn't complain.

After an hour of stopping and starting, the artisan finally reached down. "I help." He grabbed his rope with the pots and draped them around his neck.

"Good, he's slow," said the tracker.

"I know. Not much I could do about it, though. I did my best."

The artisan looked down at him. "We... tell you the... appree-chiate."

Zreyas grinned and Q-leaped to keep up and lead the way. Though he knew they knew the way, it made him feel better to scout ahead and come back in cycles. They all would need that clean water, and soon. He felt a little faint and his vision seemed to swim from time to time a little.

"Do you know of a place we can get reeds for your

pots?" said Zreyas as he came back to the two Janquar after a scouting cycle.

"We have some in our camp, but if that camp is no longer there, we know of a place to get them nearby."

"You said they wouldn't be looking for you."

The tracker spat out a grunt. "Seriously? You think they can do without us for very long? The only reason we can be gone this long is because our brothers are making up for our work. As long as what they need gets done, they don't care. But they will never let us go."

"You have a point! Maybe we should stop by the camp and get your reeds first." Zreyas suggested. "If you are going to live a life of choice, it might get rough."

The artisan looked at the tracker, then Zreyas, and said, "Now *you* have a point."

The tracker looked at Zreyas, "Yeah, we go get the reeds first."

"Okay, then lead the way," Zreyas said, feeling that nagging weird gut feeling again.

They veered off toward the camp. It wasn't long till they got there, though, and no one was there. The two Janquar went straight to where the reeds were stored. They pulled out a few extra, just in case. They also packed a few bags of tools and rations. All three of them also drank water and filled their water-skins just in case things got eventful before they could get the water made.

He tried to keep his tendency for leadership out of his tones but he heard it when he said, "Just in case we see problems, if you can drop the pots so they won't get damaged and move away from them, it will help make sure our work and time weren't wasted. We *need* that water. I can't shake this feeling something is wrong."

The two Janquar were silent, but nodded, paying attention to everything around them.

"I'll scout ahead a short way since I'm not burdened with the pots and gear."

"Good idea," the artisan said sincerely.

Zreyas Q-leaped with utmost silence ahead. "Rhom, something is really wrong here. I'm not sure if you can hear me, but I just thought I would let you know. You probably already know about the nagodara, but that Dark One is accessing things that are not of this world and using them. There has got to be more going on and I have yet to get to the Nation camp yet to find the—"

As he made it to the cave, he spotted approximately twenty Janquar warriors gathering at the landing rock formation where he killed the nagodara.

Zreyas hurried to close the distance. It didn't worry him if they saw him, because they focused on something in, or on, that formation. They weren't paying attention to their surroundings at all. They were also loud.

He Q-leaped quietly behind them.

Several warriors were trying to scale the rock formation. There were three archers with bows knocked and ready. For a moment, Zreyas was confused as to why. *Are they having some sort of competition?* No, that couldn't be it, with archers at the ready. Then he saw the reason.

In a sudden split second, he saw a tuft of white hair and icy-white predatory eyes pop up over the edge of the rock formation.

The archers loosed their arrows.

His little friend ducked its head just in time to avoid them.

Immediately after nocking new arrows, the archers drew their bows.

Rage rose within Zreyas, and he pulled the two swords on his back. *Ticking-hell, there is no way I'm going to let these piles of mag-shit hurt that baby creature!*

Zreyas yelled, "Hey!" Then he Q-leaped to the top of one of the three archers' head while the warriors weren't looking as they investigated what they had heard behind them. He raised his swords above his head and reversed the grip. As he lowered the swords with force, he squatted to get low enough to plunge the swords into both eyes of the first archer. He didn't wait for the result and leaped again to the second one.

The Janquar warriors had turned around toward the voice and they saw the artisan and tracker in the distance and assumed it was them that called. The Janquar started yelling at them, asking where they had been. Some stormed toward them and Zreyas watched them put the pots down and walked forward to meet them.

Getting distracted by the exchange, Zreyas almost lost his footing when the archer turned his head to see what had happened to his fellow archer as he slumped to the ground.

Zreyas used his swords on the archer's head like a pick or stake to grab the side of a mountain to keep himself from falling.

The archer immediately tried to swat his own head to kill the source of pain blindly. That shoved the sword in deeper, hitting bone. The Janquar let out a growling wail and his war aura erupted.

Zreyas Q-leaped out in front of the archer on the ground and faced him. Then he whispered, "I can do that too, you murdering bandhula."

He could tell he heard him in all the commotion because he focused directly on him. Pointing his swords at his eyes deliberately for intimidation, he watched the archer's eyes widen in surprise. Zreyas' size, and who he was, sunk in.

Zreyas grinned, then whispered, "Much thankings to

you for making this easier." He Q-leaped straight for the eyes. He hit his target spot on when he came out of the leap—almost *too* dead on.

His swords hit the eyes, but his chest slammed into the archer's face, knocking the wind out of himself and he felt the archer's nose crack. The archer let out a war aura, even as he fell backward. Zreyas braced himself with his grip on the swords. When the archer hit the ground, his body weight on the impact shoved the swords in so far it buried his arms past his elbows and up to his shoulders. It knocked Zreyas' head backwards.

Zreyas worked his body under himself, stood on the archer's face and lifted himself up and brought his arms out of the Janquar's head.

He Q-leaped to the third one's head, who had just taken a shot at his new friend. He changed grips, flipping the swords up in the air to hold them backward again, and slammed them into the archer's eyes just under his feet.

Concerned for his little tuft-haired friend, Zreyas Q-leaped toward the rock formation in silence to help him.

There was so much chaos going on that the other Janquar warriors did not know what Zreyas had just done. *Looks like this is my lucky day again. My identity is still obscure…for now.*

15 Save You, Save Me

ᒧᒧᒧ *Zreyas* ᒧᒧᒧ

He Q-leaped behind the rock formation on the opposite side, then again to the top of it where he had fought the nagodara. He didn't want to reveal himself to the Janquar yet, so he stayed low.

"It's okay, little friend. I'm here to help. Would you like to move to some place safer?" he asked, approaching the hole. Zreyas sheathed one of his swords, but kept the other one ready.

The rage and auras from the Janquar were pretty sharp to feel, and loud, so he figured that was why he was not showing himself.

"I can't help you if I can't see you. I'm a little limited sometimes." Zreyas heard significant... silence.

Just as he Q-leaped down into the hole, he saw the creature's head in all its glory. Poking its head around the corner of the wall of the bedding dens for the shinits, Zreyas couldn't believe it was the same creature he was looking at that he helped just days ago. Its expression was pure inner strength. He wasn't sure how he would even describe it if he had to. But, he didn't know how something could have an expression of strength, though. Maybe strength was the wrong word. Perhaps it was his aura or energy in general, but he had no way of telling with his skills at the moment.

There was one thing he knew, though, and that was how much larger the creature's head was. He couldn't see the rest of him, but his head was as large as his own body, now, and had grown several times its size since he last saw it.

It was the most unique creature he had ever seen, and its white fur seemed to glow ever so slightly now. There were brief times it went into a state of iridescence. The small flecks of silver that had been on his fur were all gold now. The predatory, soul-searching icy-white eyes communicated strength and confidence.

Zreyas looked into those soul-touching eyes. "How magnificent you are, and I only see your head and neck. But I feel your inside... and it is even more... well, just more."

He could hear the Janquar getting closer, but it was dull in the back of his mind.

"I'm glad you are safe. Something tells me you really didn't need my help, but here I am. I don't want them to hurt you."

Zreyas walked slowly toward him and reached out with his hand palm down. "Can I touch you?"

The creature jerked his head back, then relaxed, almost as if he forgot Zreyas was okay to be close to.

Zreyas didn't move at first. After a few seconds, he decided not to push it. Just before lowering his hand slowly, he said, "I understand."

Then the creature lowered its brow to his hand for a brief second and then raised it.

"I think you understand me. So what are you going to do? Can you talk? You seem way more intelligent than you are letting on."

The eyes of the creature looked at Zreyas, then nodded its head.

"So you understand at least." Zreyas smiled. "I'm not surprised. I've been through some amazing and horrible mag-shit the past week, and I realized that more creatures are a lot more intelligent than I."

Suddenly, a Janquar stuck his head and arm down through the hole and let out a war aura. Zreyas could see the warrior's eyes going through the turning and shifting that Janquar's eyes do to adjust to the dark vision.

Before he had a chance to fully adjust, Zreyas flipped his sword in a reverse hold and Q-leaped. He appeared right beside his head, both hands gripping the hilt. He arched his body, let out a roar, and shoved the sword through his temple. The Janquar slumped.

Zreyas hung, holding the embedded knife, while he watched the Janquar's arms dangle and drip blood into what he felt was a sacred place. Zreyas felt sick at how everything good on Tarq was becoming so dirty and disgusting. He swung his feet up to push against his head to get the leverage to pull the sword out, then Q-leaped back down to the floor of the cave away from where the fluids were dripping.

The creature looked at him and nodded, almost like he was approving of what he just did and didn't seem scared at all.

"The Janquar have now even desecrated this place," lamented Zreyas.

He looked around, trying to figure out what to do to get his large new friend out of here. "You might be able to go down the way I got out, but I hope you can swim. But let me make sure there are no more Janquar coming in behind us." He turned to check for any near or coming into the hole. Before he could leap up on the ledge, he felt something grab his shoulders. His whole body jerked and flew upward, almost losing his sword.

"Who-oa!"

He found the hole of the formation growing smaller below him. Too startled to even do a war aura in reaction, shocked that or something was blocking him from doing it, his stomach lurched.

"You can fly already, not to mention fly strong enough to pick me up?"

Zreyas heard nothing but silence from him.

He looked up and saw... nothing.

Then he checked to both sides... nothing.

Growing more frustrated, he yelled, "What are you *doing*? You are blowing my—"

Sure enough, the Janquar's attention was already on him. It's hard not to see something flying out from a rock.

"Ticking hell, there goes my cover. Now you've done it, now the Janquar will know I'm not the large version I used to be. You have ruined all my efforts for sabotage!"

The band of Janquar below started backing up and jumping off the rock formation with expressions unlike the Janquarian people. Their behavior shocked Zreyas. Then he realized something. "They are afraid."

They knew he was up there, but they tried not to look at him. Maybe they thought he was a nagodara. No, he wasn't the same size and looked nothing like one.

Several Janquar scaling the formation fell to the rocks below. One smashed his head on the rocks and never got up. The scene was pure chaos. Some tripped over each other, trying to get away. No one was helping each other. One killed another that was in his way.

Zreyas finally realized why they were so afraid. They had seen the three archers he had killed or maimed earlier, eyes all bloodied. Two of them reached out into the air, trying to grasp hold of something.

A death like that for a Janquar was low status, but maimed in that particular way, and still live, was worse. He just shook his head.

The two blue camp members with the pots down the beach watched it all calmly, exchanging glances from time to time.

Zreyas was furious at how they tried to kill an innocent creature. He wasn't sure why he was so upset about things like that recently. But he was glad he wasn't like them anymore, with no regard to life at all. All of them were willing to kill each other just to get a step further.

He decided he would use his anger and go with his situation.

"Yeah! That's right! I will cut all your eyes out if you ever come back here again or harass an innocent creature again!" He thought again and added, "And leave the blue camp alone or everyone of you will have no eyes." Zreyas knew that wouldn't happen, but he was angry and a little unreasonable now.

The last of the band of warriors pick up the three archer bodies and either helped them to their feet or picked them up and started running away.

Suddenly Zreyas fell. "Ticking mag-shit!"

He instinctively Q-leaped to the side of the rock formation then immediately leaped again to the shore.

Zreyas heard a faint, "Weet, weet, weet."

He looked up. *Did he just laugh at me?*

"Ha... ha." He couldn't help it. It was comical when he thought about it. How he must have looked to the Janquar and seeing him up there in the sky like that, and it made him laugh even more. "Ha... ha... ha..."

"Well, that was quite the spectacle." The artisan said as the pair approached.

The tracker looked at him with piercing eyes. "Should we be afraid?"

He looked up at him and said evenly, "That is up to you. If you feel you should be, kill me right now. I'll let you. You can have all the fame for it, turn dark, grow horns, and become just like them. It's all you have wanted, right? My life means nothing if I don't find a way to stop these pieces of mag-shit. My only other hope was to give you a chance like I had."

Zreyas sheathed his bloody weapon and held his arms out wide in the ultimate vulnerable position, head back and neck exposed.

After a long silence, the artisan simply said, "I will kill you after you teach me how to make fresh water."

The tracker belted out a single, "Ha!"

Zreyas slumped forward, looking crass. "Did you just humiliate me?"

"Yeah, if you won't teach us how to make water; no, if you are." The artisan shrugged.

Zreyas started laughing and shook his head. He looked back and saw the last of the Janquar disappear into the tree line. "Do you know where the others are?"

"They are probably working in the Nation, but they will be back at night to the camp."

"Well, let's go make drinking water," said Zreyas.

The large Janquar artisan pulled the two Zreyas size pots off his neck and draped them over his back, "Here, these are too heavy for me. Someone needs to do their part of the work."

"Ha!" said the tracker.

"I like making you laugh, Tracker," the artisan said as

they walked over and hefted the pots and gear he had picked back up. Then they looked at Zreyas expectantly.

Zreyas grinned and started leading them back to his cave. He explained how to make fresh water out of the sea water as they set up the fires and pots. They followed his example as if they were mirroring him.

As they spent the day making fresh water, the tracker and artisan seemed to be happier than Zreyas had ever seen any Janquar be. They took turns going out and bringing back wood.

They enjoyed the first remnants of fresh water as if it were the best drink in the world. In Zreyas' opinion, it tasted better than natural fresh water—probably because he had such a good time making it with his two new friends.

Zreyas used the salt left in the bottom of the source pot on the hide he had been trying to dry out for days. It seemed to impress the two Janquar that the process had more than one function.

The artisan reached in their large pot and pulled out some of the salt, moving it around between his fingers to test the texture, then tasted it. "Better than trying to mine it. It tastes different, but... I like it."

"Salt from the sea has good nutrients, too. The grandfather artisans taught this to me. I put sea water in my water, but only a little. If I had both, I would use mined salt on the hide and use sea salt for water and food."

They looked at him like he was nuts, so Zreyas spent a couple hours teaching them about what the grandfather artisans taught him about the differences between salts, nutrients, and food to keep them strong. They sucked it all up like they starved for learning.

Night fell, and the Janquar picked up the purified water pot and the salts they had made. They left the rest of their setup, because they would be back to make more.

Zreyas sat out on the rocks. As he continued to make fresh water for himself, he glanced at the source pot for the blue camp. It was like having his friends here with him. Smiling, he leaned back and ate his dried meat and the last of his berries.

He wanted a full pot and water-skin, just in case he got too busy to stop and make more. Zreyas listened to the pot boil and gently popping fire as he looked up to the stars.

Zreyas wondered what Rhom, Rtu, and Tulyata were up to. It seemed like it had been varSas since he had seen them last—not less than a week.

He sat back and took another bite of his simple meal. Since the others didn't have food with them, he didn't want to eat in front of them. It had been a good while since he had eaten anything. Zreyas never realized that simple food could taste so good... until now.

After that pot of water finished boiling dry, he took apart the system he set up carefully and put each part up in his cave to keep them safe. The large Janquar pots wouldn't blow away, but his small pots could easily if the wind was strong enough.

Once he put out the fire, Zreyas laid down for a good night's sleep. He was looking forward to it. He was exhausted and was asleep before he laid his head down.

Sometime during the night, he heard a voice in his mind while he slept.

— Zreyas, there is big trouble here. Is it okay that I use the quantum to bring you here? I can put you back at the same time as when you left if you like.

He woke, sat up sleepily, and looked around for Rhom. "Hmm? Yes, Let me dress and get my weapons."

16 Dead Eyes

Zreyas watched the distinctive particles of transporting through the quantum. He expected to see Tulyata saying something like 'the ferret is back' and 'hello little buddy!' from Rtu, but that didn't happen. One thing he knew—he was not in Tulyata's realm.

"Hello, my boy!"

"Now *that* is familiar. I don't see you, old man, but I know that voice." Zreyas turned around to see a large complex of technology he couldn't even begin to understand. Finally, he saw his friend. He was standing on a table because he was at Rhom's shoulder height.

Rhom's smile was anything but his normally bright smile, though. His face was grim.

Zreyas' heart fell. He felt his smile fade as he noticed the challenge node not expecting to see it in a strange place, but it looked like Aqum in Tulyata's dimension. Then he got excited. "I knew there was another node! Is this one the mate of the one I found in the challenge?"

"No, it's the same one that was in Tulyata's realm," Rhom said sourly. "I moved it here when Rtu and Tulyata didn't want to help anymore. It's a good thing I did, too."

Confused, Zreyas quit looking around the massive complex of what he could only assume was Rhom's science tech and focused on his friend. Something obviously upset him. "What do you mean?"

"Just after I moved the node—" Rhom paused and swallowed. "I mean... I relocated it just before the Dark One obliterated Tulyata's dimension."

"Wha-at?!" That couldn't be true, could it? His eyes wandered aimlessly as he tried to process that information. "I thought her realm was safe! Are Tulyata and Rtu okay?"

"No realm exposed to the physical planes is safe. It happened twice; once, when she picked me up, and again, when she dropped you off. She either got careless or knew it was going to happen to begin with."

"She fully expected to get out," came a voice that sounded familiar, but also strange.

Zreyas turned toward the voice, and there stood Rtu. But it wasn't the same Rtu that he knew. Zreyas looked at them both, feeling like his mind was going to blow up from confusion. "What happened?"

Rtu walked into the next room where the challenge node was, just off the one he and Rhom were currently in. They followed Rtu and watched him plop down on a large plushy couch as if he had no will to live. His glow had disappeared. Zreyas felt the incredible lack of... life had left Rtu. It alarmed him and he wondered how a visage of natural balance could be so... dead.

Something horrible had definitely happened and Zreyas was now terrified to find out what it was.

This room looked just like the one in Tulyata's dimension. The screens, the furniture, the doors, and the challenge node. The only thing it was missing was Tulyata's desk and Tulyata herself. Zreyas' guts twisted, and he suddenly wished badly to be called a little ferret again. As he paid close attention to his new feel for quantum space and energies, he noticed he didn't feel her anymore like he did before. That took him by surprise. There was a void in the multiverse somehow.

Zreyas and Rhom looked at each other. He could tell Rhom was as shocked and worried about the state of Rtu. No matter how bad the situation was, he was always happy and laughing. He guessed no one could be like that all the time. But this...

Rhom lifted his hands helplessly. "I can't feel him as myself anymore, so don't look at me. You know as much as I do. It's why I called you here. I was desperate for help... and a little moral support, if I'm honest."

Zreyas tentatively approached Rtu, looking up into his downtrodden eyes. Panic ran up through his body at seeing Rtu's eyes. They were dead. Zreyas had seen many people and creatures he had killed in his life; but somehow, Rtu's eyes seemed more dead than all the eyes of the corpses put together.

He scaled up Rtu's leg and sat down beside him. "I'm concerned, Rtu. Even *I* can see you festering. I don't know what to do to help, but maybe you are experiencing what us incarnates are going through when we experience significant loss or guilt, like when I lost Aaru."

Zreyas, respectfully slow, moved to sit down on his knee to look into his friend's face. *How do you reach a visage to help them up?* "I don't know what happened, but I know you well enough to know you would never do anything to hurt anyone on purpose. I am asking you to come back to me and Rhom. You are not only important to every part of creation, but you are important to me as a friend. I can't imagine a multiverse without you. I'm sure Rhom would like to have his brother back, too."

Zreyas shifted a little before he took a breath to say with more determination, "You both taught me that there was nothing but ego involved to take responsibility for something that you had no control over."

He didn't know what else to say and felt helpless. Then he remembered a discussion once about how ego disguised itself in many states of festering. He wasn't sure it would help, but now was the time to be blunt. Something told him this situation, left unchecked, would be dire for the multiverse.

Zreyas gently said, "Rtu, you aren't about ego, don't condition yourself to be. At least talk about it. Maybe it will help you sort it out, at least tactically, for your next move. Your next move is direction, and that gives hope in a war. And you, visage of laughter, are at war... with yourself and your creations might be a casualty."

Rtu looked up slowly, with tears streaming unnaturally fast from his eyes. As soon as they dropped on his chest, they quickly absorbed like rain on dirt, leaving no trace—another feature of a visage, Zreyas guessed.

He could tell that Rtu was having a hard time swallowing. Then a voice came from Rtu that sounded raspy and cracked. "Thank you, little buddy. Thank you for the reminder."

Zreyas looked up to Rhom, who was sitting down across from them. Rhom was not doing well himself. He looked depleted, even more than Rtu. The shimmer on his skin was gone and the colors on his skin seemed to be more of a dusty version of the tones. He wondered if it was because the two were still connected somehow.

"You are right," said Rtu hollowly. "I will talk about it. I bear much responsibility and I need to face them. You called me out and gave me what I needed to wake up and pull myself out of this. My love of my creations and family is important to me. You instinctively understand my design, and that is an amazing wonder to me. It reminds me there are beautiful things still left to live for."

Rhom smiled and let out a long breath of relief, the features of his face relaxing visibly. "Take your time, brother. Remember as much as you can. We want to help."

After a few long minutes, Zreyas looked at Rhom with a questioning expression. Rhom just shook his head and shrugged, confirming he still knew nothing. Then Zreyas turned to look at his grieving friend, focusing.

Rtu was still looking down, but said, "I really don't know much more than you two. But I will say this... It is my *inaction* that caused Mother's death."

Zreyas sat up straight in surprise. *Oh, this is bad... this is very bad.* That explained the void feeling he had.

He nodded at Zreyas. "I will tell you what I remember." Rtu wiped his eyes and lifted his face with an expression like someone that had a headache or something.

Zreyas could tell he was struggling. He couldn't imagine what a visage of creation might feel like to destroy something he loved so much. It wasn't in his nature to destroy. This disaster, however it happened, had to be started by an outside influence.

He focused his mind and heart and put himself into the peace he felt just being with his friends again. He was beginning to understand his own aura now, and Zreyas knew it would push to him naturally. Rtu seemed to breathe better, and that made Zreyas feel more at peace.

Rtu looked at Zreyas with appreciation laced eyes. "Rhom and I had a heated discussion after we dropped you off. It was about my inaction. I just felt no compulsion to do anything. But I fought it, but inside I cried for losing the joy I used to have. After Rhom convinced me to help him on Earth again, I backed out at the last minute. I had less and less inclination to watch over my creations and balances. I found myself not caring about Ayya anymore."

Rtu paused a moment in thought. "I know the Dark One didn't know about where the dimension was when Mother made the contract with him initially. We weren't in either of our dimensions when we did that, we were in *his* dimension. From what I can surmise, when the dimension was exposed the first time, the Dark One immediately found out." Rtu rubbed his face. "Oh yeah, we talked about that already."

Rhom asked, "It's okay, brother. You are talking about when you both picked me up from the dying dimension?"

Rtu nodded.

"Yeah, he was right there in that dark hall in the dying dimension. I apologize for the interruption. Go ahead when you are ready."

"Even from the time we first met with him, till the last time we communicated, the Dark One was very different. He's turned into mostly a low-frequency being, with programmed intelligence." Rtu shuddered, then moved on with the story. "When Tulyata opened the dimension to drop Zreyas off, it puzzled me why she didn't teleport him down."

"I wondered that myself, brother. But I was so distraught with Zreyas leaving and you not seeming like yourself that I didn't say anything. You are not alone in that responsibility."

"But... I didn't care enough to question it." Rtu threw up his hands weakly and let them land on his thighs. "I understood the reason for the *first* time, because Rhom had to make the decisions and choices for balance's sake. She could have made an additional dimension to hide her location afterwards, but she didn't. It was probably because we were under contract with the Dark One then.

But the second time... it just made *no sense* to me at all."

"Tulyata had a flare for the dramatic when a situation had a chance to be different from the same old routine. So I figured that was why she exposed it—that, or... because she loved Zreyas and just wasn't thinking because she was upset, too. But, it's also not like her to lose her head over something like that either. I can't shake the feeling that she did all this on purpose."

"Yes, I agree," said Rtu. "I don't think she was being reckless. I think she *knew* it would happen. She was too careful. When have you ever known her to not calculate balances on everything?"

Zreyas was listening, but he couldn't help but think rapidly firing questions. *Why are they talking like she is permanently dead? Even if she is dead, isn t she a visage? They never really die completely, do they?* He didn't want to ask his questions right now. He felt like he needed to just let Rtu and Rhom talk.

Rtu looked at Rhom. "You have a point."

The lack of carefulness was extremely uncharacteristic of her, so much so that he continued to obsess about it. Zreyas had a feeling something would come to the surface if he kept talking, so he said nothing.

"Why didn't she make a new one? She'd done it before many times over the course of our lives, but she didn't." Rtu turned to face him, "Anyway, Zreyas, you know about the contract we had with the Dark One, and you *did* actually break the contract with that peace aura of yours. But the Dark one knew about the dimension, *then.*" He paused, then said with a slow, thoughtful and distant cadence, "She didn't make a new dimension. But... when that door opened to drop you off, suddenly like magic, I didn't care about *anything*. I didn't care about mother, my twin brother, or whether you lived or died, Zreyas."

The grief intertwined with those last words seemed to split the visage of balance apart, both in energy and expression. Zreyas could feel it, even through his peace.

"It's okay Rtu, I'm not mad," Zreyas said matter of factly. "It wasn't your fault. I discovered the enthrallment tentacles in the quantum while I was down there. The Dark One has enthrallments on all creatures within his immediate range and you dropped me off *inside* that range."

"Interesting, my boy! I agree with Zreyas. I would say the Dark One definitely influenced Rtu."

Growing more energetic at the information, Rtu said, "Rhom tried to get Mother and I to do something with him in the portal room again as a team, but mother refused, and I didn't care. I guessed something wasn't right; in fact, I knew something was very wrong. But again... I didn't care."

"I couldn't put my finger on it, either. I wondered why she didn't change the dimension," said Rhom, scratching his head just above his ear and leaning back.

"After Rhom got angry and ranted about how complacent I had gotten, I still didn't care. He even asked me what was wrong, but I had no feelings about any of it. I cried, but I didn't cry because of that. I cried because I felt myself leave even more that time. After Rhom went to the portal area next, Mother and I watched the challenge node disappear. We just looked at each other without saying anything. I knew then he knew something was up. I'm glad he moved it, because right after that, everything went bad."

Rhom *looked* empathetic, but Zreyas could feel an anger radiating gently. He wasn't sure if it was at Rtu, or if it was at the Dark One that killed Tulyata. He supposed it was the latter of the two.

Rtu sighed. "When the dimension started to shatter and rip apart, Mother and I were on opposite sides of the room. Whatever hit us ripped her dimension up between the two of us."

Zreyas watched Rtu's expression almost show what he relived by telling the story. Rtu was in what the Janquar called war-shock. It didn't happen often, but if it did, they sent them to the blue camps. He could tell Rtu was watching the scene as he explained it. It gave him chills.

"I just watched it happen—numb. Mother worked hard at her balances to make a quick decision while debris was flying everywhere. Tiny black holes appeared all around us. I barely understood when she yelled across the breaking dimension to tell me to go home. She had frantic love on her face, but she also had that Tulyata Prime Visage of balance determination and fire in her expression, but that didn't even make me act."

Rtu sighed and flipped his palms up weakly on his thighs in a grief that was palpable. "But... I didn't even care enough to port myself out. So, I'm assuming she used what little balance she had left to port me out instead of herself. She is now lost because I didn't care enough to get myself out. She made the *ultimate* sacrifice."

"It might have *felt* like it, but I don't believe you didn't care. The Dark One enthralled you." Zreyas watched him shift in his chair, trying not to topple him over in the process. He climbed off and sat next to Rtu so he wouldn't have to worry about that anymore. Rtu was going through enough as it was.

"Agreed!" said Rhom.

"You know, I think you are right, little buddy, because as soon as I got to *my* dimension, I *immediately* felt like myself again."

Rhom's eyebrows lifted. Zreyas realized he was

grateful that it was the Dark One and not something wrong with Rtu.

"I saw things clearly and figured out what happened. I went back in time in my mind and it was when that door opened for you it started. Now that you have told me what you discovered, somehow the Dark One tethered into me and started draining the state of freedom, love, and purpose out of me."

"It's happening to the Janquar too," he said to Rtu.

"It probably happened to Tulyata too, but she was much stronger than I was. I mean, she *is* my mother, after all. She's been around a long time and a mother's love is something more powerful than anything in creation. Mother knew something I didn't see."

"That was probably the case, brother. Her love was fierce, but she always had her head on straight about it."

Suddenly the challenge node came to life and lit up visibly, as if someone was in it. Then a familiar voice cut in.

"—This is an Aqum interruption—Alarmed while informing you—Aqum is taking advantage of the space between rules."

Everyone looked at each other in shock, raising eyebrows, and nodding.

"Please go ahead, Aqum," said Rhom. "No need to be alarmed."

"Yeah! I'm having the happies that you are real and using the spaces. Ha!"

"—Aqum is saying with deep relief—Aqum finds hope that we will be forgiven for eavesdropping—We have something that has been recorded by The Witness that might shed light on some of the mystery of Tulyata's behavior.

"Yeah, yeah, you are forgiven as far as I'm concerned."

Zreyas chuckled. "You might be disguised as a travel node, but anyone that uses the spaces makes you practically chosen family."

"Indeed!"

"I agree with my little buddy."

"—Aqum obtained this from the one that uses the code name of The Witness, aid of a Prime Visage's right hand."

Again, everyone looked at each other in shock. Rhom seemed especially dazed to Zreyas, like he was off again in that space his mind wanders to.

"Uh oh, you broke Rhom, Aqum. Ha! You might want to wait till he comes back before you continue."

17 The Witness

The Witness

"No, no, no, no!" a voice lamented.

The Witness looked out over the desolation of the Dark One, seeing only a single wing of their friend. The cliffs were barren and black. They looked at the valley that now lacked life. The only thing still moving that they could see was the smoke and fire. The Witness walked toward the edge of the cliff where his friend lay dead. The body of the noble bird hung over the side, unseen. With an air of hopeless grief, not knowing what to do, they reached out to the ashes.

Carefully, they lowered themselves down into a squat, reaching out to touch the wing with tears in their eyes. The gentle touch caused the ash of his friend to deteriorate and break loose like a domino effect.

"I'm so sorry, my friend," The Witness said, as they dropped to their palms and knees, looking over the ledge.

They watched the rest of the body slowly waft to the bottom of the desolate canyon that had flourished with life just moments ago. "The multiverse will miss you... I... will miss you."

Sitting back, they pulled their knees up and leaned on their hands. "I thought Rhom was going to help, so something must have happened to him too... or there was some sort of problem. I will look into it. I'm angry. No, I'm furious." The soot and ash were taken by the drafts. The atmosphere disappeared slowly, cutting off clouds and landscape as it shrunk. Yet another dimension was dying.

With a hopeless sigh, they spoke to Jonath's spirit, still lingering. "You were a critical part of putting this Dark One back into its place. Ayya and the new age needed you. What, dear friend, are we going to do now?"

They peered down into the canyon at the bleak darkness and devastation. They felt numb, and the loss destroyed their heart. Then they spotted a little light at the bottom of the canyon. Not much, but enough to catch their vision in such a dark place. Hope rose in their heart.

They immediately made the trek down the pathway that wound down to the bottom of the canyon where the dim light was.

Near the ashes of their friend, they saw an egg... much different from their friend's species. "And who might you be to still be alive in this disaster? Maybe this is what Jonath tried to show me before..."

Drawing a deep breath, they squatted down, looking inquisitively at the egg, reaching their fingers out to move away the ash that fell on it gently. "Our hunt wasn't all for naught after all, Jonath... looks like you got us to the right place in time."

A screeching rush of sound filled the canyon. They looked up. High in the sky was a snake-like trail of fire that seemed alive and was seeking something. It turned and headed toward them in a winding way. It almost seemed like it was tasting the environment.

"Rhom, you came after all, but I'm afraid you are too late."

The fire grew angrier and much larger. It seemed to look straight at them and the egg.

The Witness stood and backed up. "It seems we have a survivor, and I'm not sure what it is. It's not in my realm of things to understand each of the species."

Almost as if in realization, the thick snake of fire rushed quickly toward them with the speed of a diving predator bird.

"Whoa!" They jumped back further. The fire stopped just above them and swirled like a storm, but in a consistent pattern. The ferocity of the fire, though stable, was still intimidating, and it burned everything around it. The ash that remained flew out of the area.

"So, this is the one to aid us," The Witness said, not affected at all by the heat. "Looks like you got here on time, my friend, albeit dramatically too late for Jonath. You must have had trouble too. I felt your separation a good many weeks ago. It's not like a visage to have trouble getting somewhere."

The fiery hurricane-like storm above them, still constant and steadily circling, seemed like it was going into a swirling, dormant, yet agitated, circling pattern. "You seem furious, Rhom. Then again, nothing about fire is exactly calm. You are incomplete. Where are the other parts of you? The fire is great and all but..."

A cracking sound emanated from the smooth egg, now a fiery red color.

Fascinated, they spoke to the egg. "You look much different now, little one. Come out before this dimension folds forever." They looked up, regarding the atmosphere vanishing in places and the line of disappearance hurrying toward them. "Talk about last-minute drama!"

The fire of Rhom continued to circle and hover like a hurricane above them. The egg suddenly cracked open slightly. Rhom immediately dove right in before they saw anything in the shell. As soon as the fire was all inside, it exploded out and emerged in the shape of a bird made of pure fire. It spread its wings, blasting The Witness back many meters. Unharmed, The Witness stood and closed the distance again, looking up at the magnificent fiery bird.

"A rising phoenix... I guess you are not a myth after all." The Witness bowed slightly. "It's an honor to meet such a new visage of the ages. We most definitely need you here and thank you for coming. What name do you choose or have you chosen already? I apologize. I'm not sure if this is a first birth or if you were born again."

The majestic bird turned its fiery eyes toward The Witness, and with a booming and echoing voice, said, "I am sorry for the loss of your friend. I am Samsara and it is my first birth in a form of my own."

The visage of pure fire began looking around, as if sensing things that were beyond sight. "I do not need to be offended, that would mean ego. I have no need for ego... Something is coming."

A rumble sounded soft at first and grew louder. A golden ball of light raced toward them.

The Witness said softly, "Looks like today is a day of surprises."

The screeching ball came right up to them and stopped just in front of Samsara in a slow-moving swirl of golden light.

Samsara said, "What is it? Something amiss?"

For a moment, nothing happened. An otherworldly, echoing, and androgynous voice announced, "A death proclamation to be delivered to the visage, Samsara." Not waiting for a response, the ball of golden light became a hologram of a scene of devastation in a visage's dimension.

The Witness moved closer, watching. "Oh, no!"

They noticed Samsara was suspended in curiosity and had an expression of gravity as well. A scene played out of an event of two visages in a dimension talking when critical mass devastation blew up between them. The Prime Visage sent the other one away in time, and just before the entire dimension ceased to exist, the last words of the Prime Visage of Balance were said.

The Witness couldn't understand all the words because they broke up just before the dimension snuffed out of view.

Samsara looked at the now swirling, glowing light. "I'm assuming you understood what they said. Tell me. I have much to do and we don't have long here."

The otherworldly voice was silent for a moment, then said with an emanating vibration of everything around the area. "The result is This Prime Visage passed their powers to you until which time they are born again. They did not want the Dark One to gain their powers. They saw your coming ahead of time and gave them to you. Do you accept?"

"What if I don't?"

This visage is wise to ask this question, The Witness thought to themself.

"Then they will go to her killer—But the original Prime Visage's soul will be snuffed from existence in the past as well as in their current dormancy."

"Oh, that would not be good. Then Rhom and Rtu would

never have been born and Zreyas would never have met them and become—I can't finish that sentence." The Witness looked to Samsara and waited for their reply.

"That is a lot of power, but is it not too much for one to have one's own, plus that of another? How will this affect balance? Can this power go to the killer, since it is no longer incarnated?"

The voice from the glowing ball of light replied, "Yes, the Dark One now has a status of visage-hood because of the numbers following him."

"Even though the followers are intimidated into following?" The Witness asked.

"The status is valid, no matter the reason. Either way, it is a choice, even if they don't realize they have the courage to make their own choices."

The fiery expression of the new visage turned slightly in thought. "If the Dark One receives the powers, would they bind it to balance?"

"No, because the dead Prime Visage's powers didn't bind them to balance, it was their choice to help the multi-verse. Everything is a choice in how you react to empowerment or things that happen to you. It can use the powers when it serves it or not."

The Witness asked, "Why do you call it an 'it'? I get they are no longer in a body, but it is still who they were."

"The dark form is no longer the entity it was as of this day. It no longer thinks, it no longer laments, it no longer celebrates, it is now only pure hate generated by automation. It is a thing acting on its automatic program. It taught and conditioned itself while it lived."

"So now it *is* truly more dangerous than we ever thought possible." Samsara shifted her body, testing out her movement. "Then I choose to accept the powers, if there is no better a visage or incarnate. Is there more worthy of an entity with a better capability to help the current situation and defeat the Dark One without killing everything else in the process?"

The golden ball of light replied with nothing but silence for a long time. "There may be, but not ready or accessible at this time."

"Can I turn around and give the powers to someone later?"

"Yes, until which time the deceased Prime Visage is born again. But they will not be born until the need for them is strong again. You do not need to worry about balance, Samsara. Nothing about this age now has anything to do with it. Balance within itself is both taskmaster and liberator. One side is liberating, and the other side is oppressing. The rules of balance are distorted right now with both the anomaly and the 'it' that is destroying everything. Balance is impossible until certain events take place."

"What will the effects be of me taking these powers on, since they are the powers of another?"

The golden messenger flared brightly a moment. "It will render you subject to cycles. You will become a new Prime Visage of guidance for the new age. The late Prime Visage recognized this. It seems they foresaw much. They identified you were coming. They foresaw the future, and they were very adept at using their gifts to help us all. If you do not accept, everything will cease to exist and creation will start again after an unknown amount of time that none of us can foresee as existing at all yet. The source of all we are may choose to see this multiverse as a failure, and may not try again."

"So, we just blink out of existence," The Witness observed out loud. "That has good and bad points. On the one hand, it would seem a waste and the source would undo all its progress and the Dark One would quit making everyone miserable. Then again, the downside is those that are of the higher frequencies would snuff out, too."

"And I can see further implications on both sides as well that you did not mention," contemplated Samsara.

"Do you accept the visage's gift?"

"Yes. I choose to hold their powers in my trust, as long as I always have the choice to use them or bestow them as I wish. I suspect there is more than just the obvious in these powers I have yet to come to understand. Until they are born again, I will be caretaker of these powers. Not accepting would be like telling those that have sacrificed so much that it was all for nothing, and it would be a nasty killing blow against them."

The messenger glowed brightly. It was so bright that even Samsara turned her head and shielded herself with one wing. The golden powers of the dead Prime Visage left the orb and swirled around Samsara before entering her. It gave her fiery body an overall golden glow.

The only thing left of the messenger was a tiny pin light that immediately warned, "Time to leave," and snuffed out of sight.

The Witness looked at Samsara, noticing the walls of the dying dimension were only fifty meters away. "I will stay with Jonath."

"That would serve no purpose, and I need a right hand until the age dictates differently. Would you accept this position of helping a new Prime Visage bring in a new age?"

The Witness looked toward Jonath's ashes one last time. "Thank you, dear friend." The Witness looked up and smiled with a single tear in their eye. "I accept... for now."

Zreyas

The replay of the recording stopped and everyone sat there, stunned, for a long time.

Rtu finally spoke up, "So *that* is where your fire went! I understand why you couldn't tell anyone. So now a visage just born is now a Prime Visage by inheritance."

"We just saw the old man give birth to a visage. Ha! Then the visage advanced to a Prime Visage because Tulyata gave herself. Rhom, your baby became your mother, and the mother is your baby. It might not be the same, but that Prime Visage will understand Ayya and Aaru real good!"

"I hadn't thought about that, though you are right, my boy, it's not exactly the same. Aqum, are you sure you should have shown us this?" Rhom asked. "It would be big trouble if anyone found out too early."

"—Aqum says with highest security confidence—yes. The new Prime Visage of the new age issued the request for The Witness to tell Aqum and for Aqum to tell you when the time was right to pass it along to you of the three.

"I see. Thank you, Aqum."

"—Aqum is saying with eagerness—we have a message specifically for the Rhom of the three from the late Prime Visage of Balance."

Everyone in the room perked up.

Rhom's eyebrows were both raised and eyes wide. "Go ahead, Aqum, thank you, I'm ready to hear it."

"—Aqum relays the message—Rhom, find me where you know best."

Everyone waited, and after it was evident that was probably it, Rhom repeated the words in thought.

"Well, science is your thing, bro," Rtu offered.

Zreyas' eyes brightened with realization. "Are you—"

"That was what I was thinking." He scratched over his right ear.

"But it is kind of broad. Find you in science?"

Zreyas shook his head and tried again, "It's not that har—"

"You are right. It doesn't sound right. We need an objective point of view, I think."

He palmed his forehead as they talked. Zreyas got up and went over to Aqum and remembered from when he was in the challenge before that they could talk privately through his thoughts. *How long do you think it will take before they ask me?*

— Aqum says as if we were a betting challenge node—Aqum will put up a timer.

Sure enough, Aqum did. It seemed to be superimposed in the corner of his vision that he assumed started when he initially gave the message because it was already at one minute forty-nine seconds.

Hey, that is a nice magic. I say it will take them over five minutes.

— Aqum converses with an implied voice of excitement—over two but less than five. And it is not magic. —Saying with an air of confession—We had a little help to do that. Aqum calculates that Zreyas of the Atra will meet them soon, too.

Paying attention more to the bet than about his friend, *And the time has to be at the end of the question, not the beginning. Wait, what are we betting?*

"I agree, bro. Hey wait, do you think it might have anything to do with your Viduri incarnation? You loved that tower of yours and you spent a lot of time in that research room!"

Two minutes and fifty-nine seconds.

"That is a great idea, brother. Let's step into my lab in here and see if anyone is in there at the moment. If not, we can browse around and see what we can find."

— Aqum replies with secrecy—space—

"Ha!" *Ticking-hell, I might have just messed up my chances of winning, but I agree to the bet. Nothing like betting potential.*

— Aqum replies as a safe betting node—We agree Zreyas of the Atra.

Are you ever going to explain to me what Atra is?

Zreyas watched Rhom and Rtu gather around a screen, chatting and pointing about what they were paying attention to. He couldn't help but think about how two extraordinary visages that were so wise and smart could be quite thick in some things.

— One moment please while we look into this question.

You have gone official on me. Forget it. I want the unofficial Aqum back. It doesn't mean much to me, anyway. I am what I am.

Zreyas sat down on the challenge node and turned sideways so he could lean up against the edge of the wall just inside the node. It was a good spot to see the twins and at least relax a little.

Four minutes and twenty-two seconds.

Zreyas sniffed. *Looks like you are going to lose this bet, Aqum. They aren't even showing signs of stopping.*

"— Aqum says with dampened spirits—Yes, time is running out."

Four minutes and thirty-six seconds.

"Wait," said Rhom. "We are missing something here."

Zreyas thought, *Mmhmm, yes you are.*

"You should ask Zreyas. He's objective enough to probably know the answer."

Ticking-hell.

— Aqum imagines to laugh like Zreyas—Ha!

Four minutes and forty-eight seconds.

Zreyas sat up straight, watching the timer. He tried to keep his voice down. "This is going to be close!"

18 Thinking Tactically

Both twins walked into the room agreeing that they should ask Zreyas.

Four minutes and fifty-five seconds.

— Aqum puts extra excitement into our words—We will win!

Zreyas mumbled to himself. "No, no, no..."

Rhom lifted his finger and started asking the dreaded question of shattering bet wins. "My boy..."

Four minutes and fifty-nine seconds.

"What do you think the answer is?"

Five minutes, zero seconds.

Zreyas froze, then remembered what time he bet and slumped, but also chuckled. "Okay, okay, you win, Aqum. I said over five minutes."

Rhom and Rtu looked at each other with questioning expressions.

"—Aqum says with melted words—We don't win either, we said under five."

Zreyas started laughing hard. "That was having some fun, sending you the thankings, Aqum."

Rhom and Rtu both cocked their heads, hung their

jaws, and looked between Aqum and Zreyas with confused expressions.

He looked at them and lifted his arms and slapped them back down on his thighs. "Well, hello twin visages... the *quantum*! Old man, you have been teaching me about it since I met you!"

They simultaneously face palmed, then exchanged glances.

"Were you two betting on when we would ask you, little buddy?"

"Look, Aqum, Chuckles has brains after all. Ha! And the question ended exactly at five minutes. You heard the rest."

They all laughed, but with the distraction gone, Rtu seemed to melt back into his state of whatever it was beyond guilt and grief.

"Alright, all I know to do right now is think tactically. Can I ask a few questions? They might seem stupid to you, but things are not clear to me." Zreyas' head drifted to the right as he concentrated out of his left eye.

Rhom turned and faced him in his seat, leaning forward.

Rtu looked at him, turned toward him and pulled his right knee up on his seat, right arm flopped over the back of the couch, to face him comfortably. "I think we need to start with tactics right about now. I'll answer what I can."

Zreyas Q-leaped over to the back of the couch and started pacing. All kinds of questions were bouncing around in his head. "My brain is flooding with tactics and questions and I'm trying to place them where they belong visually in my mind."

Rhom and Rtu looked at each other and grinned. It was good to see Rtu grin. It wasn't a laugh, but it was a start. As heavy as the situation was, that was about all he could hope for from either of them.

Though he didn't understand what it was like to have a mother, much less lose one he loved. But he knew how he felt about losing Tulyata as a friend. Aaru's death was too fresh, so he understood them at least a little. He didn't know why, but Tulyata was special to him, and it wasn't just because she was now dead. He just couldn't believe she was dead, though. It didn't seem to settle inside him. At least, that is what he told himself.

"First, something is just weird. Rtu, you feel more like a normal person to me now. I'm not saying you lost power or anything, you just feel sealed up and heavy. Do you feel the difference?"

Rhom sighed. "He has a point, brother. We both need you. I've never seen or felt you like this. I can speak for both of us. It hurts to see you die inside. I feel it."

Rtu looked at Rhom, puzzled, in deep thought. "I think I do feel that. I wonder what it is."

Rhom opened his mouth to reply, but Zreyas cut in, unable to contain what he wanted to say. It was like his throat was wide open and everything was coming out. "Well, I have a theory, and it might be a load of mag-shit."

Rhom's left eyebrow went up immediately with an expression that he was interested.

"Because of my anger compartment and learning how to change an energy's frequency, I have been noticing other things as well. One thing I noticed is that when I am in anger, sadness, or guilt, I feel the compartment close and seal off. I feel separated from you two and... Tulyata. I even feel separated from Aaru, no matter how much I think about him. It's so heavy it makes us feel the separation."

Zreyas turned to look at Rtu. "I wonder if you feel the grief so much that you have separated yourself from Rhom and Tulyata because of the frequency differences. Also, now that Tulyata is not here in the dimensions anymore, I'm assuming you feel separated from her because of your grief. I don't think I'm the only one that has a center compartment, it's just that a different species handles it differently. Rhom would know better than me probably, but it is just my thoughts."

The second eyebrow rose to match the other on Rhom's face. He grinned and somehow made his face glow. He looked at Rtu and held his tongue.

Rtu thought a moment, closed his eyes, then a smile started creeping across his face. "You know, little buddy, I think you are on to something. When you left, I was not happy, feeling bad about what we had to tell you about our involvement with the Dark One. I was ashamed, and I left myself ripe for the Dark One's enthrallment."

Zreyas sat down on the back of the couch. "Now we are getting somewhere."

"It's not the Dark One's fault, either. I did a handshake, albeit it was unconscious. In a way, I'm an incarnate, because I'm not used to having to work through these things. My frequency is normally so high that I didn't have the capacity to do that handshake unless I consciously wanted to. Thank you, little buddy!"

There was silence. Then Rtu grinned. Then his grin grew. "It's so simple, isn't it?" He abruptly let out a laugh so large and booming it made both Zreyas and Rhom jump.

Rhom beamed and Zreyas wasn't exactly sure why such a reaction, but he didn't care. He was just relieved to see the old Rtu again. But he wasted no time getting to the next question.

"Rhom, did you find another portal or node yet?"

"No, my boy. I've gone to Earth a few times and been working on a project I think might be useful in the future for us.”

Zreyas Q-leaped over to the couch Rhom was sitting on. “Rhom, can you tell me more about what happened to this universe? I didn’t get much from Tulyata’s description at the time she told us about it. We need to know for strategy’s sake.”

“Come with me.” Rhom got up and moved into the room Zreyas originally entered.

Zreyas Q-leaped down off the couch and followed. “This is some room you got here!”

“We told you he was the science geek.” Rtu said, as he followed the rest of them. “There’s no place to sit in here, Rhom! Maybe this is why I never got into science. I can’t help it. I love to sit when I create.”

Rhom laughed and shook his head as he pushed a button on a console. Zreyas watched him move his hand in the air like he was sliding something around.

He cocked his head and Q-leaped up on the console, “What are you doing? There is nothing there.”

“Oh, my apologies, my boy! Here you go. You should be able to see it now.”

Zreyas gasped in wonder as a hologram appeared in front of him of a living universe. He could feel it all moving inside him, too. “Whoa!”

“Give me a moment to make a few more things visible by representing frequencies by giving them a color. Incarnates can’t see those frequencies without aid. They still won’t be easy to notice, but we can work with it.”

Zreyas nodded as he watched nine galaxies come to life with colors. The top three were lined up vertically. He found it odd that something organic would be lined up like that. Zreyas shrugged and waited for Rhom to start his science talk. He needed to learn more, and he almost hungered for it now that he had gotten a taste.

Rhom pointed, directing his eyes. "See these first three galaxies? The top one is Serens, following that one is Centaurusan, and the third is Calesius. These galaxies have been in this universe since the beginning. I'm still integrating back into my visage-hood, so my memory that far back is still fuzzy."

"That is correct, brother," said Rtu. "Those three, and the last two lined up at the bottom."

"Ah, thank you."

Zreyas noticed he could almost draw a line from top to bottom and six out of the nine were lined up perfectly.

"The next one down, the fourth, is where you come in, my boy. This one is Vela Eubeleus System. We just call it Vela for short. We chose this galaxy to house the Viduri light people, and we created it before the rest of the universe."

Rtu nodded, confirming, "Correct. Your memory is just fine."

"And the planet, called Vela. It is only habitable by the Viduri for long periods, but its atmosphere is okay for most species for short periods. That is its design."

Zreyas started to ask a question, but Rhom held his hand up.

Rhom chuckled. "Don't ask me why. Though I have the information, we weren't around for the creation of this galaxy, and we don't have that kind of time to explain. Maybe another time for that. Anyway, your fracture showed up in the capital city of Whitemyth."

"That's all very... weird. Who set all that up?"

"That is weird, even to me, little buddy. It's been there since before my consciousness came to be. We would have to ask Tulyata that one."

"Let me enhance what I want to show you next." Rhom spread his hand apart and moved a few things around. "Do you see this line of particles starting to the right of the vela system running southwest, in this view, to here?"

Zreyas scrunched his face up in concentration, looking closely at where Rhom was pointing. His eyes finally dialed in on a faint particle line. "Yy-yeah."

"That is fracture remnants. It's no longer a fracture but there is remnant energy from it. It's almost like two galaxies gave birth, giving a part of itself to the new one. Both are new and the planets and suns within are still new in scientific age. But there are many energy signatures that used to be in the original galaxy."

Zreyas nodded, then pointed to the map floating around the room now. "None of these are Tcaktranot, the galaxy I came from. Where is that?"

"That is the amazing thing, my boy. The Janquar Nation is seven Universes away, with a large amount of space between each of them."

Rtu flipped his arm over conversationally, "Your galaxy was in an area called 'The Outer Reaches.' A new area of the multiverse, still in its lower frequency stages. It doesn't have much awareness associated with it, just as the life there."

Rhom said instructively, "Before I incarnated myself, they didn't exist. I find it interesting that is where the Dark One showed up. It's probably why it never progressed as fast naturally. It's only theory, though."

Rtu nodded his head. "I think so too. Your race was one that was most in line with the Dark One. It might be why it thrived, though still very primitive in technology and of pure primal energy."

Zreyas felt conflicted for a moment, but then decided it was a fact and put it into his tactical mind. "If the Dark One's prison was there all along, it makes sense. That pile of mag-shit has some seriously low frequency energy. It would help to know how he got that way."

Rtu lifted an arm as he explained. "Though your species is primal and primitive, your inner design is powerful and advanced, like your war aura mechanic. However, because of your inner design, you discovered its exponential power. The ability to convert lower frequencies to higher ones and direct it is only one of them."

Rhom picked up where his twin left off. "Yes, as it stands with the Janquar now, even if the Dark One didn't have a hold on them, there would be no advancement in potential because they view everything through a lens of fear. They are used to it. Sometimes what we are used to feels safer. However, they are progressing, though... in deterioration. It's because of the frequency they were growing toward. Though the Outer Reaches were born recently compared to the rest of the multiverse, they are dying fast, where others are thriving."

"Ticking-hell, it all makes so much sense now!" Zreyas paused a moment, then noticed they had gotten off track with his question. "Wait, we got off track."

Rtu laughed. "It's okay, little buddy, you are helping us make connections, too. And something tells me you will need this information in the future."

Rhom nodded. "I think you will find this next part interesting. The galaxy off to the left is the Zagreus System. It is one of the original ones as well, but this one shifted its position slightly after it divided and birthed a twin! That is unheard of, as far as I know. I've never seen an entire galaxy give birth to another one and move that far away so fast."

Rtu's expression grew serious, features crunching. "Yes, I've never seen it happen, and though I create these things, I didn't do any of this, at least consciously. I'm beginning to think I've lost power to someone else."

Everyone was quiet a moment.

Zreyas shook his head, "No way, Chuckles. First, even if you had no power and not a visage, you would be important and have power in my eyes just being who you are. I mean, look at what you do. Even if you are an extension of something else, look how important you are!"

"Here, here! Well said, my boy!" cheered Rhom.

Rtu grinned, but totally focused on Zreyas in thought.

"You said I could say anything I wanted to you so I'm going to school you on change as an incarnate!"

The two visages laughed.

"When I was forced from my command—"

"Little Buddy," interrupted Rtu, "Would you let me experience your life a moment?"

Zreyas tentatively nodded, not really sure what he needed him to do or what he wanted. But he trusted him.

Rtu closed his eyes and Zreyas felt his connection. A part of Zreyas couldn't believe that a visage would want to live his life. He figured they already knew.

Zreyas looked at Rhom, who was looking at him with tears filling his eyes. He wasn't sure why he would cry.

"Go ahead, my boy. He's ready," said Rhom.

Zreyas took a deep breath. "When I was forced from my command path because I defended Aaru, I fell from grace and approval from all that I knew in my life. I thought I was nothing. I felt lost and angry. Well, I had always been angry then, but I was *more* angry. The only thing that kept me from killing myself was finding Aaru. And by the way, I was even angry at Aaru! I had nothing left, no purpose, and I was no longer important. I had no like or excitement for anything anymore because all that I had liked, or had worked for, just disappeared, even my body. The memory of it all was all I had, which seemed useless after a little time. I seemed to go backward."

Rtu's eyes started streaming with water, though they didn't open. A few seconds later, he quietly said, eyes still closed, "Please continue."

Zreyas looked at Rhom again, not sure what was happening.

Rhom nodded to him.

"Well, if all that didn't happen, I wouldn't have gotten the chance to meet Rhom. Through him, I got to know myself a little more. I didn't like it at all at first. In fact, I had plans to kill Rhom as soon as I found Aaru. But Rhom was maddeningly patient and pleasant. Though it made me suspicious, on top of the anger, I discovered new things. I didn't even want to say his name, even though I knew it. As much as I fought it, I liked the old man."

He sat down and let out a breath. "Now I am sending the lovings to who I am, even more than I did before, and learning more and more every day about myself. I don't care if my old people like me or think I'm someone to look up to—or if they think I'm an abomination. I don't want to lead them, or myself, in fear anymore, nor have those familiar problems. My new problems are something I am almost glad to have, because I know they are because I am choosing to... move higher."

Rtu cried more with his eyes closed, but he had a distinct look about him.

Rhom nodded to him to encourage him to continue.

"It's amazing watching the problems fade as I conquer them, only to see new ones appear to climb on. There are many things I can't do anymore and I have to do things differently almost in every way now. That, and a lot of other things, are really scary, too, if I'm honest."

Zreyas moved over to Rtu and climbed up on his lap. He sat and talked to the closed-eyed visage. "The Janquar see it as a handicap, but I see it as something that is amazing. Now I love water, and the Janquar avoid it at all costs. I just have to learn to think differently. I got a long way to go, though, but change has meaning now."

He paused a moment, then said, "It's scary but I know that every time something changes, I will learn something more and it will add to my tactics and who I am." He looked at both Rhom and Rtu, "Seems to me you are both going through the same thing in different ways. Maybe not, but it is just how I see it."

Rtu opened his eyes slowly, eyes draining profusely, with a bright, peaceful look on his face.

"Thank you, little buddy. You just gave me the most amazing journey of my life... sincerely."

"*That* is why I loved incarnating, dear brother. Welcome to a new awareness."

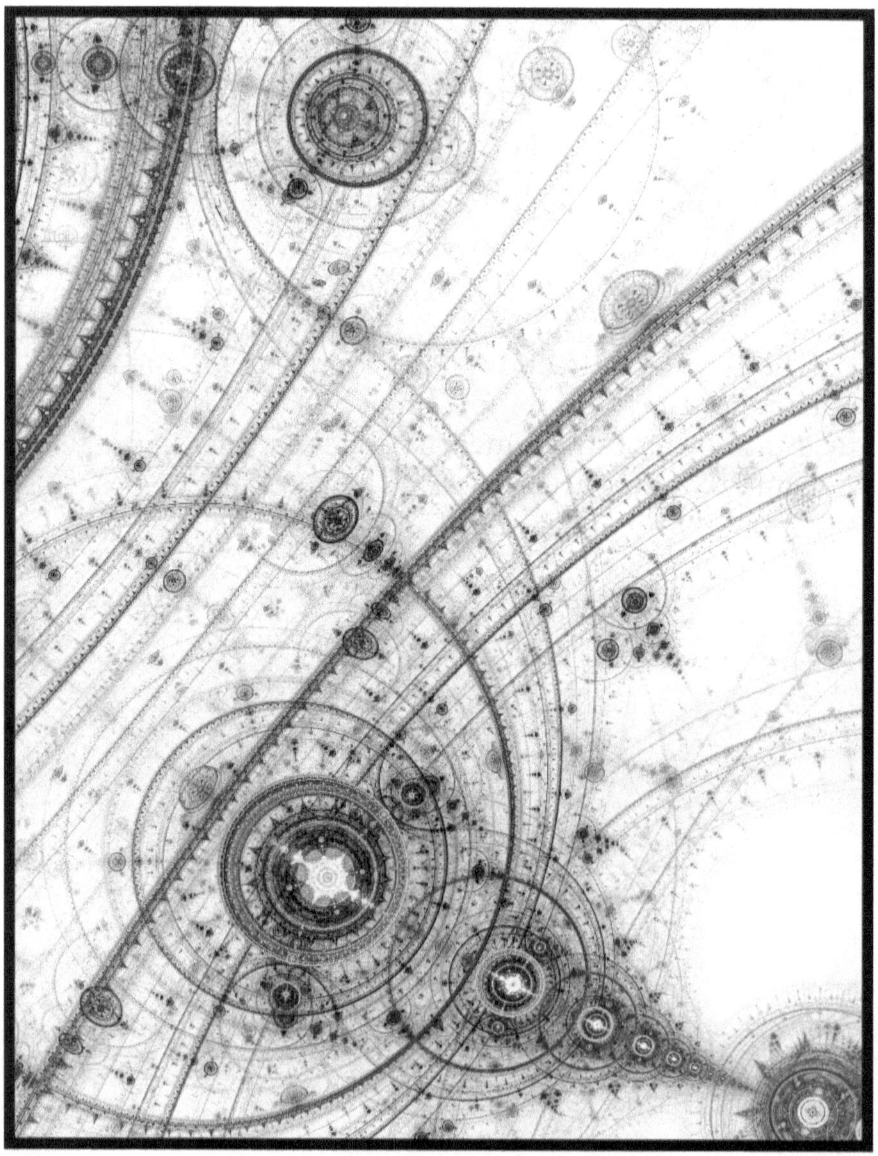

19 Phoenix Ray

Rtu sat up straighter with a bright look on his face again. "What a great reason to get sidetracked!"

Zreyas grinned. "Chuckles is back, better than ever!"

"Indeed! Now back to the Zagreus System that moved over. Its sibling is Canis Lyrae. None of the fractures ever went to Canis Lyrae, though. It's new and pure. No one knows about it yet."

Rtu shook his head. "And there is only one planet in that system that is ready for sentient life, but only barely."

"Not surprising," said Rhom. "I hope this answered your questions you had earlier."

"It's interesting that this universe is the 'Phoenix Ray Universe.'" Zreyas took his time to look at the layout of the galaxies. After a few minutes of the visages waiting patiently while he thought, he finally said, "There are a lot of phoenix references with you, Rhom. I don't even really know what a phoenix is. Does the shape of the galaxy look like a phoenix or something?"

Rtu laughed. "The irony is that it looks nothing like a phoenix, unless you are looking at it from a certain angle, then it looks more like an aircraft called a jet rather than a bird."

"So a phoenix is a bird."

"It's a mythical creature, little buddy. Several species like to use it for symbolism. One of them is Earth, ironically."

Zreyas thought as he watched the hologram in front of him. "Well, it looks like it is pointing at something to me. What is at the top direction that this 'ray' is pointing to?"

Rhom laughed, "You know, you can be a little scary at times." Rhom looked at him again with an amazed and puzzled expression.

"What? Why?"

Rhom chuckled and pointed at the top galaxy. "When the galaxy was chosen to be the Vidurian home, we knew nothing of anything past this top galaxy. Rtu and I didn't exist then either. The multiverse just hadn't grown globally aware and progressed enough to allow us to see it. Maybe, just like us at the time, it just didn't exist. It makes no difference, at this point."

"But now there is something there?"

"Yes, but let me explain something. Between these galaxies, I have found faint channels and there is one at the top going somewhere we don't know yet. I am just getting my visage legs on again and we have been busy. Remember Tulyata talking about how the Proioxis system seemed sentient, reaching out to others?"

Zreyas nodded. "I remember, yes."

"This is what she was talking about. These channels that I enhanced so you could see them—they are a sort of like long black holes, but both ends are known and they are more of a passage than the behavior of a black hole. What brought them to my attention were the fractures and where they lead. Other than your home system, some were being created, while other patterns and places ceased to exist, like the dying dimension we were in."

Rtu's face beamed. "It's fascinating, isn't it, little buddy?"

"Yeah, it really is! My mind is sort of fracturing in a way, thinking about how big this is. And to think Rhom and I were in the middle of all that happening. Ha!"

"I never thought about it like that, but you are right, my boy! Some of these weird channels are very clear, but others are vague or almost don't exist at all." Rhom looked at the hologram, then pointed at one channel. "These channels seem to have a two-way current. Some are clear and defined, some are not. We can still track where they go when they are not there by the energy signatures."

"Is there a way to find out for sure where they are going, instead of guessing?" Rtu asked.

"I already have. It's like there is weather, but on a universal level. Sometimes they appear for short or longer periods of time, but then disappear again. And some of them I have never seen show up at all, but the signatures are there. I have cataloged everything that I have found so far, and I have a monitor on it and it's gathering that data as we speak."

"How many are there?" asked Zreyas.

"As I discover them, I number the gates at each end of the channels. So far I have found forty-two but I see there are more popping up on the data readout. I just haven't had time to number and chart them yet."

"So what can we do with them if they are so unpredictable? Are there any that are stable all the way across?"

"Yes, there are five complete connections that have never wavered so far. So those will be easy to use."

"Like... how?"

"Let's say for something like fixed travel routes. There are fourteen of these pathways so far that have half of them showing all the time. There are seventeen that are never stable in any part of them. They come and go."

Rhom pointed over to another hologram and slid it over in front of Zreyas and Rtu. "This is a design for a fueling station I've been working on."

"For what?" Zreyas felt his eyes glaze over, not understanding anything he was seeing.

Rhom smiled and stared at him, making him feel a little uncomfortable. Then he continued. "Before I incarnated, I worked on a special ship."

Rtu butted in with excitement, "He has a lot of ships that are special but this one is supersonic amazing!"

"Thank you, brother, but I can't take all the credit, as you know. Anyway, it uses a fuel made of what we call element eighty-seven. E-87 for short. But it has its difficulties."

That threw Zreyas. He just couldn't understand what was so difficult about fuel, so he asked about it.

"It's difficult to handle E-87 and is extremely explosive because it only has a half-life of twenty-two minutes of Earth time. After that, it explodes... powerfully. It makes it good for ship fuel *if* you have the right containment system, but it is difficult, if not impossible, for incarnates to use because they lack the technology."

Rtu leaned against one of the tables nearby. "One species in another universe is close, though. That's a little scary."

Rhom turned his head to one side with a tentative expression. "I hope they are wise enough to handle that kind of responsibility."

Zreyas couldn't understand why Rhom would mess around with a ship. "You can go anywhere you want... at any time. So why would a visage need something like that?"

"He has a point, Rhom. Why follow this science project?" Rtu added thoughtfully.

Rhom stood up straight and looked at them both. "Rtu, I thought you were excited about this because this ship was extra special." He grinned and held his hands out, warding off replies for the moment. "Aren't we supposed to be creating our universe in balance? Shouldn't we know what is in our realm, and the potentials of it, so that we can design and create the world we want to create—not to mention help when they get in trouble so horribly that it breaks balance? It's one thing to have data, but it is another to have the *experience* of what is at our fingertips to explore."

"Visage or no visage, we *all* have that responsibility, old man."

Rhom chuckled. "A fine point, my boy! It's the only way we can gain wisdom and insight to potentials in any level, with anyone, and with any subject. If we don't experience what our creations are experiencing, how can we ever have real empathy or understanding of what is best for the balance and their potentials? Numbers and letters are representations of data. They are not sentient."

Rtu said, "I think Zreyas was on to something when he talked about how there might be something, or someone, bigger than even us. I don't feel like I'm at the top of the chain anymore."

"I don't think we are, either," said Rhom.

"All I know is ever since those fractures started and the Dark One appeared, I haven't felt balanced at all," said Rtu.

Zreyas cocked his head and contemplated Rtu's words. "Well, you are the visage of earth and air. When you create, are you creating from yourself?"

"Yes."

"Well, hello! There were fractures, disturbances, parts of you were under the influence of a Dark One, parts of you created, parts of you grieving, parts of you fighting, and parts of you... dying. It's still fluctuating, isn't it?" Zreyas turned back to the fuel station plans, staring blankly at it, not waiting for an answer. "I know it's not the same, but I know that *this* part of you," pointing at himself, "has not felt normal since the fractures have appeared."

Rhom beamed and gently added, "Rtu, you are much more involved in physical creation than I am since you have all the earth. Though I have the water, it's also cleansing by nature. Maybe Zreyas is right. If you know it is going on, it might be easier to work through as you go about your work. In that process, you will teach your creations to do the same thing."

Zreyas watched Rhom go back to the Universe chart, then he pointed at it. "These new channels, the accelerations, the new galaxies, it's like everything in existence, including us, are gaining more awareness—whether or not we like it."

Rhom put the fueling station plans aside and brought the universe hologram back. "If we weren't gaining awareness, we would have never found these new channels, for example. We know they weren't there before, or maybe they were all along. Who knows? The weather of them... something is influencing that. I would have investigated none of that if it weren't for Zreyas and Ayya."

"I wonder where it points to?" Zreyas persisted again with the question.

"Where does what point, little buddy?"

Zreyas pointed at the hologram of the universe at the top system. "It points somewhere important."

"Like I said, I did find a single channel that is connected to somewhere. Honestly, I'm not sure."

"So why was my home world part of this fracturing if it was seven universes away?"

"The best I can figure is there are two contributing factors, but I still don't have a definitive reason. One, the Dark One's prison dimension, was in the outer reaches where your home world was. And two, your Janquar race was close to the Dark One's frequency and nature that was pulled into the events. Remember, the quantum is everywhere, and so is attraction. The wave patterns' attractions, just like when you use the quantum to leap. There are many visages at work and some of them we have never met."

Rtu nodded approvingly. "Smaller visages are created out of the wants and fears of sentient creations. It happens all the time. Though they don't have to be in the physical, incarnates create visages through the quantum because that is where they put their energy. Most of the time, they don't realize what they are doing."

Rhom flopped his hand over in the air. "There are even two visages of currency exchange. Though they are often never acknowledged as a visage consciously. One of them is of a lower frequency, like the dark one made of greed, envy, and resentment. And one is of a higher frequency for the opposite reasons. And it is all because cultures, no matter what type of species, have some sort of currency system."

"This is too science for a not-so-science Janquar right now… or whatever I am." Pointing at the hologram toward the top, "But I don't have to be scientific to know that it's no coincidence that this universe is called the Phoenix

Ray. It's way too coincidental to be coincidence."

Zreyas shrugged, "Well, I guess a phoenix it's no longer a myth in any case... Like you said earlier, visages get created all the time from sentient people of all types, putting their wants, fears, and needs into the quantum. That's the key to this whole mystery, I think. We just need to learn to work with it, rather than against it, just like I did with water."

Rtu cocked his head with a grin. "What do you mean, little buddy?"

"The list of all the events and chaos going on are results of choices of something. It could be the universe is taking on a life of its own—becoming Sentient... or was sentient all along."

Zreyas suddenly missed Tulyata tremendously. Tears set his moisture intolerant eyes on fire. He took a breath as he watched their bright faces and continued. "Tulyata said things were sentient with the galaxies. It can't be affected without someone or something creating the effects. I'm not-so-science right now, but it seems logical to me."

He shrugged. "You did such a good job at what you did as twin visages that every creation makes choices, even if the choices weren't conscious or sentient. Maybe there is another visage or large group of incarnates that did the same thing but chose the not-so-great stuff, like the Dark One or... the Janquar."

20 Spatial Spectacle

"You might have told me this before, but how can Ayya age so fast when it's only been a few weeks for us?"

"Ah, simple science, my boy. Ayya is a different species on a different planet that rotates at different rates than, let's say, Tarq or on Vela. Different species have a different life cycle. And don't forget, we are timeless here. There are a lot of factors involved."

"Ah!" Zreyas thought a moment, then asked, "Is there a habitable area in the new galaxy that hasn't had fractures?"

Rhom chuckled. "I just started a scan on that just before I called you here. We know there is life there. But it is all new life, not long-established races. If there are sentient species, they would be more primitive than even the Janquar, but not necessarily low frequency sentience. Let's see what it says."

They walked over to another console and Rhom pulled up a hologram.

Zreyas Q-leaped onto Rtu's shoulder. It seemed to comfort Rtu a little because he turned around and looked at him with a warm smile. He did just lose his mother. *I wonder what it is like to have a mother. Are they all like Tulyata? I'm too old for a mother now, but I'm still curious what it would have been like.*

Zreyas looked at Rtu's ear. After all, it was right there next to his face. The way he was bent over and propped up on the console made the height too perfect. He thought about Aaru when he was only a few days out of the tunnel and gave him ear squeakers to make him mad in order to help him develop his war aura. It never worked, it just made him squirm and grin. He knew it wasn't the time for stupid stuff like that, but sometimes he just couldn't help himself.

"Hey, Chuckles, Rhom said I should always inform people because of my design. I'm just informing you ahead of time, just in case it might happen, that I have an urge to give you an ear squeaker like I used to give Aaru to tease him. But I get it is harder to do on you with my size." Zreyas cocked his head, assessing the situation, saving up his spit.

Rtu cocked his head questioningly. "What's a—"

Zreyas hocked up the spit he saved up on his hands and rubbed it on the inside of Rtu's ear. It was the perfect opportunity.

"Aaauugh!"

Zreyas Q-leaped away for safety. One never knows the mood of a visage. He grinned while Rtu stuck a finger in his ear, fervently cleaning it out. He paused a moment and looked at Zreyas.

He held up his hands in peace, "I informed you!" Zreyas looked at Rhom, who was doing his level best to compose himself.

"You know, it does squeak a little," said Rtu as he used a handkerchief to clean out his ear.

The entire room erupted with laughter.

Rhom wiped the tears from his eyes, shaking his head. "Well, he warned you. But your question was too much of an invitation to resist."

Zreyas started executing a mock bowing motion of his hands and body, "Peace, oh visage of elements, you are the amazing and all-encompassing visage of earth and air, and... stuff."

The twin gods couldn't hold it in. They both lost it. They howled in laughter.

Rtu slid himself down to the floor and laid back laughing.

Zreyas noticed that when Rtu laughed that hard, he couldn't do shit, but roll over. "Ha!"

He Q-leaped on Rtu's belly to say something clever, and he found his belly was unstable, like a bouncing quake, and had a hard time standing. He finally lost the battle and fell. At least the landing was softer than the floor.

That made him laugh worse.

Rtu's belly giggle was a serious training exercise in Zreyas' mind. He did his best to gain some balance and stand up on the quake under him. He almost got up once, then lost it and landed face first on Rtu's belly again. His war aura started emanating out of determination, causing the twins to laugh harder, and Zreyas didn't think that was even possible.

Then something strange happened as he focused... He saw the image of his compartment inside himself that held his rage and anger for his auras. The vision superimposed itself over what he saw, and it reduced in size. He felt the joy they all three had from the silly stunt he pulled.

Things started to look different. Everything around

him changed. The two visages and room looked more and more like moving energy.

At first, Rtu looked normal. In a few seconds, particles of energy blurred his outline. It wasn't long and Rtu wasn't in a body at all really—his body, made of concentrated energy, spread out everywhere.

Zreyas turned to observe Rhom as he sat and bounced on Rtu. The same thing, but Rhom looked different. He supposed it was because they were made up of different elements. Zreyas looked down at himself and he was much denser, but he still saw the energy more than the body. He was all around himself and overlapping with them. Rhom's lessons in the dying dimension all came back to his mind when he talked about energy.

Zreyas gained his equilibrium back in the bouncing. He stood and his legs stayed fluid to keep his balance. The wonderful visions of energy faded, though. He didn't want them to fade, but he couldn't help but feel energized and happier than he had ever been in his life.

He held his arms up straight at a forty-five degree angle and closed his eyes just a moment before he erupted with the success. "Yes! I did it!" He let out a breath. "Okay, what did you guys do to me this time?"

Rtu propped up on his elbows behind him, gaping at him.

He turned and faced Rhom.

"We didn't do anything!" Rhom confirmed with a grin. "You just had one of those moments that will change you forever, is all."

"He knows what he is talking about. He is the visage of aether. Thanks for the laugh, little buddy. I needed that... badly."

"So did I! Things have been so serious for so long. You always bring us joy. Thank you for that, my boy. And...

thank you for helping me get my twin back to his normal self.”

Rhom went over to a chair and plopped down, and closed his eyes. *That is the first time I have ever seen Rhom rest like that.*

Rtu just laid back on the floor and closed his eyes too. “That was a good laugh.”

Looking at them both, not sure what to do, he sat down where he was and laid down himself, closed his eyes, and just stayed in his peace for as long as they were resting. *Today is a very good day.*

Zreyas opened his eyes to find he was still on Rtu’s belly, but he was staring at him.

“Have a nice rest in the lap of luxury, little buddy?”

Zreyas rubbed his face and sat up, still feeling tired. “Oh, I guess I didn’t realize how tired I was.”

Rhom said, “Well, you *have* had a lot going on. Don’t be so hard on yourself. If it makes you feel better, you didn’t sleep long. Why don’t you head in there on the couch and get some proper sleep? We can do this after you rest up. I did wake you from your sleep, after all.”

Feeling a little drugged from sleep, he didn’t argue. Zreyas nodded and walked into the area with the couches and leaped up sloppily. He curled up near the arm and fell asleep.

ꕥ ꕥ ꕥ ꕥ ꕥ

Sitting straight up, Zreyas rubbed the sleep from his eyes and asked, “So, what did the scans show?”

Silence was the only reply. Something felt unsettling in the quiet, even down to the energetic level.

He slid down the edge of the couch to the floor. Zreyas landed and walked into the next room, looking for the twins. This was beginning to feel a little too uncomfortable.

"Chuckles? Old man? Where are you?"

Zreyas Q-leaped to the console where he had watched the galaxies earlier. He figured he would get some exercise in while he looked at the galaxies again, so he ran in place as hard as he could while he looked at the Phoenix Ray map. After fifteen minutes, he had committed the Universe to memory and the channels Rhom showed him that were permanent.

That is about all he could expect himself to do in one setting. His memory was excellent, but he could only do memory work like that in short spurts. He loved the learning, so only doing brief spurts was annoying to him. Zreyas wanted to have more attention span.

It felt weird because his mind felt like he had learned something he already knew, but wasn't exactly sure why. Maybe it was because he had watched it so much before he slept.

He turned around, still jogging, and noticed a partially opened door he hadn't seen before.

"Rhom? Are you in there?"

Zreyas walked over to the edge of the console and started ranting. "I can't believe you guys just left me here in this boring dimension!" Zreyas knew no one would hear him, but he noticed he was growing angry. He wasn't accustomed to having to wait for people. It had only been a couple weeks at most since he was a Janquar commander, so he couldn't expect for habits to just go away just because his life changed without a little conscious work.

"Well, that is a little... Get your shit together, Zrey." He Q-leaped over to the door and pushed it open.

Then he halted. "Whoa!"

As he walked through the door at a reverent pace, his mouth gaped. "Wha-at the ti-icking-hell?"

Ahead of him was a walkway that was suspended in space. Zreyas wasn't sure how he was even breathing. On both sides of the wide, futuristic walkway, as far as he could see, were ships of all shapes, designs, and sizes. "Tulyata was right, my race *is* primitive... I've never seen anything like these before."

"This is so... this is... ticking-hell, I don't have the vocabulary to describe this!" He didn't care if he was talking to himself, at least someone was listening. There were even ships for species that must be his size!

He continued down the runway, a little unsure if he was supposed to be here or not. Zreyas couldn't believe Rhom's collection of ships. Some of them seemed just too odd for general use and were probably for something specific.

Some ships had a whole bunch of things mounted on them, while others were sleek, smooth, and mysterious. He couldn't always tell what their purpose was. These ships looked nothing like the ones he had to ride in back home. Those were basic boxes meant for carrying warriors, and they were painfully slow. He remembered aging several years just for one battle that only lasted a week.

"This is..." Zreyas started jogging slowly, looking at each ship as he went. The awe he felt at each one of them just made him want to see more. Some ships had to sit *on* a platform, while others floated next to one. They built some for one or two passengers, while others would carry thousands. He saw one off in the distance, away from the others, one that would probably carry tens of thousands or more. As far away as it was, it was hard to judge, but it looked like a city ship.

The further down the walkway he moved, the higher technology the ships seemed to have, at least by his untrained eye.

Zreyas stopped a moment and looked down at the walkway strip. The more he looked at it, the more he saw details under his feet. It had neon blue lines on the edges all the way down as far as he could see.

He hopped up and down on it to see if it would do anything... nothing. "I guess it is just a fancy walkway." He looked back where he came from and the door to Rhom's lab was so small now it would disappear soon in the distance if he kept going. Zreyas shrugged. He had nothing better to do, and Rhom could no doubt find him. He turned and continued his journey.

He was loving these ships! It was almost like he could feel the stories behind them, at least in general. It was fascinating to him. There was a ship in front of him to the right that looked almost like a squashed crustacean with two sets of wings on each side that had weapons attached that he had never seen before. *Clearly built for war.* It almost made him sad, but he couldn't help but be fascinated.

The next ship just past it was a long way off, and the ships were getting so big now that it would take a while to walk to it. The shape of it attracted him, though. *I want to get to that ship as soon as I can so I can see it closer.*

As soon as the thought came, he saw ribbons of blurred light. In the next instant, he stood in front of the ship he was looking forward to see. The ribbons of light seemed to linger a few seconds, but they moved on past him before disappearing.

"What the... Ticking hell, that was so... so..." Zreyas sighed, dejected. "I really need to figure out a word for good stuff like this that is ten times 'really good.' No, a hundred times."

Zreyas looked up in awe of the massive ship. The entire front was a huge white sphere with an open slit horizontally in the front. The upper half had circles imprinted on it. One of them on the side was open, but he couldn't see much of anything in there.

He backed up to get a better view because the ship was so large. He wondered how someone got to the door. *I wish I could get higher so I could at least see this ship better.*

Ribbons of light appeared again, and in the next instant, he was standing on the walkway, but it was higher at the slit level of the ship.

"Whoa! I need to ask Rhom for a portable one of these. Ha!"

There was a vessel that almost looked like a bubble inside the open circle, hovering inside. He also saw the rest of the ship. Part of the body looked like a fish skeleton and at the tail of the ship was another, smaller sphere. This ship was a little too odd for his taste, and more than a little creepy.

Zreyas intentionally used the walkway this time and said that he would like to see each of the ships from mid-height. The ribbons of light passed by, and as he walked, his height would adjust depending on which ship he was looking at.

Just ahead, there was a gap in the line, and he headed toward it. Sure enough, the gap seemed strange and vacant. He had the walkway take him to the normal ground height, and he just paced around the walkway looking around at all the ships and wondering what he should do.

"This is bizarre. I bet they took this ship out. I wonder why they left me?" Zreyas felt like a forgotten piece of rusty armor and it made him realize how spoiled he was. He had always gotten attention in his position in the

Janquar Nation. And if he didn't, all he had to do was bark out a command to get it.

"And maybe it is none of my business where they went, Zrey," he said to no one in particular. He laughed at himself. "And I need to stop talking out-loud to myself. I'm not sure why, but I feel a presence here *and* a vacancy."

Zreyas walked further down, "Well whoever you might be, walk with me."

He almost fell when a disorientation hit him from the walkway ribbons that showed up while he walked. His walk pace was ultra-fast, but hadn't increased his speed.

Zreyas stopped, and everything seemed normal. He started walking again and the ultra-fast speed scaled to his walk speed and the hints of ribbons appeared.

"Oh ticking-hell, this is so... so... argh!" Excitement and frustration both filled him. "Its... *so*... I give up!"

A twinkle caught his attention in the distance that spread out briefly. He rushed to the gap in the ship line-up using the walkway. As it approached, he couldn't believe the ship. It was the best he had seen so far!

The ship was sleek, fairly large, and oddly shaped. It could house a large crew from the looks of it. However, it was so oddly shaped that he wondered if it was really a ship. He felt drawn to it. The shape was unexplainable at this distance. About the only thing he could come up with was it was sleek, round and square at the same time and round and flat at the same time. He wasn't an artisan of shapes. Was it changing shapes?

Zreyas couldn't see the entire ship at his angle either, but from what he could tell, the outline of the ship was like a loose resemblance to a curved triangle and there was a gap at the bottom. He cocked his head, then decided it wasn't really like a triangle when it came closer. *I could have sworn it had a different outline earlier.*

As it pulled up to the gap in the docking bays, it shimmered as if its skin was reacting to something. He noticed movement on the surface. He decided to get closer, so he told the walkway to move him as close to the ship as he could get. Ribbons of light flowed and dissipated, bringing him right to the ship at the edge of the walkway.

"Ticking...-hell," he whispered as he strained to keep his stomach stable as he watched Rhom and Rtu come out of the ship's doorway. They seemed further away than the ship itself. It was an odd illusion. The sight of the spatial spectacle gave him a sudden wave of nausea. *I m glad I haven't eaten in a while.*

As he fell to the floor, he could tell Rhom saw him fall and started a panicked run. Then his vision faded. The last thing he remembered was Rhom doing a Q-leap toward him just as things went dark and heard him say, "I'm so sorry, my boy!"

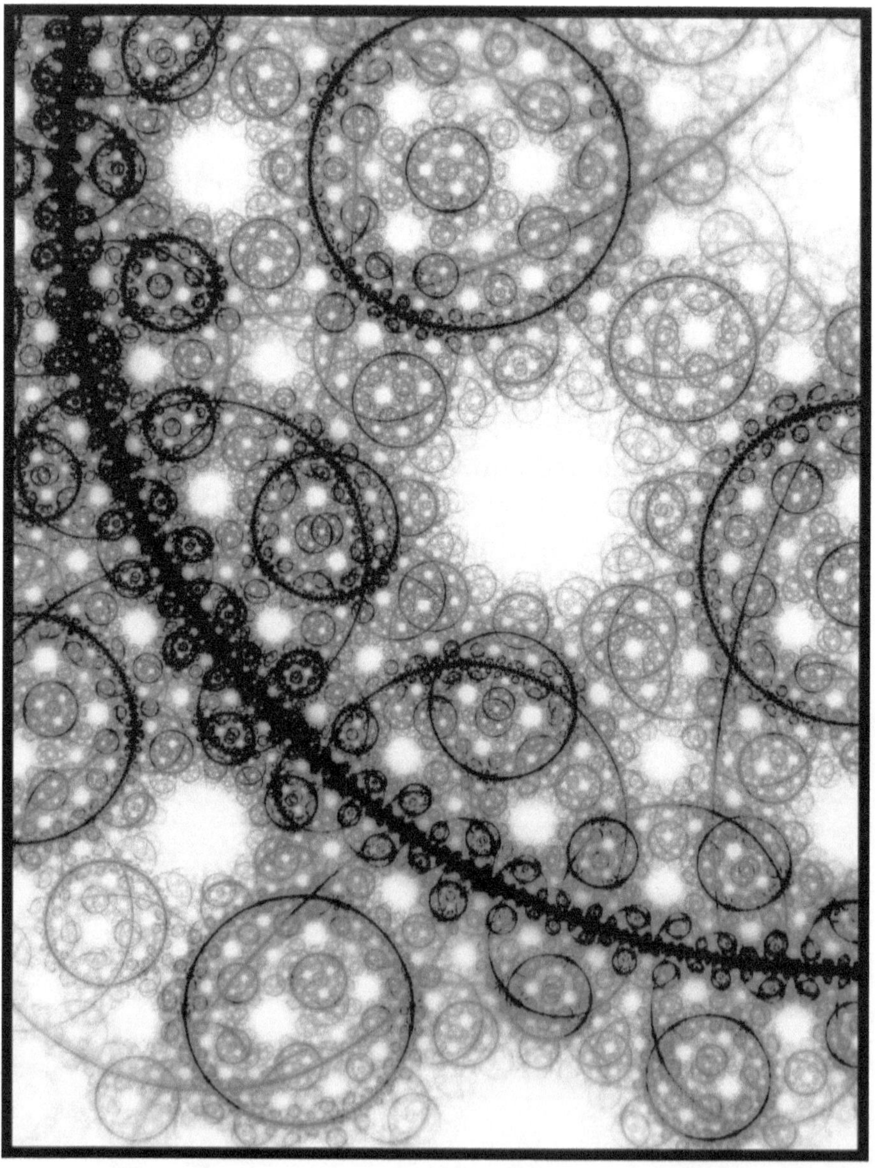
ishKiia Paige

21 The Defenses

Rtu panicked seeing his little buddy laying there but his sense of humor tried to go on. "You killed him Rhom, seriously? Was that your plan all along?"

"No! I just forgot to turn off the ship's defenses! They are *devastating*! If we weren't here, it would have killed him in a *horrible* way. Thank the universe that his body energy wasn't at the frequency the defenses were set to target."

Rtu forced himself to half grin at Rhom and winked, trying to help him feel better. "I know you wouldn't have killed him... on purpose, anyway."

"Well, look at the bright side, he doesn't know he is sick right now at least," Rhom said with a look that had worried features that betrayed how bad he felt. "I was just in my science mode and—"

"Yeah, yeah, I know. Let's get him in your lab and fix him up. He will feel much less hostile when you tell him he has a present coming to him. *If* he wants the responsibility that comes with it, that is."

Rtu felt bad for the little guy as they used the walkway

to get Zreyas back to Rhom's lab faster. He thought about what Rhom wanted to put in Zreyas' lap. He couldn't help but feel for his little buddy. "Are you sure you want to do this to him?"

Rhom looked at him with a shocked expression. "We have been over this before. Who else have we got that we can trust and still stay within a reasonable range of balance? Besides, he won't be on his own for a good while. Everything within my being says he is the one that is supposed to do this and he will do it willingly."

"Yeah, well, he shouldn't be manipulated into it either, just because you feel it in your gut!"

Rhom looked at him with incredulity and stopped walking. "You *heard* her say he is the one."

"I know, I'm sorry. I'm being overprotective. You wouldn't manipulate him, and I *did* hear her. He's just been through so much already. I just want my little buddy to have time to enjoy life, like you did when you incarnated. Besides, that is what an incarnation is for... learning and enjoying being in a body, not some serious hell experience to waller in as punishment or work off some currency of karma only! The most fun he has had was being on Tarq for a couple days and even *that* was serious."

Rtu opened the door for Rhom and they carried Zreyas over to a table that Rhom was quick and careful to lay him down on.

Rhom's voice cracked. "I'm so sorry, my boy. I never meant to hurt you. And you are right, Rtu. It must be his choice."

Rtu watched his beautiful-hearted brother look at Zreyas. He was so glad to have Rhom back.

Rhom started the arduous process of taking off Zreyas' clothes, and for the first time, Rtu noticed he had no armor on. It seemed odd to see him with no armor. Then he remembered how Rhom told him about how Zreyas freaked out in that nagodara fight and the aftermath. He was in his dark place when all that had happened.

Rhom shook his head in empathy. "I know you are strong, my boy, but I hope you are stout enough to say yes and take on this burden others are putting on you indirectly... for all our sakes."

Zreyas

Zreyas moaned and woke up slightly, holding his head as he rolled to his side. He tried to open his eyes, but he shut them quickly again.

"You will be okay, little buddy, just rest. Rhom will give you something for that whopping headache of yours."

Rhom stepped into view. "We will have you patched up in no time, my boy!"

Zreyas winced and moaned as he brought up bile from his innards weakly, turning to the side toward Rhom.

"Ooh, this is bad." Rhom went over to a cabinet on the wall and he pulled down a bottle and syringe. Zreyas barely understood a distant conversation about how they would need a reinforced syringe for his skin.

"Where did I put those?" mumbled Rhom.

"You are a visage, Rhom, not an incarnate anymore; just make one!"

"Oh yes. That's a good idea. I'm not thinking clearly."

"And you are still adjusting to your... loss from your donation."

"True."

Rhom rushed back to Zreyas, almost making him sick from the fast movement. He watched Rhom carefully fill a clear tube with what he assumed to be the medication he was trying to find. Though blurry, Rtu watched the fluid, and it seemed to have miniature chips of something in it that glittered.

Rtu held out a hand to stabilize Zreyas. "Is it safe to say that those floating things are the part that we talked about before that will prevent his brains from scrambling in case he is caught up in the ship's defenses?"

"That is correct. They will allow Zreyas to progress in whatever frequency he grows into and attunes to; however, they will prevent sudden change bombardments changing his own body's frequency. I should say sudden bombardments from the ship. It emits the waves in a signature pattern no matter what setting it is on."

"Clever! So those floaty things won't help him with something other than when your ship bombards him with another pattern frequency?"

"No, only because of balances. That is why the ship's defenses emit a specific pattern. These will only react to that pattern."

"I see. Still, pretty smart. Balances have to be accounted for. I hope I got his brain unscrambled right. I'm used to creation, not fixing."

Rhom grinned, and then turned and smiled a moment. "Yes, it's a normal reaction of the chemicals in his body to scream with the adjustments."

"There is an upside to all this. We don't have to test that part of the ship now. At least we know the ship's defenses work."

"True!" Rhom carefully pulled Zreyas' ear forward. He wondered what he was doing when he felt a prick and a sting just under his ear, high on his neck. He jerked in surprise. He tried to listen to them talk. He knew it was interesting, but he couldn't quite assemble words in his tactical awareness, but he heard what they said.

"But will it work on Janquar or other low frequency creatures is the question? The effects might not be quite so severe even if we adjust the frequency, we don't know yet. I need to check what I had that defense system set on when this happened."

"Have a little faith," said Rtu. "I wonder if he has tried his converted aura on the Janquar."

"He just had a run-in with some, but I'm not sure what it was about yet. We were busy. Zreyas is more quantum based now and has a much higher frequency than his counterparts. Do you remember if I set the frequency back when I was fixing it? We could have set it on the higher frequency. Maybe I forgot to turn it back down to the *low* frequency."

Zreyas felt the area around where he felt the sting fill with pressure and he opened his eyes. It was uncomfortable, and he wanted to hit Rhom, but he was too out of it and sick to care.

Rhom pulled away and wiped the area of the neck. Then he whirled around and looked at Rtu with horror in his eyes. The fast motion almost made Zreyas hurl his already empty guts up.

"Oh, my... I think we best find out now while he sleeps some!"

ꙮꙮꙮ *Rhom* ꙮꙮꙮ

They both scrambled to get out to the ship as fast as they could. Rhom was worried beyond anything he had been through except for Ayya's demise as a Viduri and another time long ago. If he did anything to kill that boy, he didn't know if he could take it.

"Ramsey's ass! I had it set wrong! I did indeed forget to set it back when I fixed it!"

"Who's Ramsey?" asked Rtu.

"I don't know, it just came to mind."

"You're... interesting, Rhom."

Rhom looked at him. "And? It's not like you didn't know that already."

Rtu laughed while Rhom worked frantically to finish the instrument so they could use it in normal operation, rather than in its experimental state.

Rhom looked concerned as he worked, and it didn't go unnoticed.

"What's wrong?"

"I need to pull myself together... I'm not adjusting well to being a visage again, I don't think, and I seem more absent minded than the normal 'periodic every-once-in-a-while' kind of absentminded. I wonder if I'm under some sort of Dark One influence like you and Tulyata were."

"Maybe so, but I don't think so. I know that feeling and I don't feel it in you. I could definitely tell the difference after Mother—"

Rhom reached over and patted his shoulder and looked at him sincerely. "It's okay. Remember, we all make our mistakes... even Tulyata. I miss her too.

22 Ridiculous!

Zreyas rubbed his eyes and stretched. He felt like someone had squished him under a rock. When he tried to open his eyes, it was a little easier, though things *were* blurry.

He wasn't aware of his surroundings, but he heard Rtu whisper, "Here goes... let's hope his brains aren't scrambled enough for him to rip us apart."

He had no idea what he was talking about, but curiosity lit up distantly in the back of his mind.

"Oh boy," Rhom seemed to echo under his breath. Then, he heard, "Uh, welcome back to the world, my boy!"

"Yeah, little buddy, good to have you back with us. We were getting tired of bantering back and forth without you."

Zreyas closed his eyes and opened them again to a world that was still blurry. He rubbed them, frustrated. "Where did I go?" After growing irritated at the blurry vision after rubbing them again, he sat up. He blinked a few times, "Ticking-hell, what happened?"

His head pounded, but at least it was better than it was before. He blinked again several times, trying to look at the two in front of him, but figured he was having delusions of blurred stone warriors again in the challenge. Afraid to say anything too loud, he murmured, "Where are we? Are we in another trial?"

"No, you aren't in a trial... but... we *do* have armor on," Rtu admitted.

One of the blurry warriors elbowed the larger of the two, causing a familiar sound to him, a clash of armor. When Rtu giggled, he knew he wasn't in a trial. The large one on the right was Rtu.

"Well, my boy, I'm going to tell you that you were subject to an unfortunate oversight. We forgot to set the ship's defenses back to the normal settings in our test. I apologize with all my heart for that."

"Yeah, Rhom..."

Rhom elbowed Rtu again.

Rtu giggled again. "Stop tickling me! *We* forgot to change the setting back when *we* were fixing a problem. You were an accidental test subject. But the good news is we were testing something out that works very well, as you can tell!"

Zreyas moaned as his head told him something bad had just happened to him and blinked more. He heard them, but the meanings of what they said still seemed a little farther off in his mind. He couldn't even remember where he had been, much less testing something.

"How are you doing, my boy? Would you like some water or food? You must be famished by now."

"No... Yeah, I'm starving," he said, still groggy. Whatever this mistake was, they seemed sincerely aplo-po-getic. "And it's okay. We all make mistakes."

"Whew! I'm so glad to hear that! Now I can take this armor off. It's incredibly uncomfortable. I don't know how you do it!" Rtu began taking off the armor. He took his helmet off first and put it down, then untied his bracer.

Zreyas felt confused, trying to put it all together as he held the right side of his head. "But, I'm not sure—"

"Rtu, um... he's still not..."

Zreyas' frustration flared at how bad he was feeling and his eyesight not being good. He rubbed his face with vigor, and then let his hands drop to his thighs. The meaning of what they had said trickled into clarity. "Wait... you did what?" He opened his eyes again, and at last, he started seeing things clearer.

In front of him were Rhom and Rtu, standing there with armor on, looking utterly ridiculous. Rtu appeared frozen in the motion of taking off a bracer. "Your armor looks like the Hasya made it. There are so many gaps and it looks like someone splattered colors on it."

"Uh oh..." Rtu slid his bracer back on, reached down to pick up his helmet, and put it back on his head. He lowered his head and raised his shoulders.

"What are you afraid of?"

"You!" Rtu shifted nervously.

"What?"

"My boy." Rhom reached out and put a hand gently on Rtu. That seemed to help calm Rtu down. "Please hear me out."

"Okay," said Zreyas as he rubbed his head, looking at their ridiculous armor.

"We were trying to fix the ship's defenses that I re-designed from inspiration that I got from how *your* aura works. We didn't realize you would be there standing at the dock." Rhom sighed and said with remorse in his voice, "I forgot to set it back to normal settings after the test run, making you an accidental test subject. It was unfortunate timing, but the good news is, it works! I apologize. You would have been dead had we not been there."

"It's not just his fault, I failed to catch the mistake too," Rtu added and visibly relaxing more. "But please don't make us hurt. I would rather you kill us, but you can't really kill us. I mean, remember, if you kill us, you kill everything! And... well, hurting us... well, it hurts and I don't li—"

Rhom elbowed him a third time.

Zreyas could finally focus again. He looked at each one of them in their armor. "I'm afraid I couldn't kill or hurt you if I tried."

The twins questioned together, "Why?"

"Because... because..." Zreyas couldn't hold it in anymore and broke out in hysterical laughing fits. He rolled back on his back and laughed. "Ha!... ha... ha ha..."

Over the next few seconds, Zreyas' laugh became more and more normal, rather than the struggled, single laughs.

The twin visages exchanged surprised glances. Then they turned back toward him.

"Bugger-me-britches, Rhom, he's laughing normally!"

Rhom cocked his head with a thoughtful look. "I think you fixed him a little too good, or... his body has changed so much in his transition that it can happen now because he has the flexibility to laugh."

Rtu sobered a bit, then said hesitantly, "Either way, this won't change his potential reaction to what happened."

They both went silent, but Zreyas was so excited about laughing normally that he didn't care why they might be a little nervous, though it felt a little like he was using someone else's laugh. He never heard a peep from the twins after that over the next few minutes. Each time he looked at them in their armor, the urge to laugh started all over again.

He finally sat back up to see two very nervous visages looking at him in their armor. They looked so ridiculous that he thought he must still be dreaming or drugged. Tears streamed and his eyes sealed shut.

"I think we need to do a little update," Rtu said to Rhom.

Rhom looked at Zreyas. "Yes, maybe I will invent a new set. He's going to need a new set, too."

He opened his eyes again and looked at them.

"My boy—"

Howls of laughter erupted again, causing Zreyas to lie back in a helpless state. His face and stomach hurt from the laughing.

Rtu started taking off the armor. "I know when I've been had."

Rhom did the same. "Okay, I give up, too. He won't talk to us until he comes out of that laughing fit. And if we don't, I'll start laughing with him just because he is laughing."

When they both got all their armor off, Zreyas sat up and his laughing abruptly stopped. He looked at them with a war glare.

Rtu elbowed Rhom this time. "I think he manipulated us, and we are in big trouble."

"You did *what*?!" Zreyas growled with force.

Rtu put his two hands out, palms down as if to calm him. "Now calm down, little buddy. We were honest with you. No need to get hostile. It was an honest mistake."

Zreyas reverted to his normal mode of personality with a grin, bouncing his head back and forth with his words. "I know, I was just messing with you."

The twins looked at each other and started laughing.

Rhom turned toward Zreyas. "We deserved that."

"Yes, you did! That was some nasty ticking mag-shit your ship did to me! That was the defense system?"

They nodded vigorously, and he could tell they were still a little nervous.

He continued his rant. "That was some ticking mag-shit, devastating, dark ticking, bandhula inflicting, death magic! I don't want to be at the receiving end of that again!"

"You won't, my boy. I have put small neutrinic based chips, particle sized, into your head. It makes you immune to frequency patterns like that from the ship. It might come in handy in dealing with the Dark One at some point if you are ever unfortunate enough to face him. But who knows... he seems to know everything that is going on somehow."

"By the way... I'm impressed at that string of expletives," Rtu said nervously.

"Peace, Chuckles, I won't lay the pain on you."

Rtu sighed in relief and leaned up against the nearby console.

"Well, as long as I don't have to go through that again, I'm feeling the happy. I have so many questions." Then he remembered all those ships and immediately got excited again. "And those ships are so... so..." Zreyas sighed, "I really need to expand my higher frequency vocabulary. I got the lower ones down pat."

The twins laughed.

Rtu laughed. "It's an adjustment. I'm sure you will learn or make many words up before long. But I will have to say, judging by that string of explicatives, you use what you know well!"

Zreyas grinned. "So, tell me... what were you doing?

And I want to look at your ship! I am... I feel...”

"Excited about it?” Rhom finished for him.

"Yeah! I'm excited to see it! It's so... so...”

Rtu and Rhom looked at each other and waited with grins.

Zreyas realized he had no references in his mind for the brighter side of vocabulary. He shook his head then blurted, "It's so Ticki-tastic!”

Silence assailed the room for a long second, then all three burst out laughing. The twins patted Zreyas on each shoulder.

Rtu finally ebbed his laughter away enough to say, "That is a great word!”

"Agreed! It's a fine word, my boy!”

"See, old man—I got word skills!” Zreyas shook his head and started laughing at himself. "Now that I'm a word creator; seriously, you can't wear that armor again... ever! No one will ever take you seriously. Now, are you two old men going to feed me and show me around?”

Rtu started tearing up and pulled out a handkerchief, started dabbing his eyes, "Oh I love you, little buddy! You have given this visage so much joy! I'm so glad Rhom didn't kill you.”

Rhom looked at Rtu with a traitorous expression.

Zreyas cocked his head at Rtu, "Don't make me cry, then I'll really be ticking-angry.”

Rtu sniffed sharply and did his best to stop the wave.

Zreyas Q-leaped over to his shoulder, "Don't make me do it!” and pretended to hock up spit.

Rtu slapped a hand over his ear. "You win, you win.” He started laughing.

Rhom shook his head and laughed, "Come on you clowns, we got a lot to talk about. You can eat on the ship, my boy!”

Zreyas felt his stomach and looked down. He couldn't believe how different he looked. He really never paid attention to it because he really had never been fully unclothed but once and he was so busy then, and he had been through changes since. "Uh, old man."

"Yes, my boy?"

His light blue skin, where joints were, didn't have cracks like they used to. They were smoother. Distracted as he turned his arm over to see his elbows. "Where are my clothes?" He wasn't sure if he should be upset at the lack of armored skin or glad about it.

"Oh, I apologize." Rhom walked over to a table and picked up his clothes and vest. "Here you go. And don't worry, we will make more armor for you."

As they approached the ship, Zreyas' mind reeled, and he backed up a step. He was apprehensive about getting near it, the last experience too fresh in his mind. The sudden, all-encompassing fear caught him off guard. Images from his recent fight assailed him right after.

The twins turned and looked at him with reassurance in their faces and body language. They both held out arms and motioned him on.

"Trust us, my boy, it won't happen again, I promise. And remember how you coached yourself back in the cave. Remember what you want more than to—"

"Smash my face against a wall and die." Zreyas suddenly needed to pee, and he felt his legs rebel as he walked forward slowly, almost stumbling. But he realized he was closer than he was before, so he was satisfied that he was indeed safe.

He took in a deep breath and rubbed his sweaty hands

together, then he let his breath out telling himself that he wanted to see the ship more than die.

Excitement bubbled up again as they walked and said, "Show me the way!" He rubbed his hands together and looked at the twins. "And I'm *hungry*."

Rhom waved a hand toward the ship in introduction. "You can do the honors. You deserve it. It is ceremoniously appropriate for you to do, anyway."

Zreyas looked suspicious and frowned. "How? What do you mean ceremoniously appropriate? I just want to eat and see the ship, then go back to Tarq and put a knife in the Nation's side."

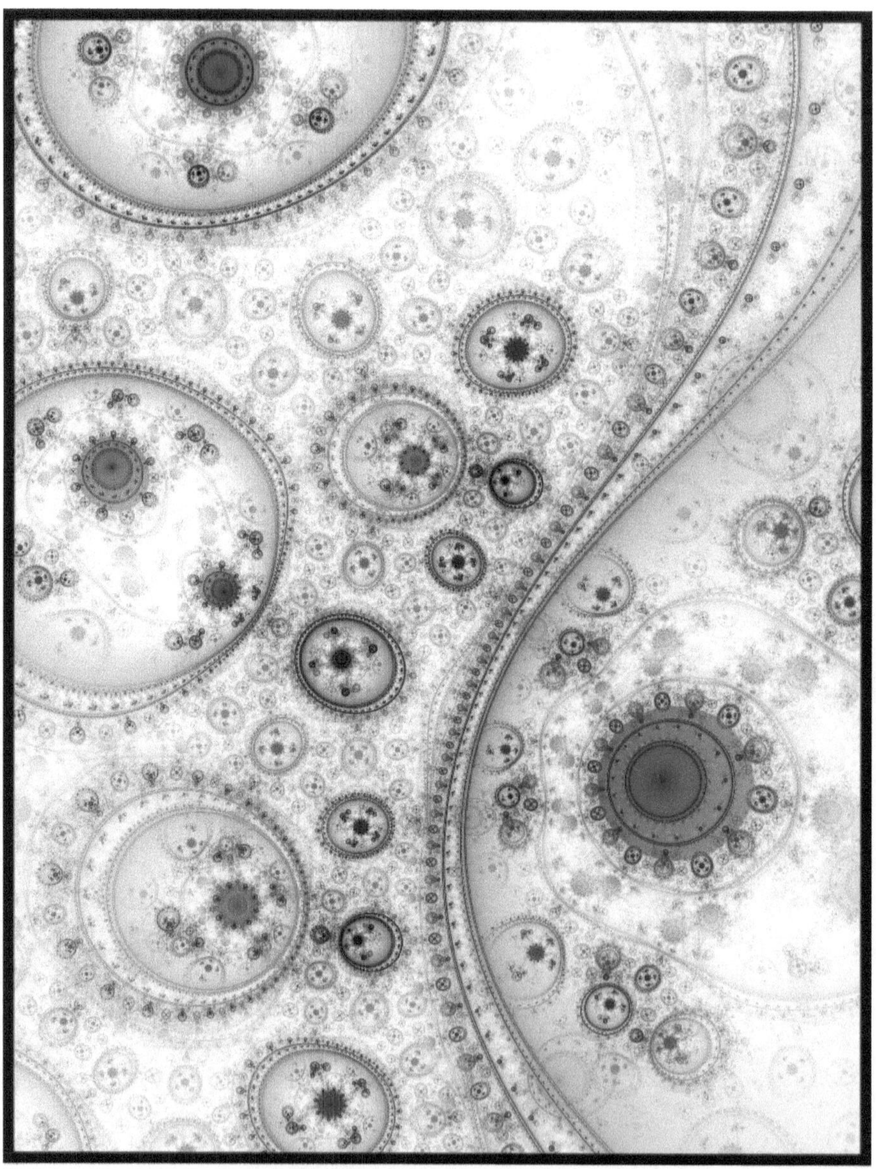

23 Pass-code

Rtu laughed. "Look, little buddy, do two old visages a favor and entertain our thoughts for a few minutes. Besides, Rhom went through a lot of work over the past few centuries bef—"

Rhom elbowed Rtu hard, making Rtu laugh.

After Rtu stopped laughing, he continued. "With the ship, you need to come up with a name for it that only *you* know. We have our own name for it. It's like our own access key. Of course, we will know your name because we created the ship, and it is part of us in a sense; however, no one else will know it."

"He has the right of it, my boy. Take your time though... make it special. We are in no rush. Time doesn't move here compared to the physical world."

"That is convenient. I keep forgetting that," Zreyas said as he considered. "Wow, my own special name for it."

"Just so you can get familiar with the multi-verse's ancient way of referring to ships. They always refer ships to as 'her'. It's not so much gender anymore as much as energetic orientation of relationship."

"Oh! So I should have said... 'special name for *her*.'"

Rtu clapped excitedly. "You got it!"

"Hmm, everyone would expect me to name it something having to do with Aaru, so I won't do that."

"Smart thinking, my boy!" Rhom started walking down the walkway.

Zreyas followed in thought. "I think I need to be with *her* first before going any further."

"Another smart thought, little buddy."

When they arrived at the ship, Zreyas stood there, frozen. He was in wondrous awe as he took in her features. "Is there any way I can move around her to see more details? I can't see much from here."

"Most certainly, my boy!" Rhom made a presenting hand gesture toward Zreyas' feet and a disc appeared underneath him. It was plenty big, with room to take a couple of large steps to the edge in any direction.

"It will act like the walkway, but easier," said Rhom. "Just think where you want to go and it will react."

"Whoa! That is... is..."

"Tiki-tastic!" the twins said in unison.

Zreyas tried to mimic that knowing scholarly expression like Rhom sported from time to time. "Yeah! Now you are learning."

They all chuckled.

Zreyas looked up at the ship and thought about walking higher toward the front of it. The disc moved smoothly at a running pace without feeling the momentum to put him off-balance. He let out an excited 'woo' and raised his fists.

The main body of the ship would have been hard to describe in words, but in his mind, the ship was pleasingly sleek and there were no sharp corners anywhere. The nose of the ship had a suspended ring around it about twenty meters in. Nowhere did it touch the ship. No matter how he moved around the front of the ship to get a look at it, the ring turned slightly to face him.

Zreyas looked back toward Rhom and Rtu. They were smiling and nodding. Rhom gestured for him to continue and sat down cross-legged. Then he turned back toward the ship.

"Hello," said Zreyas softly as his eyes wandered across the ship's surface. "You are huge now that I am here up close and can see you better." He raised himself up so he could see the overall shape of the ship from above, but that wasn't as easy as he thought it would be. He had to get very high before he could really see it well.

It was smooth, sleek, white, and modern—more modern than anything he had seen so far in all the ships in Rhom's collection. In the Janquar culture, there were no white objects. They were forbidden. So, to him, just the color was a luxury.

He took in the ship's shape and tried to come up with a way to assimilate it in his mind. It didn't seem like it would fly at all. Cocking his head as he considered the simplest part of it, the body. It had an aerodynamic nose that widened out. Then, accounting for three-quarters of the length, it gradually got thinner as it went toward the tail end. It had a smooth and aerodynamic raised section at the top for the command deck that slowly tapered down to nothing three-quarters on the way back. Windows for it started large in the beginning, but the smaller that raised section got, so did the windows.

The problem he saw was the wings. They really weren't wings. They were more aerodynamic molded semi-circles that looked almost like a fancy water pitcher handle, but flatter. They hovered next to the body, and weren't attached to the it at all—at least that he could see. There was a cyan-blue flat shaped beam of light between the front of the wing and the body that seemed to serve as the connection.

In the back, hovering behind the body in the circular space between the semi-circle wings, was a skewed cube-shaped light. A flat extension of the square light seemed to be pulled from the cube to the gap between the ends of the wings to a single point. Those ends were way beyond where the body ended and it created a triangle shape of light attached to the square.

It was way more than odd, but it looked ticki-tastic. Though his mind couldn't quite understand the science behind this ship, he was in awe.

He moved toward the twins again, who were both standing now. "I don't know how to describe this ship, or understand how it can even fly, but it's... tiki-tastic! No, it's better than that." He absentmindedly leaned toward Rhom, still looking at the ship. "You have so many ships that are just indescribably interesting, but there is something about this ship that I'm drawn to. I don't know why. And I was trying to come up with a way to describe her, but I failed. It's just too unusual. It looks like you made it for... for—"

"The quantum?" Rhom smiled.

"Yeah! That's it! I bet it's fast! I mean... I bet she's fast!"

Rtu looked at Rhom and smiled as if he was confirming something with a resignation.

"I'm not sure what this ship is for because I know nothing about it," he said, looking toward the ship, "but I think I will name her something that is for you, not me, that has to do with the new age and Ayya." Zreyas turned his face toward Rhom to look at him as he said, "What do you—"

Zreyas stopped talking when he saw Rhom had tears in his eyes. *Ayya means so much to him. I know things probably seem hopeless to him sometimes, even as a visage. He gives here the lovings beyond anything I could ever understand. The old man has done so much for her, the balance, and me.*

He looked at Rhom in a new way. No matter what he had done for others, he had done it *his* way and never sacrificed who he was to do it, yet worked with and honored others.

Zreyas turned to Rtu, who was sniffing again in his handkerchief, then back to the ship.

As if Rhom sensed his confusion, he said, "My boy, our tears are the joy we feel at how far you have come and the choices you are making. The name will come to you."

Zreyas nodded, feeling awkward, thought about it. He knew what he would call it if it were his. Since it was made for the quantum, he would call it The Potential. But it was not his ship, so he wanted to name it in dedication to him.

Rtu patted him on the back.

"This might seem... emotion, but—"

"Emotional," corrected Rhom gently.

"Yeah, emotional. But I want the name to be a sign of the bright future and still relevant to *our* path, not just my path. It's *your* ship, after all. You might think this is weak to say, but I never thought I would be anywhere doing anything other than killing and leading others to kill. Thanks to you two, and Tulyata, I've woken up some. I'm giving you... the thanking of... appreciate."

"It's not weak at all, my boy. The feeling is mutual. We thank *you* and appreciate you, too. You have helped us wake up to many things outside ourselves."

Something came to him that was so obvious that he couldn't believe it had to take him this long to figure it out. "Well, since it is your ship and you will know anyway, I'm going to call her 'The Awakening Phoenix.'" Zreyas turned to face Rhom, "Like you talked once about her cycles of growth in Tulyata's realm, she will always wake up and sleep doing those cycles, and I'm putting that in the quantum, old man."

Rhom cried explosively. Streams of water flowed down his face so much that it startled Zreyas.

"That is a beautiful name with a lot of creative energy, little buddy! I love it!"

Rtu followed Zreyas' gaze as he looked back toward Rhom's state. Zreyas' feet were getting washed over like he was in surf.

He and Rtu backed away from Rhom.

Rtu said, "Uh oh, now you've gone and done it. Route the water Rhom, or it will wash us out in space and I'm not ready for a bath! That water element of yours is out of control!"

Zreyas wondered what he had done to Rhom. He watched him route his flow of tears to his right and over the edge of the walkway. It all looked surreal, like in a dream. The waterfall was massive... and otherworldly beautiful. The love that came from Rhom and the water was intoxicating and it penetrated all parts of him.

The further it flowed, the larger it got. Zreyas watched the water flow up the sides of what he guessed was the border of his dimension in the far distance. He followed it upwards until the many flows met way above him. Instead of flowing down on top of them, it dissipated into particles of glowing light that floated back down. "Whoa!"

It compelled Zreyas to sit down beside Rhom on his more dry, un-flowy side. "I'm so sorry you lost Ayya, as the Viduri you knew. I know I don't understand the size of your loss, but I just know in my chest she will wake up and save your people. Well, you're old people. I know you are still there in the heart, just like I'm still with my old people. It's part of who we are, I think. I... I..."

Zreyas swallowed and felt a huge knot in his throat. He physically had a difficult time uttering the words, but he was determined. He slowly mouthed the words and what came out was guttural in nature, "I... giving the lo-ovings... to you... old man."

He breathed in a deep breath, swallowed, and then continued to give him the stuff in his cracking chest. "I am giving the thankings to you for having faith in me when no one else did. You could have killed me, but you taught me instead."

He turned to look at Rtu, taking the simple route for him. "The same goes for you, Chuckles."

24 Why?

After Rhom properly pulled himself together and stood, he continued as if his emotional outburst never happened, "Now, even if someone guesses the ship's name, they cannot access it with *any* clearance, because it also needs your—"

"I'll boil it down simple, like I like it," chimed in Rtu. "They won't have your living energy signature, which is a combination of your spirit and your body, and they won't have your willing consent. And it takes both together to validate the name."

Zreyas sighed in relief. "Oh good! But how does *that* work?" He would panic if he messed their ship up. It was just too good to get into the wrong hands.

"Now, my boy, all you need to do is think about the ship and say her name in your mind. This ship is quantum oriented."

Zreyas took in a deep breath, as if he was starting something new for Rhom. *I would like my pass-code name for you to be The Awakening Phoenix.*

"Good, you've imprinted it officially. She already knew, but now it is official."

Zreyas shook his head and waved both palms in front of his own face in a warding way. "But how did she know?"

"She knew long ago that you would be coming and you would already be welcome. We just had to make it official."

"Even though your access word could be stolen, and no one can board safely, you must never tell anyone what the key is to opening it because they could do horrible things to her. It would be better for them to know your name than for them to know how she utilizes it. Otherwise it will be exploited, even by those with the most well-intentioned beings. You will find out more why as you get to know her and learn more about her. Does this tell you how much we trust you?"

Zreyas turned around and looked at them both with scrutiny. "Why? I'm not sure it is wise to trust me that much. I'm no visage, and I'm far from being one of your Viduri light people. Full of anger, impulsive, and explosive, I'm wild and I can't help it, it just flares."

He frowned and turned a circle, almost in place, feeling frustration and anger rip up through his gut and chest, then turned and held out a hand in question. "Why did you put this extra burden on me if you knew this? If this ship is as immensely powerful as I think it is, then why would you entrust this secret to my kind of person?"

Zreyas pointed at himself. "See this?" he growled. "Right now, you are looking at a creature who doesn't even know who he is anymore. I'm no longer a Janquar. I'm no other species in existence... nowhere." Zreyas paced in a circle. "I'm wild, untamed, *and* a lifelong killer!

Even you just said the most well-intentioned person would exploit this." He stopped his pacing to look at Rhom and Rtu. "So why would you put this knowledge in my head?"

Rtu and Rhom didn't flinch or make any motion to say anything.

Zreyas looked at them and felt that explosive nature rising up inside himself. He watched his own gaze turn into a piercing, dumbfounded, and angry focus. He was *furious* that they would put him in this kind of position. "Well?" he said in a growling yell, louder than he intended.

"Because we knew this would be your reaction, little buddy."

"You say you are nobody," Rhom said as he shook his head. "Even if you were Viduri, or whatever species, it wouldn't matter your color, type of skin, frame of build, whether you roar, sing, kill, or heal. Each person... each *creature*... is unique and has a design of their own."

Rhom's expression was that of ultimate patience and the new word he learned in the dying dimension from him—compassion. "You have had the unique circumstances to get the chance to see all of that up close. You have *chosen* to accept it. As an example, you didn't ask us to make you who you were again in size. You have come to embrace the new you, and your ways of doing things— all that you have discovered on your own."

Rtu smiled and added, "Neither one of us has ever asked you to change. Your uniqueness has helped us grow and realize that we are just part of a larger whole. You have helped *us* grow through you and your incarnation. You have risked your life for a bigger purpose, not your own selfish needs or wants."

"Yeah, but it's not like I had a lot of choice in the

matter, either. I was thrown into a position I couldn't get out of."

"Really, my boy?" Rhom flipped a palm over and said, "They *forced* you to save your brother before he fell into the fracture? You were *forced* to defend good nature and kill your own brother to protect another? And you mean to tell me I *forced you* to help with Ayya at the expense of your brother? You wer—"

"I get it, I get it..." Zreyas held up his hands in a warding gesture, "You have a point."

"I'm not sure you do fully '*get it*,' little buddy. You had so many choices you could have made that we never mentioned, but you chose a higher purpose each time. Zreyas, you chose to care. You chose the betterment of all, *and* you chose to defend against a foe whose entire purpose is to take *away* choice.

"No one prompted you, and though you are not used to thinking you are more than a warrior, you are so much more than that to us, your brother, and the multiverse that has never met you yet.

"They do not know what you have done for them, and they may *never* know. If it wasn't for you, and the ripple effects you created, the Dark One would have had us all by now. Sure, we had a part in it too, but the point is, *you*... are... *part* of it."

Zreyas stared at them in shock, losing all sense of communication. It was like he forgot how to talk or think. After a minute or two while they patiently waited, he found his voice again. "I guess we really never know how much good or bad we do. But all I have ever heard about before you two was what I did wrong and how I didn't meet standards. The list of bad is big, but it's not something I want to focus on because it won't help anything. I know my struggles and what I lived; but to hear you tell it, you think I'm some sort of guardian spirit or visage. I'm not!"

Rhom smiled gently. "Being a visage is no different from being you, my boy. We all have different growth patterns, design, skills, and purpose."

Zreyas rubbed his hand along his now soft and flimsy horns.

Rtu held up his palms. "I'm not perfect either; I mean, look at what I did by just letting things happen in the past! Though I can't do anything about it now, I am a better Rtu from what I learned from it. There is only so much we can do, even as a High Visage, because choices are motion that we make by living life, however long that life is. But Zreyas, like it or not, even the Dark One is part of us all."

Zreyas looked down at his feet as he thought a moment, "Well, I know I feel dark and angry at times, but it reminds me to focus on purpose, what brings me peace, or makes me feel good. I remember having to do a lot of that on Tarq. Oddly enough, when I looked at the dark stuff, I felt peace, so I thought it meant *I* was dark. But now I'm not so sure. I think I understand your speeches at least a little."

"Your design as an incarnate has a signature of peace when you are living your design well by listening to your inner authority, not your mind. When you are not being yourself and not living your design, all you feel is unconquerable anger. It is easy to let it take you over and condition yourself to it. If you watch it objectively, which is what you are doing, that is another matter, and it becomes a powerful tool."

"Little buddy, you have seen the damage you and the Janquar Nation can do if they live in that unconquerable anger. But—"

"Despite that," Zreyas interrupted, "knowing how

destructive I can be, you give me this responsibility to know something this important!"

"My boy, you didn't let him finish. We trust you, the problem is, *you* don't trust you." Rhom paused a moment, then added, "Do you trust us?"

"Yes, of course. You know I do."

"Then why not trust us now, since you are in no position to be objective about trusting yourself? You are just having a wave of doubt, and trust me, more severe doubts will arise soon enough. But I ask that you trust us now."

Zreyas sighed, "You are right, I don't trust myself since I realized what damage my people have done." He rubbed his head, then slid it down the side of his face. "I know I trust you with my life, and I have got to trust that you did this for a good reason. It's the only way I can wrap my head around why you would do such a thing. You give me trust. I must give it back in the hope I understand one day."

"Thank you for that, little buddy. You might get angry with us again soon enough, so get ready," Rtu warned with a laugh. "Maybe I should put my armor back on."

"No way! Ticking-hell, you cannot wear that mag-shit covering ever again! So what's next? I'm really starved. But I want to see your ship."

Rhom smiled and put his arm out in a gesture toward the ship. "Open our path for us, dear boy, and lead the way."

The Awakening Phoenix, open the way for us so I can meet you, thought Zreyas.

Rtu smiled. "Nicely done. You are already treating her as someone special, not a thing. She is quite incredible once you get to know her."

When the opening revealed itself and the ramp raced

toward them, Zreyas jerked back in reflex, bumping into the shins of the two visages standing side by side behind him. That unpleasant experience was just too fresh in his mind.

"It's alright, my boy, she won't hurt you again, we made sure of that."

"You old men are tiki-tastic."

The two visages chuckled and stepped beside Zreyas, one on each side of him, waiting with smiles, looking down at him.

Zreyas smiled and looked at each of his friends and the ship behind them. It was weird, but he had one of the most profound moments of clarity he had ever experienced before; so much so, he felt he may never have it happen again in his life. He realized that if all the things hadn't happened to him since the fractures, he wouldn't be here now talking with two visages, doing something that would help many like his brother had the chance to do.

He decided that it was okay if he didn't understand it all.

25   T.A.P.

The three walked up to the ship and up the ramp. Once they entered the ship, he saw nothing but mist. Zreyas checked to make sure the twin visages were still with him—sure enough; they were. But no matter which direction he looked, he saw nothing but mist.

Zreyas finally said softly, "Okay, I get it, it's some sort of test or experiment of yours, right?"

"No, my boy, you are within the quantum space of the ship. The mist you see is the ship's generosity in trying to keep you from getting disoriented as an incarnate, since you are not used to being in 'the nothing'. Look at it like this: the quantum is another word for potential. Just be with it a moment and get to know her."

"Yeah, little buddy, we are in no hurry, anyway."

Zreyas didn't dare move too much. He couldn't see anything, including his feet. *So, you are a quantum-based ship... a ship of potential.* He didn't know what else to do but talk to her.

This was so bizarre for him. Zreyas took in a slow breath and decided to just go bits to the wind. *The Awakening Phoenix, my name is Zreyas. I thought I would ask you a question. Other than for entry, is it okay if I shorten your name to Tap... T... A... P? I know it s short, but I can think of many ways to use tap. You tap potential; I tap the quantum when I leap. And it s easier to say. What do you think?*

Zreyas didn't expect to hear anything, but it was the only way he knew of to get to know the ship—just blurt out what came to mind.

Just as he started to ask Rhom what he needed to do next, a gentle, but strong, female voice entered his mind and out in the open for his ears at the same time.

"It is okay with me, Captain. Tap is a nice name since you gave it to me."

Zreyas jumped slightly at the odd multi-dimensional response. He whirled around toward Rtu, who grinned like he just did something naughty and got away with it. He turned to Rhom, but his eyes fell on him with that familiar knowing and peaceful look he got on his face a lot.

"Alright you two, you might be visages and I should show you some sort of mentally half-cocked brainy etiquette, but I'm not going to do that because... really?... Captain? As in, you didn't ask me about being a captain? As in... take over something I have *no idea* how to take over and operate kind of captain?"

Rhom held a hand up and closed his eyes.

Zreyas narrowed his eyes in frustration. Then he realized he was missing an opportunity. He took in a deep breath.

"Tap, I'm... not good with words, but it is good to do the meeting with you. I don't know what got into these two, but I have *no* qualifications to be any kind of captain."

"It's nice to meet you too, Captain. I too have problems with words. I'm learning to communicate, just like you. You will teach me my potential, just like I will help you with yours. I have been waiting to meet you for a long time."

"You have? I'm confused, I thought Rhom made you." Zreyas considered the matter for a moment. "But if you are of the quantum, you are much bigger than me. My head can't understand why you have been waiting for me a long time when Rhom and Rtu just finished making you."

"It is understandable, Captain. Rhom just figured out a way to incarnate me... sort of. He gave me a way to speak so that your ears and mind can hear and see me. I have always been part of you, but now you know I'm here."

"Oh! Well, doesn't that mess up the multiverse-balance? It seems powerful."

"It *is* powerful, Captain, but we are up against something *more* powerful."

"Are you the creator of the visages?"

"No, Captain. I am potential—*your* potential. I am your pallet, empty page, and the tools which you use... and more. I am where everything begins, ends, and transitions for you."

"So you are the larger part of me, however big that is, I can't imagine."

"I can't imagine either, Captain. Now that I am partially incarnated, we will both be learning together to imagine this."

"Why do you call me Captain?"

"Because I chose you when Rhom brought me to a consciousness, Captain."

"What? Why not choose them?" Zreyas pointed at the twin visages, incredulous. "They are the ones that *made* you… I mean like this, anyway. They have the wisdom to handle that kind of responsibility!"

"Captain Zreyas, they did not incarnate me for them. They incarnated me for me and you. I am already a part of you. That is why they cannot be a captain. They are visages and the balances would not be in order. However, even if they could, I would still have chosen you, my captain."

"I don't want power and leadership, never have. I've had it, and I did nothing but destroy with it."

Rhom moved ahead slightly to let Zreyas know he was willing to chat any time he was ready to talk to him again. Rtu did the same, but he heard him sit in a chair. He couldn't help but laugh, imagining him sitting in the mist with nothing under him.

"Old man, you outdid yourself this time. But when did you make this ship?"

"Before I incarnated."

"Seriously? That long ago? But when did you first talk with Tap? How can she choose me when I wasn't even born then?"

"I first spoke with her before I incarnated. And she chose you, like she said, because she is already part of you. Why would she choose any other?" Rhom answered gently, with a straight and honest tone.

"So,…" cocking his head to one side, "did you know I would be a captain then?"

"Yes, but I did not know your name or who you were after your new incarnation for balance reasons."

"New incarnation," scratching his chin, repeating his words with thoughtful suspicion. "So you knew me in a previous incarnation?"

"Yes, but don't ask about it, because I won't tell you."

"Don't worry, I don't think I want to know!"

"But I didn't know who you were when we met in the dying dimension. Remember, I was an incarnate at that time as well."

Rtu had a grin on his face that was as bright as the sun. "I love when things happen with such synchronization like this! Isn't it amazing, little buddy?"

"Captain, you use the quantum naturally. That is important to remember because it is how you will control the ship. I like talking about you. You are the first incarnation in history with the ability to control me naturally and have the multiverse's best interest in their heart. Your last incarnation prepared for this."

"What if I choose to not take this... opportunity?"

The twins suddenly looked horrified, though he could tell they tried not to show it.

Then there was a brief silence before Tap responded.

"That is a possibility, Captain. If that takes place, then that means I have misplaced my trust in part of myself, which is you, and I will learn from it. And the next one—"

Silence filled the room. After several long seconds, Zreyas broke the silence. "Tap?"

"Yes, Captain?"

"Did I break you?"

"No, Captain, I'm trying to calculate when the next one I would choose comes."

Zreyas sighed in resignation. "It doesn't seem like I can avoid this whole responsibility thing. You haven't forced me, but I feel forced to do it. It's okay, you can stop. It doesn't matter, I accept. I trust all three of you here. And though I just met you, Tap, I can't imagine you would be full of dark intentions unless Rhom and Rtu put them there. And Rhom and Rtu would never do that."

"That is correct, Captain. And for the record, I wouldn't want to hurt you, even partially incarnated... at least for now."

"Well, I would hope that if my heart turned dark like the Dark One, that you would."

"Would you like me to record that request, Captain?"

"Yes!"

The twins laughed and both of them did an odd high slap of their hands to each other that he had never seen them do before.

Rhom turned to Zreyas with a bright smile. "So, my boy, we have a lot to do and plan."

Zreyas looked around, still seeing nothing but mist. "Well, can you show me the part where I can actually see the ship we are in? Either that or feed me. I'm starved."

The twins laughed hard with nods of affirmation.

26 Impossible Possibility

"Captain, you can create the design you want me to be."

Zreyas sobered from watching the twins' expressions, "What? I thought Rhom designed you already."

Rhom remained silent and watched with a smile—as did Rtu, but he had a grin on his face with a touch of wonder.

"All potential of this ship is still here, Captain. As you learn, things will appear as you wish them to. As I learn, things will appear that you can accept or re-design with me together."

Everyone in the room responded with some version of, "Whoa!"

Rhom looked shocked and added, "I didn't even know that."

That surprised Zreyas. "What? Really?"

He nodded with a raised eyebrow, scratching his head over his right ear with an amazed expression on his face. "This is far more than I imagined it would be. That one sentence tells me the depth of how far you two can go. However, Zreyas, listen well to me."

Zreyas knew this was serious if he used his name. He focused and listened.

"It isn't any different from the depth you can go *without* Tap because she has always been part of you. You just didn't know it. The only differences is that she is incarnated now, too, because of multiverse's needs and balances and your previous choices to come here and incarnate. Together, you both have more potential in different ways. Is that correct, Tap?"

Silence filled the room with no response. After a time, Zreyas' instincts kicked in, almost feeling her.

"Tap, speak with Rhom and Rtu as you would me."

"Yes, Captain. I will note that for the future until you instruct otherwise. That is correct at the percentage of ninety-eight point six seven percent."

Rtu chuckled. "That is pretty accurate in my quantum book."

Zreyas crossed his arms and thought a moment about the ship's design because it was bugging him he couldn't see anything around him. A few moments later, he smiled, having decided.

Uncrossing his arms, he said, "Tap, I don't want to make you into something you might not feel is right for you. Create the ship design that expresses who you feel you are at the moment in a design that I can relate to. Then we can make adjustments together. At least the base core of who you are will be represented."

"Yes, Captain. I like that idea."

Silence filled the room again, but this time for a long period.

ᕲ ᕲ ᕲ ᕲ ᕲ ᕲ

"I think you broke her," Rtu quietly whispered, still listening for her.

Zreyas turned toward Rtu. "Can I eat now? I'm hungry and there is no distraction."

Rtu laughed, "I like that idea!" He waved a hand and a table of food appeared with seats around it. "I don't have to eat, but I *love* to eat!"

All three of them sat in the chairs. Rtu had made a special chair for Zreyas that put him at table height. They all sat together in the midst of the quantum ship and they ate a meal together.

For the first time, Zreyas had a small idea of what an actual family might be like. He had heard and seen the ones before he had killed them doing things like sitting around a table eating, but he had never had that experience for himself.

When they ate at the Janquar nation, it was always standing or while traveling. Sometimes they would sit but not at a table, and it certainly wasn't around a group that gave the lovings to each other. He would add this moment to the list of things he would remember for the rest of his life.

They were all so caught up in their wonderful meal together that Zreyas hadn't realized what was happening around them until he felt something changing inside himself. Things started to look and feel different inside and around him, even the food. He shoved the last bite of food into his mouth, pushed his plate away, and stood on the table to find out what was going on that would have his whole torso feeling like it had tidal pools in it.

He had to blink a few times while he wondered if his eyes were playing tricks on him in the mist. The longer Tap manifested herself a little at a time, probably for his sake, the more Zreyas hung his jaw.

Rhom and Rtu stood and walked around the table to stand next to him. Zreyas looked at each one of them and their expressions were as dumbfounded as his were.

At first, the mist receded from the floor slowly, revealing a black, oddly blurred floor. It was big enough that he could tell the design of the room would be fairly large. He didn't know why, but it felt... comfortable. The detail wasn't there yet, so he waited patiently. What fascinated him was that he felt the changes within him, like something was slightly shifting and moving inside his body. It wasn't painful or pleasant—he just felt it.

The mist began to recede up the forming vague walls. The general idea of large windows emerged, though he couldn't yet see through them. Everything he saw, though not yet formed, seemed nice and in a design that appealed to him.

He glanced at Rhom and Rtu and their hanging-jaw expressions told him they were as full of wonder about it as he was.

Everything so far in the room seemed like a molded, blurred-vision variant of grey tones. Simple and sleek ornate-shaped trims began to mold, giving it some opulence. He liked that a lot. One thing he knew about himself was that, though he might be primitive and rough, he loved a touch of a simple, ornate royal look in his surroundings. He had no idea where he got that from because, until recently, he had always just seen rustic and rough around him. Maybe that was why he always molded his horns differently than other Janquar.

"Whoa!" Zreyas finally closed his mouth and swallowed and couldn't help but bounce slightly on the balls of his feet in excitement.

"My sentiments exactly, my boy," said Rhom with awe in his voice.

"I can't see it all yet, but I'm *loving* this!" added Rtu.

The mist stopped receding, and he realized it was

because there was none left. The blurry greyness of everything around him made it seem like mist. Then, in what seemed like the same order, Tap started revealing the true form of the floor under him. Black marble with crystal veins started filling in, working its way out. It gave him warm chills as it manifested throughout the room.

Zreyas walked slowly toward the middle of the room, his arms out slightly with palms up. All the changes Tap was doing, he felt inside. He closed his eyes and felt the moisture pool at the crevices of his lids. He could still see the room but also the energetic flow of her creating process made him gasp.

He felt Tap more inside himself now, as if she was getting inspiration to discover more of her own likes and dislikes. Zreyas watched her work in awe.

Finding he felt like it was almost an invasion of her privacy. *Sending the thankings to you for showing me.* Then he opened his eyes and watched the rest of what she was doing from his view, yet still felt the work inside his body. It was the oddest feeling.

The materials continued to emerge, and some sort of black shiny stone on the consoles was trimmed with the strong pattern of the wood he saw in Tulyata's dimension. Though there was a lot of black, the room didn't seem dark.

The subtly used ornate trim phased in. It was a beautiful shiny sculpted gold color and texture. All the consoles started lighting up with many lights, dials, and buttons. Then the glass seemed to melt away as it turned clear and he could see Rhom's massive air strip and all the surrounding ships.

Zreyas was in awe and had a hard time finding words, and apparently, the twins did too because they were still standing there with their jaws hung. "It's strong, striking, official, yet soft, warm, and comforting. I like the marbled crystal floor and whatever black shiny stone that is on the consoles there," pointing toward the console ahead of him.

The twins looked at him in shock.

"I don't see it like that at all," Rtu said, astounded. "I see a solid earth and rock texture there. It's nice and smooth and wonderful stone work with earth texture marbled in."

"I see something different as well. For me, it is a solid crystallite with aether mist," added Rhom. "Well done, Tap! That is quite the feat to have everyone get their own experience from the same thing you created!"

Rtu added, "Yes. The different perspectives from each of us are powerful in their own way."

As soon as Rhom and Rtu talked about what they saw, Zreyas saw a version of their descriptions mixed in with his, in tiny areas in just the right places. He guessed that now that he understood their view, he could see it add to his own. "Tap, well done. You look very good!"

"Thank you, Captain. I'm glad you are pleased with your interpretation of my vision of me."

Both visages shook their heads, and it was obvious in their faces that they were pleasantly surprised, too.

Rhom looked around wistfully. "My boy, I did not know. She never showed us this side of her... personality before. She was always nice, but more... robotic. No offense meant to you Tap!"

"None taken, Master Rhom. Is it okay to call you that? It is the name you are most fond of. It means a lot to you... the Viduri experience. But there is a close runner behind it."

"Yes, it is okay," Rhom said, smiling fondly.

"Master Rhom, you helped me incarnate, but you never

asked me to be myself. The Captain did from the start.”

“I understand, Tap. I didn’t think about it because I was too caught up in the fine details of creating a vessel for you. If I ever have another opportunity to do something like that again, then I will not forget that important detail.”

“Captain, the station in the center of the room is for you. When you step on it, or sit in the chair, you will connect with me. I will be an extension of your skills that you have. However, they might be modified to translate to a ship.”

“What?! Impossible!”

Rtu asked in return, “How can you Q-leap? That *was* impossible, too,” then gave him a wink. “Just because you have never seen it done before doesn’t mean it isn’t possible.”

“I hate to say it, but you have a good point, Freckles.”

Zreyas looked down at his armor-less body, battered use showing even on his vest and under clothing. He turned to the captain’s station in front of him, wondering how he got to this point. It was all surreal.

He shook his head and uttered, “I... I really don’t think I can do this, even though I know the possibility is there.”

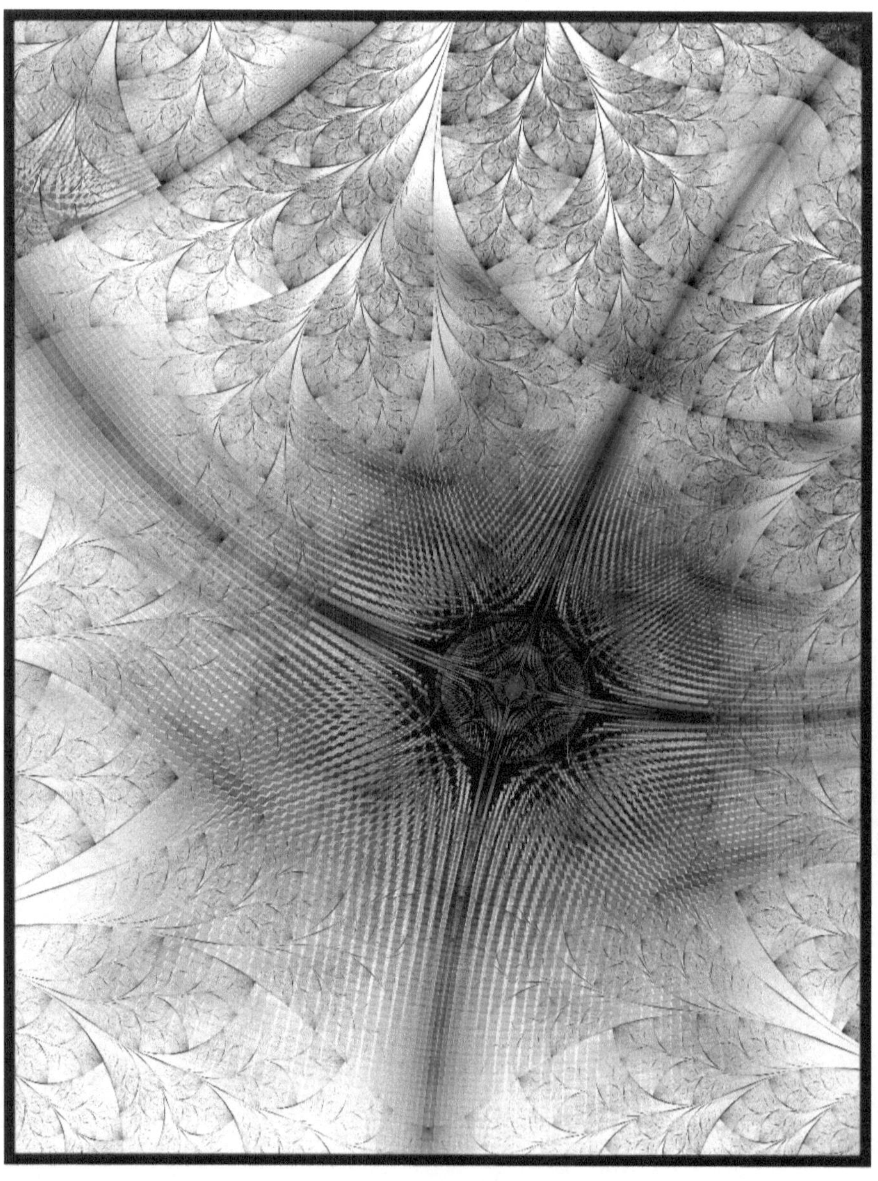

27 A Manifestor's Strategy

ריה *Zreyas* ריה

"Why do you think you can't do it, my boy?"

"Yeah, little buddy, you are the perfect person to captain this ship!"

"Look, I know I seem squishy and weak, but I know my flaws way too well," he said, holding up a finger. Then he held up two, as he listed another reason. "I know my aura pushes out and affects others. I'm okay with all that and I'm okay with me as I am. But to push all that out through my aura and force a ship to change and affect everyone in it? — That is another matter entirely."

Zreyas sighed and dropped his hands. "My oscillating emotions are one thing for *me* to manage, especially the anger, but it is another thing to push them out on others. I've destroyed life with those waves and I don't trust myself to control it. I've had enough of hurting others. I know I will have to do more to those that want to take away choice, but to push that out and make others live *in* it... No! I won't do it. I'm sorry Tap, you have waited all those years for nothing."

Rhom asked in a way that was more the Master Rhom than his friend. "Would you like some of my thoughts on this?"

It was gentle, and he had encouragement and peace in his voice, not judgment, but it was still that Master Rhom tone that made him turn to face his friend and teacher. "Yes, I guess I would, actually."

Rhom smiled and nodded, then sat down near him and looked straight at him. "Do you remember what I told you that you needed to do concerning interfacing with others because of your pushing aura?"

Zreyas thought for a moment, despite his overwhelmed and overloaded mind. *My aura pushes out... and I must...* "Yes... yes, I need to inform others."

Rtu clapped, and Rhom nodded.

"Your pushing aura is your strength as well as your weakness, depending on how you respect it and work with it... or not."

"And that is what I am afraid of," admitted Zreyas.

The nodding Rhom smiled. "There is the problem, not how your aura works. You are no longer accepting yourself as you are because you fear who you are. It doesn't matter the reason. You are in a fight you will never win unless you do one thing."

Curious, Zreyas asked, "What's that?"

Rhom looked at Rtu and nodded. Rtu said, "Stop fighting, little buddy. You were perfectly happy with yourself until you thought about what others might think of you, or how you might hurt them accidentally. It's okay to be mindful of not wanting to hurt others, but it is debilitating to freeze yourself out of fear of it. That isn't being mindful... that's being fearful."

"But how can I stop fighting myself? I don't ever think

I fought myself before, but I'm not sure how it started—not like this, anyway."

Rtu smiled. He had a strength in him now that Zreyas had never seen before through all his laughing and joking around. His power was immense and he couldn't help but listen; not because he made him listen, but because he wanted to, out of respect.

"You always accepted who you were before. You knew your limitations and your strengths. And yet, you still accepted that and worked with it strategically. You knew what you did well in and used that in your strategy in life, along *with* your weaknesses, to help the weaker parts along. You know and understand yourself... but just because others do not, doesn't mean you have to stop accepting yourself."

"So..." Zreyas turned to Rhom. "I just need to inform others for *two* reasons—to let others know what is coming their way, *and* to keep my waves of emotion in check at the same time like an equalizing observation?"

"You have the right of it, my boy! You can say things like: 'You might see this happen from my excitement,' 'This is my plan, and this is how we need to do this,' or 'Hey, I'm angry, you might see the ship change—get ready for the impact.' Rhom pointed sideways. "Inform others, then release whatever energy you have to go where it needs to go, or do what you need to do, just like you normally do. Do not change the mechanics of who you are unless your growth changes it. Just inform others."

Rtu happily added, "By informing them, you are avoiding confrontation with yourself as well as with others as much as possible. If people don't like how you operate and who you are, then they are at least well informed and they can decide if they want to be there with you or not. Though that strategy won't work for me, Rtu, or many others because we are not of the same design aura, it is perfect for you. You can probably see it in Aaru, even though he was a different *type* of manifestor in his *Janquar* body."

Everything the twins said made so much sense to him. It seemed to take the weight off his shoulders *and* his heart. He consciously stopped the fight in his mind with images of how he thought it might look and replaced them with pictures of who he was in different scenarios.

After all this time, Zreyas realized that Tap had never said a word, but she probably knew he had to work things out on his own.

"Well, I'm *informing* you three I'm unsure of myself, but everything you said makes sense. I'm trying to put it together in a strategy that I feel comfortable with. If you are all okay with that, and willing to give it a trial *without* commitment, then I will consent to this."

"That is all any of us could ever hope and expect of you, little buddy. Every day is a trial run for everyone, anyway."

"Thank you, Captain. Go ahead. Step up on the platform if you like. I promise I will not hurt you, and you will not hurt me."

Zreyas nodded and eyed the center platform suspiciously. It was a couple of hands high off the main floor, and it seemed huge to him, but he Q-leaped onto it anyway, where he saw nothing but the low foot wall.

The entire center area he was standing on started morphing and resizing itself. He felt himself rise up, and he looked toward the twins with surprise.

The twins pulled their heads back in amazement as their eyes grew wider. The wonder in their faces lifted his spirits somehow.

Zreyas was now standing on the same center console

pedestal, but only slightly higher than it was before. *I want to see better, Tap. Lift me to the height that I can see what is going on in the room as well as outside the ship.*

The floor of the pedestal lifted slowly and adjusted in the room where Zreyas could see everything, just like he asked for. He took a step back and bumped into a chair that was now there behind him, making him involuntarily sit. His jaw hung, astounded.

"I'm afraid I don't know how to pilot a ship."

"I have a funny feeling that even if you knew how to pilot a ship, it wouldn't be much help when it comes to working with Tap," chuckled Rtu.

"You know quantum at least on a surface level, my boy! That is more than anyone else in the multiverse that isn't a visage and a good start. But we do need to make you some new armor. I knew that part would be a factor whether you lost your armor or not."

"Ha! Well, I'm not putting on any new armor until you update yours!"

"Fair enough, fair enough," chuckled Rhom.

Rtu laughed. "We definitely need a change in that department."

"Well, there is good news—we created a special inner armor for Zreyas, but since he now needs outer armor, we can do all of ours at the same time!"

Zreyas palmed his forehead. "You already made armor?"

Rhom laughed, then smiled broadly. "Tap, would you like to do the honors?"

"Yes, Master Rhom, I would like to do that."

Just ahead of Zreyas' station, the floor opened up and a beautiful ornate gleaming chest emerged. He knew that material.

"Is that the material the Viduri build from that I saw

at the ritual?"

Rhom seemed to glow, then nodded. "Neutrinic-gleam."

"Captain, this is one of our gifts to you. I helped make it too. I'm inserting a laugh here."

Zreyas and the twins laughed, who were watching him with interest, probably to see how he was reacting to all this. He liked the sense of humor emerging in Tap.

"It is a happy emotion moment, Captain."

Zreyas stood on the platform laughing. He wanted to get to the chest, but his station was in the way. Before he had a chance to do anything about it, Tap interjected with a suggestion.

The platform slowly adjusted so he could see and he reverently stepped closer to the chest, watching the material's living and swirling movement. He had always loved that material ever since the first time he saw it and how it drew him in.

"Forget the armor, this chest is... I'm going to touch it if that is okay."

"Certainly, my boy!"

The neutrinic-gleam seemed to brighten, and he heard a faint tone ring out if he listened.

Zreyas reached out and touched the chest, the chest rung out soft gentle harmonic tones in response. Zreyas looked at his hands. The light blue of Zreyas' skin seemed to draw the light from the neutrinic-gleam chest, almost marrying with it in a way.

The chest sprung open. Zreyas jerked back reflexively. The slight shock turned into wonder as he watched the armor rise up out of the chest.

A half-corporeal gleaming suit of armor floated up in front of him. Its iridescent material seemed alive, like the chest, but different. A balance of a marbled dark and light swirling patterns flowed, morphed, and flipped continually like the fractal shapes on Tulyata's scales used to, neither one overcoming other. They seemed to work together as a team to Zreyas.

"Ticking-hell, I don't think I have ever seen any armor so beautiful, or the magic to make that armor rise like that."

"It's not magic, it's science, my boy. The—"

"Another time, brother," interrupted Rtu, chuckling.

Zreyas hesitated as he tried to figure out a way to tell them this armor was not normal, and *way* too bright. "You know... not being normal and feeling okay with it is the best part of my life now..."

"But?" Rhom questioned with an understanding that seemed to make Zreyas feel a little less awkward.

"Well, it's dazzling, radiant, mesmerizing, and... thin."

"I had a feeling that was what was on your mind, my boy. It's okay, it won't look like that when you put it on. It will look like whatever you want it to look like. Remember, it is an *inner* armor. You can even change it with a thought in appearance, depending on the situation."

His mind couldn't quite grasp the ramifications of what they just said, but he understood enough to know that it seemed way out of balance.

"Also, Captain, as your moods change and awareness grows, others will see it manifest in the ship's appearance."

"That seems, I mean, that is..." Zreyas didn't want to hurt them; after all, the three of them put so much into something like this.

"But out of balance?" added Rtu with a smile.

"Yeah! You made that easier. I know so much work goes into normal armor, but this... it's beyond anything I could have ever dreamed of."

"Thank you, Captain, for your sensitivity. I was afraid you might hurt my one feeling."

Zreyas tried to grasp what Tap just said, and a good full two seconds of silence passed through the ship, then the entire room busted out laughing.

"Captain, if I knew how to laugh I would insert a one-'ha' laugh here."

After a few minutes passed full of laughing and chat, Zreyas looked at the armor again and went silent. Everyone in the room seemed to follow.

Tarq Map

Portal
Janquar Nation
Blue Camp
Janquar Landing
Zreyas' Cave
Zreyas' Landing

Acid Pools
Blue Camp Cave

Tarq Map

28 Quantum Protection

ᕮᕮᕮ *Zreyas* ᕮᕮᕮ

"So... tell me about this armor. I want to like it more than I do already."

Rtu grinned. "Besides what Rhom previously said, I'll give you a list of general features you can discover the details about later. Tap, can you put the list of the armor's features up on a holo display, please?"

"Certainly, Freckles."

Hundreds of holo images with walls of text in small print appeared all around the room, overlapping each other so thick the walls were totally covered up.

Zreyas' eyes immediately glazed over, not really looking at the print. He wouldn't know where to start, even if he could read.

Rhom laughed and said, "Uh, brother?"

"Oops! Okay let me revise that request," said Rtu. "Okay, Tap, just put up the general features of the *individual* usage at the surface level—Omit the tandem and global use for now."

Tandem and global? What the ticking-hell?

One panel of information popped up and everyone in the room seemed to sigh in relief, including Zreyas.

Zreyas rubbed his face then said, "That's better for a not-so-science Zrey."

"I apologize, little buddy. As you can see, there are a lot of features you will just have to get to know as you use it. But here is a list of some of the general features for individual use. We will start with that. This is your inner armor. You will also need outer armor, more like what you are used to."

"So, I can have double layers of armor?"

"Yes, my boy. And once you put this armor on, you will never feel it and it will not add to your weight or movement burden."

"Whoa! Magic! I mean... Whoa! Science!"

They all chuckled, then Rtu continued. "Some of these features seem bizarre on the surface. Most of them are automatic, but those that are not, you will know when the right time to use them is."

As Rtu told him the features, Zreyas looked out of the window while he listened carefully.

Quantum Armor (Individual use)

1. Wearer can change the surface look of the armor at any time without a wait time.
2. Once worn, it becomes part of the wearer's body.
3. It can be taken off after it has been put on.
4. Wearer can absorb fifty percent of what the wearer *chooses* to accept
5. Wearer will also take fifty percent of any type of damage that is inflicted on the wearer.

"Now these next two are big ones, little buddy, so listen up."

Zreyas nodded enthusiastically, amazed and excited about the features so far and eager to hear these next ones.

6. Wearer can choose to adjust the percentage of protection as long as it adds up to one hundred percent. For example, fifty percent protection for dark matter damage can be adjusted to seventy-five, with the balance adjustment that all other protections suffer the balance cost.

   Or the wearer can choose specific single or multiple elements to pay the balance cost instead. The extra balance cost is a wait time to change back to the default of one hour per five percent.

Zreyas shook his head at the implications of that freedom and cost strategically. But he knew it would take time to be mindful of that feature.

7. Wearer may change forms with the following limitations:
   a. The form uses the owner's base attributes, not the chosen form's attributes that owner turns into.
   b. Wearer cannot use quantum mobility while in that form; for example, no quantum leaps.
   c. There is a balance wait time to change back to the owner's normal form.
   d. Physical damage protection of any type - None
   e. Quantum and elemental armor protection - Yes

"You are right. As a list, it seems bizarre. But *some* of it makes sense."

Rtu smiled and happily explained. "It is what we call quantum protection. The protective energy will become part of your body when it is put on. And if for some reason you want to take it off, then all you need to do is think about it and pull it off like any other armor. And before you say it, it's not magic. It's quantum science with the material doing most of the quantum work for you."

"Ticking-hell! My head is exploding with trying to apply the strategies."

Rhom continued where Rtu left off, pointing at the armor casually. "Also, that colorful iridescence you see if you look close is the representation of the elements! So Rtu, Tap, and myself are represented in both symbolism and protection. All three of us gave a part of ourselves to create this armor. The way it works has Tulyata's balance as the backbone."

The entire room went silent for a few seconds at the mention of Tulyata.

Zreyas broke the silence in an attempt to lift his friends' spirits. "I'm glad Tulyata is there too. See, she's not really gone. We are keeping her alive in the quantum by including her. It wouldn't be proper armor without the balances and elemental protection, too!"

Rtu chuckled proudly, "You've got to have us along with you, little buddy! Earth, fire, air, water, aether, and then add the quantum balances for the big win!"

"This is ticking-crazy!"

"This armor has features you don't have time to learn about all at once, and the ones we gave you are only the basic features of individual use. Part of the balance is for you to learn about them as you go. But there is one important thing you need to know, and Tulyata's balances coming along with you will help you feel better about all this.”

Zreyas watched Rhom lean forward to stress the importance of what he was about to say. He knew he better listen to every detail. This was the Master Rhom speaking again, not his friend.

“Memorize this list. This protection is all about frequency, which means the base statistics are based on the science of *who* you are at the moment. Notice I *didn’t* say, ‘*what* you are, *what* you are wearing, or what species you are’... I said ‘depending on *who* you are’—your ‘yan,’ as you called it in the dying dimension, meaning your intention, and the frequency of it at the time.”

“Oh, so it uses the frequencies and the intent of them as Tulyata’s scales!”

Rhom and Rtu nodded with bright grins.

“I like it! It’s strategic on many levels. I like having Tulyata on the ride with me too. It will help me be... a better Zrey. Now if my armor calls me a little ferret, I will come back and tell you to make a modification. Ha!”

Rhom laughed, then said, “You will understand more as time goes on. But the important thing to remember is that *you* are the best part of that armor... or the worst part. It’s up to you. *You* are the base alchemy. Everything else that armor has to offer stacks on top of that, and dictates the rest of the available features, protections, and abilities.”

Rtu scratched his cheek then said, “Do you remember what Rhom said about how technology had to match the wisdom and maturity of the holder in the dying dimension, or there would be disastrous trouble? Yes, I watched that science lesson.”

“Yes,” said Zreyas.

“That applies here. You are up against a *lot* you can’t

fathom right now, but the technology of this armor is dependent on your wisdom, maturity, and who you choose to be at the time, dictating how effective it is. The more wisdom and maturity you have, the more you will have access to, thanks to Tulyata's balances."

"Ticking hell, it just seems... too..." Zreyas let out a frustrated sigh at the lack of vocabulary and laughed at the new problem in his life. He smiled as he thought to himself; *I like having this kind of problem and not the past problem of just being a killer following orders.*

— Yes, Captain, I'm glad you are out of those past problems. And yes, I am speaking directly to you in your mind. You would have ended up being a very evil being had you continued on your old path. You were very good at that way of living and it was painful to watch your dark progression, but also wonderful to watch you break that progress. I have been waiting a long time for you to wake up.

That was sobering and a little scary to hear Tap talk about what he would have become and remembered the red-eyed statue of himself he had seen in the challenge. *If it wasn t for Aaru, I wouldn t have. And no privacy in my thoughts, I see!*

— Did you really *ever* have it to begin with, Captain?

"Little buddy, you are up against a lot, so don't get the idea you are invincible. We just felt you needed as much chance as you could get to succeed."

"And, Captain, if you die while we are transformed in tandem mode, which we can learn more about in time, I die right along with you. So, before you take a chance on that feature, we really need to read up on that set of rules."

"That's sobering, Tap. Nice job sucking the joy out of that armor!" Rtu laughed and shook his head.

"That wasn't my intention, Freckles. I'm finding... I want to live now. I'm growing to like Zreyas a lot now too. This incarnation has made me forget many things. You all are... I would insert an entertaining descriptive word here if I had one, but instead I say the one-'Ha!' laugh, just like Zreyas learned how to do."

"I think she more than likes you, little buddy!"

"Yes, Freckles, I like him. What is more than like?"

"Love." Rhom smiled. "There are many types of love, but the love you are probably likely going to feel is an all-encompassing high frequency like this..." Rhom closed his eyes a moment.

"Yes... Yes, I understand now, Master Rhom. Yes, Freckles, I love Zreyas, just like the Captain loves Aaru. I'm finding I am doing the same thing as the Captain is doing, reaching to find the words. Thank you for the help, Master Rhom."

They spent about an hour bantering with each other, and they all laughed. Rhom laughed so hard that he had floods of water coming from his eyes again, and Zreyas got under him and took a bath, making them laugh even harder.

Zreyas needed that because he was seriously stressing about the new leadership and responsibility thing.

"I'm saying the 'ha!' Like the Captain says the 'ha!' Captain, you are entertaining."

"Hey! I laugh normally now!"

"Not all the time," all three of them said together.

Zreyas laughed. "Well, the ingrained ticki-tastic-ness still comes out in its own way, I guess. It's what I do." He grinned at them all, holding his hand to his chest strutting around in a circle for fun.

"Captain, is it okay to ask Freckles a question about the weeping term?"

"Ask all you want. It's up to him to answer if he chooses."

"Freckles, since Rhom is the visage of water, when he

cries, water comes out of his face. You are the visage of earth. Do you drop pebbles when you cry?"

The three of them lost it. They laughed for a good long time over that one.

29 E-87

Zreyas

Finally, Zreyas sobered from all the laughter. "Well, I guess I should put this on. We have a lot to do. How do I put it on?"

"Touch it. It's already attuned to you, little buddy." Rtu rubbed his hands together, looking excited about the armor as much as Zreyas was.

He took a deep breath. *This is going to change everything in my life... again, even more than I could possibly imagine. Am I ready for this? I m just now getting to know myself.*

As he reached out for the armor, he noticed his hand was shaking and he hesitated. Then, mustering up determined resolve, wanting to be *part* of the solution instead of running from it, he touched it.

Zreyas slightly jerked when the armor started flowing over and around his fingers and hand like a thick liquid. He felt himself panic inside as it made its way up his arm. He felt the anger rise as the panic set in as it flowed up to his neck. His breathing was erratic now, watching it take over his body.

"What have you done, old man?" he yelled. Zreyas roared out a war cry as it continued the journey across his face and head. When he realized he could still breathe and see, he calmed down as it covered the rest of his body until there was nothing left of him that was uncovered.

He went still inside for several minutes, allowing his anger to recede and slow his panicked breathing down. As those few minutes passed, his awe increased. The armor felt like it was integrating with his body, like exhilarating warm liquid flowing through all the tissues inside him with massaging tingles.

His awareness altered for a few moments, and he watched energy move around him. Zreyas watched himself integrate with the armor and realized that he was adding functionality to the new armor as much as it was adding to him. Now he understood what Rhom meant when he said about his yan and who he was mattered.

When his normal vision returned and he examined his arm, turning it over, he found the marbling of the texture of the armor had changed. The white and black swirls of the armor were now an almost black purple and brilliant gold.

"Unbelievable," he whispered to himself. "You made this... you three are truly higher than Prime Visages."

"Quantum science that marries physical science, my boy, that's all it is. We just have a unique way of seeing things because we have more perspectives. That is the only difference. You also have the same potential. We are just further down that path than you are."

"Yeah, little buddy. Like the old saying of many cultures, 'Flowers bloom at different rates and times.'"

"Captain, you can put the outer armor you make on top of that now. It will adapt and integrate, but you must make that a conscious choice. It's a safety precaution.

Another... feature."

Rhom held a hand up and calmly said, "We talked about it briefly before in my lab, but I want you to remember that we fueled her with E-87. It's not a problem for us, but it is a potential problem for you, Tap, and those around you."

"Little buddy..." Rtu scratched his freckles a moment on his left cheek as his expression grew serious. "It's *extremely* volatile. However, Rhom figured out a way to harness and condense it within a special containment system."

Rhom nodded. "I used the regulated explosion design for fueling the propulsion and quantum leaping. While even a crash is not likely to breech the system, we are dealing with a quantum-oriented foe as well. You need to be well aware of what Tap holds in her belly."

Rtu scrubbed his face with his hands, then dropped them to his knees. "Yeah, when we say volatile... we mean more volatile than you can imagine with that kind of technology and concentration of E-87. If it releases simultaneously, the potential damage is way beyond planet devastation level. That wouldn't do the most damage, though. The aftershocks and other types of misaligned rotations, explosions, and imbalances that it would cause could take out hundreds of times more than that, at the least."

Zreyas knew he wasn't exaggerating. The intensity with which Rtu was speaking at right now scared him.

Rhom explained further. "Yes, she is full and you will not have to refuel her often, but if you need repairs or fuel, we have set up three refueling and repair stations in three places so far. As we see the need, we will add more.

"However, for balance purposes, you will need to find them on your own *without* our aid. Tap will detect them if you move within range of them, but I will not tell you what that range is. They are not inside galaxies. They are hidden in a special type of dimension in null space, untouched by normal physical science rules because of the danger the stations may be, if destroyed, breeched, or by someone tampering with them. We didn't want them to be accessible to *any* life already established."

"But don't worry, my boy!" said Rhom. "It would take quite a trick to expose it, even in a crash. And we will leave it all up to you as an adventure to find, dock, and refuel when the time comes. But that will be a long time from now, even if you use the ship in a physical mode for varSas.

"Quantum travel will use less in the quantum space, but more before and after, so if you do a lot of quantum travel jumps, you will need to fuel a little more often. Tap will keep you informed of her fuel level, but it wouldn't hurt to keep an eye out for the stations because you just never know when you might need a repair... or—"

"Upgrade," finished Tap.

Rhom chuckled. "Right you are, Tap."

"Explosive topic, Captain."

Zreyas chuckled. "I need to think about something familiar for a few minutes. That subject makes me want to quit and run. How's that for informing? Ha!"

He placed his elbow in his hand, thinking about his outer armor. "I would like to ask about making the new outer armor, as you make yours. You promised after-all to update yours. I would like to at least have some sort of skill, or at least the knowledge of it, for the future, especially since it's closely integrated with me and Tap and I really don't know the technology of the world. How high a tech is it compared to what I know?"

Rhom looked at him gravely. "I thought you wanted to think about something familiar."

Rtu jumped in quick in an obvious attempt to steer the subject, which made him more curious and anxious. "I can help you with that armor. The physical areas are my strength. Rhom here adds and blends his extra special perk sauces as we make it."

Rtu smiled and looked at him as if he noticed something, "But you need to change to the size you prefer to be before we do it. It's not like the quantum armor. As you know, we cannot change it once we do it unless you take it apart and cut it or melt it all down again, at least some of it."

Zreyas smiled, "I won't be changing myself to my original size. Nothing but good has happened since I became who I am today, even in the struggles I have faced. And that is partly due to my size. I'll take the struggles and accept what has happened as a gift from the ticking-hell-this-happened visages."

The twins both smiled with glints in their eyes.

Rhom nodded respectfully with a proud smile.

Rtu placed his hand over his heart in silence, then said with excitement, "Now *that's* my little buddy! Besides, I would have had to change my pet phrase for you to big buddy."

Everyone shook their heads in silence.

Zreyas wanted to move the chat in a different direction and said, "If we are lucky enough for them to consent, I know where we might get a crew after we make the armor. We can go talk with the blue camp members."

Rtu clapped his hands together once with excitement. "Good idea! We were hoping you would say that!"

"You know, Freckles, you really need to learn to be excited about life a little from time to time." Zreyas Q-leaped onto Rtu's head, making Rtu wobble in surprise.

Rhom laughed and then said, "Let's go make some armor!"

30 The Fitting

Approaching the finished sets of armor on their stands, Zreyas smiled, happy with himself and their combined work. His armor had a washed and subdued navy-blue color with a brushed matte finish to it.

He loved it because it was at least a little reminiscent of his old skin, yet still different enough to be new. He didn't want to be his old self, but there were parts of himself then he liked. He still couldn't believe they had just made them with all the features they had put into them.

Excited, he finally said to the twins, "Are we ready to put them on?"

Rtu's whole body bounced in his excitement. "We must! It needs to conform and adjust to our bodies before it all sets in! The sooner we do that, the better the fit will be."

Zreyas jerked and started to scramble to pull a piece of armor off the stand, taking what Rtu said literally. His intent was so focused that his war aura appeared, making the two visages laugh beside him.

Rhom laughed. "You don't have to rush *that* fast. We have time, my boy!"

He slowed down, but only slightly, because he was as excited as Rtu about trying the armor on.

"I hate to say it, but I am giving you the thankings." Zreyas grinned at the twins. "You are the best family I could have ever dreamed of, and not just because of the armor."

"My boy, I quite love your contribution to the armor. Your knowledge of how your aura worked at different times was invaluable. Brilliant suggestion of the amplification materials for all of us on the chest and torso areas, my boy!"

Zreyas smiled proudly, "Sending the thankings to you for both sets of armor." *Thank you, Tap, for your part as well.*

— You are welcome, Captain. I'm looking forward to seeing the other set on you too.

Zreyas thought about the blue camp members. He couldn't get them off his mind. He looked at the armor. "The blue camp members agreeing to be part of the crew is unknown, but it is worth a try to go back and see."

"Good thinking!" said Rtu. "You are already thinking like a strategic leader, again. The multiverse needs that, and you have trained all your life for this role. Du-ude, I have this awesome feeling about you!"

Rhom started laughing. "You have been practicing earth slang, I see. It fits you though!"

"That is a different part of their country, though," Rhom said, grinning at his brother.

"I'm an implant! Besides, it fits me," said Rtu as he winked.

"Well, I have to get into the roles of helping with Ayya,

don't I? I know you said there was a gap where there was little opportunity to help. But in order to help her, we need to either recruit those blue to hurt them more than burning supplies. They are what is threatening Ayya more than anything. They are a supply of bodies in addition to an army for the Dark One."

Zreyas grinned at the twins, but still thinking about his future potential crew. "How easy is it to replicate this armor?"

"Very easy once we have created it the first time, my boy. Why? What do you have in mind? I'm beginning to enjoy my new apprentice's ideas. It's so... scientific and strategic!"

Rtu laughed at his brother. "You know I didn't realize how much science I knew and enjoyed until we worked on Tap, then this armor together."

Grinning, but still focused on his thoughts, he said, "I don't know if we will have anyone that is of the fighting type, but it seems anyone with me will be in danger. I don't want them at a disadvantage with what we are up against... whatever that might be. I would not feel comfortable with..."

"Say no more, my boy! I thought maybe this might come up eventually, but we weren't sure because of choices you may or may not have made. We already added a device on your ship to distribute armor or suits in the colors that you want your people to wear in what job they take on. There is no reason we can't make those colored suits, colored armor instead... or both... or a combined both. However, once the suit is printed, it will not adjust at all because it is *all* physical, unlike ours."

"Just put in a measuring thingy inside the machine beforehand," Zreyas said, coming out more like a command than an idea.

The twins exchanged glances.

Realizing how that sounded, he said, "I mean, can it be done?"

"Certainly, my boy!"

"Yeah, we just never put the masters in the device yet because we didn't know how things with you would turn out. We are not disappointed! You came through and did as we hoped without influencing you." Rtu held up a hand in joy. "And I have a new little buddy that has the awesomeness factor!"

Zreyas laughed at how bubbly Freckles was right now, "You know I don't know what... awesomeness factor is, but I'll take it as it's a good thing." As an afterthought, he said, "I'm informing you that I am focused and need to get this worked out. He rubbed his nose, sizing up the armor in front of him.

"Uh oh, here comes another idea. I can smell it, Rhom!"

Rhom laughed and nodded. "Me too!"

Zreyas turned to the twins with a concern brewing in his mind for his ship and his future crew. That made the twins' grins dim a little, but they said nothing.

"Can we put a loyalty indicator in the armor? Or... I'm not sure if what I'm trying to say is coming out right. Um, frequency indicator. If someone is growing dark or their motives get questionable in helping with our purpose."

"That... is tricky business, my boy... because everyone has to live according to their purpose. But..." Rhom went off in that distant land he journeyed to when he thought things through.

After a few moments, he got the typical 'solution face' that Zreyas recognized. He leaned forward. "And?"

Rhom spent the next few minutes talking about a solution that will be within balance without interfering with a crew member's life purpose. He talked about how he would install an alarm system that would only go to him and Tap that would show up on his vision interface.

"I'm putting *this* armor on now." Zreyas rubbed his hands together, egging Rtu on and admiring the distinctive features of the armor. The living neutrinic parts of the armor made Zreyas breathe better just being near it. "Oh, did we remember to put the odor and self-cleaning features in? I can't remember."

"Du-ude! It's in!" Rtu said brightly. His voice echoed from his face already inside the chest piece of his armor as he put it on.

"Good," Rhom said, sliding his lower parts of the armor on first. "But I won't look much like a scholar anymore."

Both Rtu and Zreyas said, "Good!"

Zreyas laughed as he looked at the emblem on his chest piece in front of him. He picked it up, inspecting the flaming phoenix on the front that seemed to animate, burning with subtlety. He knew the neutrinos were living and at work. They caused the tiny fractal shapes to flip and turn. He smiled at his contribution and rubbed a hand over it reverently before putting it on. *Thankings to you, my friends, for helping the cause and coming with me.*

The sides of the armor stretched like a shirt with no clasps or ties. There were small interlocking pieces at the joints that separated to allow him to slip into it. They made them of a pliable material that he didn't yet understand, deceptively almost as protective as the rest of it.

They all finished putting on their armor. Zreyas put everything on but the helmet, unlike the other two. Then all three of them held their arms straight out to their sides at shoulder height and put their feet at shoulder width in unison.

"Nice, you remembered, my boy! Now we just need to

wait for the activation and fitting."

Zreyas smiled and nodded with excitement as the armor activated. He felt it vibrate, almost like a hum, and when he looked down slightly to make sure his position was correct, it was shimmering. The burning phoenix changed from its two-tone red and orange to royal purple and cyan-blue.

Rtu laughed. "This tickles. This reminds me, I need to make a massage chair!"

Rhom laughed. "You and your comforts."

"There is nothing wrong with liking the comforts of life! The fact that I like them, more than most, is beside the point!"

Part of Zreyas' head piece started forming up his neck and onto his head to his specifications that Rhom helped him with. He wanted to keep some semblance of his old identity—at least the feature he liked. This was a function that was partly the work of his gifted under armor activating when he put the new outer armor on.

His flimsy limp horns, that Rtu had described as branching dread locks on Earth, morphed. "Here we go Rhom. Now we find out if our modification to the gifted armor worked. Here's to always remembering where we came from and how far we have come!"

Zreyas felt his head tingle in waves back and forth from front to back as if something was scanning his skin. Then he felt his horns shorten, lift, and change shape. The horns adjusted where they exited his head. He could tell they were shifting because his newly grown hair shifted position that was now lapping over his forehead. The horns exited at this forehead hairline only two-and-a-half centimeters apart.

"Oh, it's happening, little buddy! Best test it all out now so we can make modifications if we need to."

He did as instructed. He reached his hand to the front and top of his head. Feeling the horns, they weren't as thick as they were before. His horns ran over the top of his head like twin lanes, a hand's thickness away from his head. As they got to the hollow of the back of his head, they turned and arched over his ears, keeping the same clearance from his head. They ended in a downward arch between his ear and his cheek.

All along the horns, they started branching out like subtle tree branches with fresh leaf growth, just like how he used to mold them with leaf patterns on the spikes that emerged. *Now they are like how you used to like them, Aaru. I wish you were here to test them with me.*

Rhom's armor finished adjusting, and he went over and pulled out a mirror that was recessed in the wall. Zreyas thought it was quite clever as Rhom rolled it over in front of him so he could watch the changes.

"It is looking good! But adjust them soon if you need to," Rhom encouraged.

Zreyas let the armor work, for now. He watched his horns morph and mold as if he was doing it himself. The golden color came back to them and they had grown more brilliant than he expected, but also the color of raw gold metal. That part he expected.

Rhom had a tear running down his face. "Oh, I like that, my boy! The old but with a new understanding! It reminds me of the day I met you in that dying dimension. I like the hair that is coming in. I just noticed, it's dark navy blue like your skin used to be! And I like the clean skin on the sides of your head."

"Yeah, that hair was something I wasn't used to, and it drove me crazy, tickling my neck and ears. So I made it not grow anymore on the sides and back."

"Classy and strong, too, little buddy."

He concentrated and subdued the golden glow that came on its own and manipulated the design to show both leafy shaped spikes and a few shorter, pointed spikes with no leaves.

"You can move your arms now while the head part finishes." Rhom smiled and had a look of awe on his face.

Zreyas moved his hand under his horns to make sure he could put his entire hand between his horns and head in every area. Then he rubbed his itchy face from the tingles. He noticed it didn't feel scaly anymore at the edges of his face.

He let his hands down and looked into the mirror, and he no longer had a rough skin resembling scales in spots on his neck. Zreyas had an androgynous appeal and appearance.

"Oh, I think we did a great job!" Rtu exclaimed as he tested his own armor.

"Now put on your helmet and let it adjust, my boy. Don't worry if you can't put it on all the way with the new design of your head. It will adjust and still allow you to take it off."

Zreyas reached over and picked up the minimal, flexible helmet with the slits in the right place for his horns. He put his chin down and put it on from behind his neck, sliding and pivoting it up under his horns and over his ears, then closing it around his jaw.

Rtu looked down at himself and wiggled once more to adjust his armor and then looked at Zreyas, "This armor is as comfortable as my normal attire!" He gestured at his head, "Oh, and once it adjusts to your head, you can hide it, remember?"

"Oh, I almost forgot about that!"

After all the adjusting was complete, Zreyas looked at the two visages' armor critically. He realized their designs were a newer style of their previous armor but also with the phoenix crest of a smaller size over the heart, rather than covering the front of the chest.

"You look presentable! And you look... more like how I feel you are in personality with a new hint of... strength!"

"Thanks to your vision. Thank you, my boy!"

"Yeah, thanks, little buddy! I love the new, but familiar look. And, man oh man, it feels nice."

"It really does! Glad you had the idea to do this with us too. We are all better off for the teamwork."

Zreyas smiled and watched them, taking in their new looks, with a sad knowing creeping in. His smile faded a small bit. "You won't be with me much longer, will you? Are you going to slap me on that ship and in some fancy armor and send me on my way?"

Rtu slumped his shoulders with a sigh. "Aww, don't say it like that, little buddy. You are breaking my heart."

"My boy, we won't part like that. But you are not a visage, and it would be unfair to keep you here with us. You chose to come here and live for a purpose. If you were to stay with us, it would hurt your growth and your purpose."

Zreyas felt a lump in his throat forming fast, his eyes burned like fire from the moisture mounting up. After a few breaths, he smiled. "I'm just being the grateful for the time with you, and I have so much to learn yet to update to the age everyone else has been living in. I'm guessing the Janquar were lost in time."

The twins gave Zreyas a genuine smile with tears in their own eyes.

"Well, I know you are in a hurry to get back to the Janquar, but we still have another gift for you when we get back to the ship. Something that will help update you to the times."

"More gifts?"

They both looked at him gravely before Rhom said, "You are up against more than you can imagine, or us for that matter. Let's head out to the ship."

31   School of Hard Knocks

The three of them reminisced about all the fun times they had laughed at each other, their discoveries, and the horrors as they walked down Rhom's special runway without using its functionality.

Then silence ripped through Zreyas, and it seemed to do the same for the two visages that had grown on him. All of them took a deep breath here and there, the air heavy.

Rhom broke the silence. "You know, my boy, though the gifts we are about to give you have a specific purpose, we will always be with you and give you love and aid when you need it. The gifts will always be there for you. All you need to do is remember us. And you will always give to us because your example of hope is an influence has changed us forever."

"In a way, little buddy, you are like a visage. You give to us eternally."

Zreyas smiled and looked down as he walked toward

the ship looking up to the sleek unusual build. *The awakening Phoenix.* As the ship opened, he turned to them. "Okay, but I have a few questions."

"What about the challenge? Aren't we supposed to be a team in this? How can we do that if we are not together? Where I come from, teams are forever till death." Zreyas paused at those words, remembering his oaths.

Rtu must have sensed his inner conflict because he said, "You are no longer bound by the oaths in what doesn't exist anymore. Even if you belonged there, they are no longer the people you knew and have broken their oaths to you. The Dark One saw to that. And before that, they severed that bond by declaring a hunt for you, and for nothing more than you trying to protect your brother from nasty acts of jealousy and fear. Let it go, Zrey."

Zreyas looked up at Rtu's face. It seemed to glow with something he couldn't put his finger on. His look radiated strength. He wanted to tell him the thankings, but it seemed hollow compared to how he felt. Zreyas smiled and looked straight into his eyes and nodded. He hoped he would understand what he was feeling—he was a visage, after all.

Rhom turned toward the ship. "We are a team, and we will see each other again after the time we need to part. And that is part of what we will still talk about. We just have different jobs to do." Zreyas could tell he was hiding his face by how he positioned his body to walk up the ramp of the ship. He understood why, because he wanted to do that himself.

Breathing out a sigh of relief, "Oh good. I don't like quitting on things I commit to. You are family. The one blood family I had is now gone and I'm hanging on tight. You two have saved me in ways I would never have the vocabulary to explain. I know I told you that before, but it's just wrong to quit on family."

He had a thought about his old people and couldn't help but ask out of curiosity. "Is it wrong to leave a family that isn't good for you, like the Commander and Nat, if they were still alive? Ticking-hell, why am I suddenly thinking about this mag-shit?" His war aura erupted with force from the anger of thinking about this whole thing.

Rhom turned around with urgency in his face.

With gritted teeth, Zreyas ground out his words. "I've gone too soft. I'd rather someone break my limbs and die."

He watched Rhom back up from him, shaking his head without a word.

— Captain, observe yourself.

He noticed her tone seemed more edgy than before. It made him take notice just as Rtu stopped, stooped down, and sat right on the walkway where he stood. His expression looked serious.

"Little buddy, I want you to understand something."

Zreyas walked up to him as close as he could get without bumping into his crossed legs. The anger still churning, but he noticed it was more pain. *Get over this mag-shit, Zrey.*

"This is one of the most difficult things for any species to fully comprehend, and that includes Janquar." Rtu reached out and touched a finger to Zreyas' chest and said, "*Everyone...* wants to belong." He paused a second and emphasized, "Even machine races. Everyone wants a family of some type or variety, even if that family is a home with no one in it. Everyone wants a place or purpose to be and live. No matter how well you know, or don't know, yourself, this is so."

"So, what? How does that help me?" It sounded more edgy than he meant for it to come out. Zreyas couldn't help himself. His pain was real, and he also noticed it seem to consume him while he stared at Rtu.

"This is important… for yourself, for your friends, *and* for your enemies. You are lucky to have had the opportunity to see two extreme sides of life and their perspectives. You have done an amazing job of adjusting to it when you could have easily just gotten what you wanted from us, and stayed as you were in that dying dimension, rejecting anything new. But you chose differently. You *chose* change. Remember this perspective advantage you have.

"That understanding is one of the most significant boons *and weapons* you could ever have in discerning the nature of anyone. I don't mean judge it—I mean perceiving it objectively. Use it to understand your enemies as much as you would your friends and family. Most of the time, that kind of strategy will eliminate alienation."

Zreyas mouthed Rtu's last words, trying his best to integrate it while the anger seemed to surface no matter how hard he fought it. He wanted to punch Rtu right in the face.

"Now, to answer your question; it is *never* wrong to put distance between you and family if they are creating hurt and havoc without regard to one another. It isn't wrong to put distance between family or friends that are not aligned with you or your purpose in life. We *all* have turmoil in life creates pain or havoc unintentionally as we learn to live life." Rtu held up a finger and stressed, "As long as they are choosing to grow and taking action to do so, it's worth sticking around and helping if they want it."

Rtu paused, but it didn't look like he was done.

"But if a bad kind of pattern continues, even with love and understanding going toward them from you, then it is time to put distance between you for *both* your sakes. It is just as easy to love them from a distance as it is up close *if* that love is real, and in motion.

"Sometimes letting them go—*really* letting them go—with love intact, is their best teacher and friend. If it is done in punishment, it becomes a manipulation, and that hurts and destroys both parties."

Zreyas felt his fists start to relax slightly, and his breathing slowed. Just when he thought he was about to calm down, his anger flared again like the old days. He couldn't seem to suppress it for some reason. "So, what is the strategy in all this for me?" he said explosively.

And that's when he realized he was doing his best to *stay* angry and *not* calm down. It was a habit he had trained in all his life. What scared him was right now, he had no desire to change it.

Rtu smiled with a focus Zreyas had never seen before. "Learn to recognize these things in yourself, then you can recognize them in others. Most people think it is easier not to care, because it can be painful and they won't have to change—like you are doing now.

"But *not* changing, and staying in that kind of state is not your true self, and it is the most difficult thing a living being can do—*and* the most destructive. Recognize when your enemies are doing that because it will be the time to strike," said Rtu. "It's actually easier to change as change is called for, both biologically and mentally."

Zreyas' anger flared hearing those words, thinking he had nerve spouting off flowery words of useless grandeur as an excuse to—

Rtu punched Zreyas hard in the chest with lightning speed, knocking him several meters back before he hit the floor.

— Captain!

Zreyas slid a long way down the runway while he tried to get his breath under control and think. He focused to put together what just happened in his mind. *I m okay, Tap. Let me think. I felt no anger or threat, which is confusing.*

When the sliding stopped, he was already sitting up. He popped up to his feet and estimated he had slid thirty or more meters down the shiny and smooth walkway.

Zreyas looked at Rtu, who had not gotten up, sitting there vulnerable. His expression was calm, caring, but it also had a gravity. As he stared at Rtu, understanding came to him as his now acute mind calculated and put together everything Rtu had just told him.

I deserved that, Tap. He was trying to help me in a way I understand... and I just got a lesson that might have just saved our lives. I got punched into a serious training school.

— I noticed, Captain.

Zreyas confidently strode toward Rtu. He felt himself transform on the walk back to his new teacher. His emotions were even, and he was focused like his old commanding days—anger gone, all business. He realized he was on a new kind of mission... to learn for the best chance of their success as a team.

He stopped right in front of him, looking into Rtu's infinite eyes. "My words... 'hanging on tight'—" He paused, trying to find the right vocabulary in a realm he was not used to being in. "Hanging on tight to you and the old man as family because of the loss of Aaru, and because I want to belong to something worthwhile. That was *fear*, not the lovings or friendship. That *fear* made me weak and unaware, *not* giving you the lovings as my family. I understand if you want to put that distance between us that you talked about."

Rtu shook his head. "We don't need to, or want to. You want to learn and grow and you understand we have our own paths to live. Saying goodbye to that would be a very bad choice on our part, both strategically and for the heart. You will always belong, because you are always choosing what to belong to.

"The trick is to be *aware* of what you choose to belong to. I will ask Tap to put this whole interaction in the ship notes for you to read later. It's a lot to remember and sometimes we need a reminder, if that is okay with you, Captain." Rtu smiled brightly.

Zreyas stood frozen a moment and looked down.

"What is it, little buddy?"

Despite Rtu sitting down, he still had to look up to meet his eyes. Embarrassed, he said, "I don't know how to read. I'm not saying the sorries, it's something I learned to do to survive in a non-death way. I've pretended in the past and got away with it because I was aware of every bit of conversation and asked the right questions to get the right information. It was not in our... ticking-training. They wanted to keep us ignorant, I guess."

Rtu leaned forward, putting his hands on both sides of Zreyas' head, almost smothering him, and kissed his head. "It's okay. Tap can read it to you, but I think you will find that in time, it will resolve itself." His freckly face smiled brightly and then asked, "Now, are you ready to finish your questions?"

Rtu got back up and Zreyas could only stare at his armored boots for a moment in front of him. They seemed extra-large to him now. He had underestimated Rtu, but that would never happen again.

Rhom stepped in next to him and Zreyas realized he had been calmly watching the entire interaction. "We understand that you are still adjusting, my boy."

Rhom gestured toward the ramp, and they began walking again. "We will not leave you high and dry like trash thrown away. You can count on two things. We will never give up on you, and we will always be with you, even if we physically part."

Zreyas sighed, emotions welling, but keeping his composure. "Big thankings to you. I don't want to admit it, but I have this feeling inside me right now that feels big and... wrong. I'm not sure what it is. It's the kind of wrong I felt when bad things started to happen to Aaru, or when they were going to punish him. Right now, though, it's big."

"It's called fear, my boy."

Zreyas thought a few steps up the ramp, then said, "Fear seems to have many forms."

"Not really. It just isn't always easy to recognize why it might be there. It often gets mis-interpreted as something else and causes a lot of reactions and bad things to happen. Keep observing it." Rhom chuckled. "Don't let it have power over you like it did earlier when Freckles over there punched you into the next varSa. The armor did its work, though. And it seems my brother has hidden his skills well, and he didn't even use the quantum." Rhom chuckled. "Today is a day of discovery."

All three laughed. But they were like a reflective kind of laugh.

"So, if I understand myself, I will understand my friends and enemies."

"As soon as you do that, my boy, you will understand things about your enemies you might not expect. That is your own adventure to discover and experience."

"That seems powerful. I wonder why they didn't teach us that?"

"Because that would require choice and awareness, and they can't control that, little buddy. That very thing is one of the largest reasons why you are critical in helping Ayya bring in the new age. The old way of leadership will begin to crumble across the multi-verse."

Zreyas grinned and ran up in front of the twins and turned around to look at them.

They stopped and watched him.

"Here is one of my questions. Would you like to come with me on this Tarq thing? I know you said we wouldn't be together all the time, but it just doesn't seem like the time has come, or am I just wishing it isn't the time?"

Both of the twins smiled and exchanged glances, then responded together as one, "We would love to go with you, Captain. We were hoping you would ask." Then the two smiled with excitement on their faces.

Zreyas cheered and waved them to come with him. Walking up the upper half of the ramp, he didn't hear them. He turned around and noticed they were not walking. "Are you coming?"

They both said in unison, "We can't."

— Captain, you need to give them access.

"Oh!" Zreyas responded, so they all could hear. "Give them access as my second in command, because I trust them with our lives as long as they are not in league with the Dark One, consciously or unconsciously. I know that is an over-precaution to put that stipulation in there, but I don't underestimate our enemies anymore."

— Yes, Captain. Done.

Both visages smiled and exchanged glances.

Then Rhom said, "Wise, my boy!"

"My little buddy is back! Wise indeed!"

"Come on! You have full access! I figured if you screw me over, then I wouldn't be the only one dead. Everyone else would end up dead, too. Why didn't you have access anymore?"

"She is not ours, my boy. She never was. Tap is an extension of you that you have just gotten acquainted with. We just facilitated her coming and the design. We could force it, but then we would be no better than the Dark One."

32 Tech Shock

With sudden realization, Zreyas turned to the twins. "Oh, I forgot my weapons in the lab! I'll be right back. I can't forget those." He Q-leaped to the doorway immediately.

"Wait!" Rhom interjected quickly. "Tap, would you like to give Zreyas his gifts from you now?"

"Yes, I would like that, Master Rhom."

"Captain, would you wait a moment before going to get your weapons?"

Zreyas walked back to where he was standing before, curious and a little leery about what new thing would blow his mind again.

Grinning, Rhom smiled and nodded toward where the floor opened in front of Zreyas.

He watched what looked like a weapon's rack rising up. Light poured out from behind it. It was so bright that it obscured any detail of what the objects were on the rack, though.

"Nice presentation, Tap! It makes this more exciting and I know what it is!" said Rtu, clapping.

Fascinated, Zreyas' eyes widened and his heart jumped as he recognized a set of five weapons. Not four, but a glorious five! When he saw his favorite type of weapon on that rack, he couldn't help but jump and raise his fists up into the air. "Whoa! This is so... so..."

"Tiki-tastic!" Rtu finished for him.

"No-o! That isn't good enough this time! It's... pheno-mi-tastic!"

"Little buddy, that is a pheno-mi-tastic word!"

"Agreed, my boy!"

As he gazed at all the weapons, his breath caught, feeling tingles from them as he reached out. Chills ran through his body as he reverently touched the bow. His favorite weapon looked beyond amazing with all the workmanship. "Giving the thankings to you, Tap. Maybe you might better explain these weapons before I pick them up."

"Yes, Captain, and I'm glad you like them. The old man and Freckles helped me, but I designed them. I also helped make the materials for them a long time ago. They have been made and sitting here since that time. And though I didn't know exactly who you would be, I knew your potential and what it felt like when I thought of you."

Rtu's eyes were wide, and fascination radiated from his expression. "I have not seen them in so long and they still amaze me. You are wise to ask about them first, little buddy."

"Yes, my boy, these are very special. I will let Tap explain them, since she was the mastermind behind them."

"Thank you, Master Rhom. Captain, I made these from the energetic signature manifestation of your highest potential crafted into physical material. The material make-up is something I don't have time to explain because

I'm not sure I can with words because there is a lack of them for this kind of science. In addition, Captain, they also have your favorite material you discovered recently through the Viduri."

"Neutrinic-gleam! I knew it!"

"Yes, Captain."

"My boy, I want you to know how special these are. What she speaks of, *I* can't even fully understand it. This comes from something bigger than all of us. Nothing in history has ever been made of this combined set of materials before. They are an extension of you. I did not know neutrinic-gleam would be your favorite material then, either. Another synchronization that amazes me. We could never duplicate these tools for someone else. If each person had a set of tools made like this, they would all be unique.

"That material is a living, five-dimensional energy arranged in a special design that carries the information about your full potential. They are what allow the manifestation to occur and they are willingly choosing to help you connect with them as an extension of you."

"Captain, that is why you felt the tingling. I made every weapon there with it. They cannot break. You cannot break eternal living potential made with information and energy of the stars that the neutrinic-gleam is holding. It was also made with a portion of—" Silence invaded the room as they waited a few seconds.

"The spaces?"

"Yes, Captain, the spaces—the nothing, because that is what potential comes from, so it allows for more potential."

Zreyas stood there shaking his head in disbelief, "This doesn't seem... possible! This is... a pheno-mi-tastic gift. It sounds cheap to say, but I don't have any words that will work."

No one said anything for a long time while Zreyas stared at them. There were two swords, a dagger, an axe, and a wondrous bow. Oh, how he had missed his bow. "I know they are primitive weapons in today's technology, from what you said before. But will my skills ever be enough? And... they are very... bright."

"My boy, you are seeing them in their purest state without a physical face. You can make them look however you wish them to look, just like your armor."

"Yeah, little buddy, Tap knew you would come from a primitive race and she wanted you to have something that was as comfortable for you, just as you were. That is why they seem impossible for balance... because of the difference in tech levels, you are now up with technology but in your own style."

"Yes, Captain, your advantages and disadvantages will differ from other technologies, but they are more advantageous for you than theirs are for them, in my way of thinking, because I made yours with your ultimate potential."

Holding up a finger to emphasize his words. "Which is limitless," said Rhom. "You only have to discover it for yourself."

"You keep schooling me on the quantum. My head keeps going back to what isn't possible, rather than what is. That might kill me one day. I never expected a gift like this."

"That is why it is fun to give them to you, little buddy! And by the way, your horns sparkle gently in the presence of those weapons. I bet you can figure out why. And I think I forgot to tell you, I like how your horns turned out. Now they are really amazing!"

"They look nice, Captain, and they are functional, too."

Zreyas felt his face get hot for some reason. That was foreign to him. He shook his head in awe of what he was seeing. "So, what do I need to know about these weapons?"

"Captain, the weapons work the same way as the weapons you are used to, but there are some differences. The bow needs no arrows, so no quiver is needed. You only need to think about the type of arrows you want to use, and they will stay that way until you change it."

Zreyas was so stunned at this news that all he could think to say was a simple, "Oh!"

"Also, Captain, at the cost of no quantum usage for a period in relation to how extensive the change is, you may change the weapons to any weapon or tool you don't have. The larger weapons you have, like the bow, change to larger weapons or tools. That is the balance advantage, the transformation ability, to having primitive weapons."

"All of you keep talking about how I came from a *primitive* race and these weapons are *primitive*. What do you mean?"

The entire room went silent for a moment.

"Captain, primitive weapons are any weapon you could make without involving physical science chemistry. It's not as much about the complexity as much as it is about how it is made. Early civilizations started with wood, bone, and stone, for example."

"So, the Janquar Nation *is* a primitive race." Zreyas couldn't help himself, he had to ask. "What is an example of something that isn't primitive?"

"Little buddy, do you remember those weapons you were up against called shotguns?"

"Y-yes," he said warily.

"Well, that is almost primitive in a lot of the multiverse now."

"Ticking-hell, no wonder everything you have given me seems too powerful and unrealistic."

"Yes, my boy." Rhom looked a little uncomfortable as he leaned in to say what he wanted to say next. "If you are up against many of the Janquar, it will seem like you are a visage in comparison. However, you need to remember that you are up against millions of Janquar and advanced technology in many parts of the multiverse."

The room went silent again, and Zreyas went to the next level of nervous and on the edge of anger.

"I can show you some advanced technology, Captain. Look out the window ahead of you."

Zreyas watched through the glass where a target appeared in the air above all the other ships docked. He waited only a heartbeat before he saw a thin rip of light hit the target in less than a fraction of a second.

He jerked and squatted in a defensive stance as the target was shredded into bits with nothing but a few particles left floating off in different directions.

Zreyas' jaw dropped as he staggered and his eyes widened in the accompanying horror of what he was up against. He immediately started shaking with unused adrenaline.

"How... how can I fight... *that*?" he whispered, incredulous and completely overwhelmed. A sense of hopelessness filled him. "I can't even *blink* that fast, much less react!"

"This is a ship weapon, Captain. There are less powerful, yet devastating ones, that species carry."

"Like shot guns..." he said, remembering the thunder spears those men had. "That doesn't make me feel any better, Tap."

"I'm sorry, Captain. I won't say anything to make you feel better about something that is that destructive. You need a healthy respect for it."

Zreyas paused a moment and turned to look at the twins, his face still warm and pulsing with the aftershock of what he just saw.

Deadly focus calm came over him. He was so calm in his anger he scared himself. "You... *knew*..."

— Captain, please check yourself. You are doing it again.

His anger took him over, way past filling his compartment. It flared so big he almost just went into a killing rampage right there and then. Something seemed off, but it seemed like a little tickle in the back of his mind and paid no mind to Tap.

The words seethed through his gritted teeth trying to hold back the death rampage state he was in just so he could get a little more information before he ripped them apart. "You brought me here, showered me with encouraging words, gave me fancy weapons and armor, and all so you could get me to do your killing work, only to obliterate me when I couldn't go any further. *That* is just like what they were going to do to Aaru!"

"Little buddy, it seems like that, and it's also a lot to take in at once, but we are here with you and will watch over you when we are not with you. Imagine yourself if you were still with the Janquar. You would already have fallen to the control of something hideous. Now you have a chance in a world where you can live free."

"And a chance to free others, my boy," added Rhom.

"Alone, yes, it would be impossible, but now you have Tap, who has the highest technology in existence. You have myself, the old man, and Ayya with Aaru within her."

Rhom reached down carefully and picked him up. Zreyas' shock was so substantial that he couldn't even think to reject the old man's desire to pick him up. He stood him up on Rhom's lap, who had a seriousness and love in his expression.

— Captain, please listen to him and let it sink in as much as you can. It will make things easier. I am with you. I love you already, and you are not alone in this.

He tried to grip his fists harder, but they were already in such a firm grip that he felt his knuckles pop from the pressure, distantly feeling pain.

"Zrey, my boy… there is a history you are not yet aware of. It is best you discover yourself when you are ready. That will help you understand more about why you have so many Janquar."

Zreyas knew he was trying to distract him with information he would be interested in, and it almost worked.

"When the time is right for you, go to the 'Order of History' and speak to the Master there. Tap has the location for you in her data banks. We ask this of you for two reasons, for you, *and* for us."

Tap, can you remember this stuff for me? I can t think straight right now. I might need to hear this again.

— Yes, Captain. I can record the whole conversation.

Good.

"Tell them you were the one the ship chose. Tell them the 'brothers of the elements are three' and 'the phoenix has been captured.' They are code phrases.

"There will be a test they will give you. Then, when prompted, tell them all you know of what happened since the day the fractures started. Give him all the details they ask for and what you think is important that you wish."

Zreyas was focusing now on what they were saying, but barely.

Rtu took his turn about something Zreyas had not thought of yet. "You need to come up with a name for the ship that the outside world should know, then give them that name. The one you chose for entry will not be something you want to give out."

Rhom nodded. "In turn, the master of the Order of History there will give you information about two things, 'The Heart of Odium' and 'The Mothers of the Janquar.' The master will ask you if you are ready to hear it, and you must make a choice then, or *never* hear it. You need to make sure you are not in a high or low state of mind, and your emotions are even about accepting news of horrible things."

"Little buddy, you are not ready now, and you need time. Much has happened in the time your world has flipped upside down. You are extremely angry, and you need to be kind to yourself right now and let yourself process, or you... *will not*... survive."

The more Zreyas heard, the more he seethed, grew more overwhelmed, yet felt numb. Why hadn't they told him this stuff before? He concentrated only on what he could feasibly think about in that moment—Tap. They were part of each other, just like Ayya and Aaru were. *'The Potential, do you like it Tap?*

— Yes Captain. I like it a lot. It is what I am, after all.

A long silence held the room hostage.

Sounding almost robotic, Zreyas re-affirmed, "Tap's world name is 'The Potential.'"

Rhom said sincerely, but with apprehension laced on his face. "That is a perfect name."

He would almost swear Rhom pulled his head back slightly and saw something. That confused him. But he was fully aware of his state of mind right now at least, remembering Rtu's punch, and he took a long, deep breath. Some semblance of equilibrium came back to him, ever so slightly.

Robotic, yet heartfelt, he said, "You have never asked anything of me except to survive the dying dimension, so

I will do as you ask to return at least a portion of what you have given me, despite what you just set me up for. I would have been dead already anyway had it not been for you."

He still felt angry, manipulated, and unable to resist feeling a mistrust, but he knew they were in a bad situation too. "I'm glad you are here to soften the blows. It was better I had that tech shock now, rather than find out with mine and Tap's death."

Rhom nodded. "I'm sorry about all the news. We would not give it if we didn't think you were ready for it, and we have faith in you. We see your potential and have for a long time. Most incarnates go through life without ever knowing their purpose. You have the blessing... and the curse of knowing."

Just when he thought he had himself under control, something grew within Zreyas so much it overwhelmed him, yet it was way too familiar... his old anger and how it used to feel, but this had a little extra something in it.

He had forgotten his old raw, low frequency companion in such a short period of time. He looked at Rhom and his words seem to ripple the surrounding air. Impatiently, he spat out, "Yes, yes, you did all this to get me to help save the world. You said all these encouraging things to get me to feel better about it. I get it... just a means to an end and you fully invested in your little changed Janquar tool."

Rhom smiled gently, but with gravity. "You are right, and I respect that."

"Of course, I'm right!" Zreyas started waving his arms around as he ranted, "Yeah, just get the primitive little piece of ticking-mag-shit to work for you! Ticking-hell, he's expendable!" The pressure of the anger built up with so much force, his neck stretched forward slightly as his war aura pushed outward.

Rhom and Rtu's expression never wavered, as if it did not surprise them at his outburst. This made Zreyas angrier.

He watched his anger, but he felt the compulsion to cut his head off. Just as he was about to Q-leap over to get his weapons, that very thought threw up a flag distantly in his mind, but he was so angry he didn't pay as much attention to it as he should have.

The only reason why he didn't do it was a flash image came into his mind—the statue of himself with the red eyes that he had faced in the hall of statues. Then he realized something that caught him off-guard. He -was- that red-eyed statue.

🔯🔯🔯 Statue *Zreyas* 🔯🔯🔯

When he looked down, he saw the little rebellious Zreyas sitting on his heals in the hall. It felt good to stand over that weak and puny little Janquar. He might have his uses, though, with his new skills and size. Then he heard the little mag-shit talk to him, refusing his leadership. He felt himself swell at the anger, and the red light from his own eyes grew brighter. He could now see that it shined down on the little piece of mag-shit.

Then the Zreyas, who liked to sit on his heels, said, "No, this is just the influence of the Dark One. This is not me. I can't let this statue of anger influence me. This is not me anymore, and no one will make me be anything I don't want to be. That is my pledge to myself and to those I'm trying to help."

Then the little mag-shit heard a wailing scream from one of his new allies. He laughed as the little mag-shit struggled to keep himself from breaking apart from it.

Now he would understand that science lesson the betrayer gave him in the dying dimension that he watched from the hall. They never knew he was there. It was a pity he would have to kill this little Zreyas. But maybe there was still a way to use his body, though. The one he was using would be dead soon enough.

A flag that went up earlier in his mind started waving again as he watched the little Zreyas repeat his words again but, he stood this time, pointing towards him so defiantly.

"This is not me anymore!" he said. "And no one will make me be anything I don't want to be. That is my pledge to myself and to those I'm trying to help."

Then the little Zreyas stopped pointing and asked, "How do you feel now? What kind of power do you have now? You are a slave to anger and fear. You will never be free... *never* be free."

33 This is not Me!

Zreyas held his head, now on his knees, still on Rhom's lap, full of the all-consuming anger he had built up. It felt like a volcano he didn't create, but about to erupt. Then he remembered his conflict with Rhom and Rtu.

This is not... me.

With gritted teeth, he asked, "If you agree with me, then *why* didn't you at least tell me that is what you were after to begin with, rather than be so deceptive!?" Just when he thought the anger couldn't get more intense it did and he found himself yelling out the words, "Betrayer!"

"Because, little buddy, that is not what we did, or intended," Rtu responded softly.

The scream still resounded through his body and mind. *Has the Dark One found me? This... is not me.* Zreyas' anger grew more heated due to the confusion. "Rhom *just said* I was right!"

Gently smiling, without a patronizing air, and full of sincerity, "You are, my boy, you are."

"How... can one of you say it wasn't what you intended,

and the other tell me I was right? Explain it!" *This is not me!*

"It is simple, my boy. Everything you see in this situation is your perspective with facts you have assimilated from your point of view. That is your summed up reality. It *is* valid, and you are right. You *aren't* crazy. However, it is not ours."

Rhom smiled that... *s-sickening* smile, and he gently bent his head down to attempt eye contact, but the illumination from his eyes was too powerful. It was hard to face the old man, so Zreyas turned his body.

This isn t me. I don t want to be like this! The light from these two visages was just too bright. This ship they were in was too bright. *Everything* was too bright.

"I didn't know that you were going to be the one Tap spoke about over twenty-four hundred varSas ago. Remember, I was incarnated when we met. I grew to love you as you were... rough, but with an inner moral purpose.

"You were, and still are, refreshing for an old Vidurian High Seer and Astrologian. I grew to love you just the way you were, not because of what you could do for me. I *still* see you as an equal. And that is *my* reality. And it is *also valid,* and I'm also right."

Zreyas listened, but had to close his eyes, but it was too bright even with his eyes closed.

Silence filled the room and Zreyas froze in his radiating war aura, letting it all sink in slowly. The screams started to get quieter and the pain in his body subsided. His mind started to work again, and he thought about what Rhom said. He was still angry, but he could think.

"Strike us down, my boy. We are not stopping you. You know it can be done now, because of Tulyata's... death. If you cannot find peace in all this, we are all dead anyway. Fact is, you would be blind if you didn't know how special you are to us. Think about our good times... did they seem fake? You are not blind—you are scared, just like we are, I might add. We know much more about the scope of what we are up against than you do."

Rtu leaned forward, propping his elbows on his knees. "The scale of what we see we are up against makes us freeze sometimes in panic, too. We are *out* of our elements, and just like you, we get angry about it. We didn't coax you into anything. You have driven every choice you have made since this started. The only thing anyone convinced you to do was when Rhom asked you to run from that dying dimension. He wanted to save you. He could have saved himself much easier. Another fact for you is that you are very used to getting your way, and that is not a bad thing. But you are *not* used to surprises or things being out of your control."

Rhom nodded. "Everything in your world was simple, except the one thing you loved most, the situation with Aaru. And yet, it was the most valuable part of your past with the Janquar, no? We as visages don't have control either, and most of the time *we* don't even know what to do in all this mess."

"Remember our talk about fear, little buddy, and how it is often mistaken as other things?"

Zreyas nodded.

Rhom asked, "Do you remember that statue in the challenge node that looked like you but with red eyes and darkness about it?"

He nodded quick as he closed his eyes, squinting. *If they only knew.*

"My boy, all those statues were of actual people and their potentials. You saw three potentials of yourself. One full of darkness, anger, and hate. Another was strong, void of the hate and anger, but with no purpose... no life. And the third, the one that was broken apart just to birth a new way, feeling like shit, but finding out the victorious new you."

Zreyas rubbed his head, feeling a major headache from not letting out all the anger that he had built up. He decided to convert it slowly to the love he really had for these two visages, so he didn't have to do anything explosive. Trying feebly to lighten things, he said, "I guess sometimes shitting yourself is a good thing."

"Little buddy, you are not a means to an end, you are an end to a means that has been around a long time that no longer serves healthy life. You are hope. You are joy. You are laughter. You are strategy. You are even death, if you choose to be, though it is not your core. We see you as part of a team doing your part and us doing ours. We will not be sitting around in a room when we part, waiting for you to save the multiverse. You can't do it alone. You are our brother... our family."

"Yes, you are, my boy. You have taken on so much in what has only been a few weeks, but it seems like it has been varSas since we met. I do not know of anyone in existence that would have done as well with it all, though I'm sorry that you had to go through that. Please forgive us for what part we might have done to cause it unintentionally, though we still can't figure it out."

Zreyas filled with emotion, his eyes filled with painful tears that felt like were ripping them apart. They sealed. He Q-leaped off the walls and floors of the command room to blow off the anger.

Then he realized something; he could see Tap's walls and inner workings with his eyes sealed. It was like a living hologram blueprint. It looked like the blueprints he saw of Rhom's in his lab, but with movement. He now understood the different materials more just by seeing how fast the particles moved and how close they were.

He stopped his leap in the middle of the room, but he didn't fall, and felt Tap on a level he had never felt before, as if he was looking and feeling her as his own body. *Tap, are you doing this?*

— No Captain, we are… discovering us. You are my heart.

And you are my potential and… the rest of my body.

— Yes, Captain. Without you, I cannot really live. Never forget, *we* are not alone.

Zreyas turned to see the twins, eyes still sealed. They were pure energy, just like he had seen before once, spread out all over the place. But they were part of Tap and him, and he was part of them.

— Captain, the twin visages have tears too. They are feeling the anguish at what you are going through, just like the joys you feel. Rhom and Rtu understand how overwhelming this is for you… us. They feel your pain as if it was their own.

"Because there is no separation." Zreyas' eyes unsealed and he Q-leaped back to Rhom's lap. "I apo-apo-jo-lize, I never want to hurt you. And… I think the Dark One found me through the statue."

"We know. We saw, and it's okay," said Rhom. "We are proud of you for listening to yourself through that. You did that all on your own, my boy."

"Can we change this dimension so he can't find us here?"

"Tap can, little buddy."

"No need to ask, Captain. It's already done. I did it as soon as you ended the exposure. I couldn't let him hurt you, Freckles, and the old man like he did Tulyata."

"Giving the thankings to you, Tap. Does he know about you?"

"No Captain, he only saw a physical manifestation of a room in a ship. It is separate from me."

"Wouldn't he see the big energy signature I just saw? How could he not?"

"Little buddy, the physical ship is like a manifested physical shell, not her. Just like how you just saw all the frequencies of all the materials in the ship, that isn't really her. There is a term called quantum mirroring. It's a potential manifestation, just like your spirit and potential are using your body, but aren't really you. All she did was hide the ship again in another quantum dimension."

Rhom grinned at Zreyas and got back to business. "Thank you. Your *apology* is accepted, and you are forgiven. But we only do that for you, because in our eyes, there is nothing to forgive."

Rtu nodded emphatically.

Zreyas felt himself flip a latch inside himself somehow, deciding to move on. "Well, we have a lot to do, so let's do it. So, what's this good news you have for me, Freckles?"

Rtu suddenly looked very serious. "We are going to give you some *s-sacred* words to use, much like you do with Tap to enter the ship. When you mentally say these words, it will do two things. One, it is a signal for us to pay attention to what is going on around and within you. We will be watching and listening for your words. In turn, when you hear that name, listen. We will try to speak to you. Quiet yourself so you can hear or sleep as soon as you can. It is more difficult for you as an incarnate."

"Oh, okay, what is the other thing it does?"

Rhom smiled. "If you say the words to get our attention, we can validate if what you are seeing is legit or an illusion. With the Dark One using the quantum, he is becoming a master of illusion as well, just like what you saw in the hall of statues. If whatever you want to validate persists, then it is legitimate. If it changes or disappears, then it is an illusion."

"That is also nice to know. What's the sacred words?"

"We made it fun and family like, little buddy. 'Namdlo

dna Selkerf.'"

"What?"

Slower, Rtu sounded it out for him, "nam-dlo d-na sel-kerf." He paused, "Namdlo dna Selkerf"

Zreyas mouthed the words with him, then said, "Namdlo dna sel... kerf"

"Right, my boy! Well done!"

"Namdlo dna selkerf. Got it! What does it mean?" He watched the twins excitedly, waiting to hear the meaning.

Rtu leaned forward secretively, looking around, "It means... Old man and Freckles." Rtu leaned back and said with a grin as if to push it into Zreyas' brain more, "Namdlo dna Selkerf are the words for Old man and Freckles spelled backwards."

Zreyas' jaw hung slightly for a second, then he narrowed his eyes. "Should I hate you?" Then he let out a laugh.

The twins couldn't hold it in any longer, either.

"You two are ticking bandhulas! I thought it was going to be some big secret that was sacred."

"It is! But not everything has to be solemn, serious, and miserable, does it? Even *I* tire of too much of that." Rhom exclaimed in his laughter, "You are calling us! Do you want to advertise it? We can always make it more complicated and put pompous theatrics on what we do, but why do that?"

"True, Namdlo!" Wiping the moisture from the laugh away from his eyes. "I don't think I'll forget the name Selkerf."

"You won't, little buddy. You just applied them, so your mind will be more apt to remember them."

"I'll help too, Captain."

"Zrey, just use it when you want us to watch something, tell us something you think we need to know, or to validate."

"Well, let's do this then. Teach me how to fly this pheno-mi-tastic bird, Tap!"

"Yes, Captain, please step on the platform."

Suddenly, Zreyas felt a warmth at his chest and a faint high-pitched tone. He knew that warmth and reached for his chest pocket. "Oh, no..." He turned to tell the twins, but he could tell they already knew. "Ayya's in trouble. We need to go help! But how did time pass while we were here?"

Rhom and Rtu were almost to the door of the ship when Rhom said, "Say no more, my boy! Let's go! I'll explain on the way."

As he scrambled out of the ship behind the twins and ran down to the walkway, he had already concluded. "It was that Dark One episode that I had that made the time go a little, wasn't it? Are there more of those statues?"

"Maybe, my boy. We need to do some research on that," said Rhom as he ran to the strip.

"Little buddy, you are getting sharper and smarter," Rtu said. as if he was sitting in a chair and not winded or shaky from the quick pace. His voice was a picture of normal calm and bubbly excitement. "Let's go have some Earth fun! Beat you to the challenge node!"

34 Needlework & Lightning

Aqum Interruption:
— Anxiously informing you with secrecy —
Revealing time period: 1 hour in the past
Discovered by: Aqum friend challenge node
— Transmitting Event —

Emperor Rok Phaar

Emperor Rok Phaar barked out a command for the four warriors with skins of a wolf, German Shepard dog, a Janquar that would take the form of a tree, and a human girl. "Get ready to go."

The four walked up to a black and red portal in a suspended room with a walkway.

He looked at the screen in front of him, then turned to the slightly pudgy girl form with dark brown hair and large dark brown eyes about ten varSas old on earth. "Go! and don't come back till you are either dead or the girl is. What is her name?"

The four at the portal were dead silent.

Another moment passed, and it came to him. "Ah yes, Ayya. If I can't have her, then kill her."

The one in girl form looked nervous as she stared at him. A hissing sound filled his ears, and he remembered he was not alone. He fought it, but then the pain he felt brought him to his knees.

As the Emperor gasped, he looked up at the girl and said in strained tones, "Your name is Jackie."

Rok Phaar worked so hard to wrestle his mind free from the grasp of what had him that he almost fell. He leaned against the console to pull himself up. It was a lot easier to right himself now that his horns had long broken off after becoming brittle, whatever the reason was. At least they weren't in his way anymore.

All he knew right now was that he was miserable and felt hopeless. He wished one of the commanders would challenge him soon so they could put him out of this misery. Rok Phaar did not know where this... thing that called himself a king came from that was inside him.

This was his own fault, he remembered. He hadn't listened to Aaru's words of warning about someone being in his chambers. Zreyas had tried to help in something too, but he couldn't remember what it was. He couldn't remember who and why he was hunting.

"No... not again," he whispered as he felt his mind drown again in the thing's grasp. He fought hard, but he knew it wasn't enough again when he heard himself say, "The storm should be just right, so make sure the one taking that tree over doesn't move. But I prefer she barely be alive so tha—just try to keep her alive!!"

As the black mist came from Rok's body, the four faces widened in fear, then they ran into the portal and disappeared.

Alone in the room, Rok Phaar said quietly, "It shouldn't be long now, my King."

A hissing sound and black mist wafted from his own face, swirling visibly in and out of his eyes for a few moments. He felt it. Its voice was so much stronger now in his mind. He couldn't hear himself think anymore, and he didn't want to fight it anymore. He was tired... so, so tired.

"Yes, my King," he finally said, bowing his head sharply as if someone was in front of him.

—End of Aqum interruption—

ꊦꊦꊦ *Ayya* ꊦꊦꊦ

Sitting at the kitchen table, Ayya thought about how everyone was there that needed to be... just her and grandma. She usually always had people around because she had ten children, eight living. She couldn't imagine what it was like to have that many kids, but she bet they had no problem getting a team together to play stuff.

She felt so lucky she had her grandma all to herself for an entire week, and today was the first day.

Her mom and dad were good at keeping secrets, so she didn't know why they had brought her up there to stay. They had taken her sister to her other grandmother's house across town.

The kitchen still smelled amazing, even though all the food was put away, and the dishes were done. Today was her seventh birthday and lunch had been something she would remember for a long time. Her cousins had come over and they ate, played Rummy, and had a great time.

She was sitting at the table in the kitchen while her grandmother was finishing up putting things away.

Ayya kept looking at her heavy-set grandma. Her build made her almost giggle affectionately. She had short, wavy, grey hair. When she walked, she walked like her legs wouldn't move well. Maybe it had something to do with how wide apart her legs were. Ayya cocked her head. They looked like they were attached to hips that weren't wide enough or something. She couldn't help but wonder why some people were big and some were small.

"Grandma, why are you so big?"

"Well, your grandpa used to say that somehow I got sand up my crawl."

"Oh, okay." She didn't know what her crawl was, but she thought maybe one day she might be like an oyster and make a pearl. "I think I might be as big as you one day, so I can give hugs like you do. I love your hugs!"

Her grandmother laughed and turned to look at her. Her dark tan skin and dark eyes seemed bright. "And I like giving you hugs, girl." Then she turned back and started loudly putting pans back where they belonged.

Ayya loved her grandmother more than anyone other than her mother. Then she started giggling, thinking about what her grandmother had done earlier that day at the bank. She had told her to stay in the car. Ayya hadn't minded because she loved her car.

Another one of her uncles had given her what he called some 'car smarts.' He was a well-known mechanic, and he had taught her all about different kinds of cars. Her grandmother's car was a 1950 Red Chevy Bel Air with white trim. It was fun to ride and sit in, so she hadn't minded having to stay.

As she sat on the front seat on her knees, she had noticed her grandmother stopped right in the middle of the bushes and mulch that decorated the front of the bank. Her grandmother had always gotten dressed up to go to town, so she had on a red necklace, red purse hanging on her arm, her Sunday hat, and a red and white dress on.

Her grandmother loved red.

At first, she had no idea why her grandma had stopped and just stood there, but then she had realized what was going on. She was peeing, and no one was even paying attention to her!

Ayya had thought about it as she watched her. She had tried to pee in the woods many times, but unless she squatted, she always got it all over her. It amazed her she could stand normally and just pee and not get a single drop on her. After she was done, she had walked into the bank like nothing unusual happened. Ayya giggled, still thinking about it.

When her grandmother had gotten back into the car, she had asked her why she peed out there and how she didn't get any on her. "I need to learn that trick for when I'm out in the live oak woods."

Her grandmother had just shrugged like it had been normal and said, "I always have to pee when I get in that line. I just figured I would save myself the trouble of walking out and finding a bathroom. As far as how I didn't get any on me, I suppose the Lord just gave me the gift of gap."

Ayya giggled, thinking about it as she put the deck of cards she had been playing with in the box. That would be a memory she would have for the rest of her life, she thought.

Ayya felt a thrumming growl inside her. *Shut up Aaru! Why are you so angry all the time? And by the way, I can't hear you talk anymore. I don't know why, but don't get mad at me if I don't reply to what I don't understand.*

Ayya frowned, frustrated, but soon forgot it all when she followed her grandmother into the living room and watched her take out her needlework. She laid down between her feet and watched the needle poke through from below. She knew little about it because her mother never did anything like that before.

It was so peaceful there with her, and she felt a satisfaction, like things were right. As she thought about it, the needlework got messier and messier.

"I've never seen anything like that before, Grandma, but it sure looks messy."

She never flinched and said calmly, "Well, girl, it might look messy to you, but it looks beautiful to me."

Ayya watched her a while more, then out of curiosity, she got up and looked at what she was doing from the other side. She could tell her grandma knew she would get up and look—she had that grandma expression that seemed to know everything.

Her mother had said once that she was a no-nonsense kind of person and it was from having ten kids and working on a farm all her life. Her mother was the youngest of the ten, so she was much older than her other grandmother. Ayya didn't know what no-nonsense meant, but she guessed she liked it because she didn't say one thing and mean another.

As she stood beside her and looked at the needlework, she hung her jaw. It was the most amazing thing she had ever seen, with all different types of stitching. "What is this kind of needlework called, Grandma?" she said, astounded.

"It's called crewel," she said as she continued to finish the bottom stem of a wildflower near a large tree with the sun behind it.

"I don't think it is cruel, Grandma, I think it's beautiful!"

Her grandmother laughed. "Same word, different spelling and meaning."

"Oh! One of *those* words." She cocked her head as she

thought she saw moving and flipping shapes within the picture. It made her feel weird, and it reminded her of her camel saddle cap she wasn't allowed to play with anymore. Tears started running down her face at the beauty of the work her grandmother did. She didn't know why she was crying, but she felt good, so she didn't care.

She couldn't help but feel how much she loved being with her grandmother. "It's the most beautiful thing I've ever seen, grandma. Something that beautiful can only be made by someone beautiful."

Her grandmother looked up at her from her chair. "Nah, an ugly person can make beautiful things, too."

Ayya couldn't help but look at her grandmother with more love than she had ever felt for anyone before. She hugged her neck and looked at the needlework and said, "Grandma, now *you* are looking at the back side of the needlework."

She smiled and pulled her around into her lap and gave her a big hug. Ayya thought she would squeeze her to death... literally. She was a hefty and strong woman, and Grandma's hugs were deadly. She finally let her go and put her down on the floor.

As Ayya thought a moment, she finally said, "Now I just need to find the front side of Daddy."

Grandma smiled with warmth. "Let's work on seeing the front side of him together."

They both smiled at each other and nodded.

"You still have some time to play. Go see if Jackie wants to play outside for a bit before it gets too dark," Grandma said, rocking in her chair putting away her needlework.

"Thank you, Grandma. I lo-ove youuuuuu!"

Her grandmother laughed. "I love you too, baby girl. Have fun."

Ayya opened the front door and pushed the rusty

hinged screen door open, feeling content. She glanced back at her grandmother and felt like she just wanted to get one more look at her.

Grandma smiled, then leaned her head back and closed her eyes. She did that from time to time.

Ayya looked up at the sky outside and she could tell a storm was coming. Her grandmother had taught her over the last couple of years all about what she called 'weather sense.' She sniffed the air to see if she could tell what type of storm it would be.

Her uncle that lived near her grandmother had also taught her a lot about it. He had told her that she was a natural at it. She loved the smell of some types of storms. She had grown up in storm country, and the smell was a telltale sign. "Storm's coming, Grandma, and it smells like a thunder and lightning storm."

Her grandmother didn't open her eyes, but said, "That's right. Best keep watch, but it's a little ways off yet I think."

"Yes, ma'am. I'll be careful." Ayya shut the door and started skipping down the packed dirt road that was covered in sand between her grandmother's house and her uncle's house where Jackie lived. She decided it was a good time to talk to Aaru, since no one was around. She didn't know if he was really listening, but she wanted to give Aaru the description of where they were in case he could see.

"Aaru, my grandma and uncle live on the same land, but built their houses an eighth mile apart. Jackie is my cousin, and she is fun to play with. Look at all these lovely trees along the road, they are sycamore trees. Isn't their bark the neatest thing? I love the different colors the peeling bark shows under it. They are really good for shade too! Grandma says the one by her library over there is over a hundred years old. It's huge!"

Ayya felt her guts lurch and that thrumming growl again.

"There you go again. Stop that! I'm just trying to show you around. We are passing what Grandma says is the library. It's an enormous garage full of books. My Grandma loves to read. I'm surprised she wasn't reading when she was doing the needlework. Most people think Grandma is stupid and uneducated because she lives in the country and worked on farms all her life."

She faced the library, feeling a little angry that people were so mean about their thoughts. She loved counting the books in the little windows up top. "One, two, three..." She stopped. The library looked much odder than she remembered. "I thought there were four walls and four windows on each wall, but..."

Ayya walked around the library out of curiosity, counting the walls and windows. She came full circle and stood back out at the road. "There are six walls and six windows."

She felt her guts jerk again sharply with that familiar growl thrumming inside her. "I know it is really weird, Aaru, but you don't have to get upset about it. Maybe counting the books will help you calm down."

"One, two... three, four, five... six." She counted the other windows coming to the same number. She thought that was odd, too. That never happened before because the books were different thicknesses. "Six book spines in each window."

Ayya skipped in a circle. "That is a lot of sixes! Six, six, six. I wonder what the total number for that is. Let's see..."

Ayya walked toward the edge of the road to look for a stick. Aaru lurched inside her again, hard. The growling thrummed, but never stopped completely. It just evened out. She learned to ignore him, but he was really getting irritating. "Aaru, you are grating on my nerves. Please stop."

She loved being barefoot in the sand, but she didn't like going out in the grass of the sand hills, so she didn't step out in it till she found the stick she wanted. She didn't want to step on those sand spurs in the grass. They were nasty when you stepped on them.

Ayya balanced herself carefully as she walked off the grass and onto the sand again. She started drawing out lines and numbers to figure out how many books were in all the windows. Before she could finish the multiplication of the first two sixes, she heard a few soft footsteps.

"Whatcha doin', Ayya?"

She looked up and saw her dark-eyed and dark-haired cousin and smiled. "Hi, Jackie! I'm counting Grandma's books in the library windows." She pointed toward the library. "Did it always have six walls, or is that new? It all still looks old, but I don't remember that many."

"No, it used to have four walls, but yesterday it suddenly had more. And look..." She pointed and walked toward her house a few steps. "Here. I already figured that out. I did the same thing you did. See?"

Jackie pointed to the marks on the driveway road. A few tire marks messed up part of it, but it was clear she did. "Two hundred and sixteen books in the windows. Want to see how many there are inside?"

35 Where s Bill?

"We better ask Grandma first. Her hugs are strong, and I would hate to see how strong she is when she is mad."

"Okay, but I know she will say it's okay. She always said, 'if a kid is curious about a book, then I aim to please.'"

They giggled and started walking toward their grandma's house, squishing and twisting their feet into the sand as they walked for fun.

"But yeah, when Grandma gets mad, I run, just like we did when we ran from Aunt Martie that one time."

"Oh yeah, I remember that!" said Ayya. She shook her head as she stepped onto the sidewalk to the front door. "When her snuff changes sides of her mouth, run for your life! But... she was right to be mad. Uncle El conked you on the head with his arm cast while he was drunker than a skunk. That knot on your head was huge."

"But I often wonder how many times that snuff changed sides when she cracked her cast iron frying pan on his head, knocking him out with it."

Ayya reached out and turned the doorknob as she felt

Aaru's thrumming growl jolt. "Well, I wasn't going to go back and find out."

"Me either, but that doesn't stop me from wondering."

They jerked when they heard the sharp crack of thunder, not expecting it so soon.

"Wow, that was fast coming in," Ayya said. Not finding her grandmother in her chair, she looked into and through the kitchen.

"Yeah, it's odd. It shouldn't have been here for another hour or so, judging by the smell."

"That's what I thought." Ayya went through the kitchen and to the bedroom. "Grandma!"

"Where are you, Grandma?" yelled Jackie.

"By the way, where is Bill? He's always with you."

"He ran off sniffing something when I came to see you on the road. I'm surprised he isn't back yet. He never leaves me alone."

Ayya looked through the window to see if the car was still there. "Well, her car is here. She must be here somewhere. But this is weird."

"Well, come on, she won't mind us going into the library. She's probably in the bathroom or something, and I don't want to be here when that door opens!"

Ayya nodded, scrunching up her nose. "Yeah, okay, let's go." She ran to the door and almost shut the door in Jackie's face, catching herself. She was excited. She loved old things, how they felt, and trying to guess their history and who might have touched it. Sometimes, when she was concentrating on the object, she would get an image in her mind or superimposed visions. Sometimes she even felt she was being helped to remember things.

Aaru jolted inside her again, and that thrumming growl was extra loud this time. She had never felt these strong reactions from him before. It made her stop just in front of the looming shed that was the library. *Are you going to settle down? This should be fun! Why are you being this way today? I know you give me warnings sometimes, but you been doing this all day and nothing is happening to be afraid about.*

"What's wrong?" asked Jackie, looking a little concerned.

Ayya shook her head and sighed. "Nothing, I just had a thought that something wasn't right. Maybe it is the six walls."

Jackie propped her elbow on her other forearm against her stomach. "It does seem weird." She looked up at the shed, but then she said, "But we should still have fun checking the inside out, right? It's not like the building is some evil spirit."

What she said made sense to Ayya. She looked up and said, "You are right, let's go! Where's Bill?"

As they ran to the entrance that was opposite the road, she told her that he would be along. Ayya never understood why the entrance would be away from the road, but she kind of liked it that way.

"It's really neat inside," said Jackie. "She has ladders we can climb to see the books up high now, too." Then she stopped as if in afterthought. "Wait a second. Now that you asked, I'm getting worried about Bill."

"Yeah, you can't even go to the bathroom without him. It just seems weird he isn't with you."

Jackie turned around and cupped her hands around her mouth and shouted, "Bi-ill! Here, Bill!" She looked around the area and finally dropped her hands and said, "Stupid Dog, he's been acting weird today, now that I think about it."

Ayya followed her cousin to the door and watched her lift the latch. The old and frustrated hinges creaked open. She saw nothing but darkness inside, except for the lighted windows up high. Being outside in the brightness didn't make it exactly easy to see inside.

Jackie took a step in and said, "Oh, the flashlight isn't here on the little shelf. That's *weird*. There is *always* one there. I'll run to the house and get one." Jackie started running and turned back partially to holler, "Be back in a jiffy!"

Ayya started giggling as she watched her cousin run up the road because the sand flew up behind her from her fast feet on the sandy road, running full speed. She admired her running that fast on thick loose sand and figured she was used to it. The land was so flat that she watched her open the door and disappear into the house.

While she waited, she looked around. The area around the shed for a good way was a mixture of sand and grass. When she looked toward the house to see if she could see her grandma, Ayya could have sworn she saw Jackie walk behind the car. She moved away from the shed to double check. No one was there. She sure felt Aaru jerk her insides in many directions, almost making her sick. The thrumming roar was so loud in her mind's ears that she thought she might go mad. *What... is wrong with you today, Aaru? We can't live like this. We need to find some way to talk again.*

Ayya noticed the wind picking up as she looked back toward her uncle's house. Jackie was on her way back, running fast, sand flying up behind her. When she was halfway back, something caught Jackie's attention to her right, and she stopped. She changed course and ran into the tree line.

She must have found Bill, Ayya thought. Just as she shrugged, a crack of lightning hit so close it rumbled the ground with the thunder right behind it. "Wow, less than one second between them. That storm is almost right on top of us, Aaru. I better yell for Jackie. We need to go inside. I bet Grandma is going to get worried."

Ayya yelled for Jackie, but she never heard a response.

The lightning cracked again, lighting up the whole area.

"I better step inside the library, Aaru. I hope Jackie and Grandma are okay." She cupped her hands around her mouth. "Grandmaaa! I'm in the library! I'm okay!"

After Ayya stepped inside, it took several seconds to let her eyes adjust. Sure enough, she saw the ladder that Jackie talked about on the opposite wall. The walls were full of books to the ceiling. Last time she had been here, they were only a little over three quarters of the way up.

Then something grabbed her attention. There were only *four* walls in here, not six. Ayya walked out of the library, no longer paying attention to the storm. Sure enough, there were six. Suddenly, that inner growl of Aaru sounded, but this time, it was menacing and low. *That* got her attention... that was *way* too different.

"Aaru, what is wrong?"

A loud crack of lightning lit up with sharp thunder that felt like it would crack her ear drums open. It seemed like it was amplified somehow.

Aaru's growl started again, just as she saw Bill coming around the corner, head lowered, stalking, and hair raised on his back. Ayya noticed he had blood dripping from his mouth.

"Oh, no! Are you okay, Bill?" She approached him with concern.

Aaru sharply growled and jolted inside her.

Bill launched himself toward her. Somehow, she reacted faster than she thought possible and threw her forearm up just in time. The rest seemed like a blurred whirlwind.

The dog knocked Ayya to the ground, hard. Over the

course of the next few seconds, she felt the sharp pains as teeth punctured her skin in different places, especially on the right side of her shoulder, neck, and face.

Just as Bill had her pinned, she realized Bill was too strong for her. She started crying and couldn't think.

"It's okay, Ayya, I'm here! Keep defending yourself. That's not Bill!"

The voice was not familiar to her. She couldn't see well with her right eye—something was coloring her vision red. But out of the left eye, she could see something small with what looked like sticks in their hands sailing through the air toward Bill.

The animal yelped, it startled Ayya. She quickly hit the dog in the face, surprising herself, knocking the dog off her.

A blur of what looked like a miniature man was stabbing the dog twice in the side near the front and several times in the neck and face.

He looked familiar as he approached her, putting what she realized was his weapons back into their holders. Who was this little person again? Oh! It was her old toy! She had lost him when her daddy threw him into the woods. But now he was here again, but he looked different.

He walked up to her. Someone had changed his clothes and now he had a bow on his back. As small as he was, he helped her sit up. He was strong! She leaned up against the library doorway. Aaru was silent except for an almost harmonic hum. She watched him come around in front of her.

"Ayya, I'm Zreyas. You aren't safe here. Can you slide inside the library and shut the door? Get up on the ladder and climb as high as you can. I need to go help protect you from the others. Aaru will guide you... listen to him. His instincts are good."

She nodded and slid inside as she shook, and Zreyas closed the door. She sat there a moment, trying to understand what had just happened.

Aaru's growl vibrated menacingly through her again.

Ayya's eyes grew wide when she remembered her toy had told her to climb the ladder as high as she could. She staggered to the ladder as she wondered why everything looked red. She willed herself to climb that ladder. At least she could move the books out of the window to see outside if she could get up there.

That thought gave her motivation. She climbed one rung at a time. Then she thought about her grandma and felt herself panic. She climbed faster and threw the books in the window to the side. She watched them hit the floor. "Sorry, Grandma, I need to see out."

Just as she turned to see through the window, she saw the enormous sycamore tree first. Just then, lighting struck it right at the fork with a crack that shook the entire building. The lightning ricocheted off the fork of the tree and split it in two, then hit the library right where she had been sitting on the floor just a minute earlier.

Ayya screamed as she held her ears, feeling her body shake all over. She felt herself starting to fall, but she gripped the ladder just in time. She heard someone call her name, but it didn't register who it was in her mind.

"Ayya!"

She knew it sounded familiar, but all she could do was shut her eyes tight, waiting for another strike. Then she registered a soothing crackling sound. It reminded her of a fireplace, and Ayya was feeling warm, as if she was sitting in front of one. It relaxed her.

"Ayya, it's Uncle Ben! Look up out the window! Hurry!"

She opened her eyes slowly and lifted her head as she stepped up one more ladder rung. There he was, down at the road just below her.

"Listen to me, Ayya. Someone is at the house to get a ladder, but it won't be in time. I need you to be brave and do something!"

Ayya sniffed and nodded to him.

"Grab one of Grandma's old hardback books and use it to smash the glass. Wrap one of your legs around the rungs of the ladder like I taught you last time you were here when we were painting the house. Safety first! Don't panic, but hurry, the library is on fire!"

Ayya whipped her head around. Just behind her, the whole door side of the library was burning and shattered away. It was angry.

She heard a tap on the roof and a voice said, "You can do this, Ayya. Listen to Aaru. He will guide you." Then she didn't hear him anymore.

The wall fell apart where it was burning and she thought she could get down off the ladder and run through it. But she heard Aaru's thrumming growl. Then she looked back out the window and nodded to her uncle.

Ayya grabbed the ladder and stiffly through the pain lifted her bloody leg over a rung and hooked her ankle around the rung below it. Then she reached to the next window over and grabbed a large faded hardback that had the title 'Heart of Odium' on it. She didn't know who odium was, but she picked it up with both hands, letting her legs hold her steady. It was heavy and hard.

She grunted as she straightened herself, trying her best to get balance.

"Hurry, Ayya! Break the glass and make sure you knock off all the sharp edges!"

Ayya nodded, and she heard Aaru's gentle hum within her. She paid attention to the difference in his voice. She didn't hear the words, but she felt the voice.

— Yes, do this... this is the correct way, they seemed to say in the vibrations.

She grunted loudly as she shoved the spine of the book into the glass. The pieces of wood frame kept it from breaking. So, she tried again, and yet again, she couldn't get it to break.

"Try harder, Ayya. Use the corner of the bottom of the spine!" coached her uncle.

Ayya turned. The fire was almost to the ladder, and her back was hot and stinging now. She started to panic, but she saw Zreyas where the book used to be. Had he been there the whole time?

"I'll help. Lean back and hold the book so I can stand on the ladder rung."

She nodded in a spastic way and leaned back, holding the book in her arms.

Zreyas pulled his axe out and climbed in front of her. "I'm not supposed to do this because of balances, but..." He swung the axe hard at the bottom and it cut the wood divider through in one hit. The glass cracked. He moved out of her way and popped back to where the book used to be on the shelf. "Now try. You can do this, Ayya."

Ayya nodded, feeling a determination. If her little toy could do it, she could. She felt Aaru's hum, and she focused just above where Zreyas had cut. With all her might, she hit it with the spine of the book and it cracked the wooden pane dividers, cracking more glass.

"That's it! Again, Ayya!"

She did it again, and it broke all the way through, losing the grip on the book. It fell into the fire that was burning the ladder now. She looked toward Zreyas and he smiled and nodded.

"Good job! You know what to do."

Ayya grabbed the book nearest to her and used it to

break the rest of the glass away until there were no sharp edges. Ayya grinned, proud of herself, and she looked at Zreyas—only he wasn't there anymore. Had she imagined him?

She unwrapped her leg and used it to step up.

"Good girl, Ayya," her uncle praised. "Now crawl out of the window and hang on as long as you can till you are ready. Then let go and I will catch you. I promise I *will* catch you!"

Aaru's hum was loud now.

Ayya nodded to her uncle and did as instructed. Her body shook badly, but Aaru's hum seemed to help.

She almost didn't fit through the little window, but somehow she did it. Ayya did a thing she did when she was climbing in the live oak trees back home. She got a reverse grip on the edge of the window and went out head first and flipped through the window slowly. She used her feet at the edge of the window to catch and steady herself and let her hands go. Then she held on tight and let her feet go.

Her heels slammed against the wall of the library and she let out a yelp of pain from the shock with her already hurting body. Tears streamed down her face as she hung.

"Are you ready, Ayya? I am. Let go!"

Her uncle sounded confident, and she trusted him. She let go. Sure enough, he caught her, though she bumped her head.

She wrapped her arms around him and cried.

"It's all right, Ayya. You were so brave! I'm so proud of you. You did it!" He pulled her away from him for a second and his eyes went wide.

Ayya noticed her uncle's clothes were wet and red, but his expression was full of panic. She heard Aaru's hum, and she knew she would be okay.

"It's okay, Uncle Ben. I might look bad, but you are just seeing the back side of the needlework. Grandma and I just talked about that. I'll look okay when you see the other side after I heal."

Her uncle wrapped his arms around her firmly and he ran up the road toward the house just as the fire department showed up, driving up their driveway.

As she jostled from his run, she noticed Jackie sitting on the porch and sobbing into her hands. To her left, she saw Bill, with his throat ripped to shreds.

She laid her head down against her uncle's neck and shoulder. Her mind and body went numb and all she could think to do was talk to Aaru. *Thank you for saving us. I understand now when you growl; it is a warning. I'm sorry it took so long to figure that out.*

Ayya barely had the strength to ask her uncle a question, but somehow, she already knew the answer. "Uncle Ben?"

"Yes Ayya?" he said, winded as he ran.

Tears spilled down her face even before she asked, "Where's Grandma?"

36 The Ones

Zreyas poked his head around a part of the shredded and broken tree. The tree was monstrous, and he walked through large splintered parts peeking through them. He directed his attention on a spot of the tree where the rings were exposed. "Whoa!" he said with a lowered voice, standing in the rain. "You been around a long time."

After doing some calculations, he estimated that it had to be at least one-hundred ten varSas old. "I'm bringing you the sorries, old one. This Dark One has really messed up a lot of..."

He suddenly noticed Ayya being carried toward the house. Knowing his brother was part of her made his heart crack a little. She seemed so much more grown up than before.

Her cousin looked up from sobbing over her dog and saw Ayya. She went wide eyed, and he heard her ask if Ayya was going to be okay, then got up and followed them into the house.

Zreyas sighed and wondered about her grandmother. He hadn't seen her while he was skulking around.

Paul, the fireman and his sidekick paramedic, came scrambling up with gear. He was glad Rtu and Rhom were there. Rhom and his fire crew were making their way to the burning building while Rtu and his partner paramedic were taking a stretcher into the house.

That off his mind, Zreyas looked at the tree. Black mist sneakily oozed from the exposed rings of the tree.

"You have murdered a beautiful species of plant by taking over its form, but you have my vow, you won't live to leave it." His anger filled his inner compartment and his eyes moistened when he thought about what had happened here today.

Zreyas did not know what he was doing, but he put his hands on the tree. As he was getting ready to convert his energy to a high frequency, he attempted to put himself into that state he had been in twice before. One of them being when he converted energy to give to Rhom while they put Ayya and Aaru together to save them.

It was so distinct there would be no way he could forget what it was like. Even if he couldn't get into it, he would pretend he was and open his mind and senses enough to kill that mist. He hadn't forgotten he was a target and hunted, and he intended to use it to his advantage.

He went over it in his mind to make sure he got it right. It was still new to him. To achieve that state, he would fill his anger chamber. Then he reminded himself to picture creating a high frequency filter door on the chamber by sending good thoughts and emotions like laughing, the feelings of freedom, the love, good memories, and peace.

Then when he would let that war aura go through that door to raise the frequencies to something that would heal or create. The frequency would be too expansive, too fast, for a low frequency to adjust to quick enough with the force. It wouldn't hurt the tree, but it would kill the dark mist.

He was in a hurry and he only had one shot at killing this Dark One's game piece that took over that tree. He wondered who the Janquar used to be and if he knew him. Whoever it was, it wasn't them anymore, and they were a slave now, enthralled by the Dark One, he told himself.

Zreyas began converting the pent-up anger to a much higher frequency, trying to help the tree and kill the minion at the same time. He might not be successful in helping the tree, but at least he would kill the minion of the Dark One. He focused and used his aura to push it to the tree. *I hope this doesn't hurt you, tree, but I don't think you would want to house who is inside you now because they would end up killing you, anyway. I hope you accept this gift for you on this day.*

Zreyas felt the struggle of the dark mist, almost like it tried to push his hands away. He knew then it was working, and he renewed his efforts. It wasn't long and he couldn't feel the presence anymore.

Then he heard what he had expected to hear at some point—at least some type of threat. This was a long, deep growl that made his neck tingle.

His senses were extremely acute at this point because of what he had been doing. Zreyas did a Q-leap to flip himself around but waited a second in the quantum to see what he was dealing with.

In the crisp darkness of the quantum, he saw enough in that short time to understand it was either an enthralled wolf or a form taken as a wolf for the challenge. He hadn't learned to see the difference yet, or he couldn't think fast enough in that time to let all the visual information set in. He wasn't sure which. His guess was that it was a form from the Janquar challenge node.

As soon as he thought about how he wanted to land, he came out of the quantum with his weapons drawn, facing a wolf much larger than himself, about two meters away. With a lowered head and slow prowling step, the wolf lowered his center of balance, ready to pounce.

Just as Zreyas started a Q-leap, he barely heard Tap say, — Captain, watch out!, a split second before it knocked him so hard sideways that he heard his head and neck do a sickening series of cracks right before he went into the quantum.

Zreyas turned to see an enthralled form of Ayya's cousin. She was hitting him with a sanded club with a white ball imprinted on the side. It was almost as if the scene had frozen, but he watched the image of his body stutter and flicker. He instinctively tried to separate himself from his body as it started to break apart in slow motion.

He had no idea what to do about it. All he knew right then was that his body was going to die, and he was glad he wouldn't have to feel that impact. His horns were strong, but they could never hold up to impact like that without breaking. That was a Janquar with full base strength in that form.

He consoled himself with the thought that Ayya was safe for now, at least with Rhom and Rtu around.

Whether it be from delirium or him passing away, Zreyas saw the energy signatures of all the firemen and people at the house nearby. Paul the firefighter was near at the burning shed with one arm up in the air.

The fire had energy too, so it was difficult to see what he was doing, where he started, and where the fire did. Knowing him, he was probably doing a good job fighting the fire. Rhom would find out soon enough that he would be dead.

The entire scene slowly dimmed and faded into black. *I'm sorry Tap. We just found each other, and I've gone and done what most tunnel newborns do when they first start learning to fight. I guess we are always newborns, no matter how much experience we get.*

He heard no response from Tap. *Everything* was silent. He never realized until now that there were always sounds around. No circulation sound in his ears, no breathing sounds—he had always taken those sounds for granted.

— Don't look at your body in the physical. It will alter the quantum potential. Even here, balances must be kept.

He didn't know who that was, or what to say, but he knew what they said was genuine guidance, and did as instructed. He would have said something, but he couldn't. The quantum space was now looking raw and bumpy everywhere. He realized it was signatures of energy he had never seen before.

— You can now see energy that the incarnate eyes can't see of any species. Don't be alarmed.

Zreyas' awareness tried to blink to clear his vision, an old habit learned from being in a body, and how odd that was to try to do things in the quantum as if he was in one. He thought it was interesting.

— I don't know why you are so surprised. You still have the energy signature of your incarnation. Why are you having problems with your Q-leap? Ask yourself.

He wasn't sure why he had issues with his Q-leap or that he was even doing one. Then he saw the energy around him and since he literally -was- the quantum leap, he never thought twice about it. He guessed as an incarnate he would see it as a separate action because of the limitations. But he also knew that he, too, was limited because he was still attached to his body. Oh yes, he had almost forgotten the body they had instructed him to not look at. He couldn't remember if it was attached or not. No, it was... mirrored. He felt the knowledge come to him, quantum mirroring.

Zreyas remembered Rhom as he saw waves of energy and his science lessons in the dying dimension. But he noticed something he hadn't fully realized before. Waves and particles, caused by thought, could exist in the quantum at the same time.

— You are getting closer, keep learning. It will also make your Q-leaps... more.

He wondered what it meant by more.

— More than 'just is.'

That was cryptic, but he continued learning. He felt his awareness becoming more educated. He was finding out differences between what was going on around him.

— Your life is moving fast. Faster than your...

Zreyas remembered his life. So much had changed so fast. He learned so much. But it was so fast he felt like he couldn't take it.

— I see you are not ready for the next expanse. Why is that?

The numbers 1111 came toward him, but as a frequency. How did he know that? He didn't know, he just did.

He didn't know who this was talking to him. It wasn't male or female, robotic or organic, but it *was* of both high and low frequencies. Zreyas realized he was still thinking separate. He wasn't an incarnate anymore, but he still thought like one.

His life had changed so fast, and he realized that his perceptions of everything, except for one, had changed too.

— 1111 Now you ar—1111—ight track. 1111

The energy signatures representing 1111 images started flying toward him faster, yet they were also part of him.

— 1111 1111

Then he remembered the dying dimension and Rhom telling him about the tick-tock number 1:11. The old man had said there was more meaning to it than he had explained. That stuck in his mind more than the explanation itself. More...

— 1111.

Everything in his life had progressed, except... more. No, not more. Think like an incarnate to understand, he told himself. It was so hard to think as an incarnate now. All his perceptions had changed except... more.

What would Rhom, Tulyata, or Rtu say to fill in that blank? Nothing came to him. He would have to rely on himself for that answer.

— 1111 came toward him.

There was that number again, and it felt like it came from the same source. Whatever was keeping him here in the quantum was connected to that answer. He decided to *be* the answer. Maybe it would come just like being in the place he wanted to Q-leap to.

— 1111

He felt like he was coming close, but he still couldn't see himself objectively. Maybe that was the answer, he told himself. His life as an incarnate had grown so fast and all his perspectives changed and grown but one—how he perceived himself.

— 1111 Now you ha—1111 the answer to both problems.

Both problems? He thought back to when he first found himself here. The energy signatures changed to follow his thoughts. He was using the quantum and also part of it. Then the words that had been said to him replayed.

— I don't know why you are so surprised. You still have the energy signature of your incarnation. Why are you having problems with your Q-leap?

It was right after he had been told not to look at his incarnate body and he started noticing wave-particle duality. Then he noticed the energy signature of his Q-leap. On the right end of the arch wave, there was the part of him that was currently being hit, well killed.

— 1111 the perception of yourself.

On the left there was the part of him that was where he was going to land perfectly fine.

Why was he having problems Q-leaping? He felt numb, like he was losing who they were and all their memories.

An '1111' energy signature swished past him four times and each of the four times came a word.

— You

    — are

        — not

            — alone.

That felt good. They needed to know that somehow, and they were glad they weren't alone. It made them feel better. How could they feel better if they weren't still alive? They had grown so fast and all their perspectives changed. Their frequency had risen tremendously, and... *they* were helping with something important. Wait, weren't they... *male? Yes, We seem to remember that part.*

Another '1111' signature swished through him this time and the echoes said, — Hear...

Waves ran through him again. He was feeling more awake now and remembered he was an incarnate individual having some sort of experience.

— 1111... Deceased in your body's world...

Someone was trying to help him, but right now, it didn't make sense or mean much to him. The understanding of what that meant would be nice to know.

Someone once told him he naturally used the quantum.

He remembered that part. So he had the idea of putting himself out in the quantum as if he already understood all this, as if he knew what it all meant. So he did.

The understanding came to him in wave frequencies. It was a language that he was beginning to understand consciously.

Who do I know that died that might try to help me? And with those words, waves of energy and frequency streamed through again, as if in answer to his question.

He found himself being just a little more defined in his mind now that he had a focus, rather than an all-encompassing numbness.

— 1111

The tick-tock room came to his memory again, seeing the hands on the clock. Then he thought about the portal Rhom talked—

— 111

The portal was what saved Rhom.

— 111

Tulyata and Rtu were who—

— 111

He found himself repeating things over and over. Tulyata an—

— 111… 1111

Tulyata... who made the portal.

— 111… 1111

He had stood up to her defending himself and who he was, that he was just as... wait. Looking at his body in the world, he knew he was dead now.

He looked toward where the energy that waved through him normally came... nothing. Then he looked back at the energy signature of his Q-leap and then recognition hit him. It resembled a scale, something like... Tulyata's scales. It was tipping toward the dead side.

Zreyas realized he didn't want to die, but wasn't he

dead already? He shifted his gaze over to the result of the Q-leap where he was supposed to be. The image of him was now faded, but not gone. That was where he would have popped through the quantum, weapons drawn, and ready to defend himself... defend Ayya and... help try to wake her up. He was glad he remembered something specific.

He noticed the scales were now tipped evenly again.

— 1111

There it was again! He must be headed in the right direction. When he saw the result of the Q-leap again, it was back to being clear and easy to see, and he started repeating things again. His life and growth had progressed faster than his mind could keep up with.

He looked at the result of his Q-leap. A good representation of that. He never thought he could ever do something like that... but he did it naturally now.

But his mind still couldn't believe it. After all the things he had done to hurt so many, he didn't feel he should be one of the ones that could do that. He looked at the version of him, now splattering from the impact. That is what he judged he deserved.

The scales tipped rapidly toward the dead Zreyas. Now he saw the pattern.

Zreyas looked toward the result of the Q-leap again and it was almost gone. Instinctively, he put himself there. The more he did, the more he remembered.

— 1111 Quantu— —irroring

What he heard sounded cut off, but he understood the frequency language. Quantum mirroring. He had no idea what that was, but hadn't he heard that term before once? He was not-so-science compared to Rhom.

Then he heard a song from far off. A song of tones that touched his essence. He felt warmth in his existence as he watched the result of his Q-leap become more real and the scales tipped over in its favor. The love he felt from the sources guiding him was overwhelming, but he now saw the quanta frequency coming through him. He would never forget how it imprinted on his mind and it had the lovings for him.

He sent out thoughts in a song to them all that were helping him, wherever they were:

During my falls, into doubt and fear,
I will put myself in the eye of my storms,
I will know it...
I will feel it...
Your love and guidance are there.

He realized it had always been, and always would be, his choice how he saw himself. Everything had progressed for him except in how he perceived himself, and it always jerked him back.

Zreyas looked at the result of the Q-leap and thought, *I m already there.*

The scales of the Q-leap tipped to stopping toward the result of the leap, and he imagined the clink it would have made in Tulyata's dimension.

Zreyas planted his feet on the ground, weapons drawn, and his war aura immediately converted to the love he felt for everyone he knew he had grown to love.

Still high on his quantum experience and discovery, he let his aura blast out with the most incredible force he had ever thought possible.

When it was over, he said, "The only thing holding me back is the perception of myself. And that, you piece of soul killing mag-shit, isn't a problem now."

The wolf and the impostor form of Jackie were

collapsing from the high frequency blast, but he wasn't taking any chances. Zreyas walked up to the wolf and girl and said, "Eat some love and compassion for a change. It's to *die* for!"

With that, he gave all that anger, guilt, and remorse he had into the conversion and both bodies exploded out away from him. The viscera hit the burning library and hissed, making Paul the fireman look his way. He gave him a thumbs up and Zreyas nodded.

There was one more thing he had to do while they were finishing up their jobs, and that was to find Grandma. Ayya would be okay in Rtu's hands, but he also knew, no matter where he found Grandma, many would cry for her that day.

37 The Answer

As soon as Zreyas, Rhom, and Rtu approached the ship, Zreyas spoke to Tap and gave her the access phrase. The door opened, and he just stared up at it. The walk to the ship had been quiet.

"Well, that ticking stunk like a rotting pile of mag-shit, but at least Ayya is okay."

"I would have to agree, my boy," said Rhom. "That will be a large hump for Ayya to navigate."

"It is sad," added Rtu. "That dog really chewed Ayya up, but I don't think she will scar or have any permanent issues."

"Thanks to you, Freckles." Zreyas gave Rtu a good hard pat on the back of the knee.

Rtu started laughing. "That tickles!"

Zreyas grinned as he started walking up the ramp. He shook his head in thought, then decided to just say it. "As much as I don't like to say it, I have to admire the perfect strategy in all that they did. It shows what we are up against. I'm confident about what I do, but that was some ticking-cunning strategy. It's like they learn each time. It makes me a little nervous. I'm used to fighting brute force vs brute force, not intelligence."

"My boy, don't let it get to you. We have some intelligence on this side too, remember?"

Rtu made a fist and threw it up in celebration. "Oh yeah! We certainly do! We won that battle, though it caused scarring inside for those that made it through." He let his arm drop. "But we need to take the wins we can get."

"Well said, brother, well said."

All three of them entered the ship, and they all sat down.

"Welcome aboard Captain, Master Rhom, and Freckles."

Both of the twins returned their greetings, and they all had a little small talk. Everyone seemed a little... awkward to Zreyas. He didn't know why. Then he noticed the twins were looking at him and their faces were the picture of visage expressions, not his friends.

"What?" Zreyas said sourly, tired of feeling more than a little awkward in his already dark mood.

He figured he would break whatever awkwardness they were having with something that would interest them. "I think Tulyata was communicating with me when I was in the quantum."

The twins hung their jaws, staring at him like he was crazy.

"Really true. Do you remember that 1:11 on the clock in the dying dimension?"

They nodded and looked interested.

"That quantum experience was... something I'm not sure how to explain." He told about his experience in the quantum the best he could. They apparently hadn't had a clue what happened then because they were shocked. After he thought about it, he reasoned just because they were visages, didn't mean they were consciously aware of everything, especially if they were incarnated in a partial way.

"We were going to ask you if something happened in the quantum because your Q-leap looked odd. The air warped and fluctuated. One moment I saw your body splattered all over the place, then the next moment we saw you getting hit, and the next you were back on the other side of the dog. I figured some sort of quantum mirroring was going on. But as a firefighter in a body, it was hard to tell for sure."

"And that converted war aura blast was akin to a small nuclear blast," said Rtu.

Rhom nodded with a grin. "Being semi-incarnated as a challenge form, we know mechanics of it, but we just didn't know how you got the force capacity or what prompted it. I don't think you need to explain now, my boy."

"Anyway, I told you I didn't think Tulyata was dead. Now I *know* she isn't. In the future, maybe I can help you contact her... somehow."

"How so, my boy?"

"I don't think I will ever forget the energy signature she communicated with. But I'm not so sure how I can relay that."

"What a great idea, my boy!" Rhom turned to his brother. "What do you think? Maybe we can all three do that project together like we did the armor."

Rtu raised both fists in celebration with a smile. "I love our group projects, and that project will be for the historical records when the time is right."

Zreyas spent the next hour trying to explain his experience with his so-called death. He then asked Rhom about quantum mirroring and he gave him a short explanation and said it would take more than a few minutes to explain that. He had basically told him that the vision of both sides and the scales was a perfect replica summation of it.

"Giving the thankings to you, we will work on contacting her, but it won't be today. I got business to take care of on Tarq!" Zreyas clapped his hands together, ready to move on.

Rtu and Rhom exchanged glances and grinned as Zreyas turned facing forward on the platform. Everything adjusted to his size and raised the platform up.

"Don't be surprised if you get sick the first few times doing this, my boy," warned Rhom. "But, we can help do most things right now so you can get the feel of connecting with Tap. One step at a time. You can gain more steps as we make more trips."

"I'll be *fi-ine*! So how do I do this?"

38 The Show

When the ship stopped, Zreyas stumbled off the platform and heaved up what his stomach had in it, violently.

"Captain! Are you okay?"

"He will be fine, Tap. We expected this. It's why we didn't want him to try controlling you until he got his quantum space stomach regulated," Rhom said, chuckling.

"Here, little buddy, let me give you a little medicinal aid. I brought it along, expecting you might need it." Rtu approached him and stooped down, opening a jug. He held it close to Zreyas' face. "Breathe in deeply."

Zreyas heaved again, then did as instructed. As he took the fumes into his body, the spasms of heaving began to subside almost immediately.

"Ticking... auu-hell," he lurched out, then took in another long breath of the medicine Rtu held for him.

Rtu handed him the bottle, jug sized for Zreyas.

He held it protectively, rolled to his side, and closed his eyes. "You warned me... I didn't listen. Serves me right."

Rtu sat back down and plopped his elbow on the arm of the station chair. "A few times under your belt and you will be quantum traveling with Tap like a veteran. It will get easier each time. When I was with Rhom the first time, even *I* got nauseous." He chuckled, "I feel for you."

"It's a good thing we could make it in one jump, my boy!"

Rhom's voice seemed annoyingly loud to his stomach somehow, and he pulled the stopper from the jug and inhaled again.

"We are going to try to get some gates in soon for you to make travel quicker, with more stability."

Zreyas stood and staggered over to the platform, lowering for him already. "Tap, can we make a place for this at my platform here so in case this happens again, it will be ready?"

"Certainly, Captain."

The stem of the console morphed and a round shelf with half walls emerged.

Zreyas walked over and lowered the bottle carefully into it and took another whiff before putting the stopper back in. Tap gently tightened the grip around it and sealed it so that it would not jump or slide out.

"Giving the thankings to you, Tap." Zreyas turned around. "So, are we ready for this?"

"No, we are not. We aren't going," Rhom said. "We will stay here on the ship doing some work, along with watching you. However, I would suggest one thing: put Tap in stealth. We don't need anyone knowing she exists for as long as possible."

"Tap, until I say otherwise, stay in stealth unless you need to do something critical. Then we can talk about it. I don't want anything to happen to you."

"Good idea, Captain, and thank you."

"How will I get down there? And here is something else I don't understand. If they decide to join me, this room will be way too small for those giants."

"I can answer those two questions, Captain," Tap said with a little more enthusiasm than she had shown before in normal conversation. She almost sounded... excited.

In front of Zreyas on the platform, a hologram popped up that displayed the ship's layout. His jaw hung as he saw a three-dimensional view of the ship, including crew quarters, kitchens, meeting rooms, baths, shower rooms, offices, leisure rooms, and even a library. As he saw the engineering room label, he realized with a shock that he was reading.

Zreyas whipped his head around to find Freckles smiling with that comical, but knowing, look.

He wanted so bad to Q-leap over to him and hug him for giving him the ability to read. But, if he did, he would lose his emotional stability, and he needed his war focus. He knew when it happened, because he had a strange smile about him after he kissed his head after his hard-punch-down-the-runway lesson. Then he remembered his words about how his reading problem would work itself out soon enough.

Zreyas finished turning to face Rtu. With one single tear's worth of moisture in one eye, he swallowed and gave him a respectful nod of appreciation. Then he turned back around to the hologram.

Rtu smiled and nodded back to him before Rhom's excitement interrupted the silence.

"Nicely designed, Tap!"

Everyone joined in on congratulating her.

"Thank you, all. I like it myself. Well, of course I would, it *is* myself. One-Ha!"

Everyone chuckled.

"Captain, we can bring them up in the living quarters common room if you like. You also have your own living quarters that are secure in a dimensional pocket that no one can breech while you sleep. There is also a teleportation room like that as well, so no one can board without access. That access can only come from you, Captain. Think of them as encrypted addresses that, even if found, could not access it without you willingly, and consciously, doing it yourself."

"I don't understand encrypted."

"Encryption means that something is mixed up and scrambled with some sort of logic that others can't understand or see at all. It's all scrambled so no one can recognize it or access it, unless it's *de*-crypted. It's just like what Rtu did with the names we gave you, but it's a very simple way to encrypt."

"That is so... so..."

Everyone, including Tap, joined in with him to say, "pheno-mi-tastic!"

The room erupted in laughter, including Tap's 'Ha!'

"I like the plan," Zreyas said with a chuckle. "I guess I need to get ready to teleport down. Do you know where the blue camp is, Tap?"

"Yes, I do, Captain."

"Then I would like to teleport there."

"But, Captain..."

"Tap, let's just do this."

"I think you might want to listen to her. It's part of being an excellent commander," Rtu advised.

Zreyas exhaled and said, "What is it, Tap?"

"Captain, Janquar bands are surrounding them. They are close and coming fast. The blue camp members are in danger of being taken as prisoners, tortured, and killed if they don't come willingly."

"What?! Can you show me?"

"Yes, Captain, right away."

The entirety of the walls in the command room turned into a 3D viewing experience of what was happening at the blue camp as if they were there but elevated. Several huge bands of warriors were surrounding the camp and closing in, and the blue camp members looking uncomfortable.

"They don't stand a chance, nor would I, if they all get there before we do, or at least get them out. What do you think we should do?"

The room was silent. Zreyas turned to see the twins' faces watching him, but said nothing, albeit they were smiling gently. He knew that look well now. *Well, I guess I m on my own a little more now. They are forcing me to take charge, aren t they?*

— Yes, Captain, they are - and they should. You are stronger and smarter than you think you are.

Zreyas willed himself to stay calm. He slid into the tactical mind-space of the commander he trained all his life to be as he watched the Janquar bands close in from three different directions.

"I have two questions. How quiet is this ship? And, if you open this ship, are we susceptible to the Dark One, like Tulyata and Rtu were?"

Rtu sat up with a grin, interested in what Zreyas was calculating. "It sounds like a gentle breeze. It would take a keen ear to tell the difference between real breeze and this ship's sound. Being near an ocean or waterfall, it would be near impossible to hear."

Rhom scratched his head just over his ear. "It's hard to say on the other question. That depends on how much the Dark One has progressed in his new visage-hood. He uses the quantum consciously, and this is a quantum based ship. However, this piece of the quantum is now an incarnation... basically an encrypted dimensional being. I cannot advise you one way or the other because these circumstances have not been scientifically traced and tested yet."

"Thank you both for your input. Tap, make sure the defense system is ready and set to the frequencies that will hurt those Janquar, but not at one that it affects the blue camp members. Close in. Get as close to them as possible without blowing plant life too much, at least more than a breeze in that area would naturally."

"Yes, Captain. The defense system is ready as you wished. The frequencies between the two groups are quite a bit different. We will be in a position in four, three, two... we are there, Captain."

"Where is that teleportation room? I want the ramp let down without opening the hatch. Stay in stealth so they don't see it either. I would like to use the teleportation room to travel to just outside the door since it is... how you said... encrypted."

"Yes, Captain. The teleportation room has been revealed, and the ramp is down and low enough that it is just above their head level. They won't see it, but you will, because it is... us."

She was right. He could see a hologram version of the ramp on screen. "Good." Zreyas picked up his weapons from the racks, focused. He didn't have to think where to put them. He set the swords in their crossed place on his back. The bow hung on the clip over the swords. He checked to make sure he could still access his swords and pull them. He nodded, then put his axe and dagger on his hips.

"For now, I want these weapons bright. In fact, I want them so bright they have a hard time seeing me because of the light shining in their eyes and all they see is a silhouette. I want their living nature to shine like a beacon! They must be bored to come at them with those numbers. I'll give them a show they won't forget."

"Little buddy, they know you might be around. Don't forget that," Rtu advised.

"Thankings to you, Rtu, for the reminder. If they want to come at them with all that flare against men that have no desire or ability to fight, they are going to know Zreyas *is* there. I might not be advanced technology, but I got Tap and a little flare myself. Time to get sick, you ticking-bandhulas!"

The twins exchanged grins and glances, giving each other a high hand slap. Zreyas wasn't exactly sure what that meant, but he liked the looks on their faces.

"Tap, how do I use this teleportation?"

"It is easy for you, Captain. You don't have to use it in the physical, using coordinates. You can just use the quantum and show it where you want to be."

"Good, at least that is familiar. Be ready for my signal to turn on the defense system."

Rtu stood and did a fun-loving bow. "We are with you, little buddy. Watching with interest."

Rhom stood as well. "I'm liking what I see so far, my boy! You do what you do best... be you!"

Zreyas stepped into the teleportation area with a grin. "This reminds me a little of the challenge node. Anyway, I will see you soon, hopefully with a new crew."

He took a breath and closed his eyes, then thought about where he wanted to be as he got angry at what they were doing to the blue camp members. He didn't know much about anything anymore, but he knew intimidation.

And with that thought, he saw particles for a few seconds. And then, he was standing on the top of the ramp looking down at the blue camp members and the approaching warriors, listening to a breeze that felt like Tap.

The light from the pure weapons shone everywhere, grabbing the attention of the blue camp members and the Janquar immediately behind them first. *Tap, can you amplify my voice so they can hear it without a doubt?*

— Yes, Captain.

Starting to back up, the blue camp members looked like they would rather take on the Janquar, rather than whatever it was they were seeing.

The tracker held a hand up, whispered something to the one next to him who nodded, then said, "He's back!"

There was a pause as if it hadn't sunk in yet, then the blue camp members cheered and the Janquar warriors started throwing up their war auras.

Putting himself into a frame of mind like his father would have was difficult now, but he did it for the show. Sarcasm oozed out in his voice. "Aww, so the mighty Janquar warriors can't cook their own meals and dig their own latrines by themselves?" His amplified voice seemed loud to his ears, but he continued. "They need the ones that they see as *weak* to help them! How ironic!"

As expected, that made the warriors extremely angry. He didn't need to *hear* the growls to tell him that. Zreyas could see the communicative war auras as they all turned to face him, still unsure of what they were dealing with.

As the warriors stomped closer, drawing weapons, yet their head turned slightly, wincing at the light, trying to adjust their vision. Zreyas knew bright light was difficult for Janquar to adjust to. It didn't seem to bother the blue camp members near as much, though.

"So.... you want to kill or abuse the ones you deem weak, yeah? That seems frail, like an old one about to be slaughtered for lack of usefulness to me. *Shame* on you for straying from your orders to find and kill Zreyas. But I'll help you out. You know me as the one you hunt, who used to be the third strongest in your Nation. Turns out, I was the third weakest, till I discovered how your nation really worked and lived."

Zreyas laughed hard for show as he walked down his ramp slowly. He could only imagine what it all looked like to them. Zreyas *almost* felt ashamed to be putting on such a show, but only almost. He was not here to show humility—he was here to save lives and help the balance.

The growls of the Janquar grew when they heard the laugh even though they still had issues with seeing. Their eyes were not made for bright light, but even so, they started swarming toward him slowly, still careful because of their vision problem. They knocked the blue members aside as they passed.

"You have *failed* your hunt miserably! I should put you to death if I lived by your rules."

One of the blue camp members standing beside the tracker crossed his arms and taunted the warriors.

Zreyas wanted to laugh hard, but he was too focused to let it break his aim and continued sharply. "*But* I *will* make you wish my simple weapons killed you. You *will* remember who and what you are up against *if* you live. And I will make you remember that if I ever see you killing blue skinned Janquar, what you will be up against."

Even the distanced Janquar came rushing towards him after that speech. Those that hadn't already drawn their weapons, did.

Zreyas pulled his bow and thought about the arrow he wanted in a split second and nocked it. He didn't know if it would do much, or how it would react, but it was more for the show right now than devastation. He pulled back the neutrinic-gleam arrow and aimed at the center of the Janquar warriors at a bowman drawing his bow.

These numbers are not even a drop in the sea of the numbers of Janquar, but don t kill them, Tap. Make them live just above death. When I let this arrow go, I want you to make them sick and permanently disabled the rest of their lives. I want the others to look at them and see that they are not invincible.

— Yes, Captain. Understood.

He remembered Rhom's lesson in the dying dimension about shattering glass. That lesson kept coming back to aid him over and over. The neutrinic-gleam would be too high a frequency for his target's body to handle all at once, with no time for his body to adjust. He whispered to the arrow, "Help me save more lives through the death of this one."

Only one Janquar would die by his hand today if he could help it, but he couldn't help but feel the sadness in it. He knew a lot of them would be left to die, or ground up for building—but *that* was not his responsibility. He would put an end to their Nation's torment and what they did to others at least a little today.

Zreyas let his arrow go. *Now Tap!*

39 There are More?

ᚱᚱᚱ Zreyas ᚱᚱᚱ

Tap didn't turn the defenses on as soon as he gave the signal. She turned it on when the arrow hit the Janquar. It added illusion that it was the arrow's power that did it, not the ship. That left mystery in their minds, and to Zreyas, that was an extra benefit for the future.

Nice strategy, Tap. I am giving you the lovings already!

— I know, Captain.

Zreyas grinned openly and chuckled at her, out-loud for show as the serious empathetic sadness ripped through him when the masses of hardened Janquar warriors dropped, reeled, and heaved. The blue camp members started backing up over bodies in horror.

"Now you know what is coming for you if you ever hurt the artisans, cooks, and workers again!"

I don t want to be their judge. I just want to get the blue camp out of there. They deserve a chance like I had.

— Yes, Captain, I'm glad you don't want to kill them. It would be the wrong time and wrong reason.

After it incapacitated all the hardened warriors in the area by the hundreds, Zreyas spoke to the blue camp members, "It's okay, my friends. Your bodies were too high of a frequency to be affected. I just came to talk to you."

Zreyas didn't realize how it must have looked as he walked down the ramp to the blue camp members until they all fell to their knees.

He stopped and waved a reflective hand. "Oh no, no, no, don't do that. Stand." Zreyas jumped off the ramp with a Q-leap. *Close the ramp now, Tap. I don t want anyone running into it or accidentally hitting it.*

He watched them get up with thankful, but also wary, expressions, breathing a sigh of relief. The blue camp members towered over him again.

Their inquisitive, but stony, faces looked at him. The blue Janquar shifted around him so they could see him, but they didn't go behind him. Zreyas knew it was out of curiosity, not for intimidation.

Zreyas asked them, "Would it be okay with you if we spoke about a few matters?"

One of the Janquar stepped forward. "I am Cree," he said gruffly, putting a fist to his chest and nodded. "We will speak with you. You just saved our asses. They were going to take us and use us for food since we would not come back willingly to work for them."

"Well met, Cree. You are the leader?"

The artisan that Zreyas knew stepped forward to affirm, "He is. You can trust him. It is good to see you again, Zreyas."

"And you, my friend."

Cree spoke up. "You helped our people with gaining water technology. It seems we owe you quite a lot. What is it you want from us?"

"The only thing I want is for you all to make your own choices. I respect you as a leader, Cree. We all need good leaders as long as they don't take away the will of the individual like the Janquar Nation has."

Zreyas put his bow back on his back as he addressed them all. "I would like to speak to all of you as *individuals* that have the freedom to choose."

He focused on Cree and said, "That is... if it is okay with you, Cree. *You* must start the wave since you are their leader."

He gestured to all the heaving, delirious, and unconscious Janquar. "It doesn't take much bravery to kill those not willing to fight."

Cree's expression changed from harsh to a slightly melted version. "So, you are truly the one that introduced choice to us. Your influence on my people is why we chose not to work for them. We thought it would mean our death, but we did it anyway."

"It still may mean death, no matter what choices you make from here on out. But we all die eventually, and we might as well die living free. Can we all sit around your fire a moment?"

Cree shook his head. "We need to get out of here. They will rouse and wake."

Zreyas shook his head just after him, "No, they won't wake till I leave. And if others come, they won't make it to us before the same thing happens, I assure you."

All their faces lit up with surprise.

Cree finally said, "Okay, come... we sit." He motioned to the others to help move the bodies of the sick away from their camp to the outskirts. It took a few minutes, but they were either unconscious or too weak to fight it.

Zreyas knew the importance of sitting around the fires for the Janquar and he wanted to honor that. He also wanted to send a silent message that it was important that they listen—the tradition of sitting around a campfire was a place to listen or reflect. At least that was one tradition that was a good thing.

After they all sat and got settled, Cree was obviously uncomfortable with the respect Zreyas gave them by his expression. "Are you truly the same Zreyas that your brother Aaru spoke of?" Cree gestured to a stump that was left empty, apparently his own make-shift throne of leadership.

Zreyas Q-leaped up on top of it rather than struggle to climb. He had a little dignity and pride when it came to those that were not his chosen family. However, he went against Janquar tradition and gestured for them to sit first. *Then* he sat.

"I've not gone crazy. I'm visiting in *your* home. Thankings to you for agreeing to listen. I've learned a new way of living that might seem strange to you. I'm still a commander. It is what I have learned to do all my life, but I do it the way I want to now, with what the visages call compassion. At least I try."

He watched them all exchange glances and gasps. He let it sink in. "To answer your question, Cree, I *am* Aaru's brother. Does it bother you?"

Cree shook his head. "You tell us why you have come and then I will talk about Aaru."

Zreyas nodded. "Very well. I come to you with an opportunity to consider. However, it is important for you to understand what is really going on here. You already know of the Dark One and what he is doing with the Janquar Nation."

The artisan spoke next. "Yes, and they are getting worse. Of those affected by the dark taint, their skin is not just dark anymore, it is rough and porous like coal. We do not know how some of them are still living.”

The tracker to his right added, “The Emperor doesn’t look like a Janquar anymore. He looks like charred meat that moves with the help of black mist. We scouted and saw it. We were trying to figure out what to do when we found out they were coming for us and were trapped.”

Cree said, “We already talked about it. If you came back, we wanted to join you.”

All the Janquar nodded in agreement with as much excitement a Janquar could show living the life they had lived so far.

“You have not heard the length of what I have to say about the situation. Do not join with me out of fear of what you face here. Always run toward something you want rather than run from something you don’t, because that fear of what you don’t want is put out ahead of you in the quantum and is still your focus, and you will *almost always* run into it.”

— Captain, those were wise words. The old man and Freckles look impressed and proud of you.

Zreyas let the silence live and let it all sink in a moment. “I think it is important that you hear what I have to say first so that you are informed. I don’t want anyone joining me without as much information as possible.”

“Okay, talk,” said Cree. “A few will pack while we listen. Either way, we have to move.”

“Fair enough.” Zreyas had a sudden awareness that something was nearby that he couldn’t see.

Many of the blue camp members got up and started packing, but with attention to what was going on in the talks.

Tap, am I crazy, or is there something near us that is extremely powerful?

— Slowly look behind you, Captain.

Zreyas turned his head, noticing the blue camp was

oblivious. Either they didn't sense it, or it was something he didn't understand.

When he looked behind him, he saw nothing. Then he looked down at the ground just in time to see a large paw print sink into the dirt with imprints of sharp claws in the prints' orbit a respectful distance out.

"You have some massive claws on you, but I suspect there is more to you than those claws. You have my respect, whoever you are," he said, barely audible.

The members of the blue camp were looking in the direction Zreyas was looking. He noticed their confused faces. They slowly gathered around behind Zreyas quietly, curious.

"You are not threatened here at the moment. Show yourself if you wish to speak to us. Remembering the words to get the twins' attention to validate, he sent out a thought. '*Namdlo dna selkerf.*' *Tap, are the twins watching this?*

— Yes, Captain, they were before you said the words. But they said to tell you, 'well done'. Rhom is especially intrigued.

Zreyas noticed the sun was about to set, feeling a little familiarity about the situation. *Something seems familiar about this energy. Whoever this is, they are no threat to us.*

Zreyas trusted his gut and turned around to face the blue camp members. "Shall we continue?"

The members looked at Zreyas like he was addled in the head and more than a little wary. They continued standing, though.

Cree looked at the ones that were packing before and nodded to them. "Go with you or not, we still need to move." They broke group and started packing nearby within hearing range.

Zreyas cleared his throat, letting some of the nervousness out. "I would like to offer to take you away from here with no obligation to me. I can take you to a place you can start fresh without threat of the Janquar immediately, where you can live in peace, at least for a time.”

The group exchanged glances in silence, some of them nodding.

“However, I do have another offer for you as well. After I explain that option, take your time and talk about it if you like. I can come back, but I will at least help you to another spot on this planet before I leave, because when I leave, they will start waking up. They *will* try to kill you, incapacitated or not. They will be furious and you know what that means.”

They all nodded emphatically. For a few minutes they talked among each other, then Cree turned, “We want to hear your other option, now.”

“It’s quite simple.”

Zreyas spent the next hour updating them on what he had not told them yet about the interstellar challenge, how the Dark One initiated it to kill or control Ayya to prevent the light balance. He also explained that if Ayya, also called little phoenix, couldn’t help her people bring in the new age, then an all-consuming darkness would eventually cause all of creation to cease to exist, including all visages. He also told them he had a ship called The Potential and ended the story with a deep breath and exhale.

“So, the other option is to become part of my crew for a long and very dangerous life as a member of ‘The Order of the Sleeping Phoenix’.”

The blue camp members mumbled words and seemed stunned at the offer.

“However, if you choose to join us, each one of you as free individuals will give up the Janquar culture and pledge on your honor to be loyal to the cause, or if you choose to betray or leave, you die.

"I can't let you go once you start this journey because there is too much information to exploit once you leave. I'm sure you can understand with what you know has happened with the Janquar Nation. But if you want to fight what is going on here, then this is the way to do it."

While the Janquar talked, Zreyas turned around to see what the entity was doing by its footprints. He didn't see anything new. He looked up and noticed the moon was coming up well and full. It's fairly bright for night time.

Something occurred to him that made him curious. *Tap, when I was here the first time, I heard a voice that talked to me a few times, telling me to survive. I also heard voices in the challenge. Was that you too?*

— Yes, Captain… no, Captain.

I see, I wonder who that was in the challenge.

Cree interrupted Zreyas' thoughts, "We have come to a decision."

Zreyas turned around and replied in a matter-of-fact tone, "Good. Time is of the essence."

Cree looked to those around him who were watching him, then turned his gaze on Zreyas with decisiveness, and said, "We would like to choose to be free and make our choices individually. You have impressed us, and we would like to learn to choose."

"I don't think you will regret it. It can be hard sometimes, but it is worth it. And Cree, that says a lot about you that you would give up your leadership to help your brothers be free."

"There is one more thing, though." Cree looked at the others pointedly. "Some of us would like to become small like you, some would like to learn what you do, and others of us would like to help you *without* fighting."

"Diversity is preferred. Each one is valuable in doing

what they feel a passion for. There is nothing like feeling your purpose if it was you that chose to enjoy it. I'm not sure about the size part, because I didn't purposely change myself. I was shrunk when I went through a fracture running from you in that dying dimension. I'm not sure there is much I can do there to help you there."

— Captain, there may be a way to do that.

I see. Hmm.

Then Cree said, "There are more of us. We have told them the stories of your actions."

"Where are they?"

"They are hiding in a cave to the east. The opening is concealed. They were afraid to be in the open because of what the Nation would do. We feared it too, but stayed to help conceal the others."

"How many more are there?"

Cree replied with an unsure expression. "I don't know. Some were caught by the Nation while hunting for food. We have not been back yet to see the full damage of the losses, but there *were* one hundred twenty-seven."

"What? I had no idea there were so many that refused to work. Show me the way, and let's find out. The rest can stay and pack without danger of the Janquar waking up unless I move my ship."

Cree nodded to the others, then looked at Zreyas. "Come, I show you."

Zreyas turned to follow Cree. "Let's hurry. I have a bad feeling about something I can't shake in my gut and it is growing."

Cree, the artisan, and the tracker ran together with soft footing. Zreyas kept up easily with Q-leaps for ten minutes in his estimation, then leaped onto Cree's shoulder so he could see better without leaving them. He never flinched, a good sign in Zreyas' mind.

"I knew you would do that," said Cree.

"Me too." Zreyas chuckled.

Cree turned his head toward him slightly and said, "I think you will get me killed if I adhere to your path."

"That is why you must follow your *own* path. Sometimes it aligns with others, sometimes it doesn't. If you die, you will at least leave this place of your own accord and choice, and that is the best way to die, not someone else's honor or purpose."

Twenty minutes later, they came to a place that looked like a rock outcropping. Zreyas had never come that way due to the hordes of Janquar at the shore in the beginning.

Cree sent a soft chirping call.

After a few minutes, no return was heard or seen.

"It's okay," Cree whispered. "They were not supposed to return it. They are scouting us."

From a distant location, Zreyas heard a different type of call.

"Now they will again return it."

Zreyas nodded. Sure enough, they returned the call and brush moved out of the way in a place he did not expect.

Cree walked forward carefully, and they entered the cave mouth between two growing bushy trees.

40 Painted

Zreyas

The cave tunnel wasn't lit, though it wasn't a hindrance to any of them because of their night vision. Zreyas felt his eyes turn and open, almost like a mechanical device, to adjust to the lighting. Though the color saturation faded in his environment, they took on white-ish hues of the color to show depth of field.

He couldn't see as well as he should have been able to, though, so that gave him pause. Probably because it had the same creepy darkness as what had been in that structure in the dying dimension. Though he couldn't see that well in the cramped tunnel, he could tell they took a right, then a left, at the first two forks.

This is quite the extensive cave system, and it is hard to see in here. That makes me nervous.

— It is difficult to see, even for the twins there. Are you okay, Captain?

I m fine. Let s hope it all works out. We could use some good people on our side. But there is something... off... about this place.

Zreyas ducked in time to avoid a dip in the ceiling.

Cree said nothing, but gave him a look of apology without stopping.

— Yes, Captain. The twins told me to tell you to observe, watch, and listen.

Something important is here, though I m not sure if it is good... or bad.

— Captain, the twins said this will be an important and momentous fork in the road, even if it doesn't seem like it's that important.

I will pay attention. After all, they are going through a lot too, just like I did... and am.

— It is true, Captain. I'm glad you are thoughtful. It will serve us all well.

The three Janquar stopped, and a soft call went out from the tracker, who was in front. Then he whispered the words, "Zreyas' will."

Zreyas jerked his neck and head back in surprise, but said nothing. Cree looked up at him slightly, feeling the movement in his reaction. It tempted him to say something to Tap, but he curbed the urge so he could pay close attention.

Dim light came through the blockage as they opened the doorway. Cree crouched and walked in first through the doorway so Zreyas had to adjust his footing quickly. After they were through, Cree stood slowly, giving him time to adjust as he stood.

Cree didn't just stand—he stood proudly.

Zreyas' mind felt like it had been blown to bits. He panicked and froze in shock as all the Janquar in the large cave dropped to their knees and went prostrate.

Zreyas whispered to Cree, "Tell me they do that for you."

"I cannot," said Cree.

Everyone, with no exception, went prostrate.

“My friends, *get... up...* and sit with me. You are as good a station as anyone else here, including me,” Zreyas announced, feeling extremely uncomfortable enough that he felt himself squirm in his stance slightly. “Why do they prostrate, Cree? Did you teach them this?”

“No.”

Zreyas remembered the Janquar were not great at discussion and almost forgot about that. “I understand we are used to not speaking. I have learned that staying quiet all the time is not a great way to get answers. There is a time for it, but now is not the time. So, I would like to ask you to all raise a hand if you would like to ask a question.”

All the blue members exchanged glances silently, looking like they felt very awkward.

Zreyas expected this. They were not used to having a voice. “It’s okay. I understand you are not used to having the freedom to speak or ask questions. Times are changing and there are many opportunities and choices about your life you need to make. If you want to do something other than hide in a cave, now is a good time to ask questions. If you don’t want to start with questions, I will ask Cree to update you on some important information.”

No one raised a hand.

Cree nodded after a few moments. “Zreyas saved us from the hunting circle. He made them lay down and sleep after making them sick and delirious while he spoke with us.”

Zreyas wanted to pipe up and tell them it was the ship’s defense system, but he heeded the advice of the twins and watched. They had almost created a new culture since they left the Nation and he wanted to see just how deep it went and what it was like. He could always update them on details depending on what they chose. Zreyas watched and listened carefully over the next hour as Cree gave them the updates and choices.

He noticed there were many crates and packs there already. They had seriously planned an exodus, and it looked like this might have been the rendezvous point. Several more came in, surprised to see Zreyas there. They bowed slightly and sat down like the rest. Cree continued to finish the story and all the updates. Then, he turned his head slightly and looked up at Zreyas, "Would you like to give them their options?"

"Go ahead, you are doing fine," Zreyas encouraged.

Cree nodded and almost smiled. He stood proud and Zreyas could feel an air of excitement around him. That was one thing Zreyas learned in his years with the Nation, how to read the auras of different variances of pride and intimidation. Cree briefed them on the crew option first, then the planet-side option. Then just stopped and waited quietly.

Zreyas then had another idea, something he had not thought of before. "On the planet-side option, you can also choose to be part of The Order of the Sleeping Phoenix and be part of the base of operations that will grow over time. If you want to join The Order of the Sleeping Phoenix at planet-side, we have important missions that they will be part of, just as if you were on the ship. So, the same rules apply as being part of the ship's crew. I want to make sure you are informed of what you are up against ahead of time."

Everyone looked at each other as the information was given to them. Some shifted excitedly and some more uncomfortably.

"If you choose to go your own way, we will drop you off on a different planet in a different system so you can take transport to anywhere you would like to go on your own. You will have complete freedom, but you must learn to work with other races to get to the place you would like to go. I won't do it all for you—it is *your* life. If I do it for you, that isn't learning to be free, and it isn't my responsibility to take care of you. I'm just a simple person doing a job no one else will do. Now... any questions?"

One in the back slowly raised a hand.

Zreyas nodded at him.

Tentatively, the Janquar asked, "What if we don't have any skills for The Order, whether it be planet-side or ship?"

"Great question, and I'm sure others would like to know the answer to that as well. I think you might be surprised at how many skills you have. As often as we can, we can make sure you are given the training you need to get better at what you *want* to do. I can't guarantee you will get what you want right away, though. There are only so many resources we have right now. However, if you are willing to do whatever type of labor is needed at the time, then eventually we will get you placed and trained in a position you want, then you are perfect for The Order."

They all started nodding, and their faces seemed to lift a little.

"We need all types of jobs. But I have some... connections that might be willing to teach you in what you desire to do. However, I can't speak for them or promise that. I'm only one person, and I, like you, started with nothing. But look at us now. I have not updated you all on everything because you are not part of The Order, so there is no point. You will be safer without the knowledge."

Everyone in the room nodded in agreement. It just made sense not to clutter their minds with information they could do nothing about, unless they were involved.

"Anyone else?" When no one raised a hand immediately, he said, "I have a question for you now, if that is okay."

All the blue looked at each other in shock. Cree looked at Zreyas sideways toward his shoulder and translated for them, "They are shocked why you would ask them anything." Then he turned back to them. "As your leader at the moment, I say ask what you want."

"Thank you, Cree. It's important for me to understand your motivations and where you stand as much as it is for you to hear all the information I can give. It's the only way to make a good decision. Since they will not ask questions, I will ask you one. Why did they use 'Zreyas' will' for a pass code?" *Tap, are all the Janquar out of the blue camp?*

— Yes, Captain. They are being scouted now for entrance approval.

Good, move the ship and the defense system to this location area, but as far away as you can be and still affect where we are. I want to filter out what I can t see because I want so badly to trust. It is too easy to be blinded by my own desire. I have a responsibility to those that are true.

— Wise choice and thoughts, Captain. The twins are proud of you for that wisdom.

Cree looked at the crowd, then turned his head again toward Zreyas on his shoulder. "Because you are now the visage of choice for many of them. They have abandoned their old gods. They don't know anything about you, but they revere you because of your strength and kindness that you showed us that day, offering a chance for freedom. There are other reasons, too."

Zreyas looked at them all for a moment, trying to buy time. *Tap, let me know when you are almost in position. I must do this right... and in the open.* He looked at the large group watching him. "How willing are you to test your loyalty? Raise your hand if you are *not* willing to test that loyalty?"

— Captain, we are in position. I have an idea what you want to do. All we need to do is turn it on at your word.

No one raised a hand. After a few seconds, Zreyas gave them one last opportunity. "Last chance. Is there anyone that doesn't want to test their loyalty to choice and The Order of the Sleeping Phoenix?"

Still, no one raised a hand.

Zreyas nodded. For those of you that are lying, I'm sorry. For those of you that are true to your word, you will be safe from anyone posing to be one of you. If there are any traitors to you, I must find them for all our safety. *Now, Tap. Dial in on the low frequencies and kill them.*

As Zreyas looked around, he saw two Janquar fall to the ground and started violently seizing. The others close to them backed away quickly.

Cree declared to them that what they were doing now was like the ones that fell at the camp. The crowd gave the thrashing bodies a wide berth.

How low is their frequency, Tap?

— Very low, Captain. We think they painted their skin and assume they are spies.

Zreyas continued Cree's declaration. "Except these will not wake," said Zreyas.

When the bodies went still, the odd darkness dissipated and Zreyas Q-leaped over to one of the two and inspected them. "If you want to verify the spies you had in your midst, rub the paint off their skin."

The artisan that Zreyas knew offered his water-skin, then poured some water on one of them, then rubbed the skin with a knife edge. The paint was thick to disguise the porous black charred skin.

The artisan backed up. "He's right, it's the char of the Dark One."

The group looked at Zreyas and their faces showed anger. As Zreyas Q-leaped back to Cree's shoulder, the mob of blue camp members moved into a state of outraged anger. Zreyas forgot just how brutal they were with traitors and prisoners. However, he did nothing to stop their anger. It was time to be angry for at least a little time.

Zreyas felt an urgent gut feeling rise quick to get out of that cave. It was so strong he felt like he would explode if he didn't get out of there. "Cree, take me outside quickly. My instincts tell me, so I listen. But if you want to stay, I can—"

Cree turned immediately without the slightest hesitation. With urgency, Cree nodded to the men at the door and rushed through as quick as he could get out. Zreyas hung on while the large leader ran through the cave system, taking the correct passages at the forks.

As soon as he saw moonlight from the entrance, Cree tripped, but got up as quick as he could; however, it was too late for him. It threw Zreyas to the ground hard, but he quickly Q-leaped back to Cree's shoulder.

"Something is on the floor," Cree said as he straightened and rushed to the doorway. Zreyas watched Cree's jaw hang open as he struggled to keep upright on his shoulder. As they reached the mouth of the cave, Cree was still stumbling over the uneven ground.

When Cree could reach his full height again, he slowly walked the next few steps. Both of them were stunned at what they saw. Then a clear understanding of what Cree tripped over rushed into Zreyas' mind.

41 Deserter s Dessert

Zreyas

Scattered all around them for one-hundred meters were Janquar bodies. Thousands of hardened Janquar warriors, charred by corruption, lay dead like the aftermath of a war involving fire.

There was one thing that didn't seem right to Zreyas, though. Having seen so many scenes like this in his past, there was something profoundly missing. There was no stench of bile and shit. It occurred to him that there wasn't much of anything left of the original warriors. It made his heart heavy.

The blue members apparently followed because Zreyas heard many gasps behind them as they poured out of the mouth of the cave.

Cree walked out further and shook his head. It clearly stunned him, just as much as he was.

Why didn t you say anything, Tap?

— There was no need, Captain. You had already made the decision that would take care of the problem. It might have caused you to stall too long, anyway.

All the blue members gathered around Zreyas and faced him but were silent.

"I wish I could say it was easy to just use this to kill the Dark One, but it's not that easy. This is just a defense system on my ship. Not every creature or Janquar is of the same frequency. It's only designed to protect the ship if anyone that gets near it is uninvited. This time, I had my ship set to kill because I can't let traitors go. I gave you too much information. Trust me, the lighter version isn't pleasant. I was an accidental test victim and almost died. It seems we need to be more in a hurry than we expected."

One of the Janquar he didn't know raised their hand.

Zreyas nodded to them to let them know it was okay to speak.

"Can I tell you what I wish to do now?" When he saw Zreyas nod, he continued. "I don't know what the others want, but I would like to be on your crew. This Dark One is bad. If he is allowed to keep doing what he is doing now, we won't be alive much longer, no matter where we are living. We will either be doing his bidding or dead. And from the looks of it, both are dead. If Zreyas' will accepts, I would like to join The Order of the Sleeping Phoenix and help fight this." The Janquar thumped his fist to his chest hard, knelt down, and bowed his head.

Nothing but nature, ocean waves, and breezes filled the air. Zreyas Q-leaped off Cree's shoulder toward the ship to the ground. Then he smiled and inclined his head. "I accept your pledge. Stand behind me."

The Janquar stood and jogged and took his place behind Zreyas.

Zreyas watched many hands raise. "Listen to me, we can do this properly later, but for now, those that would like to be on the ship's crew, whether or not you think you have the skills, stand in line to my left," gesturing to his left in front of himself. "Those that want to be in the order but be planet-side form a line to my right in the same way."

Tap, keep an eye out for anyone lingering behind, or in, that right line. Pay attention to their frequencies. My gut tells me there is another traitor. I felt a frequency change over that way. Maybe someone was on the border of commitment, and all those bodies pushed them over the edge. Either way, no one can get out of here with the knowledge I have given them, sadly.

— Yes, Captain. I understand, and the twins agree, as well.

Zreyas noticed a Janquar slowly backing up, moving toward the cave mouth.

"You there!" pointing to the Janquar backing up. "Are you leaving us without making a verbal choice?"

All the blue camp members turned around to look at their brother, who was backing up faster toward the cave.

"All of you can see now what is at stake!" Zreyas pointed at the suspect. "Are you all willing to let this one betray your efforts and help the Dark One? Are you willing to let this Janquar take away all the hard work and suffering you have been through to get here now?! I respect your decisions either way, but there is no position of medium ground now. To take no position is to betray the chance of a future." He lowered his hand and added, "We might not live to see it, but at least we have the opportunity and choice to help make it happen."

The Janquar continued to back up. "There is *no* guarantee he is telling the truth."

"You are right about the lack of guarantee, but I *am* telling the truth. At the very least, I have non-violent intentions, or my skin wouldn't be the color it is. Telling a lie about something with such dire consequences to hurt so many takes a very dark energy indeed."

Cree quickly looked at Zreyas. "He will run."

"I know. But if he runs, I want him to leave this life knowing he had that chance to make a choice. But... I don't think *I* need to be the one to kill him, do you? Sometimes it feels good to show ourselves that we are willing to commit to something important. What do you think? Tell you what, here is a question for you all. If he is too afraid to stay with those three choices, trying to sneak away, do you really think he will stand on his own? Or... do you think he will run back to the Janquar Nation?"

The entire group of blue Janquar turned to face the one backing up and started their low raspy hums of their war auras. It surprised Zreyas how strong their auras were. After a few seconds of watching the deserting Janquar, they walked toward the deserter slowly.

Cree started toward the deserting Janquar faster than the rest. "I will rip you apart myself if you desert! I saved your ass at my brother's expense. Had I known it would kill him, I would have let you die. But now you want to cower and run to the Dark One and become one of those... things! I am going to rip your body apart and let it rot by itself alone!" vowed Cree.

Zreyas winced at Cree's decree, understanding it to be the ultimate dishonor. The Janquar believed that when they died, they should be eaten so that one could nourish the tribe line—and horns used for building. It was much more preferable than to be left to rot.

The deserter turned and bolted. The blue camp members started the hunt. Zreyas watched in amazement as Cree ran through the crowd at the speed he was running. *Tap, before he gets out of range, tune into that Janquar's frequency, but let them take care of that traitor if he can. Cree has quantum talent.*

— Done, Captain.

Zreyas Q-leaped on the top of the mouth of the cave, "Build up the rage!" He watched Cree's aura max out, then instructed without saying his name, "Now think of your future that you want, and let all that rage turn into that future and how that future feels!"

Cree shimmered and ran faster. It didn't surprise Zreyas that he didn't Q-leap because he had not given that instruction, but he saw his quantum potential and that was enough. Giving others hope it was possible for them too was important in his mind. It seemed to encourage others, as a lot of them ran a little quicker from the psychological push. *Good progress, for starters. It will give them a taste of their potential, I think. But Cree looks promising.*

— Yes, Captain. I agree with you. I just hope he goes with you. Remember, he has not yet decided.

You are correct. I shouldn't assume he will come just because I gave him a brief lesson or he let me ride on his shoulder. Giving you the thankings for sobering me.

— You are welcome, Captain. I find I enjoy sobering you. One-Ha! Captain, they are getting close to the edge.

Zreyas continued to watch the chase as they got closer to the outer range of the ship's defenses. Cree was almost to him and passed a blue camp member that had horns. *Tap, pulse the defense system to make him stumble so they can catch him. I think it would be better if they did this.*

The deserting Janquar lurched from the effects of Tap's nasty defenses. He almost fell but caught himself. He slowed considerably with his body reacting to the pulse. Cree was now second from the front—impressive since he started from the back of the crowd. Just as the one in the lead reached the deserter, Cree caught up.

Zreyas was curious about where the one that pledged first was in the crowd and looked around for him. He was missing and couldn't seem to find him anywhere. *Where did he...*

— Captain, the one you are looking for is beside Cree. He was the one in the lead.

"Wha-at?" he said out-loud under his breath. *Fascinating. Did you happen to notice when he started the chase?*

— No, Captain, but I can replay it to find out.

"Do that. I'm curious now," he said, mesmerized.

— I will show you, Captain

Just as he started to ask how she was going to do that, a display in his vision appeared as if he put on some sort of visor that he could still see through with numbers and lines of color at the edges. In the middle to the left, a display appeared, playing what happened a few minutes ago. Tap narrated what was going on. *You don t need to narrate, Tap, I can see.*

— You might want me to, Captain.

Zreyas watched as Tap explained the scene as the deserter started to back up. The pledge clearly put up a war aura in anger. Cree ran. And the pledge in question also started running, but started a good ten meters behind Cree. He watched as the chase progressed and watched himself yelling out instructions. The pledged Janquar also did what Zreyas instructed Cree to do. When Zreyas told Cree to turn it into the future he wanted, the pledged one suddenly became another. Tap put a pointer to the one that was in the lead, who was now the pledged Janquar.

"He switched plaa-ces!" he whispered out-loud louder than he wanted. "Whoa! I didn't think that was possible without consent."

— Yes, Captain. Judging by the energy signatures, his future wish might have been to be the first one there instead of the one that started in the back of the crowd. It is likely he didn't realize what really happened because he looked around, confused for a moment, before refocusing. The twins said he got consent unconsciously because he didn't want to hurt his friend.

Thank you Tap. By the way, that is some nice technology seeing all this stuff without messing with my vision at the same time.

Zreyas felt his stomach lurch as the leaders in the chase worked together and literally pulled his arms and legs away from his body with knives at the shoulder and hips to help break them apart. The screams chilled and ripped through him. He wasn't accustomed to that kind of thing anymore and felt sorry for the man. They drug the limbs off ten meters away at each position as if they were satellites. He watched the man die as he bled out. Every blue camp member walked up to the body and spat on him, then turned to walk back.

Zreyas Q-leaped back to where he was before the hunt to prepare himself, facing the Janquar who was still quite a bit away, walking toward him. He felt a little sick, but he reminded himself that he had given the deserter every chance to choose other options, and he *had* to protect these men. It was his responsibility that he was dead, but he knew many more people would die before this was over. He lowered his head, shed a painful tear, then breathed it away. He looked up and waited for them to approach.

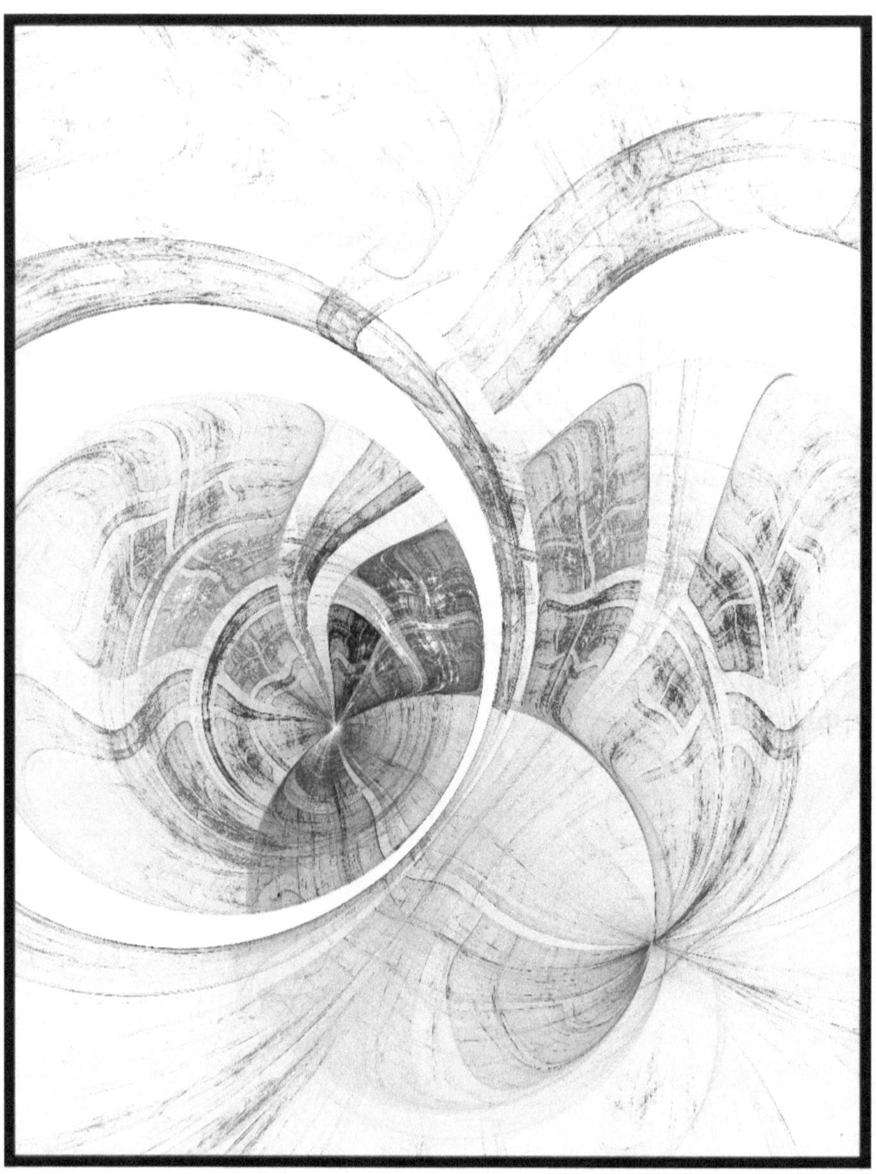

42 Washing Off

The blood-splattered blue camp members reassembled. They apparently saw his mood looking down and all went silent. Zreyas knew they were looking at him, but he took his time gathering himself.

The weight of his responsibilities and what had just happened settled on his shoulders. He suddenly felt very alone. He thought back to when he had been with the Janquar and realized that being a leader had always been his destiny. Zreyas decided right there and then to not fight it anymore. He had been fighting his design for a very long time. It was why he had not challenged the Commander earlier than he had.

He took a deep breath and looked up with a smile that came from being grateful—grateful that he was leading these people for a different, more meaningful, cause.

Of everyone who had either picked the crew or planet-based group, no one had chosen to be dropped off for another life.

"Do you really want to leave this life with the Nation

behind you?"

They all raised their hands and nodded once in unison.

"But you are still carrying it with you." Zreyas pointed to their blood-splattered bodies.

They all looked at each other and themselves.

"Then go to the shore and wash the past off you. As you wash in silence, let your old life go, and help yourself be open to new ways. When you feel you are ready, come back and stand in the line that you chose."

None of them hesitated. They *all* walked toward the shore quietly, only the footsteps and the sound of shifting ground underneath their feet. It would take them fifteen minutes to get there if they walked.

Zreyas turned to watch them walk away. He wanted to rush them, because he felt an urgency to get out of there, but this was not something that could be rushed. This was a big decision.

Then he felt a warm breath on his back and neck, then a gentle physical nudge. It felt like Rtu just gave him one of those fun jabs he gave him sometimes. He didn't move, because he felt no threat. Then he remembered the footprints in the dirt at the blue camp.

"Are you the beautiful creature that I helped get out of that hole?" Zreyas asked.

He felt a nudge.

"Are you the one that picked me up off the cliff that day the Janquar were trying to kill you?"

Zreyas felt another nudge.

"So, can I assume you can fly?"

He felt a gentle nudge.

"It might sound crazy, but I can't assume I understand everything about you. Can you fly through space with no atmosphere?"

No nudge came.

"Would you like to go with me to another galaxy?"

Zreyas felt a strong nudge that knocked him forward a little. He felt aggravation surface from being knocked so hard with his dark mood.

He just wanted to be left alone for a few minutes. But he said, "Well, I don't blame you, I would want to get out of here too. This place is quickly becoming a load of mag-shit, with the Dark One influencing everything. I can take you to a galaxy and drop you off in a safe place so you can live your life in solitude and peace if you want."

He felt a very hard knock on his back, throwing him forward. He Q-leaped easily with the anger he felt to right himself and away from where the creature was.

As he spoke, he ground out his words. "Look, if you want to work together on something, you need to find another way to communicate other than hitting the ticking-hell out of me. Show at least a little respect for someone that is willing to help you. When you are ready to show yourself and talk, then let me know. Till then, leave me the ticking-hell alone."

Zreyas decided to walk down to the shore himself. There was some past he needed to leave behind, too. He didn't need to start this new life with mag-shit hanging around his neck, and he certainly didn't like his mood right now.

At the shore, Zreyas found comfort in thinking about the water. He realized he had just asked Janquar, who *hated* water, to go wash in the water.

Zreyas took off, Q-leaping to catch up. He needed to show them by example that it was okay.

It wasn't long, and he was at the head of the pack just before reaching the shore. As he walked across the sand, he heard them stop. Zreyas calmly said, "Just look at where you want to go before you go in. Even if you only walk a little way." His small feet touched the surf foam that seemed so large to him before. He kept walking. Small waves hit his lower half. An enormous wave sucked the water out, leaving him standing on wet sand and shells.

The blue camp members gasped, and Zreyas pointed to the familiar rock he had spent the night hanging out on to the first time he landed on Tarq trying to avoid the Janquar. He breathed in a few deep breaths just before the wave crashed over him. He dove into the wall of water and swam hard.

He just hoped he would be okay so that the blue members would see it was important to navigate their weaknesses. They had to realize they were more than they think they were. And right now, he had to do the same. He desperately reached for the rock with each stroke.

As he thought about the rock he was aiming for, Zreyas felt his eyes warm and sting like they had fire in them, as tears welled up from the fear he was feeling. It wasn't from the swimming, but of the leadership. Maybe he was afraid to be successful at leading as much as he was of failing. But he *had* to move forward, just like they were doing.

He imagined taking a slow, deep breath in his mind, even though he was underwater. His body relaxed more, and he became less desperate to reach that rock on every stroke. He knew he would get there, and he started to enjoy the feel of the ebbs and flow of the waves caressing his skin.

It was interesting to feel the effects of the surrounding waves. Maybe he was mistaking what he was feeling, he wasn't sure, but either way, he was aware of its feel as it washed him.

And then, on his next stroke, Zreyas felt the rock with his right hand and climbed up the rock in one fluid motion.

His sealed eyes didn't matter.

The blue camp cheered after the gasps of shock stopped.

Hearing the direction of the wave crashes and shouts, Zreyas turned toward the shore and threw his fists up into the air. Then he declared, "Water has been my friend *and* my peace! It has been my protection from the Nation! It can be for you too!"

He wiped the water off his eyes. Just as Zreyas' eyes unsealed, he saw the blue camp members running toward the water. Some walked in, some ran in. None of them dove in, but they did experiment with it in their own way.

After a few minutes, they helped each other wash off the blood and fluids of the earlier kill. He found peace in watching them. That was to be his joy in all this... watching them discover, watching them naturally work together with mutual respect, then watching them grow better right alongside himself.

The switcher and Cree turned toward Zreyas and put a fist to their chests. It wasn't long and all of them, with no exception, were facing him with their fists over their hearts. Zreyas lifted his own fist and thumped his heart, then held it there and bowed his head slightly for a moment.

After lifting his head, he watched them gasp and exchange glances from the surprise that he would do such a thing. "Everyone deserves respect! Remember that! When you walk out of that water, leave all you have suffered, all you have felt you weren't, and all the life you hated behind you. I know *I* am going to."

He Q-leaped to them and on his second leap; he landed in the water chest deep behind Janquar, still facing the rock he had just been on.

Zreyas turned toward the shore and started walking

out of the water. "For the future!" He didn't stop. He walked back to where he knew the ship was, breathing a lot easier and feeling a lot lighter. He knew the blue were following him, but it was their choice.

— Captain, Ayya's in trouble. Master Rhom wanted to let you know that he and Rtu were going to go help. If you want to help or stay, both are important places to be. If you want to help, Captain, they will put you back in this exact moment again when it is complete.

What if I die? Then all will be lost. The blue camp members would never get off the planet. Tell them to come get me if they know they need me. Right now, every instinct I have says something is wrong here. We have got to get off Tarq. What are your thoughts on this?

— I agree, Captain.

He considered the matter more for a moment, then said to Tap, *if they go without me and I die here, then it s not a hundred percent chance of loss. Just ask Rhom to come back at this moment when they get done. That way, if I need their help, they will be here in case I go to the mag-shit pits.*

— Yes, Captain, I think you have sound strategy.

43 Tapping Trees

Grimy and shaken after what had just happened, it relieved her to be inside the tree line of the familiar fifty acre live oak forest she spent so much time in.

Ayya wiped any evidence of moisture she might have had away from her eyes. She looked back to find no one there. They had known she would walk through that entrance, and those inky mists were showing up a lot more often lately.

Those bullies were a lot more violent this time. She hurried to the tree she liked to climb up on within that side of the forest. She loved being up in the live oaks. They felt like her friends.

She had never fallen but once, and that was about a year ago, when an inky-eyed kid had showed up behind her and pushed her down. Ayya was still unsure how she survived that.

It was after that when Paul the fireman had come by to visit when her parents weren't home. It had surprised her she recognized him because it had been so long since she had seen him. After the hugs were over, and he had let her fly in his arms again, he told her some good news. He had purchased the land of the live oaks so she would always have a place to go where she felt comfortable.

Today wasn't a good day. The bullies, during and after school, had been after her. Either a teacher that she had never met before helped her out of it or she somehow slipped away, seeing them ahead of time. She had gotten very good at spotting the inky-eyes, except just a few minutes ago.

It seemed like she was always being chased, bullied, or in trouble with her parents constantly. Sometimes she deserved it, but it confused her most of the time why she was in trouble or being bullied. She felt like she wanted to explode sometimes.

She had even gotten in trouble once because she helped someone not get hurt. She knew a beam would fall from a sidewalk construction and she pushed them out of the way three minutes before it happened. They had asked her why she did that, and when she told them that beam was going to fall soon, they laughed at her and said they were going to call her parents. Sure enough, they did. And right after they had left, the beam fell down just as she had felt like it was going to happen.

Ayya had since learned to keep all that to herself, and even from herself. Every time feelings like that came, she shoved them down and pretended like they didn't happen—or tried to, anyway.

Gripping the knots on the tree, she closed her eyes and worked her way up. She enjoyed trying to see if she could feel them and see them like she used to. But it seemed like lately, she didn't feel or hear them like she used to. She didn't care though, she still liked being there. She liked to look at things from high up and she felt satisfied and at peace.

Ayya hopped from one branch to another, feeling free from the day. When she reached the outer branches of the tree she was on, she said, "Thank you!" then she hopped across to the next tree. She was so good with balance that she didn't have to look down at her feet, giving her extra freedom to enjoy the wonderland of live oak branches that was her world, her domain, and no one had caught her when they tried to follow her... except that odd inky-eyed kid she had never met before.

Paul had told her they took him to a life jail or something. He said he was in a different kind of jail than normal ones. But even with that mishap, she still wasn't afraid of the trees and being that high up.

She climbed and jumped in the trees like she had been born a monkey with their sense of balance and no fear of heights. It just felt natural to her. Ayya loved being high with a view.

Reaching the top of the most magnificent live oak in the area, at least in her opinion, she sat down on a forked branch, bark worn from her being there so often.

It was almost sunset. She would hear the whistle soon. She breathed and sighed out a long breath, feeling like the stress of the day of survival was leaving her.

She lifted her shirt and took it off and looked at the bruises forming from getting her butt kicked earlier by three of her regular bullies. Two of them had held her arms behind her back while the third kicked her in the gut. A distinct footprint started to show on her stomach and chest.

Ayya looked out across the sky over the treetops and houses. She loved this spot. No one could see her from here, even from below. It was hot and humid, but she didn't mind. She was in her peaceful spot. She felt so tired inside, so she looked up to the sky and felt tears form.

Her breathing heaved as she said quietly, "I know I'm only seven, but I'm almost eight. I hear from some people that there is someone watching over me. I don't mind being weird or not liked, but can I always have these places so I can have some time like this to feel peace? Paul gave me this place so I could feel safe anytime I wanted. Can you thank him for me again?"

As she looked up to the sky, she seemed to see shapes flipping and turning, like that old camel saddle cap she had played with for so many years. Her father told her she couldn't play with it anymore. But when he wasn't around, she did anyway.

Ayya felt her head swim a little. She was having some sort of memory or a dream right there with her eyes open. In the sky, she saw a faint crystal triangle and a light in the shape of a body with a long white beard. It was like a replay of something that seemed familiar.

> He smiled with a gentle sternness that only he could pull off. It both calmed Ayya and put her in a balanced state. "These outbursts will end, little phoenix, when you finish the joining. It's not all your fault, your body can't handle the bombardment of the multiverse weather."

As suddenly as it came, it left. All she saw was the sky again.

Ayya thoughtfully rolled the two words out under her breath. "Little phoenix... little phoenix. Paul calls me that. I wonder..." She shook her head. "Nah! Now you are really getting crazy, Ayya."

Then she thought of her mother. The Ms. Angel queen she knew seemed to disappear more and more every day.

Momma didn't speak much when her father was around, and even seemed afraid of him.

Ayya heard something rustle, then a grunt. Several trees away, one bully that had held her arm back on one side was trying to climb up one of the live oaks using the bumps for hand-holds. But the tree was so massive, she knew he wouldn't get too far.

They hadn't noticed Ayya yet. She didn't know what it was about that spot, but someone could be right under her within sight and still not see her.

She returned her thoughts to her momma and wondered if it was her fault that she didn't seem to be the same anymore. After all, she always seemed to get into trouble. Ayya looked up extra high in the sky and said, "If there is anyone listening, save my momma. If it is my fault, I just want everyone to know I'm not trying to be bad. I think it just happens. And I see more and more of those inky-eyes or floaty inky-things around and they do hateful things and try to hurt me. Like my father, I see the inky-eyes sometimes and it happens more and more too. Can you please help him? I try to do all the stuff he wants, but it is harder and harder to make him happy. He's never happy anymore, and he looks at me with blood-shot eyes filled with... I don't know what. It scares me a lot, and I don't know what to do."

Ayya heard what sounded like a squirrel rustling in the trees. There were a lot of them this time of year. She let her legs dangle as she leaned back to lie down. *Thank you for my tree spot. I think this is the heaven some people talk about.*

A yelp, followed by scrambling in the trees behind her, echoed. She sat up and looked around as she put her shirt back on. It was difficult to see what it was through the disturbed leaves.

She got up and started running through the branches

to get closer. Her now very dirty and worn high-top red tennis shoes with white rubber toes served her well.

"Help!"

She knew that voice. It was the bully that had been trying to climb the tree. "Hold on! I'm coming to help!"

Ayya poured the speed on, jumping to tap the trees in just the right places. Sometimes she had to take an indirect route, but she was trying her best to get there, following his cries for help and the grunt sounds.

Finally getting to a spot that she could actually see him floundering, trying to hang on to a branch, and slowly losing the battle, she realized he was in a bad spot. She would have to jump further than she had ever jumped to tap a tree before. Climbing down the tree and back up the other would be the safest way to do it but by then, he would likely have fallen.

The boy screamed desperately as his grip slid. "Please! Help me!"

She felt a lurch in her stomach and a faint humming growl.

When Ayya got to the outer branches of the tree, they were still firm, but the other tree's closest branch didn't seem sturdy. The tree was older and in terrible shape. In fact, now that she looked at it, she didn't remember this particular tree at all. She looked down. The trunk looked right, but the tree seemed different higher up. She knew these trees and something was off.

"Help!" The boy lost some footing and was now hanging with his full weight on one bent arm, branch at his armpit.

Just as she backed up to run, she felt a lurch in her stomach. "I hear you, I hear you, but I can't let him fall if I can help him, Aaru. So shut up or help." She took a breath and let it out, holding her hands to each side wiggling her fingers to prepare herself.

As she started the run, she focused on the branch she wanted to land on. Ayya heard a crow call... then several a few seconds later. Ayya's stomach lurched, but she ignored it and ran as hard as she could across the branch. Luckily, it was one of the large ones, so she didn't have to narrow her stance too much because it would have slowed her down.

Ayya growled as she pushed herself to top speed and when she felt the branch giving almost too much, she used the spring to hurl herself into the air.

She watched the branch she was on disappear and the one in front of her get closer. It looked like she had just enough momentum that she was going to make it.

Thwack! Something pierced her skin as it hit her face. Then she had two more hits from something else in the head.

Time seemed to slow down in the stress of it all. Ayya started noticing feathers falling and talons coming at her from all directions. As she moved through the air, she remembered the crow call and Aaru's warning. She would have probably still done it anyway, even if she had known, but for now, she had to make this jump. She didn't know how high she was, but Ayya knew it was several stories high, and she was determined to land right.

As she started her descent, she heard a much stronger bird cry, then she saw a huge vulture gliding straight for her, head-on. Its wingspan had to be close to two meters. Wildlife was something she knew about and loved, but normally vultures stayed high, gliding high up smelling out prey up to a mile away. And they don't attack live prey, well, they weren't supposed to. But this one was coming at her talons forward as if it was a predatory type bird like a hawk or eagle.

Then she saw it... the inky-eyed mist. That explained it. Now she was afraid, and she was about to land. At least she would make it as long as—

Aaru lurched in her so hard that it made her double over involuntarily. She felt a swish of air and the tail feathers brush her head. She recovered immediately from what Aaru had done just in time to land. Her feet hit the branch, and she immediately bent over and grabbed the branch still on her feet. She almost fell over, but she steadied herself.

"Help me, Ayya! I can't hold on anymore!" The bully grunted desperately, and she could tell he was in the crying stage of panic. She had been there. She knew what it was like.

The vulture rounded and started coming back at her as she slowly stood. There was no way that thing would miss her this time.

A gun shot sounded, and the vulture flailed and fell, hitting the branch ahead of her and bouncing to the ground.

Breathing hard, Ayya tried to make herself relax. She felt tears streaming down her face, even though she didn't think she had been crying. Ayya took in a deep breath and walked toward the bully when she heard a cracking sound. She knew that sound.

She picked up the pace to hurry further in, but it was too late. The branch broke and gave way quick. She started falling. Ayya reached out to grab anything she could hold on to. On the way down, the jagged edges of the branch raked her stomach and chest.

Ayya let out a scream of pain as she caught the branch. If it wasn't for her shirt catching, she might have not held on. She looked down to see the broken part of the branch still falling, along with drops of blood.

A lurch and a surge of energy ran through her and she pulled herself up, using her caught shirt as a safety net. She let out a growling flood of tears as she pulled herself up, her body shaking.

The boy nearby started crying. "I'm sorry! Please help me. I won't ever bully you again!"

"I'm trying to get there. Hang on!"

Finally able to get up on the branch, as shaky as she was from the exertion, she crawled up the large branch rather than stand and walk.

When she reached the boy, she wrapped her legs around the large branch and reached under his arm and grabbed the back of the boy's shirt as far down as she could.

"Now you are going to have to pull yourself up because I just had to pull myself up to get here. Squeeze your arm down on mine."

"Okay. I'll try."

Ayya pulled hard on his shirt and torso, using her legs and pushing with her left arm against the branch as far out as she could push till her arm was straight out.

She felt herself giving out because her strength just wasn't up to lifting a boy larger than her. Ayya yelled at him with strain, "Pull!"

After what seemed like an eternity, they got him up on the branch and she told him to stay on his stomach and wrap his legs around the branch so he didn't have to worry about falling so easily.

"Whew, that was close! Are you okay?" Ayya winced as she sat up, her legs still locked around the branch at her ankles. The pain from the bruises and the newly opened skin were setting in.

Then she heard the whistle. She realized it was just before dark. Though she wasn't allowed in the house before dark, there was serious trouble if she didn't come right away when the whistle blew.

She was glad it was her mother blowing that whistle. She could tell the difference. Even if she couldn't, though, she knew her father was out of town. Ayya would be in trouble because of the blood on her shirt, but not as much as if her father were in town. She had that to be thankful for, at least.

44 Better Than Mine

"The whistle is being blown. I have to go or I will get into big trouble. Can you get down by yourself?"

Something caught her eye. The two other bullies were coming down the path. She yelled for them to come and help their friend.

"What are you doing to him!" said the leader of the three. The girl looked at her accusingly.

"I helped keep him from falling! Can you help him the rest of the way down? My mother has blown the whistle, and if I don't get home soon, I will get into a lot of trouble."

The boy that Ayya helped looked down at them. "Virginia, she lured me up here and then pushed me, trying to push me off!"

She looked at him, stunned. "I did not and you know it!"

Ayya heard a growl inside her so loud she wasn't sure where it came from.

— Let me help!

That startled her, but knew it was Aaru within her. Then she felt the anger that filled her. It was beyond her normal anger. She couldn't sit still anymore either, so she stood up.

The boy yelped out of fear from her sudden movement and what she might do.

Ayya jumped over him and climbed down from the tree. She turned on him and gave him a dirty, bitter look. His eyes widened a little before she said, "You can get him down your*self*. I have to go!"

She climbed down the tree and when her foot landed on the ground, she saw the dead body of the vulture, watching the inky mist waft around it. All three of them on the ground stared at it and slowly congregated near Ayya, fascinated.

Ayya started backing up when she heard Aaru's growl inside. The black mist started moving around, almost as if it was looking for something.

"Hello, little Phoenix," came a voice to her right.

She darted her head around to see Paul walking up casually.

"It seems like this vulture has broken the rules of life. I will have to report this infraction to the powers that be."

"Who are *y-you*?" Virginia asked nastily.

"Hi, Mr. Paul!" Just as Ayya started to run toward him, she remembered the vulture and stopped, holding out her palm. "Be careful. There is something wrong with that vulture," she warned as she warily checked it. "Look at the—"

The vulture was gone. She stared where it had been to see only disturbed leaves and an odd patterned black, light-grey, and yellow and white highlighted snake that slithered past. The pattern was like the pythons that she had seen and read about with her mother once. But they weren't supposed to have any of those types here. Ayya looked toward Paul to ask him about it.

She forgot all about it when she saw that Paul had a look on his face that she never wanted to be on the receiving end of. "As for you three, after he gets down out of that tree, you are never to come back to this forest unless you sincerely make amends with Ayya. If I catch you here, I *will* go to the police and report you. Just think of this place as the forbidden woods."

Paul walked forward slowly, pointing as he spoke. "That was a pretty dirty trick you three pulled on Ayya at the edge of the trees over there. That wasn't enough, though, was it?"

All three of them froze, listening to Paul. They didn't even blink.

"Still another one of you just pulled another one up there," he said, pointing up at the boy in the tree. "And a third one that you were about to pull, weren't you, Virginia?"

Virginia didn't move. She just blinked and didn't seem to breathe. Well, she was, but she had never seen her that still and quiet. It made her feel uneasy.

Paul must have sensed the awkwardness because he looked up and said, "Have you rested enough to climb down yet?"

A whiny, "No, I'm tired," came down out of the tree.

"Well, that's too bad. That means I'm going to have to call the fire department to get you down and the police department to report you three for harassing and beating up a girl several years younger that was just walking into her own property, which I currently own with her."

Ayya looked at him, shocked.

"I don't envy you when all that happens and your

parents find out."

The barefoot Virginia stormed to the trunk of the tree and looked up. "If you don't get down from there, after your parents kill you, I will do it all over again, you lazy beatnik!"

The boy up in the tree sat up quick with renewed energy. "I'm good, I'm good," he said and quickly made his way down the tree.

While he did, Paul looked over at Virginia with that weird, focused expression he got sometimes when he was going to say something that made your stomach jiggle. "You are headed down a dark path, dear girl. If you aren't careful, you will be famous for the wrong kind of thing."

He wasn't even talking to her, and that made her stomach jiggle, anyway. Ayya's pain started to reminder that she was hurt, and the whistle had blown. She touched her stomach and her shirt was soaked with blood. When she lifted her shirt up, she noticed her stomach had a large hole in it. *I m going to get in so much trouble when daddy sees this.*

After the boy got out of the tree, all three of them ran out of the live oak woods.

Ayya looked back toward the smiling Paul with his arms spread wide.

"Aww, give me that hug you were going to give me just a few seconds ago. It's been a while, and I would like to have my little phoenix hug."

"But I'm—"

"Trust me, little phoenix, a little blood won't bother me."

They met each other in a huge hug, and Paul lifted her up and swung her around in a circle while Ayya giggled. The pain seemed to disappear, and she giggled. She hugged his neck tight.

"I was just telling the sky to thank you for giving me a

safe place to come, and I saw a crystal in the sky with a light man standing in front of it, then you showed up!"

"Really?"

"Yes, sir! Honest!"

"Well, I guess that is a reminder to both of us that really great things happen for us both." Paul touched her nose with a smile and a twinkle in his eye.

"I'm so glad to see you, Mr. Paul. I lo-ove youuu!"

"Aww, I love you too, little phoenix! I'm proud of you. Even though they were mean, you saved a life today. You are his hero, even if he doesn't thank you or tell you that. And you are *my* hero!"

Then Paul squeezed her, and she felt like nothing was wrong in the world. "Mr. Paul?"

"Yes, Ayya?"

She hugged his neck and closed her eyes when they started flooding, feeling the tears hit her arms. "You have always been my hero, too. You and momma. Please don't forget me."

"Oh, my girl, I could never forget you. Even if it doesn't seem like it, I will always be watching out for you as much as I can."

"Thank you, sir." Then Ayya remembered the whistle. She jerked herself up and said, "Oh, Mr. Paul, I have to go. My momma blew the whistle. I hope I don't get in trouble, but I need to go home fast."

"I understand, my girl! Momma's worry about us even if it doesn't seem like it sometimes. But remember, they have a lot of responsibility, too."

Ayya smiled like the sun. "I will, Mr. Paul. Thank you!"

"You are most welcome, little phoenix."

Ayya started to run home, then realized she forgot to ask him a question about the land. She turned around. "Mr. Paul, do I really own—"

No one was there. She looked all around but didn't see Paul anywhere. Ayya had no time to waste thinking about it. She had to get home and ran as hard as she could. She left the edge of the woods and ran across a cul-de-sac and down the street. Two houses down, Ayya jumped the azalea bushes and ran up to the front door instead of the den door near the garage where her mother usually watched TV.

She opened the door as quietly as she could and walked into the entryway that was really like a hall with a large opening to the right to a living room they hardly ever used unless they had company.

Ayya loved that room. She always sat in the bay window behind the curtains and played or just watched the sky, especially when the fireplace was lit. The crackling soothed her, that and the ticking clock on the wall. She wondered what time it was because it was almost dark.

She heard voices as she stepped forward another step and saw it was 5:55 just before she saw her mother speaking with a woman she hadn't ever met before.

Ayya turned a little to her left, away from them, toward the hall closet to hide the blood on her shirt and face. As she tried to hurry by, she said, "Hi Momma. I need to go to the bathroom. I'll be right back."

Since Lanna was facing the other side of the room opposite her, she didn't notice anything was amiss. "Okay, sweetie. Come back in when you are done. I would like you to meet someone."

"Yes, ma'am." Ayya sprint-walked to the bathroom to get washed up as good as she could in a short time. She just got into the shower real quick, even though her mother would know something was up if she did that. But it would be better than her seeing her like this.

While she was in there, she noticed there was no more hole. It was just a bad gash. "Huh, I guess it wasn't as bad as I thought."

"Ayya!"

She started rushing to wash as she yelled back, "Coming, Momma! I'm taking my bath ahead of time. I got really dirty! I'm hurrying."

Ayya got out of the shower, dried off and put her bloody clothes into a bag and ran into her room, shoving it under the bed. She got dressed and never bothered to comb her wet towel dried hair, then headed down the hall and walked into the living room beside her momma.

Lanna smiled. "Josephine Funny, this is my oldest, Ayya."

Ayya looked at the lady sitting in front of her mother for the first time with any attention. She was plump, dark-skinned, and had a big smile.

"Hello, Ms. Funny." Ayya giggled even though she tried not to. "Is that really your name?"

Lanna said, "Ayya, that is rude!"

"I didn't mean to be rude, Momma. I'm sorry Ms.—"

"You can call me Ms. Josephine," she said with a big understanding smile.

Her fat cheeks had black freckles on them, that made her want to giggle. Not because they looked bad, but because they made her want to smile and giggle... and she did. She couldn't help it.

"Ayya, that's enough," said Lanna.

"Oh, it's okay. I'm making her laugh. It's my fault. It happens a lot. I like to see children laugh. And yes, that is my name. Isn't it funny?"

Both Lanna and Ayya laughed and said, "Yes!"

They all laughed, then Lanna said, "Now I have formally introduced you, I can say Ayya is a great helper and... a *big* hand full... but she is a *great* cook!"

"I really like you, Ms. Josephine Funny." Ayya walked over and gave her a huge hug. As she laughed and hugged her back, she felt the bouncy plump woman jiggle and it made her giggle.

She pushed Ayya to arm's length and smiled. "Why thank you my new big helper... and from what I hear, a hero too."

That made Ayya freeze.

Her momma looked shocked. "What do you mean, Josephine?"

"I have a friend that saw you help save someone from falling a long way to their death. The details aren't important but, Lanna, your daughter is a hero. She tapped three trees to get to him, and just when he was about to fall, she grabbed him and pulled him up."

"Nooo, when did this happen?"

Ayya started to open her mouth when Ms. Josephine said, "Oh, I don't remember when, but it happened very recently. Isn't that right, Ayya?"

"Yes, ma'am. Do you know Mr. Paul?" she asked with excitement. "He was there!"

"That I do!"

"Well, what a small world! Paul was a fireman we used to visit when we lived on the island. I haven't seen him in a long time, but he comes to see her while I'm usually at work from time to time."

Ayya looked at Ms. Josephine, still shocked that she knew that quick. She smiled at Ayya and winked.

The room went silent a few seconds before her mother broke it.

"Ayya, come here, sweetie. I have something I need to tell you," her mother said with a seriousness that was strange.

She walked over to her, hugging her sideways, still facing Ms. Josephine. "What is it, Momma?"

"Ms. Josephine is going to be working here for a while to help me. I hope you will be helpful to her. She will be cleaning and doing some cooking for us," Lanna explained.

That meant she would have more time. Then she said hopefully, "Oh, does that mean you get to play cards with me more, Momma?"

"Maybe." Lanna paused. "Ayya, I have something to tell you and I don't want you to talk with anyone about it right now."

"Okay, Momma." She hugged her momma. "What is it?"

"I'm sick and I need to go to the hospital a lot. I have what they call cancer, and now I need you to be a big girl and help out with your sister, too."

Ayya straightened even though her heart sunk. She didn't know what cancer was, but it couldn't be good. "Oh. Yes, ma'am," she said, feeling herself grow empty at the thought of her mother being sick. *Is she going to die? Should I ask? No, I can t ask her that.*

Just about the time she was going to start crying, her mother shouted, "Ayya! What happened?"

Ayya jumped, stunned at the sudden outburst, confused. Ayya followed her mother's gaze down to her blood-soaked chest from the gouge down her front that had opened back up.

Lanna looked at Josephine real quick and noticed her blood-soaked sleeve, and said, "I'm so sorry about your dress."

"Oh, not to worry, Ms. Lanna, I'll just dye the rest of it the same color once it's washed. It will be a great change and feel like a new dress!" She laughed, then reached out for Ayya. "Let me help you with her."

Both of them helped Ayya with her shirt and saw all the swollen bruises and the ripped skin from her stomach to her chest. Lanna ran to get some supplies and a new change of clothes and they began to get her patched up.

"Now I'll know the next time you volunteer a shower, you got something to hide."

"I just didn't want you to worry, Momma. Please don't tell Daddy." She paused only a second in thought, then said, "Momma? Are you sick because of me?"

Her mother looked at her and held her arms. "Ayya, I've been sick a while now. You didn't make me sick because of your behavior. I'm proud of you. You kept a boy from falling. At least now I can feel better when I have to replace your shoes so often now from all that tree climbing," she said as she pointed at her severely scuffed and worn shoes with a grin.

She could tell her mother was trying to make her feel better. Ayya smiled back. "I love you, Momma."

Ms. Josephine started laughing. Ayya and her mother turned to watch her. The more she laughed, the more she bounced, trying to point down at Ayya's shoes.

Ayya couldn't help but giggle. "I'm glad you came to help Momma. I can teach you how to cook fried chicken!"

Her mother and Ms. Josephine looked at each other and laughed.

"Well, I'm sure I could use another lesson in cooking. Maybe yours is much better than mine! I brought some for you and your momma tonight. It's on the table." She winked at us. "Run along and get a plate of however much you want. It's hard being a hero!"

Ayya's face lit up, and she scooted off the couch and ran to the kitchen. She stopped at the door when she saw the largest spread of chicken, buttermilk biscuits, fried okra, and gravy she had ever seen. She scurried over to the table as she said, "Almost all my favorite foods!"

She heard them laugh in there as she plopped two biscuits on her plate, opened them up and poured gravy on it. Then she ran to the other side of the table and got two huge spoonfuls of fried okra and two chicken thighs. She walked carefully to the dining area and sat her plate down just as her mother and Ms. Josephine walked around the corner to see that huge plate of food.

They just looked at her, stunned.

"This looks so good!!" She sat down at took a big bite of fried chicken, and let out a "Mmmmm," as she chewed. Even though her mouth was still super full, she tried her best to say, "bis eh beher n mine!"

"Don't talk with your mouth full, Ayya," said her mother. "And don't feel bad. It's better than mine, too!"

"Mmm hmm."

"Well, you didn't have to agree so fast!" her mother said, letting out a giggle.

Ayya looked at her momma and for a brief moment, she saw the wonderful Ms. Angel Queen shine a little bit. The one she had met so long ago. She couldn't help but smile so big her food began to squirt out of her cheeks accidentally. She hurried to catch it.

"I love to see a baby eat!" said Josephine. "Would you like to join us, Lanna?"

"I think I would! I better enjoy this great food before I can't eat any for a while."

"Sounds like a mighty fine idea!"

Both fixed a plate and sat down with Ayya. They spent the next hour laughing, telling stories, and eating.

"Ms. Josephine, you are really nice," said Ayya.

"I might not be so nice if you don't pick up after yourself at your age," she said with a grin.

"It's okay, Momma's like that too."

Her mother and Josephine laughed.

Finally, after they all decided they were full, they started picking up the dishes to take them into the kitchen. As Ayya stood to pick her plate up to take it into the kitchen, something caught her eye where the phone was mounted on the wall in the kitchen.

Wafting around the phone was an inky black mist. Her smile faded as she picked her plate up, never taking her eyes off it. She slid through the doorway as far away from the phone as possible. Ayya heard the growl within her again. "Shut up. You always get me into trouble when you start that."

"What did you say, Ayya?" Lanna called over.

"Nothing, Momma. I was just talking to the phone." Ayya turned to carry her dishes in and saw Ms. Josephine looking at the phone too, but her expression *wasn't* one of disbelief, but one that told her that she was seeing it too.

She winked at Ayya and took her plate in. "You can rinse for us."

"Oh, I like rinsing! Thank you!"

45 German Chocolate Snake

Ayya

Ayya woke up excited and got ready for school. She was excited because her mother was coming back today and she would be picking her up..

She hadn't eaten since yesterday morning, so she decided to risk the wrath of her father again. Ayya also hadn't seen her father since the night he had hit her mother. Just thinking about it made her mad.

Her momma had to leave after that, but she didn't know why. She was glad that her mother was safe, at least. Her father had been having a lot of the inky-eyed mist lately and it took a lot more thinking and strategy to avoid his anger.

She put her books in a stack and tightened the belt around them, then she picked up her lunch box and books and headed to the kitchen. Hopefully, she was in and out before her father got up.

She walked to the kitchen and opened up the bread box to get bread. The clock in front of her said it was 5:55. She had been seeing that time a lot lately.

Ayya quickly made her a peanut butter sandwich and put it in her lunch box. She closed it and put her books on top of it. Then she started to make another one for breakfast when her father came in.

He never stopped as he walked through the kitchen. He stared at her with those angry inky-eyes as he picked up all the bread and threw it into the trash before leaving the room.

She knew he was waiting for her to go over and get it, and had made that mistake before. Ayya grinned though as she picked her books and lunch box up and left the house to go to the bus stop. When she was out of window sight of the house, she laughed. "I might be stupid like you tell me, but you are making me smarter. I got my sandwich!"

— Yes, survive. Survive to fight for a good purpose.

ꆜꆜꆜ ꆜꆜꆜ

Ayya was working on a project of writing one sentence for each of the words up on the board. She had to either use them or it had to be about them. One of them was a fireman. She was excited about that one, so she used it and was writing about Paul when she saw Ms. Harrison's feet stop at her desk.

"Hello, Ayya."

Ayya looked up and couldn't help but smile at the black freckled cheeks. "Oh hello, Ms. Josephine!" Catching herself right away, she corrected herself. "Oops, sorry, Ms. Harrison. You remind me of my friend, Ms. Josephine. She used to work at our house when my momma first got sick. I miss her, but I like you too.”

Ms. Harrison bent down and put her hands on her knees. “It’s quite alright, Ayya. I have done that myself a few times. By the way, happy birthday. You are a big eight years old today, right?”

Ayya smiled brightly. “Thank you, ma’am. Yes, I am. I almost forgot about it!”

“Ayya, I have a message from your mother.”

She sat up straight and felt the excitement raise. “Is she here? She’s been gone.”

“I’m sorry, Ayya. She said in her message that she can’t pick you up today as promised, and she won’t be home for another week.”

Ayya sat back and looked down at her lap, dejected. “Yes, ma’am, thank you for telling me.”

“There is more. Your uncle had a heart attack and died, sweetie.”

“Which one, Ms. Harrison? I have nine uncles.”

“She didn’t tell me that part, Ayya. I’m sorry. But she told me to tell you something important that you should know.”

“Yes, ma’am, what is it?”

“She said to take the bus home and that your father wouldn’t be home until six.”

“Yes, ma’am, it is important that I know that. Thank you, ma’am,” said Ayya gratefully.

“Ayya, are you okay at home?”

“Oh, yes, ma’am! I got till six to fix something to eat!”

Ms. Harrison smiled and cocked her head. “Did you bring lunch today, Ayya?”

Ayya got distracted with a plan to get something cooked and still put some away in her room for the next couple of days. She thought about what was in the refrigerator and freezer.

"Ayya?"

"Oops, I'm sorry, Ms. Harrison." She pulled out her lunch box and showed her the roughly made peanut butter sandwich, grinning from ear to ear at the accomplishment. "Yes, ma'am, see?"

— Yes, survive.

Shut up, Aaru.

Ms. Harrison said with a smile that seemed to bring out the dark freckles in a special way, "Did you make that yourself?"

"Yes, ma'am! Isn't it great?" Then she had an afterthought and said, "Well, it might not look as good as Momma's, but it is a happy sandwich."

Her teacher laughed as Ayya closed her lunch box and stored it back under her desk.

Ms. Harrison stood straight and turned to walk to the head of the class and said as she clapped, "Alright, class, we are switching lunch and recess today and maybe even tomorrow... So now, it is time for recess!"

After recess, they all lined up for lunch. They all did it so quickly that Ms. Harrison said, "Whoo! You all are doing so well that maybe we will do this tomorrow too! I'm not having to tell you two times to do every little thing!"

The whole class giggled, and they all headed to the lunchroom to eat. As they entered the lunchroom, Ayya heard Aaru's low growl. As they all sat down at a table, Ayya felt aggravation. *Don't mess my mood up with your growls, Aaru. Also, I have until six tonight to fix something to eat and I don't want you messing things up. It's not fun to be hungry all the time.*

When Ayya got settled, she opened up her lunch box. She was surprised when she didn't see just her peanut butter sandwich. There was a ham and cheese sandwich with lettuce and tomato, fruit and a piece of apple pie in there as well.

She closed the lunch box quickly and looked around to see if anyone was watching her. Ayya looked up and down the long row of tables. Ms. Harrison was at the end, eating a ham and cheese sandwich with lettuce and tomato. Ayya smiled at her as she ate.

Ms. Harrison looked up and winked, then called down a boy that was about to knock over his milk.

Ayya opened up the lunch box and took only a second to decide which sandwich to eat first. She carefully unwrapped the ham and cheese sandwich so she could save the wrapper for her peanut butter sandwich for later. She was so hungry and she couldn't help but shove large bites into her mouth.

Ayya almost started choking from not having anything to wash it down with, so she raised her hand.

When Ms. Harrison finally saw her, she dropped her shoulders and shook her head. "Go ahead, Ayya. I already know what you want, judging by the gobs of food in your mouth. Slow down, you got time to eat."

Ayya nodded and went to get water from the fountain next to the door. She drank a little and chewed a little, and repeated the process until it was all gone. *Whew! won t do that again.*

It was when she walked back to her seat and looked at her food when she discovered that someone had taken the rest of her sandwich. Ayya sat down in a rush and opened her lunch box. With horror flushing up her chest and into her face, everything was gone.

Ayya put her head down on her arms and cried silently.

Ms. Harrison must have seen what had happened because she said, "Alright, class, if someone puts Ayya's lunch back, I will give them a reward for doing so. No punishment, just a reward."

Hope lifted Ayya as all the kids looked around, seeming like they were unsure of what happened. No one came forward.

"Ayya, you can have my dessert." She got up and set a large piece of German Chocolate cake in front of her. "Enjoy it, and happy birthday, child."

She thought about how she and her mother had shared cookies on the front step. "Ms. Harrison?"

Her teacher turned back around to face her. "Yes, Ayya?"

"Can we share, Ms. Harrison? It will be more fun."

Ms. Harrison walked over to her lunch box, bringing over a shining clean fork and took a bite off, holding it on her fork. "Thank you, Ayya, you are right. It is so much more fun to share. Isn't that right, class?"

"Yes, Ms. Harrison!" the whole class shouted with giggles and laughs.

Then all the kids started trading halves of sandwiches, fruit, chips, and fork-fulls of whatever was made for them, having a great time. Still, no one came forward with Ayya's lunch.

Ayya was happily eating the chocolate cake, not bothering to look around for her food anymore. *This lunch is the best lunch I ever had.*

She heard Aaru's growl again. Determined not to invite trouble, she didn't look up or around. She just kept eating.

I'm not getting into trouble, I'm not getting into trouble. I'm being good today. I'm being a good girl.

It wasn't long, and she heard the other kids in her class start screaming and scrambling to get up, knocking things over. The boy next to her stood and started peeing in his pants right there.

— Survive…

Ayya gradually rolled her eyes up to the movement she

caught in her peripheral vision. Slithering past the doorway of the kitchen, she saw the thickest head and neck of the largest snake she had ever seen.

46   Did You See That?

Ayya was familiar with snakes since she lived in snake country. Plus, she had spent so much time in the woods; she saw a lot of them. Mr. Paul had once given her snake education lessons.

She could tell by the eyes that it was likely poisonous or a constrictor, and it was way too big to be poisonous, at least from what she knew about snakes.

Pans clattered in the kitchen, along with screams. Ms. Harrison told all the kids to go out the door to the hallway and back to class. Everyone scrambled all over each other in a panic.

— Slow… survive.

That made sense to Ayya. She didn't want to flag herself as prey. And as big as that thing seemed to be to cause such a panic, she would definitely be prey size.

She didn't know why she did it because it was so large, but she slowly picked her feet up to the bench height, anchored her heels down by adjusting sideways to give herself some room, and raised herself up to a standing position.

Growls and lurches were Aaru's reaction. *Calm down!*

After she said that, she finally got to see the snake. She almost peed herself and it was looking straight at Ms. Harrison, who was trying to get all the kids out of the lunchroom.

Ms. Harrison turned to face the snake, very slowly and calmly. That gave Ayya time to look at the snake closer. And there it was, the inky-eyes. Oh no!

Ms. Harrison was so still she wondered if she was a statue. It was a tactic she had been taught several years ago. Usually snakes just went on their merry way if you did that, but it was looking at Ms. Harrison like... it was smart like a human—or stupid, depending on who it was.

Ayya rubbed her eyes, thinking she was seeing illusions, when she saw a menacing expression creep across its face. Snakes didn't have facial expressions that she knew of.

As he slithered closer to Ms. Harrison, Ayya realized it was still coming out of the kitchen and her eyes grew wide. Shivers ran up her back and panic rose inside her, her palms got sweaty.

Aaru growled inside her—low, long, and menacing. She knew that growl. It was time to leave. *But we can t leave Ms. Harrison, Aaru.*

— Good purpose.

Ayya slowly stepped up on the long table from the bench and raised herself up, trying not to hit anything on it that was left over from lunch.

Ms. Harrison looked at her in alarm. Her facial expression said 'don't you dare,' as the snake slithered up her shins and then up to her lap. Ms. Harrison stiffened and arched her back.

Ayya did not know what came over her, but she

suddenly did something unexpected, almost as if someone else did it for her that wasn't Aaru. "Hey, sir scaly-butt! You looking for some food? You slimy-slack-face! I'll give you something to chase!"

Then she felt Aaru help her say, "Your scales are like the diarrhea of the mag!"

What s a mag, Aaru?

— Survive…

The snake jerked its head around and honed in on Ayya.

Ayya turned, jumped off the table, and bolted toward the doors by the water fountain that was still open. The seconds seem to slow for her as if it was minutes.

— Survive…

I m trying, I m trying. Ayya wasn't the fastest runner, but with whatever was happening to her body, she seemed to have the run speed of a champion runner. She knew it wasn't true, but she would take the feeling she felt right about now.

Behind her, she heard all kinds of crashing and things sliding off tables and benches. That snake was powerful.

Don t look, don t look. Just keep going, just keep going, she coached herself.

Ayya had no idea what she planned to do, but she was going to run for now. She heard some glass break, and an alarm sounded.

"Ayya, run! I'm calling the fire department… and Paul!"

When Ayya turned around quick, Ms. Harrison was trying to hack at the snake's tail still coming out of the kitchen area with a fire axe.

Wait, she knows Paul?

The snake hissed, and it seemed to go through her and her muscles went weak.

Ayya felt her bladder open in the fear of what she just saw. *Nope, I shouldn t have looked. I shouldn t have looked. Run, run, run.*

— Survive…

At least it s not looking at Ms. Harrison, but Aaru, I m scared.

— Survive…

"That is not very helpful, Aaru!" she yelled as tears started to form in her eyes.

She was almost at the large doors. They suddenly seemed overly large in her panic. What was she doing? She had only just turned seven. The long handles of the door were low enough that she could reach easily, but the doors were very heavy. Ayya could hear it chasing her.

Without realizing what she was doing, she ran harder and let out a long, "Mmmmmmmmmmmmmmmm." She felt the vibration that she had not felt in a very long time. It made her tear up and more determined to really pour on the speed. Her body was fighting that, though.

Ayya reached for the large handle, almost close enough to grab it. A trash can was holding it open, but not by much. The kids she saw ahead started screaming and scattering down the halls.

Thump. She felt something hit her leg. She formulated a plan. She would grab the handle just in case, then grab the one on the other side to push the door closed.

— Run… Survive…

Thump… Thump… Ayya almost tripped, but she caught herself by grabbing the handle of the door. As she reached for the handle on the other side, the snake pinned her with its weight.

It turned out that trying for the door handles was a mistake. It gave the snake the advantage, and it started wrapping around her left shin and knee.

"Ayya! Watch out!" Ms. Harrison called out to her. She could tell she was running toward the kitchen.

Her body was no match for the large door or the enormous snake. She tried to lift her leg up to let it take her shoe and sock and slide off, but it didn't work.

The snake jerked her leg back, taking her breath from the strength of the pull. She thought her shoulders would separate there for a second. She had one thing on her side, though. The floor of that lunch room was hard and slick, so it slid back toward her. That gave her the chance to grab the handle on the other side and pull herself through.

But it turned out that the snake had a plan and used the grip it had on her leg to pull and coil around, also using the closed door as leverage.

Ayya used her right leg to push on the right closed door. She felt a thump like the left door closed. Only it didn't. It just closed as far as it could with the snake being in the way. That seemed to make it very mad, though.

She called out, "Someone help me keep the door closed!"

Some of the older kids still there in the hall started running toward her. Right behind them, two teachers ran too.

The snake coiled up her leg, but it was slower since it had to deal with being caught in the door. Ayya leaned in as hard as she could, but it had a good grip on her now and she knew she was losing this fight.

— Hold on, survive…

A teacher arrived and grabbed the handle and pushed hard with a jerk. The snake almost loosened enough to pull out some, but it recovered way too fast.

In the position she was in now, she was face to face with the snake's inky-eyed head. She realized it would have no problem eating her. She pointed her toe to give it less leverage and pulled. It did slip a little, but it didn't help much. She felt her foot go numb as it started to constrict around her leg.

Still holding on to the handle at the bottom, she noticed six hands on the handle, trying to help push. Then she heard several thumps and slides coming from the other side of the door.

The first teacher looked through the glass and said, "Shit!" and renewed her effort to push. The teacher put her grip around Ayya's hands to make sure she didn't let go. "Push hard, kids!"

The snake jerked hard, causing Ayya to scream out. It felt like it almost pulled her leg out of her hip and her skin was stinging and burning. The snake had one full coil around her now and it wouldn't be long till she would go down.

Ayya's right foot slipped free from the pressure and the snake's strength took advantage of it. Ayya's butt and bent right leg slammed up against the door.

"Hang on, Ayya!"

She knew that voice. "Mr. Paul!" But it was far off in sound.

— Hold on… Survive…

Ayya started letting out a strained and growling, "Mmmmmmmmm." Every part of her was shaking now.

The first teacher said with a strained voice, "Don't give up, Ayya, you are doing great!"

"Mmmmmmmmm."

A second teacher showed up and started trying to stomp the snake and hit it with a hammer in the head, but a little too gently. Ayya realized he was trying to make sure he didn't hurt her.

Ayya's body was spent, and she just couldn't find the strength to push anymore. She couldn't feel her leg anymore. She felt her grip slip as well as her hip. Then Ayya heard Ms. Harrison call out to her to hang on. Then she heard some voices on the other side talking urgently.

Ayya looked up to the teacher and said, "Please tell Ms. Angel Queen I'm sorry. It's my Momma."

The snake took full advantage of her weakening state and it coiled up and around her and felt her stomach starting to squish, her breath left her.

— Survive

She heard the words Aaru said, but couldn't quite seem to understand them. Then her body jerked a lot for some reason she didn't understand. But she started to breathe a short little breath.

"Open the door now!" yelled a familiar voice on the other side.

The teacher and kids let go and backed up, letting Ayya get sucked into the lunchroom. She jerked left and right sharply as the snake spasmed.

She watched one of the firemen put a noose around the head and pulled it tight, using his foot on its face to hold it down. When the grip finally let go a little, Ayya gasped for breath, but it still didn't want to let go.

The firemen started working to get her free. As she rolled away from what was left of the snake, Ms. Harrison said, "Everything is going to be okay now, Ayya."

"Thank you, ma'am," she said weakly, still gasping for breath, feeling the pain starting to rip through her now that the feeling was coming back.

"I should scold you for doing what you did, but I can't. That was brave," she told Ayya, out of breath with relief in her voice. "Let's get you to a doctor."

"Yes, ma'am," she said to her as she looked over the snake. Its face was now lifeless. Then she saw the black mist sliding out of the body and into the air. "Ummm, Ms. Harrison?"

"Yes, Ayya?"

"Did you just see that?"

"Yes, dear, but I won't tell anyone if you don't," she said with a smile as she lifted her from the floor to carry her.

47 The Crevasse

When Zreyas reached the ship area, he realized he hadn't heard Tap say anything. He was glad she didn't. She must have sensed that he needed to be alone. After they had all formed two sides, he asked Tap, *Do you see any lower frequencies that would endanger us?*

— No, Captain.

Zreyas held his left hand out toward the first one in the left group. "Step forward and make your choice."

The first Janquar in line stepped forward with a stride of confidence, but no arrogance, uncharacteristic of the Nation. "I want to join your crew. I will pledge to... be..." He took a deep breath, "... be loyal to your cause, and to you, until death. I only hesitated because I have no skills that I know of that would help you, but I would like to be someone that fixes things. I like making new things too. The artisan taught me to make water, like you taught him."

— Captain, he has an inventor-ship air about him. He is creative and works well under stress. He would be a good engineer.

"We will train you as an engineer. If you are willing to take orders from me, follow me through the depths of ticking-hell that I might need to navigate through, and if you feel it is your purpose."

"It is my purpose. I seal my pledge, Commander Zreyas."

"You can call me Captain Zreyas. I don't want to have anything to do with the word commander. That was my old life. Welcome aboard Engineer."

Everyone nodded with understanding.

The blue member that pledged originally came forward. He realized that now that he saw him up close, that he was familiar to Zreyas. He was of his Rittak line but was not considered good material by his father because he questioned him. He recognized his horn array in a pattern of the rejected.

Then he stepped up and did something Zreyas never expected. "Now that we have been to the water and left the past behind, I want to renew my pledge."

He turned his back toward Zreyas, despite the rule of the Nation to never turn a back to someone in trust because they would kill you. He didn't slowly turn. He turned without hesitation and held his arms out in a gesture of vulnerability. His brothers gasped but nodded.

"Thankings to you for your trust. You can turn around now. What is your choice?"

"I pledge my loyalty to you until death with trust. I want to go with you on your crew, but I want to scout and hunt. I am not sure what it might be useful for. I might not be fit to be on your crew."

"What is your name?"

"You."

"No, I mean what is *your* name?" pointing at the rejected one.

Cree stepped forward from the line. "Captain, he doesn't have a name." After Zreyas faced him, he continued, "All he knows is 'you'. You do this, and that. The Captain might not be accustomed to this because you were in a line that was of rank to the Janquar Nation. We were nothing. We were never given names because we were told we were all but dead to them in our weaknesses. The only reason *I* have one is because... Aaru gave it to me."

Zreyas felt a wave of horror run through him. The shock made him freeze. Apparently, they noticed from his expression.

Forcing down the tears, his voice broke slightly as he replied with, "I am of aplo-po-gies to you, brothers. I... didn't know." He paused for a time, then looked up at all of them. "You will all have names. When you come up, you can choose your own name, or I can give you one later in a more ceremonious way. The world needs to know your names. Everyone is important. No one will ever be nameless again unless they choose to."

He could feel the emotions surface from all the nameless blue. The wave was so powerful that it almost knocked him backwards because of their pushing auras. The experience was incredibly profound to him.

Then he turned his gaze back to the newly assigned engineer. "What is your name?"

"I would like you to choose later, Captain Zreyas."

He looked to the one that showed his trust from the Rittak line. "What is your name?"

"I would like you to choose, Captain Zreyas."

"Switch," Zreyas announced. "Your name is Switch. I saw what happened and what you did when all of you were running to catch the deserter. I will explain to you later what happened so you can learn from what you did."

Switch nodded. "I would like that, Captain Zreyas."

Zreyas turned back to the next rejected that stepped forward and focused on his eyes. "What is your name and your choice?"

The rejected never wavered and said, "Win. My name is Win. And I want to be on the crew, but I don't know what I will be useful for yet."

"Win, we can discuss with Tap, my ship, what your best assignment might be, until we have a need for what you love to do if that is agreeable to you."

The Janquar almost smiled, but he went to one knee throwing a fist to his chest to finalize his choice with no words at all.

For the next few hours, until dawn, he watched them make choices of their names, desired positions, and their commitments. Those that wanted him to choose their names, he told them he would do that later, after things weren't so urgent to get off the planet.

After they were all done, he turned to the crowd behind him and said, "Welcome to The Order of the Sleeping Phoenix. We have a lot ahead of us and much to do. You will have your own beds and sleep in group housing on the ship with a common area to eat and talk. I have a lot to do to help you all fit in your right places, so be patient! If you don't know the word patience, start learning it. It's a critical skill."

Zreyas suddenly heard a buzzing and screeching noise in the distance. He knew that screech, unfortunately, and there was no way he could ever forget it. He jerked his head toward where he heard it from, but saw nothing. However, in the distance, at the edge of the forest, he saw the trees start to resemble melting.

"Everyone, listen up! Run up into the ship... *now*! Tap, get everyone on the ship as fast as possible. The nagodara are coming and I'm not sure the ship defenses will work on them... *move!* Teleport them in!"

As soon as they saw the ramp appear, the new order members did exactly as they were told without a thought to look for their belongings. They all ran up the ramp and disappeared at the top.

"Go, go, go! Help each other get in as fast as you can!" Zreyas turned again to the decay coming fast, refusing to go first. Some of them waited for him, "Don't wait for me, *go*! I will make sure you are in first so you can have that freedom we spoke about. I didn't do all this work to free you just to watch you decay to nothing... *go!*"

There were still too many not on the ship. Zreyas wasn't sure what to do. Then he thought about his armor. He mentally made it bright, shiny, and easy to see at dawn. He knew he was small, so he started jumping up and down after he Q-leaped to the top of the cave entrance.

He looked back and there was no way they would all get on the ship in time. He took a breath as he saw the swarm of what he estimated as a few hundred nagodara coming his way.

"Hey! Here I am, you ticking mag-shits! Come get *this*! I almost killed your brother!" That was when he knew he had their attention, because the swarm changed course. He turned around and started Q-leaping away from the ship, running east.

Tap, close the ramp behind them and do not show yourself. I will do my best to get to safety after distracting them. The largest part of what little advantage we have is them not knowing you exist. Leave, and I will let you know when I find safety. If we are lucky, they will get on the ship before some of them can get to you. There is still one more that wants to go. And I can t leave them behind. No one deserves to die the way they kill.

— Yes, Captain. I understand your choices, but please be safe. I just found you. The twins say that the one that wants to go *needs* to go, and it is *critical* that they do. They are watching and they said to tell you that you are not alone. We are *all* there with you, Captain.

Now that he had their attention, he dimmed his armor back down to the color of the environment as much as possible while running his ass off. *Don t worry Tap, we got a lot to do together. Help them get up that ramp even if you have to teleport them without them knowing what is going on.*

— I will do that now, Captain. They still have not seen me, or the group, Captain. You got their attention in time. They don't see well.

She paused a moment.

— They are all in, Captain.

Good, now go and leave this once beautiful place. It s a shame Rtu s work is so demented now.

— Yes, Captain, going now. Freckles says that he is sad too, but another place will be made in memory of Tarq that he will gift to you one day for defending it.

Zreyas didn't know what to say to that. That was too much to think about right now. *Yeah, well, I got to get my ticking-ass off the planet alive before I can think about any of that.*

— Oh, and Captain, the twins said that they were back from helping Ayya and she is safe and doing well. She ran like you are doing from a situation and was successful. They know you will be too.

The news about Ayya made his heart feel like it was floating and he smiled so large that his face hurt. Then he breathed a sigh of relief that his new crew were off the planet and safe, and Ayya and Aaru were okay. Despite what he was doing right now, it was a good day. With a smile on his face, he focused and headed northeast toward the tree line.

He filled his chamber with the anger he had for the nagodara and what they were doing. He couldn't help but wonder who created such a thing. He couldn't remember if the twins told him, but there had to be a visage somewhere that liked to lead the living to dark frequencies and turn them into something beyond demented.

Zreyas began converting the energy of the anger slowly to gain speed and larger Q-leap distance without wasting any. He knew being small made him slower, but it was also harder to see him. He looked back and realized that even with his Q-leaps, they were gaining ground. He felt his body shower itself with survival instincts. *Ticking hell, this Q-leaping used to seem so powerful, but now it isn t as much as I thought it would be.* He needed to grow his capacity or something. He was so ticking-small it wasn't a wonder they were gaining ground.

He continued northeast right into the trees, but they never slowed, no matter how much he weaved in the thick forest. That was when he discovered they had to be tracking him some other way other than sight.

Think, Zrey, think. All these new weapons and I don t know how to use them. He Q-leaped higher to the tops of the trees and started tapping trees rather than running. Zreyas had plenty of anger to spare right now and he converted it without abandon to get the leaps he needed. He looked back to check his progress. They were fumbling but still gaining ground. As he turned back around, he saw a trunk of a tree within inches from his face.

He Q-leaped ahead and then again upward to the top of the next tree and focused ahead, "Ticking-hell, Zrey, that was close! Pay attention to where you want to go!" As he righted his course toward the northeast again, he knew the Janquar had not been there yet. Things looked too good, and no trees were cut down. He started assessing on the run. *I got two small weapons, two mediums, and one large. Think Zrey, think. The problem is, I don t know what technology is higher than what I have yet except that ship's weapon.*

— Captain, just a reminder; All weapons are tools, and all tools can be weapons.

The trees ahead coming closer were more dead and sparse, but not in the same way that the nagodara melted them with decay. They just looked dead. *All weapons are tools, and all tools are weapons... Let s see, tools can be...*

Zreyas heard the swarm s noise more clearly. That meant they were more in the open—and that meant they were on the top of the trees too. He had a sudden thought, Ticking hell!" *Tap, are grappling hooks an advanced technology?*

— Yes, Captain. They are still used today in current technology, and are self-releasing and automatically retract. They are pretty amazing for such an early weapon that went into the space technology, and many forms are used today. But they take practice to learn.

Zreyas Q-leaped to the ground and headed through the dead trees as he pulled his dagger and axe off his hips. He looked at them, unsure of how to really do this. He figured it might be like doing a Q-leap and imagined them as the grappling hooks already like what Tap spoke about.

... Nothing happened, and he heard the swarm of nagodara nearing, closer and closer.

He cursed and put them back on his hips after jumping over a dead log starting to see a greenish rusty mist ahead in the air, past the trees. He reached up and pulled his two swords and tried them. *This would be a ticking-good time for you to change into advanced technology grappling hooks.*

His swords shimmered and morphed into a glimmering set of grappling hooks that were also serrated. They had a sharp spear at the top of them and the hooks retracted into the stem. Half-way down the stem, there was a catch mechanism of some sort. He noticed lighted dots in several areas. *Now to figure out how to use them, these are much different from what I m used to. I need to learn quick, because that green and orange smoke up there ahead doesn t look healthy.*

Zreyas started to get tired. He reached up as he ran and

focused on the anger to keep himself going by letting it come in and watching it fill. He noticed he had begun to do that process a little differently than he used to.

Aiming toward the highest branch that came into focus, he squeezed the handle to prepare to throw it. To his surprise, the grappling hook shot out, but the blades looked inverted.

"Ticking-hell, they are weak and already broken."

The point stuck into the wood, and two things happened. The blades snapped around the tree, and a guard of some sort snapped around his hand, holding it firm to the grip. "What the..." The line contracted, shooting his whole body up like a rocket toward the tree.

"Ticking-hell, this is going to hurt," he growled through gritted teeth. He quickly shifted his body away from what was coming, forgetting he had another one in the other hand.

By some miracle, he missed the trunk by a fraction and sailed past it. Then he heard a click behind him as he continued to fly upward. "Tap, you were right, I should have practiced fi-irst. Shi-it!"

As his upward thrust leveled off, he realized he was extremely high and his grappling hook had released and reset. Time seemed to slow for Zreyas and somehow that told him he was in big trouble. His senses became extremely acute and hyper-focused.

The dead wood trees were under him, and ahead was a very large field of steaming pools that looked acidic colored with greens, golds, and rust colors. He had heard of these acid pools, but had never seen them before, until now.

Judging by his trajectory, he would be landing generally right in the middle of one of those pools. He could Q-leap just before landing, but it was the steam that seemed like would be the more deadly part breathing that in.

Past the pools, he saw a massive open space of a canyon. He realized he used the grappling hook on the last large tree in the area just before the pools.

Zreyas looked down for a tree. He saw one in the middle of the acid pools. He aimed and squeezed the grip.

Nothing happened.

He guessed he was too high up and the hooks knew somehow. Zreyas looked around and realized he had gone higher and faster than he thought. He looked back, and the nagodara were still coming, but further back than before. They were between the dead forest and the pools.

"Come on, you nasty bandhulas! I'm your father of death!" Zreyas turned his head back around in time to start watching his true descent. He looked again for a tree. There was no more, so he aimed for the edge of the crevasse.

Nothing happened. He was too high up and out of range, he supposed.

He took in a deep breath and spoke to Tap. *Tap, I m saying the sorries. It doesn't look like I m going to make it, but I won t stop trying until I no longer breathe. Tell the twins I am sending the lovings and to you too. Also, I m sending the thankings to you all for everything.*

He summoned his rage as his life images started flashing before his eyes and thought about all those nagodara and what they would do to the environment and wildlife. His anger at the Dark One's actions flared at the thought of him putting these things in the world.

Since going back would be death by nagodara, Zreyas focused high up and let his anger loose, making it pass through the gate he created to convert the low frequency emotion to a higher expansive one. He used the joy he had from helping the blue camp, how he liked Cree, and his chosen family of the twins and Tap for his conversion door and began converting for his jumps.

Zreyas used the extra power to Q-leap as far as he could over the canyon to reach the other side. He thought about how much he had learned from the twins and how lucky he was to find them. The energy expanded and propelled him through the biggest leap he had ever performed in his life. It was exhilarating, and he felt free, even in the dire circumstances.

As he came out of the leap, he still had anger enough to do it again. He put all his fear and desperation into his chamber to add to it. He aimed and leaped once more.

Zreyas came out of the leap and assessed his situation as he started to fall again. He looked to the other side and realized it was way too far. The canyon was much larger than he expected by the look of it. Nature had a way of playing tricks on you like that.

He looked back to see the nagodara burning and floundering in the acid pools, and he smiled. Satisfied, and he closed his eyes.

48 Remembering

ꂇꂇꂇ *Zreyas* ꂇꂇꂇ

Everything inside Zreyas got quiet... silent... peaceful. Time still seemed slowed from the adrenaline rush he heard in his ears. He no longer had anger, fear, or desperation. He couldn't muster up any more. It certainly wasn't because he didn't try. Zreyas looked down and couldn't see the bottom of the canyon, due to the mist and fog and being so far down. It seemed surreal.

He felt okay with all he had tried to do in the last several weeks. At least he got the blue camp members away from the Janquar Nation. He was at peace now and didn't know how to Q-leap yet like Rhom did. He had not quite gotten to that part of learning.

Zreyas tried one last time to summon rage, but in his peaceful state, there was no override button or magic. He decided to just enjoy his last ride.

Zreyas held his arms out, feeling the wind as he looked down. Far below, he could see a waterfall coming off of a cliff. The water fell so far that it turned more into spray than a solid stream by the time it hit the river below. It was more like a river-lake that he could barely make out. The plant growth around the area was beautiful, even from this height. He also noticed the air was thinner where he was.

"Whoa," he whispered. "Aaru, you would have loved this place. I wish you could see this. It's... pheno-mi-tastic," he said softly in his peace. "You take care of each other, you and Ayya. I'll be watching over you in a different way if I can."

Zreyas tried to be angry that he couldn't fulfill his promise to Aaru, but he couldn't feel anything but peace. He knew he had done his best, and it was good enough. It was probably why he couldn't summon the anger. It was amazing what the body did and felt like when it was in a state of pure peace.

He rolled his body in the wind, belly down, and let his arms and legs spread. Zreyas felt supported by the wind while he faced his destiny with as much joy and peace as someone could possibly experience with what was about to happen, and... somehow, he found himself smiling just a little.

He loved being alone and supposed it always brought him peace in some way because he didn't feel lonely. Then Zreyas really smiled.

Aaru, I'm flying! You always wanted to fly, and I thought you were crazy. But now, I —

The breath was suddenly knocked out of his lungs, and the disorientation made him grip his grappling hooks harder. He was headed fast toward the cliff side for what seemed like a very painful face plant into the side of the cliff. His fear was very real right now. All the peace he had was gone, and the compartment filled again.

He felt something move under him and that freaked him the ticking-hell out, because there was nothing there.

Out of pure reaction, he aimed the grappling hooks toward a ledge with a single small tree on the side of the cliff living in what seemed to be an impossible situation.

The grappling hook hit the space behind the little ledge and part of it crumbled away from where it hit. It was a bad area of stone and it looked like it would be a failed attempt after all.

Then he found out how wrong he was. His body jerked with the momentum of the pull of the hook, still not able to figure out how to stop the pulling part yet. As he raced toward the cliff wall, he couldn't help but think, *This... is going to hurt.*

Sure enough, it did. He turned his head sideways just in time before his body slammed into the newly opened crack in the side of the cliff. He landed hard on the small ledge. He quickly used the other arm to wrap around the tree that was just about twice his height, all twisted and thick from trying to survive with almost no soil around it.

"I'm saying the sorries to you for messing up what little dirt you have. If I live through this, somehow I will make it up to you." *Help me remember that Tap.*

Either he didn't hear her as he tried to scramble to stand in the pain or she didn't say anything to him. However, he *was* able to hear the inconsistent buzzing of scrambling nagodara through the crack, along with loud bubbling—clearly the acid pools. Nope, chipping his way in there would not be a good thing, but it sounded like all the nagodara had their hands full with the acid.

It was amazing to him that they would go through acid just to get to him. He could only guess two possible reasons. One, they were either so under the enthrallment of the big D.O. that they had no choice—or two, they were programmed in a way to make it their sole purpose from whatever motivation they had. Either way, he wasn't sure.

Breathing a sigh of relief, he leaned up against the cliff-side to get his breath and think. Zreyas slightly bent over and looked at the grappling hooks still in his hands. "This is definitely going to take a lot of ticking-practice but I'm not sure what other type of tools to pick when I don't know the technology of the advanced."

He leaned back up against the wall and closed his eyes a moment, trying to think. At least he was not surrounded by hundreds of nagodara and wondered if they all got eaten up by the acid pools. He listened and heard only one, maybe two, sounds of faint buzzes and screeches. At first, it was interrupted quite a few times. He guessed it was from floundering in those pools.

Zreyas realized that over the next few minutes, it transitioned, from that, to a steady screech that wasn't stopping. The longer it screeched, the louder it got.

He decided to look up to see how far down he was from the top of the cliff and there was a nagodara falling straight for him.

Zreyas' body jerked up suddenly and found his shoulders were being held firmly by something with claws. Claws that would have pierced his skin, had it not been for the new armor. He realized who it had to be. But he soon forgot that as he sailed upwards into the sky, watching a nagodara splat, spraying out acid all over the place where he had just been standing.

All he could think about was that poor tree. *Rtu, I m asking with the please to save that tree. I made it a promise. I don t know why I m so soft in the chest lately about the killing, but—*

Zreyas found himself being propelled higher up past the height he had been before when he Q-leaped out too far. He let out a roar out of pure fear. "What the ticking-he-e-ell!"

Once he leveled off again and looked down where he

was going to be falling, he could only see the top of the waterfall. Below that, it looked like a misty pit from his height. He had a hard time breathing, both from panic and the thin air.

Then he started falling. Time seemed to slow again because Zreyas' senses heightened. He had no idea what he was supposed to do at this point. He just morphed his weapons back to what they were unconsciously and returned the two swords, sheathing them on his back without thinking.

In his mind, his fight was over. He couldn't even begin to guess what had just happened. In some ways, he thought very clearly right now, but in other ways, his mind was numb and couldn't think. He just wanted to say his last words that might mean something.

"Thankings to you Rhom, Rtu, and Tap." The other part of his mind said, *Think, Zrey, think.*

Then he realized what he had been thinking about when things went crazy. His armor and how he could change shape into something else! He needed to fly or glide.

He closed his eyes a moment and thought about the birds at the landing at the ocean that were killed by that nagodara. He remembered how magnificent they were. "This is in honor of you—but Zreyas style!"

Nothing happened.

"Ticking-lack of practice and not knowing anything about it." His panic started escalating as he thought about how Tap had created her ship appearance and how he had glimpsed what she was doing on a quantum level that few seconds when he shut his eyes.

Zreyas felt his shoulders being gripped again just before being thrown up even higher. "Sh-hit!"

After another second or two, he yelled, "Whoever you

are, stop it!"

— I'm saving you from yourself, Mother. You are not good at flying.

Zreyas was so shocked at what was just said, he couldn't even get angry at first. *Mother?* Then he got angry. "I am not good at flying because I have no wings, you ticking piece of m—oh, my armor..."

He was hurled back into the air, this time something sharp sliced him slightly. "Hey! Watch those claws—well ticking hell... you are the one that made the footprints in the dirt."

— Seriously, Mother. To be so smart and strategic teaching me so much, you can be really dull sometimes. Bye, have to go, the dark is coming. Hurry with your idea to fly.

Zreyas' eyes narrowed and his anger flared at the words.

He was falling, and he felt the presence that was talking to him leave. His mind reeled in confusion and he felt his body panic in the sudden silence of voice and energy presence.

"I might have been a little hasty when I said to stop throwing me up in the ai-ir!"

He was really starting to fall fast and what he saw Tap do with her appearance didn't seem to help because her body wasn't the same, but he kept it in mind. "I want to turn into my version of a kuravy." He concentrated and closed his eyes and put out ahead of him with the words he knew now as a manifested flying Zreyas.

Then, in his mind, he heard a toned song. It started manifesting as something ahead of him instead of words. He wanted to sing it. He tried, and it just came out as a bad sounding wail. Zreyas realized he couldn't hum that song and change his body to something else because it wasn't his song.

Zreyas was now beginning to see the bottom rough

shapes of the crevasse. He closed his eyes and thought about himself and who he knew he was, and took in a deep breath. He watched as he let out a roar, but in a way that felt like his song.

Zreyas had no idea what it might have sounded like to someone else, but it felt right to him. He watched his own genes and energy signature start to change and move toward the place in the quantum to signal what he wanted to do.

Waves of images came back to him in a rush.

He took in a sharp breath as he watched his body shimmer and break apart into billions of particles rearranging themselves. Then he watched himself re-materialize into the form of a modified predatory creature that looked nothing like the kuravy, but it still had wings. "Oops, sorry Kuravy, I guess my style is a bit... different."

His arms and head stayed as they were, but his back sprouted wings. His legs and feet transformed into two powerful muscular legs with a structure like most hind legs of four-legged creatures have, complete with paws and virgin, razor-sharp talons. He noticed two things right away. One, he was still falling. And two, he had no idea how to fly.

Zreyas started flapping his wings awkwardly, causing his body to slow his fall, but still falling fast, wobbling back and forth. He had grown feathers for his wings, but he needed a set of tail feathers. When he looked back, he realized his tail was long, like a feline tail. "Whoa! This is... harder... than I thought!"

Zreyas concentrated while he flailed around and modified the blueprint of what he wanted his body to be before it was completed so he wasn't locked into a form yet. He carefully thought about the body design he wanted and slowly refined it as he thought so it gave him more time.

He decided to keep his arms as they were and he morphed his head and horns into a more aerodynamic shape, with an intimidating set of icy-white, predatory eyes. Though he didn't see his own eyes, he knew the color by the frequency.

It was working, and he was lucky he thought of it before it was too late. A curved sharp beak lay over his nose like custom armor. Then he thought about his tail. He liked the long tail, so he sprouted tail feathers at the end of it. He wasn't really sure if it would be good for flying, but it just felt right.

"Is this still science? Or have I crossed into something else? I hope I didn't break any rules." Zreyas didn't really think about what he had just done, but he always had a flare for aesthetics. But it was time to get his ticking-ass started on flying... and fast.

He moved his tail feathers around to test them. At first, his tail just whipped around, getting caught up in the wind and jerking around. He added a little more design to it to have a lot of strength, then he just held his tail out more firmly and spread the feathers... it worked! But each slight movement sent him into various kinds of spins, no matter how much he awkwardly flapped his wings.

As he struggled to use his tail feathers to gain some sort of stability, he noticed his swords were a bit awkward and kept hitting his head. He changed them too, to arm bands. They poured like liquid metal from his back, down his shoulders and around his arms. Zreyas slid each one up snugly on each one of his biceps. Out of habit, he reached back to make sure he still had his bow on his back. It was there and there it would stay. Zreyas continued to flail and beat his wings, though. He didn't gain the control he had hoped for...

— You look silly, and you will die soon if you don't fly.

No ticking mag-shit! He continued to try to flap his wings, and he was getting tired.

— Fan your tail and level it, then spread your wings out. Keep them firm but relaxed like you did when you did that free-fall. Use your tail to steer and enhance your wings' functionality to support and propel.

Zreyas did as instructed. He immediately gained more stability, though awkward. His muscles didn't have the memory yet. With each tiny adjustment of his tail feathers, the direction and speed of his body changed. "Ah! That's the magic!" *Sending the thankings to you.* He began experimenting with turning, but he didn't adjust his wings with his tail and lost his support, then flipped sideways and backward.

Suddenly, he found himself being hurled back up into the sky. He wasn't sure he would ever get used to that. No Janquar he knew of liked being thrown around, though, he supposed.

— Work with the wind, not against it. Your tail feathers are of the shape that is built for speed and maneuverability, not stability and gliding, so every slight movement will affect your flight.

He took a breath and tried to relax because he was reaching exhaustion at this point. He had to get this process down, and soon. Though his fall oscillated between slowing, falling, and almost stopped, he was getting closer to the ground pretty quick.

Zreyas spread his wings wide, but it made him start to fall backward. He forgot to adjust his tail feathers by spreading them out and cocking them down slightly for more lift. He finally leveled off and just rested as he glided awkwardly. It was the best thing he could have done, because his body started to get a feel for a good base starting position to grow his flight skills from—a gliding position. It gave his mind a starting point, too.

As he cocked the front of his wings up slightly, the underside of his wings felt more pressure, but he had less velocity. As he cocked them down lightly, he felt the opposite on the top of his wings. He bent his wings so he could flap them downward, his feathers opened to let air through. As they spread out or flapped down, they naturally flattened and closed the spaces between the feathers. Understanding started to sink in.

Once he got a general feel for how his wings worked, he experimented with his tail feathers. He looked under his body quick to see them, and they spread beautifully. When he folded them a quick second, they looked slightly forked at the end as a unit. He spread them out wide again and looked forward again. The more he spread them, the more stability he had. If he cocked them downward, he had more lift but slowed. Closing them gave him less stability and more fall. His wings had to do more work and flap front to back rather than more downward. Then he tried cocking his tail feathers more to one side to help turn, then to the other side.

Still descending too much and almost to the ground, he raised his chin and started flapping his wings hard, spreading his tail feathers wide and slightly cocked downward to raise his altitude.

Zreyas smiled, feeling the exhilaration of ascending for the first time. With the excitement, he climbed harder as he aimed for the sun. After he was at a more comfortable height in case he made a mistake, he leveled off. The view as he transitioned into a relaxed glide was breath-taking in a different way than when he was falling. "Aaru! This is pheno-mi-tastic! You would love this! I'm flying, dear brother!"

Zreyas folded in his wings and tail and turned downward. He spread his wings half way and dove. He was a little scared that he couldn't pull out fast enough, so he spread his wings and tail again and lifted his chin to pull out to climb again. *I think I have it, Tap.*

As he leveled off facing the waterfall, taking in the beauty of it all. He felt fortunate to be alive to see this. *Thankings to you for the help... whoever you are.*

— I just threw you around, Mother. You are the one that did it.

Zreyas heard a screech and shuddered. He knew that sound. No matter how hard he would try in the future, he could *never* forget that sound. He jerked his head around and saw a single nagodara flying awkwardly toward him. It flew like an ass-heavy brumble he had once seen in his home galaxy before they went extinct. The decay mist was spraying all around him.

49 Matching the Past

Zreyas' eyes widened, seeing the decaying mist spraying all over the place. "Oh no, not this beautiful place, too. This is *not* good." It looked like it might be burned from the acid, but it was still deadly, with all that mucus and decay flying all over the place. He took note of his surroundings while he had time. He was cornered between the nagodara and the waterfall cliff that was in a large U shape behind him.

Talking to himself again for sanity, "Time to learn, Zrey!"

Flying furiously upward while he still had the chance, he realized as awkward as the nagodara looked; it was unnaturally faster than the rest, and it was coming quick. Then it sprinted faster than before. *How did it do that?* Then he saw the Dark One's red eyes and black mist coming from its body.

"Come on, you piece of mag-shit!" He let the rage come, and it filled his compartment, "Let's play! you bulky-assed bandhula!"

Staying well out of range, he navigated in different directions. He would climb and dive to gain distance between them when it almost caught up. He started to get worried if he would survive longer than another minute or two because he couldn't seem to get out of the trapped scenario he was in. Every time he tried to fly around it, the nagodara would zip in and cut him off. It was fast and was like he knew his every move. He felt him, not just the nagodara, but he felt the Dark One.

Okay, Zrey, remember, he uses the quantum and who knows what other talents he has. Don t underestimate him. Maybe if I can dive and get enough velocity, I can shoot around it. Zreyas dove hard and fast, but the nagodara was right with him, and even ahead of him.

"So you can read my thoughts!" *But how... I wonder if I m so used to using the quantum that I put my thoughts out there all the time. Tap did say I used it naturally. I need to figure out how to keep thoughts in my head somehow.*

The ass-heavy creature wobbled and hovered. It looked like he was doing a demented version of a laugh using short screeches.

For lack of anything else to do at the moment while he bought time, he said, "I don't mind informing you that you are no longer yourself—now, you are worse than anything that ever came into existence! 'The nothing' is glorious in comparison! Unless you suck the life out of something else, you can't even sustain yourself. You can't act, much less live, without costing someone else their life or will. I do *not* consent to let you use me in that way or take me over... *ever*. You will not have me and you don't have permission to enthrall or manipulate me! The blue camp members have taught me a valuable lesson. Someone must choose to let you do it to them. They did not and there is nothing you can do about it."

The nagodara let out a long, overwhelming, and piercing screech that made Zreyas' guts turn. It scattered the decaying mist until the end of the screech. Zreyas felt the frequencies. Once he gained his wits again, he flew higher as he paid attention to them. He got an idea.

He could possibly convert the energy and frequency of the screeches before they entered his body, or at least as soon as they entered. Yeah, that was it. It sounded too weird to be feasible, but he needed to use his war aura to his advantage somehow.

Zreyas stopped well away from the nagodara and looked at it and laughed. "You just taught me something about you, sending the thankings to you! Teach me more, you mag-shit sucking bandhula."

The nagodara screeched again, louder and angrier than before, shuddering and vibrating, while spraying decay.

Zreyas smiled as he felt the frequencies enter him. He intentionally imagined it flowing into the compartment that he used for his war aura. To his surprise, it did. The compartment felt full, almost to bursting.

He noticed that the spray of the nagodara stopped sooner than last time by a significant amount.

"You can have it back... here, catch!" Zreyas converted all that nasty devastating energy to a higher frequency as he let it go by thinking of all the fortunate and great things he had in his life now. As he did, he used his war aura to push it back toward the nagodara.

The nagodara screeched in pain and fell a good fifteen meters downward.

Zreyas felt the frequencies again as it screeched in pain. It was like the energy had information. "Interesting. I can feel the betrayal in you. I can feel your anger from the past. I don't have to know the details to understand that you were betrayed. Every time you send that screech out, I learn more. But you are not innocent. You reek of your *own* betrayal."

The nagodara hissed and quantum-sprinted right in front of his face, sliding its mouth over its own body to ready itself for taking Zreyas' head in with lightning speed.

Zreyas could see the mucus oozing off the rows of teeth. The stress of what was about to happen was his friend this time. His mind went sharp and acute as he thought about his face melting away and ground up in the belly of that thing. He immediately let his aura go, focused on the opening mouth, as he converted the anger and fear to his last thoughts of his brother, his friends, and how much he learned to love them. He let it all go with all he had with a dialed-in focus.

As the focused aura struck the nagodara, it knocked it away so fast and hard he could barely track it. He thought he saw it shimmer slightly, but it was probably the trick of the mist of the waterfall. Nature had its tricks with limited eyes, but the nagodara *did* seem stunned, though he was surprised it didn't splatter.

Zreyas tried not to think as he flew as hard as he could away from it. *No, I can t let that thing go.* He *had* to kill it; besides, it would just keep hunting him down and kill others. This wasn't a normal nagodara—not that it was anywhere close to normal. When he turned around, the nagodara was sucking in air, readying for another screech as it warped in short spurts toward him.

Zreyas climbed as fast as he could, mentally opening himself to receive the screech into his compartment. His taunting might pay off if he could stay conscious and alive long enough. He concentrated on his thoughts and willed his mind to not push out his thoughts into the quantum, and needed to test it. *He is strong. I think I will fly up.*

The nagodara made no move and stopped, inhaling to let out its next screech.

Then he tried it again, normally. *He is strong, I'm afraid. I need to fly up.*

The nagodara moved up and a screech came with such potency that Zreyas temporarily lost his senses but allowed it to fill up his compartment. He faced the nagodara and immediately converted it, throwing it back at him hard with his war aura. It seemed to bulge and spray violently. The spray didn't last long though, not like the previous times.

This time, Zreyas got more information from the frequencies. He felt the sorries for him, though he didn't know any details. He also learned that the nagodara was running out of that spray. Its body either couldn't keep up with the screeches so close together, or the higher frequency thrown back at it was hurting its capacity to make it—he wasn't sure which.

Zreyas climbed in altitude once more and decided to imagine events that matched the same frequencies that he felt coming from that abomination. He wasn't fighting with the nagodara anymore; he was fighting the Dark One.

He remembered what Tulyata and the Twins had said about how it was more automatic than intelligent, so he didn't think it would matter what the details were as long as he matched the frequencies.

Zreyas struggled whether or not to mess with its past; it seemed far-fetched to try. However, when he thought about those blue camp members, Tap, and the twins on that ship, he was willing to try anything different from what he was doing now to help them stop this horrible new visage that was possessing this creature of... wherever it came from. He had learned all he wanted to learn from that thing. It was time to kick some mag-shit ass.

"So, your name is Less-than-nothing, now. Less-than-nothing... remember that," Zreyas taunted. "I will call you Less-than-nothing because that is what you are! Did someone take your training sword away when you were young? Awww, poor little Less-than-nothing! Less-than-nothing was betrayed when someone took his training sword. Oh, and someone threw Less-than-nothing away! Poor little weak Less-than-nothing!" Zreyas wasn't really sure what else to say, and it all sounded so silly, but he said everything with words that felt like they matched the frequencies of what he felt come from the monster.

The nagodara started shuttering as it inhaled with a growling hiss, more intense than ever. It seemed so angry now that when it ascended toward him; it seemed more distant in its focus.

Uh oh, good news and bad news. Good news... It worked! The bad news is... it s beyond angry. He continued to taunt it. "Whatever you were before, you disgrace your race, Less-than-nothing! Even if you were a mag bug, you disgrace your race!"

The nagodara swelled up and shuttered more. It seemed to be at its stretched limit. Its rows of teeth in its stomach were more part of its exterior than inside, now just from the swelling.

Ticking hell, it s going to explode. "Awww, is Less-than-nothing mad!?" He scrambled to ascend in altitude. The sunlight peeked just over the edge of the cliff and it made the mist of the water inexplicably beautiful. Then Zreyas turned to look back. Though the nagodara was still expanding and shuttering, it was flying upward, just as fast as he was.

"No ticking way! I didn't find my wings to just let a nasty Less-than-nothing take *me* out." Zreyas had a sudden thought and faced up to the sun. He flapped his wings furiously to climb as fast as he could to buy him time, whipping his tail downward to help with the speed as well as steady him.

While he climbed, he thought about something that Rhom had told him. It concerned his armor and frequencies. Higher frequencies will always win over lower ones if there is an equal battle because the higher ones have more expanse, more flexibility, and faster in vibration. *There was more, but I can t remember it, and I might not even have that right. So, what if... nooo, that wouldn t work, would it? Ticking-hell, I got nothing to lose.*

Zreyas reached back for his bow and willed an arrow to nock, holding it out ahead of him as he flew upward, remembering that the neutrinic-gleam arrows were still armed. But he knew that in this case that *one* arrow probably wouldn't be enough.

He thought about Aaru, Tulyata, and their sacrifices. Then he thought about Rhom, Rtu, and Tap, who had put so much love and work into helping everyone. The joy he felt to witness any of that nearly overwhelmed him. He thought about all the love he had for them and how he wanted to be his own version of what they stood for.

Zreyas concentrated on it and poured the frequencies of the freedom, joy, and love he discovered into the arrow, willing it to transform the frequencies higher. He used his pushing aura to hurry the process as he climbed. He even poured compassion for the Dark One into it.

His mind thought about how silly all this sounded and he had to be crazy to even try something like this. Zreyas just set those thoughts on a shelf he created in his mind to let them be until later, as he focused on pouring the converted energy into the arrow as he flew up.

The arrow started vibrating and emitting a high-pitched sound. Then the arrow glowed with a white light so intense it seemed almost blue. He continued to pour in the high frequency emotions and thoughts and said out-loud straining, "This is *way* too much mushy-and-gooey for my taste, but if it works, I *embrace* the mushy-and-gooey!"

Zreyas whipped around and pulled the arrow back, raising his right knee. He felt himself suspend in time, his whole body still. As he aimed and focused the energy, he remembered helping Rhom in the dying dimension. Rhom had talked about how they had needed frequencies so high that they healed and created. Then he remembered the reversing torus of energy he had experienced while he converted his aura to give to Rhom so he could convert it more.

He knew in his gut that kind of frequency was what it would take to stop this thing. But he could only imagine what Rhom's part was, but he would try. He poured his converted war aura into the arrow with all he could imagine it being like.

The nagodara's face lit up with the light of the arrow. Zreyas felt the sorries for it, but only for a split second. And that split second was when the thing warped right in front of him a meter away.

It almost broke his concentration, but he held it. Before it could spray, he let the arrow go. It seemed like several seconds as he watched the arrow leave his bow, but it left.

The arrow was true to its mark and entered its mouth.

Nothing happened—it didn't explode, nor did it go through it. As he felt gravity take hold of him again, he gracefully entered a gliding holding pattern, still holding his bow, shocked. He flipped to the side and flew a distance away from it as it screamed in a way that seemed to come from *everywhere*.

"What magic is this?" Zreyas asked as he held his bow, moving into another gliding pattern to watch as he knocked another arrow. He wasn't about to let that thing live, but he didn't know what was happening either. He was stunned that something with that much velocity and difference of frequency didn't explode, or at least pierce it.

Zreyas winced from the screams as they continued to come. His instincts told him to run because this was so unfamiliar, but something captured Zreyas' attention.

What looked like ash started falling away from it, starting with the wings. Then the eyes disintegrated. Its appendages and teeth dissipated as it began to fall and gain speed. It transformed into some sort of blob, but it seemed more... natural. As it fell, it shimmered almost as if it was wet, but with a little extra iridescence. The dark oily mist left and fell away until he couldn't see it anymore.

As he put his bow away, he noticed the body wasn't the same as it was a second before. It seemed more like something inside a membrane.

Then he remembered what Rhom had said about the nagodara. They were the innocent, unborn children of all different types of species that had become demons. The Dark One must have access to their realm.

Zreyas lowered his head and pulled his wings close to dive fast. He pulled his arms in close to go faster.

The ground was coming way too quick, but he couldn't bring himself to stop. Whatever kind of innocent creature was inside that membrane, he wasn't about to let it smash to bits on the rocks below. It should be put to proper rest, not eaten, or splattered all over rocks.

His cheeks stung from the speed, but he reached the falling bundle and struggled to stretch his arms out to catch it against the velocity. He finally got close enough and scooped it up close to his body. It had a semi-wet feeling.

Zreyas pulled his chest upward hard, spread his wings, and lowered his fanned tail feathers to pull out of the dive. But his wings didn't want to take the pressure of the sudden change in force and felt like they would break.

A sharp rock, jetting out of the water below, came racing toward him as his muscles burned, trying to pull up. His flying strength had not yet developed. He noticed the rock had some discoloration on it, but he figured it was because it was constantly in the mist of the waterfall spray.

Though he was doing well in pulling out of his dive, he couldn't pull up fast enough. He lifted his legs up before his feet and legs smashed into the discolored rock. It almost worked. The part that wasn't successful came crashing into his mind in the form of pain. His left leg must have been lagging behind the right, and the pain told him the facts. It shot through him and he howled, filling his compartment with instant rage.

Zreyas tried to Q-leap instinctively to pull himself out of danger, but nothing happened. He forgot that he had been on a timer and couldn't use the quantum fully yet in this form.

He struggled to breathe and grunted with every attempt. He did his best to not squeeze whatever was in his arms and flew toward the shore of the river-lake near the base of the waterfall. His left leg hung useless under him as he took advantage of the currents of air to glide slowly. He was in no hurry to land, because that landing was going to make his leg worse if he didn't land right. He couldn't imagine anymore pain than he was feeling now, but it was about to happen.

He concentrated on his glide to slow it down as much as he could, patiently circling. It pleased him that the currents seemed to work with him perfectly and he almost made no forward movement in speed. After five minutes or so, he landed gently on one foot, but bumped the hurt leg a hop later. He knew then it was shattered by the way it felt as it crunched. The pain as he fell on his good side took him out of consciousness.

Zreyas didn't know how long he was out, but when he regained consciousness, he still felt his heart beating quick so he probably hadn't been out more than a second or two. He howled as he slid his body to a nearby rock. He pulled his wings in and leaned hard against the rock, still holding the bundle protectively that was half as big as he was.

Zreyas' eyesight narrowed as he thought, *Did it grow some?* He used his pain to fill his compartment because he was about to lose consciousness again, and it kept him more alert. The membrane had split and there was wet black fur poking through. He carefully peeled the membrane off. The fur had ultra-thin jagged white stripes running through the primary black. He had four huge paws and half-pan ears. Its eyes were still sealed shut, and it flopped over limp. He couldn't get over how huge its paws were.

He stroked its back, still feeling the excruciating pain, but too enamored with the bundle to let it take him over. "I'm saying the aplo-po-jeez that you never had the chance to live. I'm sure you would have done your species proud. We didn't have creatures like you in my homeland."

Lifting his head, he experienced the paradise that he saw around him. It was lush and colorful. The beauty was breath-taking. He winced as he shifted his weight and saw parts of it melting away from the sprayed decay.

Zreyas spoke to the limp body in his lap to focus his mind. "It's too bad that this is the place where the corrupted Janquar live. I can only hope they can change in the future, if there is anything left of them to change. This place is... pheno..." Zreyas didn't have the energy to finish his new word.

He breathed and tried to regulate his pain. "This place... could change anyone if they just sat quiet here. I met someone recently that was in a dangerous situation like you. Thankfully, they are still alive—at least they were not long ago."

He leaned his head back and closed his eyes. "I'm so tired." Zreyas listened to the waterfall and smiled.

50 Meeting Silence

After a few minutes of stroking the little one gently, he opened his eyes and looked around and noted. "This crevasse is huge! It looked so small from above compared to this as high as we were—another one of nature's vision tricks." There was something about this crevasse that was enchanting to him. "What do you think, little one?"

He started stroking the back of the little one affectionately again. *Tap, can you locate me and come get me? I ve broken my leg badly and I m going to need help. Until then, I have a funeral rite I need to do, though I don t know how to do them, really. The Janquar don t do a ceremony, but maybe Rhom and Rtu could help.*

— Yes, Captain. We are on our way and we saw everything. And, Captain… thank you for not dying. You had me doing a little… worrying.

Zreyas leaned his head back to rest and closed his eyes. *Yes, I m glad I didn't die, too,* he replied to her, stroking the lifeless baby that seemed to be a feline of some type. *But right now; I hurt so bad, I would love to die in one corner of my mind.* Then he couldn't help but ask her another question. *Why didn't you say anything to help me?*

— You didn't ask for help, Captain. Even if you did, there was only so much I can do. I am your potential; you have to tap into it. Potential doesn't tap into you, because you already have access to it. It's a part of you.

That made sense. Zreyas shifted with a pain that ran from his leg up into his head, making him feel faint. He could tell the armor was helping, but not sure how. He had a broken bone before, but this felt different, more painful, and he felt a lot of grinding as he moved, even with the slightest of movements.

He rested his eyes on the bundle in his arms, then lowered it to rest on his lap. "I didn't get a chance to get to know you, but I'm sending the thankings for being able to meet you. You can rest in peace as soon as the twin visages get here. They will help make sure you do."

Zreyas thought a moment, then said, "I wonder what happened to your mother that made her become whatever it was she became. That kind of thing is out of my range of knowledge at the moment. But I'm glad you are safe now."

— We are here, Captain.

Zreyas looked up and watched the twins appear and scramble down the invisible ramp. He had never seen them run so fast.

Rhom's face looked full of both panic and relief. "My dear boy! I'm glad you are okay!"

Rtu looked like he had been a trained warrior the way he was running and it shocked Zreyas. As Rtu arrived, he said, "You had us worried, little buddy!"

Zreyas didn't think he had ever felt such joy seeing those twins again. He chuckled, even in his pain, as he noticed the oddest thing about them—the twin visages didn't make footprints.

He winced. "I might need a little help with two things...

this leg, of course, for one. I know I'm getting a little overly soft, but I need you to help me with this little one's funeral rite. It deserves that. And sadly, I wasn't able to find that other creature I wanted to help out of here. My new love for animals is going to kill me one day," he said, grinning and wincing at the same time.

"Well, my boy, we can help you with the leg, but you need to stay in the form you are in. If you change back before-hand, you will have a hard time healing. It's one of those checks and balances. I should have told you that, but there are still so many things to tell and teach you and haven't had the time."

"I understand. I'm just glad to see you." He tried to shift a little and blinding pain almost made him pass out.

"Good news, my boy! You have a new crew member that has an affinity for medicine and healing. We can patch you up inside the ship so he can learn what he *already* knows, and a little more!" Rhom laughed and seemed excited and alive.

"That is..." trying to shift again, feeling dizzy, "good news. But how do we do the funeral rite for this little one?"

Rtu stepped up, holding a hand out to assess Zreyas' leg briefly. "We can't help you with that, little buddy."

"Why not? Isn't this your realm of things?"

"It sure is! But you can't do a funeral rite for someone that isn't dead," nodding toward the little one.

Zreyas looked down at where he had been stroking and saw the little paw twitch. His heart jumped, forgetting just a moment he was in pain. "Oh, giving you the thankings Rtu!"

"Dude! You did it, not us. Seems all that stroking you did with all that love you got for it, kept it alive and stimulated breath. We can talk about all the things you discovered once we get you inside the ship while we patch you up." Rtu reached carefully around Zreyas and picked him up.

The shifting almost did him in, but he felt Rtu's touch and it helped ease the pain.

"I am sorry you have to pick me up."

"You are not Janquar anymore, little buddy." He looked straight into Zreyas' eyes and said with sincerity, "It's an honor to carry you."

"My boy, you did some amazing things, even if some of them were by accident or on a whim. But you figured out the counter science all on your own and used it to kill that horrible thing. But you also restored the life for someone that it was stolen from."

Zreyas smiled at hearing this.

"But understand this... It had been merged with the Dark One, so it will not be the normal intelligence it would have been for that species of creature."

He watched it, concerned. "Does it show signs of being tainted or dark?"

Rtu stopped halfway up the ramp. "I can't go any further."

Rhom held a hand out to the new life and assessed as if it was just a gesture to make Zreyas more comfortable. "There appears to be no darkness or taint."

Rhom gestured toward the black furry bundle. "I wouldn't worry about it now, my boy, but she will get pretty big, and rather quickly, so you will need to think about that."

The Awakening Phoenix, give this little one access to the ship.

— Yes, Captain. Done. But, Captain, you might have someone else you might want to speak with before you come in.

Zreyas never thought twice about it, but he gave Rtu an order. "Freckles, turn around and walk back down."

He never questioned Zreyas. He probably knew already, but he turned just in time to see footprints in the sandy soil of the shore.

Zreyas smiled, but had his commanding attitude on now. "Show yourself, or I will leave you here. I can't have someone on my ship without some sort of relationship. I also can't have anyone on my ship that is afraid to be seen. I feel no threat from you, but that doesn't mean that I will take that for granted. I know you understand me." Zreyas cocked his head and waited patiently as he looked toward the last footprints made on the ground.

Rhom walked down the ramp, stopping beside Zreyas and Rtu. "I know who this is. Zreyas, you imprinted it. I can see it in its life force. It seems you have an affinity with animals, my boy."

"What do you mean, 'imprinted it'?"

"Show yourself. You are safe here," Rhom commanded.

The creature shimmered and faded into view. Zreyas' jaw dropped as he watched the creature appear. He instantly recognized the face, but it was far from the creature he rescued that day. It had grown... a lot. A smile was something he couldn't help. It just happened.

The large round predatory eyes and strong brow were no longer just strong and cute, they were an intimidating group of features. It still had his tuft of hair on top of its head, though. That was his favorite part about him. His wings were fully grown and a brilliant white, along with the base fur on his body. Its talons were incredibly long and sharp, and his paws looked muscled and powerful. The muscles in his body rippled strong as it paced back and forth. His tail was long and had a tuft of hair at the end, with the same color and texture as the tuft on his head.

Zreyas imagined he felt uncomfortable showing

himself. *Ticking hell, that is one majestic creature that would be a formidable foe for someone.* He felt him and realized he had been feeling him all along when he was here, and probably the one that threw him all around in the sky.

"This species of creature... Let's see if I can relate it to something on Earth, since you know more about Earth creatures than anywhere else." Rhom scratched his head just above his ear.

Rtu piped up, "He is like what earth people would call a griffin, but this one is different from even the myths there."

"Yes, that was Earth's name. Thank you, brother. This species has a long name. But the short name for it is Zizira in the proper sense, and it only comes in the physical incarnation in times of dire need. It is male, and he lost his sister when she was still in the egg to the garavu that almost ate you."

"Is it talking to you? Or are you getting all this from your visagely-wooza abilities?"

Rhom laughed at Zreyas' new word. "Why don't you ask him yourself? He understands you. You imprinted him when you rescued him, and you are the one he will follow, and it seems he has been learning from you already. You just didn't know it."

Zreyas looked at his reacquainted friend. "Your colors are beautiful and you have grown up! I never had time to give you the thankings for picking me up that day. Do you have a name?"

His predatory eyes stared straight at Zreyas with his ice-white eyes and shook his head. He bowed his head to Zreyas and looked at him.

"He's thanking you for saving him too, little buddy."

"I'm glad you didn't eat my hand off," Zreyas said. He chuckled at him in admiration. "I felt compelled to save you." He held up the squirming fur ball in his arms slightly to shift his position. *Can you talk this way?*

The powerful and large Zizira walked toward Zreyas, extending his head to smell the newborn creature, then sat down majestically. He cocked his head

— You know I can.

"Why didn't you answer me before?—like when I spoke to you at the blue camp? I also asked you questions when we were at the cave mouth, and you just poked me." Zreyas scratched his chin and shifted in Rtu's hands again and noticed he wasn't in quite as much pain as before—Rtu's doing, no doubt.

— I talked to you, and you listened.

So you *were the one that instructed me on flying after getting my wings. Giving you the thankings to you for that. So why not before?*

— Because there were those that could listen, even in the mind. The demon ones that were killed could hear. They were near. I didn't want them knowing I was there, and I was still learning about them, scared. I was just wanting to be near you for protection, like you did before. One day I won't need your protection, but maybe sometimes. I want to learn like the blue ones said. You have taught me much already.

Zreyas watched Rhom and Rtu exchange glances, both in surprise and glee. He knew the twins were listening in, but he didn't care. They were visages, after all. The realization hit him that this already large and powerful creature was still just an adolescent. *You need to learn to speak outwardly too, or you will limit your abilities.*

"What do you think about the name Silence? In most situations, silence is wise and deceptively strong. It is also stealthy, powerful, and strategic. Your colors are like silence. It is like the white between the times of speaking and noise. If you don't like it, you can pick your own, or I can pick another one."

The Zizira's gaze seemed to bore into Zreyas, but he let

it, then the creature looked at Rtu and Rhom.

Rtu smiled and spoke up to the creature softly, "To be given a name with the honor and love that Zreyas just gave is sacred. It is much more bond-worthy than if you pick your own. And you obviously chose to bond with Zreyas. I love the name. What about you, Rhom?"

"To use Zreyas' word, I think it is a pheno-mi-tastic name, dear one. And thank you for coming to help us all."

His powerful head nodded. Without moving his mouth, in a voice that denoted a young boy, he spoke, "I might prefer it, Mother."

The two twin visages were silent and did not laugh.

"So, it *was* you that threw me into the sky."

Rtu said matter of factually, "Yep, you imprinted him. Apparently, you made a huge impression on him. That is impressive if you understand the type of species it is. No visage or incarnate has ever imprinted a Zizira throughout history. He's been tailing you to learn from you like a child would a parent in nature."

"Mother taught me how to go invisible and to leap through the potential space."

"Like it or not, little buddy, you are his parent. Maybe not in blood, but you are his parent in every other way that is more important."

"I just don't understand why you two, Tap, and now Silence, think I'm worth helping and following. But I'm not *that* amazing. I mean, I'm okay and all, and I like who I am. But, ticking-hell, this makes me feel a lot of pressure! I don't know the first thing about what I'm doing."

Zreyas looked at Silence directly. "I'm honored you chose me, but I want you to know that I'm no visage. I'm just an old Janquar who realized and learned more than most Janquar do. I'm still learning in life, just like you. But you need to pick a name so we know what to call you. It's something that we all do, even the visages."

It cocked his head the other way. "I like Silence. I choose Silence, Mother."

"Good choice, Silence! It's a fine name!" Rhom said.

"You may come with me if you wish, under one condition. Call me Zreyas. I don't even know what a mother really is. I never had one."

Silence looked at him, cocking his head again the other way, making that tuft of hair swish almost comically, "Zreyas." He stood up. "I wish to come with you. Can I come with you now? I called you Zreyas."

Zreyas grinned, "Yes, you can come."

"Thank you, Mother!" He padded closer to Zreyas as Rhom and Rtu chuckled. Silence sniffed his face and neck, touching him, then turned his face sideways, sliding it across Zreyas' face and body.

"Aww, he's nuzzling you, little buddy. That is called affection."

Zreyas closed his eyes a moment, feeling the energy from Silence and his comforting touch. He lifted one arm carefully and stroked Silence's face, experimenting with seeing with touch and feel. He had always felt him. Silence was the one that was always around him, and when he felt someone watching. It was good to finally put reason to it.

Silence started emitting tones that changed every few seconds as he snuggled up to Zreyas.

He listened to the tones and felt them vibrate through him. Zreyas surmised it was his signature sound.

He closed his eyes and remembered the day he heard him back in the cave when he was trying to find whatever was calling. He remembered the 'weet' that he used to call out. Zreyas felt it then, just like now. Though his ears heard it differently than it felt, he realized it was the same signature.

Softly, he said to Rtu and Rhom, "I didn't imprint him... he imprinted me that day. That is why no visage or incarnate has ever imprinted one. It's a choice *they* make, not ours. I might have been his rescuer, but I was the first thing that he came along that wasn't violent or indifferent. In a way, he did the same thing as I did with you two when I met you. But I still don't know why he imprinted me."

Zreyas noticed that the little one in his arms was becoming squirmier and sucking on his hand awkwardly.

"Even the worst of people walk toward something that makes them feel good or worthwhile, even the Dark One," Rhom said. "But there is more to this imprinting than we are making it out to be. Even *we* don't understand it, my boy, and right now, I don't think he does either."

Zreyas stopped stroking Silence's head and said, "I don't know how to be a mother, or a father, but I do know how to be a friend. I'll do my best to help you learn and teach you what I can. I do not, or will not, pretend to understand your needs. That is all I can promise." *Tap, give Silence access.*

— Yes, Captain. It seems our family is growing quite quickly.

"We can go now; we all have access to the ship."

As they all walked up the ramp, the cub in Zreyas' arms started trying to root around. "Anyone have any tits that can feed this furry lap-full?"

Everyone laughed and Zreyas winced as his world bounced while Rtu's belly and arms jiggled.

"Well, I don't have tits, but I can help with that issue," Rhom chucked out.

Zreyas grinned. "Don't get any weird ideas, I know you are good at making armor, but I'm not putting on tit armor!"

51 Salute and Song

When they reached the top of the ramp, Zreyas realized that the door was opening and he almost panicked.

— Don't worry, Captain, the opening door is just an outside illusion. I teleported the twins out and so I will teleport you in. I remembered your desire to keep me safe and took it upon myself to do the same to keep you safe. The Dark One won't find the dimension the ship is in.

Thank you Tap. I m very pleased. In all my pain, I didn t think about this when I was sitting out there.

— I know, Captain. Remember, I am here to help you.

Zreyas heard the echoes of her last words as he went into the particle state of teleportation. As he re-materialized inside the ship. They walked around a few corners and down a hall.

He didn't recognize the room they entered, except from the floor plan view he recalled in his mind. The room was large and full of blue camp members. It was full, but it was still a comfortable space for everyone. This room seemed much bigger than the one in the plan if he compared the command room size on the plan to this room. He reminded himself that Tap had the capacity to adjust her size. *Nice Work, Tap.*

The new members of the Order of the Sleeping Phoenix noticed them immediately. When they saw Zreyas, the twins, and Silence enter the room, they all stood, bowed, then went prostrate, making Zreyas feel an incredible sense of awkwardness. He had to do something about that. That was something he couldn't take... or wouldn't tolerate.

"I appreciate your respect, but I ask you never do that on-the-floor-thing again. It makes me feel very uncomfortable. I'm a Captain, not a god. Sit and let's talk while I get myself fixed up."

— Welcome back, Captain. They saw everything you did on the screens. The twins asked me to show them too. They wanted to keep them occupied and stop the worry that they might not have done the right thing, and they also wanted them to understand that the cause they committed to was worthwhile. They kept saying they knew you would pull out somehow. It seems they respect you to an awe-inspiring degree. The twins also wanted to show them you were an ordinary person doing great things, just like they would be doing.

A hologram of an androgynous humanoid face with no hair appeared near Zreyas. Though androgynous, Tap had beautiful eyes that seemed to penetrate everything with her sight in frequency. "Welcome aboard, Captain. I'm here to help however I can. I thought it might be nice if I had more than a voice so that everyone could see me."

"I like it! It will be helpful soon, I think." He looked out over the crowd in the room. "Who was the one that had the affinity for medicine and healing I heard about?"

A smaller framed Janquar stood and came forward. "I am, Captain."

"Are there any others that have a desire to learn medicine and healing?"

Another three raised their hands and stepped forward, slightly behind the first one. Zreyas noticed the natural tendency to rank themselves. "If you are sure this is the path you want to take, I will not ask if you want to do other things because this will take all of your working hours and probably more. There are never enough healers. If you are not directly helping sick or injured, you will be researching anatomy, cures, and obtaining supplies with my approval through Tap. If this is not what you expected and want to do, step back now. There is no shame if you do."

No one stepped back and all of them straightened more.

Zreyas nodded. "Let's do this simply, and I trust you to make your own choices. If there is a conflict, then I will decide for you." He looked at the one that had the affinity to heal and asked, "Crew or planet-side?"

"Crew, Captain."

"You will lead them all and you are responsible for keeping in touch with the planet-side staff as well. Anyone else for the crew?"

One raised their hand and moved forward beside the first. "I would like to, Captain."

"The other two, which one of you wants to lead."

One of the men pointed to the other. "I'm good at following orders, but not so good at leading. I've worked under him before and it is bearable enough."

Zreyas wanted to keep this official and also keep the twins' visagehood a secret unless they wanted to reveal themselves. That would be their choice. "Master Rhom and Master Rtu, would you be willing to help them get started and learn before you have to leave? Will there be time?"

Rhom smiled. "I have my ways of helping them learn

and I would be glad to help them. If it sounds good to you, Master Rtu will train two of them in surgeries and physical medicine. I will train the other two in disease and ailments. Then they can teach each other. You will need more staff for this, eventually. Then *all* of them will be fit to lead the rest and teach when they feel comfortable in what they know. I see an affinity in each one, and though they might not think they have the talent, they all have the talent to lead."

Rtu confirmed happily, "I would be glad to help."

"Perfect! Thank you, Master Rhom and Master Rtu. Your wisdom and knowledge are critical to help us get started."

Looking over the crowd and shifting himself carefully with a slight grunt. "There is much to do to make sure everyone is going to succeed. It will take time, so if it all doesn't happen today, or in many days, everyone needs to be patient. The world... our worlds... can't change to everyone's liking overnight. Be proud of your choices. If you find you got nothing to do during your work hours, take the initiative to do manual work. If you got time to lean, you got time to clean... or help someone else. Be proud of your choice of professions and names. It is a reflection of who you are."

Zreyas grunted and sweated profusely with the pain. Rtu slightly squeezed him and it seemed to dissipate enough that he could concentrate, focused on the future healers. "Do you want one of us to name you, or would you like to name yourselves? We can give suggestions as well, and you can choose. Since you have been placed and chosen your professions, we will take the time now to name you."

The lead medic stepped forward. "I would like to be named by you, but I would also like to be named according to my profession, Captain.”

“I’m not the best with vocabulary, especially in this profession. So, I will give a suggestion, and perhaps Masters Rtu and Rhom can suggest a few. My suggestion is Doc.”

Rhom scratched his head just over his ear and said, “Kriya is an ancient word for cure. Revata is an ancient name for a medical person that is skilled in antidotes. That one is perfect for one that wishes to specialize first in disease and ailments, because that would include antidotes.”

Rtu joined in with a grin, “If you want a fun name that is light-hearted and simple, my suggestion is ‘Curit’, as in cure... it.”

The lead smiled. “Well, I would like to learn it all, but I like the name Kriya, Kry for short.”

“Then I hereby name you Kriya. I will give you as much support in your life choices as I possibly can and still do the same equally for all of you. But you will work directly with me, Kry.”

Kry actually smiled, ever so slightly, and exhaled, the joy palpable in how he looked. “Yes, Captain.”

The lead for the planet-side camp stepped forward. “I like Revata, because that is what I wish to do. And I like that the name has meaning through the ages.”

The second crew medic stepped forward. “I would like to be called Doc.”

The last medic stepped forward. “We need fun. I like Curit.”

Zreyas pointed to the lead of the camp. “I hereby name you Revata.” Then he pointed to the other crew medic. “You are hereby named Doc. And last but not least, I name you Curit,” he said, pointing to the last one.

All four of the appointed medics did something

unexpected. They all put their fist to their forehead, the blade of their fist outward, then bowed slightly before going back to a relaxed position.

Tap?

— Captain, that is their new salute.

Zreyas turned to Rhom with an expression of inquiry, hoping for some understanding, but wasn't sure what to say.

Rhom looked at all the men. "Where is Cree?" When Cree's hand went up in the back, he asked him, "Would you like to do the honor of telling the Captain why you are all doing this action and why it differs from the chest salute?"

Cree stood and made his way forward through the crowd, taking his time. He then did the same gesture as his salute. "Captain, when we watched you fall, then gain your wing form, the light from you shined bright."

"Ah, the shimmering," said Zreyas.

"No, Captain, the armor shimmered. But the light came from you. We never saw that coming from someone before. But that is not why we changed our salute. When you pulled your bow and took your aim to shoot the nagodara, we could see the concentration, and light came into you from all around into your chest."

Cree made hand gestures and spoke as if he relived the event. "It left you mostly from your forehead and some from your eyes, like a triangle with a bright top. The beams of light shined on the creature. The arrow was bright too, and the brightness grew. It was brightest when you released the arrow."

Zreyas had no idea that this happened and listened intently.

"Then you bowed down to save the falling creature. You did not care about the taint that might hurt you that was all around. The beam of light showed the way for us. Your actions to make sure we were safe, then the bow shot and dive, made us see that you will do anything to save someone in need if it is in your power—even the baby that was dead, which is no longer dead, because of you."

Rhom explained further, "When you caught the baby creature, the entire room, *without* collaboration, put their fist to their head and bowed." He smiled and faced Zreyas. "Do you realize how close your form is to Silence's? Yet you hadn't seen his full adolescent form yet before you transformed. Though your version is your style, it is still very similar to his, down to the claws and paws. And though you don't have the same tail, you have a modified version. Your tail is like his, but has a tail feather spread rather than a tuft of hair like his. You are imprinted, as you said, but I call it connected. You are growing as fast as he is. I've been watching you evolve, and the similarities are way too coincidental."

"He's right, little buddy," said Rtu.

"Well, I can't see myself really, especially my tail. I wanted to honor the birds that were killed by the nagodara but I wanted to do it in my own style." He looked at his own feet, that were paws but with talons. Zreyas looked over to find Silence, laying down just behind him to his right, noticing his feet. "We are even the same colors, I guess. I didn't think about colors or details when I changed, just function."

"Your eyes are even icy-bluish-white like Silence's, little buddy."

Silence lifted his head from his laying position and looked straight at Zreyas with his large eyes. Zreyas felt his soul penetrated as Silence's predatory brows shifted slightly as he got up and padded toward him.

Zreyas didn't fight it. He wouldn't even know how to

fight that. To him, Silence seemed to transform energetically. It felt like he was remembering something and integrating it, but didn't know what it was. But he felt the shift energetically. Maybe he *was* connected, like Rhom said.

No one in the room said a word. No one made a noise. The entire room was as if everyone was hanging on what was happening. He himself didn't understand and wondered what would happen next.

Silence sat down in front of him, upright and majestic. In a slightly deeper voice than he had heard before, spoke calmly.

"When I was in the aether, my sister and I heard your song. We did not understand it, but we could not help but follow the song. It was our species' song, but different. We came to be where you were at the time of deciding. We loved your song. You sang it naturally.

"The Aaru you taught, taught you to remember who you are by singing his own song. We spoke to him in the aether and told him he lived his purpose. We told him not to worry about the future, his purpose was complete. But he found another, anyway, so now his song has changed."

Zreyas teared up as he listened to Silence. It was as if he was remembering something he couldn't put into his conscious mind.

"We couldn't help but love your song because it is a song of strength, a song of integrity, and the song of the—*garbled sound*—soul. My sister placed herself on top of me so that she would be the one sacrificed. She sang her song, and she lived her purpose. She is now watching us. I am grateful for her sacrifice, but I wish she could be here to live directly in your song, too. I understand the missing of your brother, Aaru. But we do not need to follow or long for their songs, because they are following ours."

Rhom and Rtu looked at each other, and they seemed a little surprised at something Zreyas wasn't sure of.

"Do not change your song, just grow it, and you will remember. If you change it, all of creation will crumble in reaction because you manifest change. And because we are all connected to the all and nothing, we all depend on the others' song to be there.

"This Dark One changed his song, too. It is far from what his song originally was, and now 'the all' is cracking. But your song is strong. You must destroy the Dark One's existence here so he can remember in the aether, and 'the all' can live on. There isn't enough left of him here to learn and grow, but his corruption here will kill the all and nothing."

Everyone in the room nodded and grunted, agreeing with realization in their expressions. Zreyas realized that each one of them in the room had their own experience of the Dark one and understanding seemed to happen on at least a small scale for everyone.

"I love your song. Though I still have much to

learn, I vow to follow your song to my death and help 'the all' live, or die with you. Either way, my song lives out its purpose."

Zreyas and Silence both bowed their heads to each other.

Silence stood and padded closer to him and cocked his brow forward to meet with his. Zreyas felt tears fall from his eyes and they didn't sting, burn, or seal for the first time.

"Giving you the thankings for coming here to help me. You have my word, in front of all these witnesses, that I will do my best to do what I can to help... 'the all' transition and find balance again."

"You have shown that already, my boy," said Rhom gently.

Zreyas lifted his head and the entire room, including Rhom, Rtu, and even Tap's hologram, put a fist up against their foreheads and bowed.

52 Critical

Rhom started gesturing more urgently toward Zreyas. "Now let's get you fixed up, my bo—Captain! Then you can change your form back. And by the way, the more you change to that form, the more refined it will get. I suggest doing more job assignments for your new crew *after* that, instead of before."

"Thankings to you, Master Rhom." Though he was saying his formal name for the benefit of the new crew to get oriented, he would be calling him old man again soon enough. "Tap, put us out of range of anything Proioxis can do without a lot of warning time, even if they supposedly don't know where we are. By the way, I like your hologram. It's a nice touch."

"Yes, Captain. And thank you."

"We need to do one more set of assignments. Do we have a route set for the new galaxy yet? And another question, can we put a challenge node here on the ship temporarily in case we need it while you are here? We are still a team in that. And maybe we can get some more teams approved just in case we need them.”

Rhom laughed. “I see some things have not changed. Remember, we talked about the unstable gates and channels? While we were gone, we put two gates in place to the next galaxy we spoke about earlier, and I’m happy to say they seem stable. But neither one of them has complete channels, so we will have to wait for the anomaly weather to complete the channels so we can travel the rest of the way. The one we need to travel through to get to the next galaxy is gate forty. We are calling it the deliverance gate.”

“Oh, nice work! That is pheno-mi-tastic!... And a load off my mind. Before we travel, I want the person that said they wanted to be an engineer to come forward.”

The engineer stood, and the crowd made way for him.

“Good. Have you chosen a name, or would you like us to name you?”

“Captain, I would like *you* to name me. But I don’t have any conditions.”

“You realize I’m not good with vocabulary, right?”

“Yes, Captain, neither am I, so whatever you come up with will be right.”

“Then I hereby name you: Right.”

The engineer grinned and nodded. “Thank you, Captain. At least some part of me will be right, and maybe even some of my work.”

A few in the room that had learned to laugh did so.

Tap’s hologram went over and scanned Right, making him overly straighten his back in surprise. “You will be an excellent engineer. You are clever and creative, and you will need that. I suggest to you to make him chief engineer, Captain. I like him and he has the skills in both engineering and leading.”

“Thank you for the suggestion, Tap. Right, will you

accept the position of Chief Engineer?”

Right looked around, a little uncomfortable at first, then straightened himself and confidently said, “Yes, Captain!”

“Good. Who else would like to fix things and help the ship run and stay repaired?”

Eight more stepped up and gathered behind Right.

“This group will be the first group scheduled to get names. Right now, I’m getting a little overwhelmed with pain. Tap, can you take these engineers and teach them as you start our journey toward the gate?”

Tap’s hologram moved toward the exit, then turned. “Yes, Captain, I would be happy to help them learn to operate me. I will also ask Master Rhom for his help too in some matters since he is the one that created... uh... engineered the ship, if that is okay with him.”

Rhom nodded with excitement. Even in his pain couldn’t help but laugh inside... Zreyas knew the old man loved science on all levels. Then he watched Tap split into duplicate holograms. One asked the engineers to come with her and the other moved toward Zreyas a little closer.

“Switch, until we understand all the details of your work, it wouldn’t hurt to learn medicine in case you need it on a job.”

“Captain, thank you. I was torn between what I spoke to you about before and medicine. Now I can do both.”

“We will need a medic too that has an interest in species that have four legs just in case,” nodding toward Silence and then the new one in Zreyas’ lap.

Switch spoke up. “I can do that, too, Captain. They might be out in the field with me at some point, too.”

“Good thinking, do it. Then teach a future volunteer.” He felt Rtu squeeze him slightly. “Master Rtu will help you with that, so make sure you see him to train."

"You can start by picking up this cub and feeding it," said Rtu. "Once I get the Captain settled—"

"I can carry him, Master Rtu, if you want to help him with the cub." Cree stepped in, facing Rtu.

Zreyas could feel Rtu nod and watched Cree come over. They carefully made the transfer and Zreyas immediately noticed how much Rtu had been doing to help his pain. Rtu's eyes were empathetic.

Rtu motioned toward Switch. "Okay, Switch, come with me and I will get you started."

The two disappeared into the crowd in the common room just as a hologram of Tap approached. Cree followed Master Rhom after being waved over and Tap followed next to him.

"Captain, your hunch was right about the challenge node in the new galaxy. I've been monitoring the gate and when the universal anomalic weather had the opposite gate connected, I picked up a signature that was similar to the one that is in Master Rhom's home."

Zreyas was sweating now from the pain and beginning to feel nauseous. He strained to say, "Get me to where you will heal me, Cree. We can talk as we go. Tap, have you got coordinates... in case it closes again... before we can get through the open gate on the other side?"

Tap's hologram, blue in color, glided along with him as they followed Rhom. "Yes, captain, I have put it in the logs for you. You can access it with your internal interface. Just use—"

"Aah, got it." He remembered the interface Tap showed him before and saw the log. He grunted, but the focus kept him from passing out. *Tap, is this our connection or the armor? You will need to explain this interface to me with all the other things I see as soon as we get a chance. Right now, I can barely think.*

They entered a room with a long bed and cabinets all around. Rhom gestured to put him down on that bed with knitted brows, obviously concentrating on something.

— Captain, it's a feature of our connection. Even Rhom and Rtu didn't create that. I was surprised we had that available myself when I discovered it. We can communicate in three ways now: voice, internal mind, and internal interface.

Zreyas' pain spiked, he gritted his teeth and said, laced with the anger that was pooling up, "It's a lot for a non-tech Zrey to take in all at once. I'm going to need a lot of *help* with this new interface."

"I don't think you are giving yourself enough credit, Captain. You pulled it up before I could even explain how to pull it up, for example."

The anger filled his compartment to the brim from the pain he was getting now. He could only reply with one word. "Maybe!"

"Master Rhom, can you help the Captain?"

"Working on that." Rhom was pulling things out of cabinets in the room he wasn't familiar with, likely since it was Tap's design.

Zreyas started to feel faint and leaned back against Cree's arm, who was still holding him steady even though he had set him down on the bed.

Silence moved forward and sniffed him. "His song is weakening."

Rhom immediately took charge and started giving the training medics instructions on what to look for and do with them when they found the items. He rushed over to the table. "Lay him down fully, Cree. Since I'm having to do this the physical way for training and balance, this is going to be a longer process. Where is Master Rtu? Things are critical, and there is something wrong we didn't expect."

The hologram of Tap, who had turned the color of a

grey-yellow, moved next to Rhom. "Master Rhom, I have contacted Master Rtu, and he is on his way. He's actually running."

Zreyas could barely see what was going on. His pain was indescribable. He felt like his leg would explode and the pain was shooting up through his body and into his head. His heart felt like it was louder than Tap's voice and he could barely hear anything. His vision was blurring but he could feel Cree's hands on his sides keeping him stable as he laid there. Zreyas could tell that Rhom was saying something to him, but he couldn't understand anything he was saying anymore. *Tap, what is he saying?*

— Captain, he is giving you his encouragement about not understanding the interface, and he said your ignorance of technology and science is fading fast, that you are learning quickly. He said not to be hard on yourself and that they were not leaving you for a while, so there is time.

There was a pause in her voice, and he nodded before she continued.

— He said to tell you that they have pledged to your cause and that they believe in you. Rtu said if you died on him, he would kill you. Two-'Ha's!

Zreyas could tell Tap was trying to keep him awake and aware by being creative with her laughing. He felt her intention and wanted to laugh, but it felt like he didn't have the tools or the will to. The pain was taking him over like the Dark One did the Janquar. *That* gave him extra motivation to fight to stay coherent. *Tell Rtu, if he lets me die, I will become a visage that makes him stand the rest of eternity.*

— Captain, it made him laugh, but he is nervous because he doesn't want anything to happen to you. I can tell.

I m okay to transition if it is meant to be. Do you think I will die? I can t hear anything anymore, and suddenly I can t feel anything anymore, except gentle waves of faint vibration.

— No, Captain, I think Rtu is helping your pain and put you to sleep. He has tears in his eyes and Rhom is working furiously with the new medics. Talk with him. You have the ability; they gave you that ability. Remember the words. Silence is by your side, helping in his way, singing his tones.

Oh yeah, the words. Tap, it s hard for me to even speak with you, but I will try. Help the crew, Tap. There is nothing you can do now, but it will make me feel better if you are concentrating on them.

Zreyas tried to remember the names for old man and Freckles. He knew them, but he couldn't think.

— Mother, it is okay. I am here. The Rhom says your body is different from anything he has ever seen. Even as a visage, he is learning. I know you will be okay, Mother. I just know it. Your song isn't fading anymore, it is stable even if it is weak. Sing your song, Mother. It will help.

I... don t know what my song is. I didn t know I had one until you mentioned it.

— Every creature has one, Mother. If you don't remember it, pretend you do, and imagine it ringing through you. Rest Mother. The Rtu one is upset about you. You are being cared for by the Rhom one. They are both helping the medical ones and they are not very good at healing yet, but they are sending your body care. But I don't think they will let you die to teach. Rest, Mother. I will sing my song for you.

Zreyas felt the vibrations of Silence's song even though he couldn't hear it. He felt comforted and at peace.

53 Sneaky little Devil

As Zreyas heard the voices disappear, he tried to force himself to open his eyes. But... they didn't comply. Zreyas felt a dull pain, but nothing like he had felt before. He still felt the song of Silence.

Thank you, Silence, for your songs. They are comforting. He expected a response from him, but it never came. He expected everyone to answer him and needed to watch that. Though he was Captain... and apparently a parent to someone, he couldn't expect everyone to jump every time he wanted an answer in non-captain affairs.

Zreyas thought about his leg. He wondered how it was doing, and he found himself no longer bound to a shell. He traveled toward his leg. What he saw was a mess. There were bone fragments everywhere.

As he watched, he saw an energy of what he figured was Rtu and Rhom pulling the pieces together, and looked like someone was trying to stitch them. He decided to imagine he was helping. He had nothing better to do, anyway.

That was when he saw an odd occurrence of what

seemed like the bone fragments melting and being pushed apart again just as the bone was about to be completely knit together.

Zreyas focused. The open skin came into view and then he remembered the discolored rock and how the nagodara had sprayed decay all over the place.

If it was the decay, then why hadn't it eaten his leg up right then, even without the cut?

Alarm shot through Zreyas as he remembered the nagodara dissipating and the oily mist stuff falling away. He moved his awareness closer to the bone fragments that seemed to be melting. Then he saw it—A black inky speck with red eyes watching him.

Zreyas shielded his mind as much as he could manage and thought, *Namdlo dna Selkcerf.* He wanted Rhom and Rtu to see this because he doubted they knew what was wrong.

He could tell they were trying to use desperate measures to save him, but with no results. Now that he saw the inky fluid, he looked around and noticed it had spread very stealthily throughout his body. The song he was hearing was not Silence's, it was the Dark One's song. He made it feel similar, but now he could tell the difference.

His worst fear was happening to him right now. As he felt the fear run through him, the inky fluid grew and he felt its hate. As Zreyas panicked, it grew more. He felt it take over more. The cycle repeated, over and over. He could hardly breathe, so he raced toward his lungs to help them. When he reached them, horror filled him, and of course it made it worse. His lungs were dying. They looked like they were turning to charcoal.

He was frozen in the fear and horror, but there was nothing he could do. Then he remembered the statues in the challenge. He remembered the voice that encouraged him, then the hall of waves and the emotions. He couldn't think straight when the fear came through and it never directly hit him.

Zreyas felt himself go silent and still, and imagined himself there, watching it all over again—*being* there all over again. He had been determined not to get over-zealous... and had been calm, even though he was in a scary place and in a bad situation. The voice had all but congratulated him for watching the waves and not making any moves while waves had been going through the hall.

He knew he needed to do that now, so he watched the challenge memory *again*. This time, he noticed that more of the statues were now familiar to him. One of them was Cree. Then there was Kry, Right, and another was Switch. He didn't know them all, but he knew some of them. Then he saw the one with the red eyes in his image. But this time, it was a grotesque version with inky mist and red eyes.

Then he remembered telling it that it would never have him, and that he vowed to not be that type of version of himself. Things felt right when he waited for the calm every time. The peace he felt that day in Tulyata's dimension broke the bond the Dark One had on her *and* Rtu.

Zreyas turned and looked toward the eyes that were now with him nearby. He felt them as if they were trying to skewer him and imagined himself sitting on his heels watching, just like he had done that day in the challenge.

He moved his awareness to where he could see the eyes *and* his lungs, then watched. This angered the Dark One, and he doubled the efforts to create the fear and hopelessness. As he watched, he felt the fear wane, and the hopelessness started to dissipate.

Zreyas opened his mind and put a thought into the open. *I told you... you will never have me willingly.*

As he noticed his lungs start to turn a little pinker and more alive again, he was slammed with a vision of Aaru skewered on a stake, out in the middle of his sterile homeland. A pang of panic, fear, anger, and hopelessness ripped through him. He wanted to cry, but he would rather be angry. *Janquar don't cry!*

Then he remembered he was no longer a Janquar, and his mind went to the day in the dying dimension when he had cried for the first time. He had felt his chest crack at seeing his brother laying there in a little lump of flesh, almost dead. When he cried, it released the emotions.

Zreyas spoke to the dark one openly. *That is what you use... the automatic conditioned responses of emotion against your victims to take them over, you ticking mag-shit-eating bandhula. That is why the song sounded comforting. It was familiar, nothing more. You have been using what you have done to yourself on others.* His mind was fuzzy, but he remembered someone telling him about how chemistry triggered things. But he couldn't remember who it was that told him. *So, if I...* He couldn't finish the thought, then tried again. *Automatic responses of fear... Dark One... frequency... low... become low.*

Then his mind fired a small spark of clarity. He talked to himself to get his thinking going again behind the shield he had put up around his mind. He had done it so well, he almost shielded himself as he stared into the Dark One's eyes. *Shield still up... now think Zrey, think.*

Then it dawned on him as bright as the morning sun. A person could *become* the chemistry that they allow in, eventually. He realized that the Dark One used the automatic responses of their mind, body, and chemistry against them to take hold of them... and they don't even know it.

Zreyas' awareness sat up figuratively. Incredulous, in his insight of what that *thing* was doing to people, and the excitement of what he figured out, he focused on working out how to counter it.

Then... he stopped himself. *I'm not calm and even-tempered.* He felt it was the equivalent of stepping into the hall. He knew things were dire, but he decided to watch, just like he had done at the tunnel in the challenge, but with his new awareness of what the Dark One was doing.

As he looked around at his poor body, he felt compassion for its state. He found himself apologizing to it for not catching this sooner. Then it dawned on him when he started really feeling bad. It was when he was transferred from Rtu to Cree. Cree wasn't the problem, though.

Rtu's energy and visage aura wouldn't allow the Dark One to prompt his chemistry. In addition, there were so many good things going on, the Dark One couldn't take hold. Zreyas remembered the immediate pain difference; and even then, he noticed how much Rtu was doing for him, but not until he left him with Cree.

Then he remembered his sympathetic expression when Rtu handed him off. Rtu might have known something like his pain would spike, but not likely involving the Dark One. Zreyas understood, though, why he couldn't say anything. He was a visage with checks and balances and he was not going to interfere with Zreyas' life purpose. But that didn't stop his friend from feeling compassion for him. Zreyas realized that must have been hard for Rtu. His heart went out to his friend. *I understand, Freckles. It's okay.*

He turned his awareness to look at the red eyes that seemed to have an expression of triumph. *You want my body to use for yourself.* Then it dawned on him that he could... understand his thoughts, too. No one *told* him about the body chemistry. He was getting it from the Dark One.

Zreyas paused. No *wonder* he had it so easy on that planet. It was after him, but not for the same reasons. *Do you want to use my body? Maybe we could... negotiate.*

The red eyes changed expression and came slightly closer. He also noticed the deterioration progress had stopped that was happening in his body.

His awareness spoke out-loud to the Dark One in his mind. "First, I want to know some answers to questions I have. If you don't answer them, then there is no chance you will ever have me. I will kill myself first and I think I know how to do that *without* your help or for your benefit. You know I have that capability, which is why you want me." He didn't know who he was mag-shitting on more, himself, or the Dark One.

He felt the energy of the Dark One's mind consent. Then he watched the energy invading his body stop moving, as if it was in a holding pattern. "Do you remember your past life you had that caused you to do this to yourself?"

Zreyas immediately felt the deception in a slow shake of its eyes in the answer of a no. But Zreyas also felt sincerity. It dawned on him that the Dark One was actually deceiving itself.

He had to try something, so he shielded his mind extra tight. But let the next communication come out. "Do you remember the body you had? If so, show it to me. I need to see if we are compatible. If we are going to work together, I need to understand you."

Then, to his surprise, the Dark One showed Zreyas what it remembered. It was in a space of a lighted area, but there were no details. He couldn't really see a body, but he saw seven lights.

Realization hit him like a stone slab dropped on him.

"Did you take this body over, or was it yours to begin with?" Zreyas paid close attention and waited for the response to come.

There was a pause... a deliberate hesitation. It almost felt like it wasn't sure, but he looked closely at the seven lights. They all had color. He knew what species this was. "You were the last Tantra of the Viduri, weren't you?"

A confirmation came with anger and hate.

"Whether you took her over, or it was you originally, makes no difference. How far you have fallen. You want me so you can go back to those frequencies, or you want to snuff me out so you don't have anyone to challenge you in this world. And that is why you want to get to Ayya—the two people in this universe that are a threat to you... me and Ayya. So, you want to join with one of us or kill us both, but Ayya is really who you are after. I'm just the bridge to get you there, right?"

The Dark one felt stunned to Zreyas, and he decided to take advantage of that. "Well, I have news for you. There are *many* raising in frequency, you just haven't met them yet. You are narrow sighted that all you see is me and Ayya... and Aaru."

He couldn't help it. If an awareness could laugh, he felt himself doing it. If you take me over, you will die immediately because I have many around me that are willing to die to keep you from doing more of your destructive work. We are a family. As I told you before, you will never have me."

The Dark One's eyes grew with rage.

Zreyas laughed. He couldn't help it. All this pressure of how he would defeat the Dark One was needless. He's going to thwart him just by letting it take him over. "Go ahead, take me. Take a chance. You will have a very powerful skill set. Even I don't understand it much yet."

He shielded his mind into the far reaches of the nothing as he could reach and said to Rhom and Rtu; *I know you are watching and listening. Take my armor off and kill me. You know this is all bigger than just me. Tulyata and Aaru sacrificed themselves for the same cause. Teleport me outside the ship and kill me. There will be no atmosphere, and nothing to for the Dark One to latch on to. I don't want this ticking bandhula to have access to you. This is probably only a piece of the Dark One inside me, but I want this mag-shit to die.*

The Dark One was in a furious rage, doubling its efforts to grab hold of his body chemistry. Zreyas laughed and tried to let it. He felt his body start to deteriorate. As he felt his body die, he remembered all the laughing he and Rtu had done together, making Rhom shake his head, and Tulyata rolling her eyes and calling him a ferret.

He laughed harder, and he felt his body tissue creek and crunch. It wasn't painful, and he was grateful for that. All his memories flooded in since he met Rhom for the first time, meeting Tap, Silence, and watching Cree and Switch use the quantum for the first time. They were going to be okay, and that gave him a sense of peace.

Growls of the Dark One started to move all around him and it didn't bother him. He loved the peace he was feeling. He let his awareness close its eyes and just be in the peace, love, and joy of knowing his friends, his family, would carry on. His body seemed to be crackling, but he didn't care, his body wasn't him. He wondered what it would be like to be with no body. His awareness smiled, and all went dark.

54 Ticking to the Mag

༺༻ *Zreyas* ༺༻

"Little buddy."

Rtu's voice seemed far away to Zreyas. He couldn't tell if it was an echo of a memory, or if it was really Freckles.

"Hey, little buddy! Open your eyes for us. We need to know your body is responsive! Little buddy, wake up. Don't make me tell you a bad joke."

— Captain, it's really Freckles asking you to eyes your open.

What? That makes no sense. Did I die already?

— I don't know, Captain, I only experienced what you did after your body went to the mags and became the shit. I became smaller and larger less and things went dark except for one minor part. But we through made it.

Zreyas knew Tap didn't sound right, but he couldn't think about that now. *Wait, I told them to kill me, right? Or was that a dream?*

— Oh, you told them us to kill, Captain. I understand why too. It was very strategic. That Dark shit of One of the mag is evil, and I found out something. He has legions is-nide the demon realm that it has… coaxed to help. Thankfully, they can't find a way in-out of their realm yet and Rhom and Rtu say it won't be only one time soon. I saw them in its mind.

Is that where the nagodara come from? If so, how do they get out? Does Rhom and Rtu know about it yet?

— Yes, Captain, they know. I them told. I hope that was okay. I guess I should have asked you last. But you gave them access pill, Captain of the Zrey. But that dark of a shit-mag is evil.

No, no, it s okay. I m having a hard time waking up though. I m trying. You seem disoriented too. Zreyas couldn't help but want to chuckle at her language.

— That is what the Rhom of a Master man old said too.

"Hey little buddy, I'm going to give you a jolt of mega juju! Get ready!"

What is mega juju?

— I don't know, Captain, I never heard that term before. Can I look that up? How do I look that up?

Now I know you are disoriented. You sound like me. I think we are all jumbled. Tap, give me back the part of myself that you remember is me. Then I will concentrate on giving you back parts of you that seem more you than me... if I can recognize them, that is.

— It's al-ever been that way, captain. We just automatically used what we were used to consciously. That much know I.

Okay, then put those parts in front of us like putting something on a table and see what surfaces. And I will pay attention to what you put down on the table. Think of it as sorting data on the ship.

— Yes, Zrey of the Captain, I will try. Hell-ing to the two-ticks, this might be hard.

Zreyas laughed hard at Tap's jumbled words. Now he understood why Rhom and Rtu always laughed at his words. The more he thought about it, the harder he laughed. Then he felt a jolt of whatever he guessed was the mega juju Freckles talked about. Then the laughter or juju, he wasn't sure which, woke him up coughing.

The twins both put their hands on their chests.

Rtu sighed. "Oh, thank all the Prime Visages, you are awake! Little buddy, you scared us."

Zreyas looked at Rtu's face. He noticed it was tear stained. The conscious awake state sobered his laugh and grew angry almost instantly with the panic of what the Dark One would do to them. He sat up, "Why didn't you kill me?!"

"Oh, we tried, my boy. Trust me," said Rhom.

Zreyas noticed no joy in his face. "What happened?"

"Little buddy, we are glad you called our names, because we were trying so hard to mend you and it was like your leg kept festering and spreading. We even used a little visagely-mojo on you because the balances were so tilted in our favor, but that didn't work, either. It only stabilized it some."

"Then Tap even started acting weird," said Rhom, panic still laced in his voice.

"I noticed that too. She was trying to curse like me and got all the words jumbled. Why are you still upset if I'm awake? Is that thing inside me still?"

Both of the twin said in unison, "*No*, thank all the visages... except him!"

"Update me on what happened and I'll try to keep from asking questions. But first, Tap, how are you doing?"

"I'm feeling more sorted, Captain. Thank you for asking."

"Good! You were funny, though."

"She almost died with you," Rhom said gravely. It almost took us all with you. We were all crammed into this room. We lost one that couldn't stay in the dimension of Tap's ship."

Zreyas looked down, sighed, and allowed the emotion to surface and leave. "What happened? I was supposed to be put out of the ship!"

Rhom sighed with tears in his eyes. "We tried, my boy. We took your armor off and were about to put you out and the ship started shrinking and we couldn't reach the doorway or teleport room and Tap started acting weird and you were—"

"What was his name?" Zreyas understood. He also noticed he had changed back to his normal body and lifted his head, unashamed of his tears.

"Captain, he had no name on record yet."

"Then his name is Everyone. He will be the reminder that everyone has a name. Everyone lived and contributed. And Everyone will not be forgotten. Tap, do you have a picture of him?"

"Yes, Captain."

A hologram of the tracker he knew and grown fond of appeared in front of him. Zreyas' breath caught, and his tears flowed so heavily his eyes sealed shut.

"I knew this man. He elevated himself from what people told him was nothing and worked hard to learn to track and hunt. Tracker was no warrior. He stayed true. But he was good at what he did. I called him Tracker because I never wanted to be so pushy as to ask his name. He loved what he did, and he saved us on more than one occasion with his skills. Where is the artisan?"

— Captain, the artisan is stepping through the crowd, aided by those around him. His eyes are sealed.

Zreyas, blind from his sealed eyes, listened. He heard a few labored breaths nearby. "I know you were close friends... like family. I'm sending you the aplop-po-gies. I didn't catch what was happening sooner. There is nothing I can do now, but do you have any wishes concerning your friend and brother?"

A few shaky breaths passed through Zreyas' ears before hearing labored words. "He took on your name for him, and he would say, 'I am Tracker' instead of I am the tracker. He knew the Captain's brother. Aaru inspired him, even though he didn't give him a name like he did for Cree. He taught me how to track, too, and how to read the land, and hunt. I always followed him and I taught him the artisan ways. I held his hand, trying to keep him on the ship until the end. His last words were,

> "Zreyas' will... follow it. His scent and tracks are good."

There were a few sniffs and coughs from him before he continued. "He taught me much about things other than tracking skills. My request is that you keep his name you just gave him, but I would like my name to be Tracker. I will keep him and his original name you gave him alive through me. And I would like to become your tracker and scout, with artisan works on the side. He is why I am who I am today." Then Tracker went silent.

Zreyas noticed he heard nothing from anyone for a long time other than breathing. "You have your wish, and I name you Tracker. Your position will be part of my personal team and inner circle of advisers if you would like to grant *me* that wish, my friend."

"It is where I belong. Yes, Captain. As we said on our outing... 'Mutual team of choice,'" said Tracker.

— Captain, all the Janquar eyes are sealed. Silence is entering the room, and the new young life with no name is here.

THE END

DELIVERANCE

The Sleeping Phoenix - Part III
DELIVERANCE

1 Countdown

“Little buddy, the balances have changed and shifted, so if you will have us longer, I would like to help as much as I can. It will be more on an incarnate capacity to keep things balanced. It might not seem like much, but the vast knowledge Rhom and I have with the extra arms and legs will help. We also have the challenge to work together on too. I will even throw in a few laughs,” Rtu said with a wide, joyful grin, accentuated by his large dark freckles.

“I would love to have you two with us longer! I’m not sure we would make it without you, honestly. It’s great that things turned out better in that area at least."

"My boy, it will help us too," added Rhom. "We are up against something bigger than us. We feel just as helpless as you probably feel. And we do need to talk about what happened more before we forget. That Dark One is using ways of war that have never been used before, and we need to understand them as soon as possible."

"I agree," Rtu said, shaking his head. "That was *not* a pleasant experience."

"Before I forget it though," said Zreyas, holding up a finger. "It's important to me to get this taken care of, so it is not on my mind constantly. Tap, do we have a room for our four-legged friends that are made for their comfort?"

"No, Captain, but I can easily make one."

"They are just as important as we are, I think. I might not know the little one very well yet, but she is a miracle I would like to help grow and nurture in a good way. I'm sure its experiences of being in a demented form that was not of their own design was horrible. She is as much a part of our family as we are."

Zreyas scanned the common room. Every Janquar had an interested expression. Every little thing seemed to be exciting for them. He could relate to that. "So, let's get down to the unpleasant experience. First, I want to see if we can put something in place so that if that dimension shrinking thing ever happens again to Tap where she starts dying, that the shell of a real physical ship gets deployed, otherwise we will need to make arrangements for another ship that we can adjust Tap to. I can't live with wiping everyone out in one swipe if we can't help it over something like that."

Tap's hologram changed colors from the worried greyish-yellow to a bright blue, almost as if she was changing emotions. "Yes Captain, I agree. I think I know a way, but Master Rhom will need to help me if he is willing."

Rhom nodded. "I understand what you are thinking, Tap, and yes, it is possible. Let me show you." A hologram of schematics appeared in the center of the room, changing from plan to plan at lightning speed. It was too fast for Zreyas to comprehend.

Rhom spoke to Tap. "Put that condition and trigger there," as he pointed to a still schematic, "and you will become a physical ship of your design with your intelligence duplicated as the AI. If you happen to survive, go here..."

All that science, for the not-quite-so-science Zrey, made his eyes glaze over and seemed to fade in the background. That was way over his head. He looked around as those two talked. Silence and the new cub came into his view.

"Hello, Silence, and hello to you, little one! You have grown already!"

"Yes, Mother, she has grown with the nourishment that Switch and Master Rtu have given her."

Rtu smiled, "The younger they are, the faster they grow on the outside. But she will be a large one. Probably about the size Silence will be, but without the wings, obviously."

The little one watched Zreyas standing on the table and climbed up the pants leg of a sitting Janquar to get to him. The poor Janquar winced at the claws piercing his clothes and into his skin, but Zreyas figured he didn't want to scare it or he wanted to kill it. Zreyas knew Janquar were not accustomed to having pets or anything living around them. They pretty much killed everything, so this was a new experience for them all. And truthfully, a new one for him, too.

"Do you know what species this one is, Freckles?"

"It is unique," said Rtu. "It has the genes of a feline, but incubated with darkness and your light. We have no idea how she will grow. Don't worry, she has no taint of the Dark One or the demons. But she likes you!"

Just as Rtu said that, the big pawed feline pounced on him playfully. Without thinking about it, as soon as Zreyas started to fall under its pounce, he Q-leaped to right himself, causing the cub to land with nothing under it. Zreyas leaped down on top of it and started scratching behind its ears. He stood and watched the cub roll over on its back, holding its front paws out to the side and up, claws spread.

"I know you want me to rub your belly, but I'm not falling for that trick. I wouldn't mind petting you, though."

The cub rolled over and stood. She walked up to Zreyas, and he noticed that the cub's back height was just about high stomach height to him. Rhom had measured him in the medical wing earlier and he was not quite thirty-five and a half centimeters tall.

"You need a name, but nothing is coming to me right now. I would like to get to know you better first if that is okay."

The cub walked up and rubbed her body up against Zreyas, almost knocking him over.

"You are stocky and solid for your kind, I think. Are you made of iron?"

Rtu laughed, "I noticed that too. I think depending on the energy she grows up in, it will change. She seems to be influenced by what is around her, just like all of us. And by the way, before we tried to kill you as instructed, that cub stood over you and growled. She was not having any part of letting us do that. I had to subdue her and have a little talk with her. I sent her images of what was going on so she would understand your sacrifice."

"My boy, we are done now. I apologize."

Zreyas looked at the cub with a smile, then turned toward Rhom, "No don't apologize, I feel better now and it was critical to make sure you all were safe in case something like that ever happened again. Plus, I got to pet our new member of the crew."

Cree spoke up, "Thank you, Captain. That was scary watching what happened. We weren't afraid of dying, we were afraid of living without you, Tap, Master Rhom, and Master Rtu. We just found you."

Zreyas looked at Rhom and Rtu suspiciously.

"Don't look at us, my boy, we weren't the ones that showed them what was going on," raising an eyebrow toward Tap.

"Uh-huh!"

"Captain, it was my duty to show that you weren't dead, so they didn't give up. They thought you were. They tried to do what you told them to do. As all of it happened, I showed them everything. The only thing they didn't get was your thoughts, so they didn't get to see your strategy and way of thinking."

"Little buddy, you did it though... your peace killed the small part of the Dark One in you. That peace and love you shine when you are in that state... well, nothing dark can survive it."

"Yes, and when we knew it was gone, we stopped trying to shove you out of the dimension."

Zreyas asked suspiciously, "How did you know it was gone for sure?"

"Tap started to expand again," said Cree.

꙰꙰꙰ Zreyas ꙰꙰꙰

A loud alarm suddenly went off, making everyone flinch.

"Warning, Captain. Incoming! I'm pulling up a screen now."

Tap pulled up a hologram and an image of the stars appeared with a huge glowing black thick mist with red veins shooting through it. It was hurling toward them at an alarming speed. "Estimated time of impact is one minute, thirty-two seconds and it is following us. I have tried changing directions. This is not natural, Captain."

"He was in our dimensional space. He knows where we are now. Get me to the control room. I'm lost in this place still. Rhom and Rtu, can you teach Tap how to create a new dimension for herself?"

Without asking, Cree scooped him up and ran hard out of the room and through a corridor as he shoved him up on his shoulder.

"Rhom and Tap, I don't care how you do it, but change our dimensional coordinates in the quantum as soon as you can or we will be dodging these for the rest of our lives with no chance. This is what happened to Tulyata."

He could hear Rhom and Rtu running behind him.

Then Rhom confirmed, "It can be done, but we can't do it right now. We have to wait till this event passes."

"Mother, we are with you. Do not doubt your skills," said Silence, somewhere behind him.

Everyone knew more about this ship already than he did. "Tap, how long till impact?"

"Fifty-three, fifty-two."

"Two rooms away, Captain," said Cree.

When they entered the command room, Zreyas

Q-leaped over to the command center. It adjusted to his height immediately. "Remind me how to do this? Or did you even tell me before?"

No one said a thing, not even Tap.

"Ticking-hell, I'm on my own again on this."

"We can't help you, little buddy. We don't understand it. Trust yourself, you figured things out before, and we all know you will do it again. You are a wizard at strategy and the quantum."

Zreyas looked over at Rtu, who was smiling with an expression of pride and confidence. *He doesn't even look stressed.*

"Thirty-one, thirty, twenty-nine…"

"Mother, I will let my song be heard for you. It will help you to remember," Silence coaxed.

Rtu snickered and chuckled, despite the desperate situation.

Though Zreyas didn't join in, the air of support and Rtu's humor at such a time made him feel at ease and more focused. Zreyas didn't feel overwhelmed at all. He felt calm and quiet, then he heard Silence's song and felt a resonance.

Then he coached himself—*Remember, Zrey, the fracture day. You made it through and it was still the best day of your life, and you didn't even know it at the time. Today will be the same kind of day. Just watch and manifest the solution. Remember the quietness you felt while you were at war? Remember the crevasse and how it brought you to your potential.*

As Zreyas went into the zone of his own focus, he began to hear his own song harmonize with Silence, and he smiled. He knew they would make it because he already saw them at gate forty, the gate of deliverance that Rhom had spoken of. Their deliverance had already happened, and he put it out there in the quantum space, shielded from the Dark One by his mind and song.

The countdown Tap was giving him faded from his ears and the last number he heard was the echoing sound of one... one... one...

The Back Matter
Glossary of Terms

All definitions are related to this story. Some definitions are fiction, some may have full or partial real-world application but may, or may not, be applied in a fictional way.

Atra - <redacted>

Aramzu - An ocean creature similar to Earth's stingray, but with a larger mouth and the teeth to match. The barbs on its tail are much larger and more deadly.

Bandhula - 1. Bastard
      2. An attendant in a harlot's chamber.

Brumble – The closest creature to a bee on Earth, yet its average size as an adult would be between 6-8 inches and red and black in color.

Dina - Earth equivalent of the term, day.

Festering - The process of conditioning one's self to a lower frequency. It can also apply to doing or being something you are not, without awareness of it. It manifests physically in the body as deterioration.

Garavu - A deadly slither that resembles Earth's Cobra, but significantly more predatory. Unlike the cobra on earth, however, they ravenously eat much quicker, and the garavu's throat has hooked serrated, bone blades with poison ducts. They slice the prey as it moves down through the body to enable faster digestion. The bone blades also prevent them from sliding back out.

Incarnates / you incarnates - Slang term of the deities referring to someone that is incarnated.

Kamyami - I love you

Kuravy - Eagle-like predator. Description in the story text.

Lutari - A giant arachnid creature that has a leg span of a meter wide (approx. 39 inches) as an average adult. It bears two fangs that are 7.5 centimeters long (approx. 3 inches). It doesn't make webs like the smaller arachnids on Earth—it hunts and builds nests in small caves or crevices in rock. Its venom is potent and uses its fangs to liquefy its prey from the inside. The lutari can carry quite a bit of weight back to its nest. A lutari can suck dry of everything but the fur in something the size of one of Earth's rabbits in an hour. Their downfall is they can't see very well at all. They use the hair on their body to detect things close to them. A Lutari also has a dulled smelling sense that helps them find prey. (Apparently Zreyas stopped in for the night in a young lutari's sleeping spot.)

Mag - A parasitic insect that thrives on low frequency species, like the Janquar. Its body is jelly-like. No matter how it spreads, or its shape, it can't attach itself to the host. The chemical make-up of the secretions of the body slowly eats away at the skin, though. The mag secretes its feces, creating a crust that attaches itself to the skin of its host. Its weak hair-like legs take a long time to attach to its host, however. It isn't until there is a firm grip of its feces that it is more stable to stay on the host, and eventually burying itself under it. The mag eats away the flesh and its feces replace the host's skin completely. It infiltrates the inner tissues, eventually rendering the victim unable to move because of its solidity of the feces. The host eventually dies a long and painful death. Depending on the host's health and lifespan of race they are, their death could take between 50 to 250 varSas (years). The feces material is so hard, it takes high technology to crack or cut it. It is often taken from victims after death to use for prefabricated armor, or used with other materials to make high grade and incredibly difficult to crack technology for space technology tools and ships.

Mag-shit - An insult, referring to the feces of the mag that attach to a host's skin and gradually kill them. (see the term, *Mag for more detail*)

Neutrinic-gleam - Building blocks of the Viduri made from neutrinos in a condensed form.

Nagodara - These creatures are pure decay and darkness. They are the Fetus stolen from entities that become demons. It is a mammal, sort of in that the back part of it is like a large long-haired oily looking rat. The mouth and stomach are lined with rows of teeth that rotate opposite the rows next to them. At the corners of the mouth fin wings with three bones with knuckles. Made for wafting mucus from the stomach and the dark mist from the open slit eyes at enemies that do extreme and quick decay damage. The center of the three bones in the fins are shafts for extending clawed thin and spindly hands like working branches of bone. The nails at the end are needles of pure toxic syringe-like nails. They slide out when it brings prey into its mouth, especially in the inverted state. The creature eats its prey alive or dead by sliding its inverted mouth, teeth exposed back over its body, pulls the creature in and then folds its mouth back over the body and grinding it up with its rows of teeth in its mouth and stomach. When it dies, it stops working when the soul of the person / creature deactivates the decay.

RSi - Singer of ancient songs.

Sana jana - old man

Shinit - A meerkat-like species much larger than the species found on Earth. Found on many planets in the multiverse.

Slither - A family of creatures similar to an Earth's species called 'snake'.

Sol - A time period of one day

Torana - Arch; portal; arched doorway.

varSa - One rotation around the sun. In Earth terminology, this would be equivalent to the word 'year.'

Vyagga - Freckles

Yan - Intention and spirit of someone's actions and its energetic frequency association.

Acknowledgments

- 4 -

I would like to thank my Patreon supporters at the time of this writing. They are all individually valued as if they were hundreds of thousands.

I would also like to thank all my wonderful beta readers and fellow authors in my groups for their time and support. They gave the gift of candid feedback and comradery.

Keep in Touch

Scan the QR code with your smartphone

If you would like to support an indie author that cares about the community, visit **ishKiia's Patreon**:

https://www.patreon.com/ishKiiaPaige

The Sleeping Phoenix **Facebook Page:**

https://www.facebook.com/IshKiia-Paige-The-Sleeping-Phoenix-Series-107707978352041/

ishKiia Paige

You can subscribe to **ishKiia's personal newsletter. NOTE:** She does this personally and promises to never sell or use your information except for this newsletter.

https://www.subscribepage.com/s9y6m0

Finally, if you would like to find out about all of ishKiia's Services, wander on down to her **website**.

https://ishkiiapaige.com